"How can any
elevates the st
sculpted prose .... and
fictional craft t.... ..v.. any of her contemporaries. ... *The
Magician* is a must-read for anyone who loves baseball, small
town life, and the pursuit of the American Dream."

—Dr. Christina Fisanick
Associate Professor of English

"*The Magician* is a book that sings to the reader's sense of
justice and fairness. Life for Stan, his long-suffering mother,
and his siblings could not have been harder. ... If you are a
baseball nut, this is required reading, in my opinion, but, if like
me, baseball is a foreign language, it is still an absorbing and
telling tale of familial love, determination, courage, and the
ability to see the best in even the worst situations."

—Grant Leishman, *Readers' Favorite*

"Shoop reaches into the soul of the story to deliver a gem to
baseball and Musial fans everywhere."

—Tammy Ruggles, *Readers' Favorite*

"Five stars over and over again! The word 'Magician' in the
title hints at the magical experience adroitly encased in this rich
and exquisite book ... fully packed with brilliant metaphors,
smooth storytelling, deeply portrayed and complex characters,
and an elaborate, vividly described world."

—Foluso Falaye, *Readers' Favorite*

"It grabs you from the first page."

—Samantha Gregory, *Readers' Favorite*

Other Books by Kathleen Shoop

Historical Fiction

The Donora Story Collection:
After the Fog—Book One
The Strongman and the Mermaid—Book Two
The Magician—Book Three

The Letter Series:
The Last Letter—Book One
The Road Home—Book Two
The Kitchen Mistress—Book Three
The Thief's Heart—Book Four
The River Jewel—A prequel

Romance

Endless Love Series:
Home Again—Book One
Return to Love—Book Two
Tending Her Heart—Book Three

Women's Fiction

Love and Other Subjects

Bridal Shop Series:
Puff of Silk—Book One

Holiday
The Christmas Coat
The Tin Whistle

A Novel

The
Magician

KATHLEEN SHOOP

kathleenshoop@gmail.com
kshoop.com
Twitter: @kathieshoop
Facebook: Kathleen Shoop

ISBN: 9798596878127

Cover Design: Jenny Q—historicalfictionbookcovers.com

To Jane Kinter, baseball's biggest fan.

No matter what the Pittsburgh Pirates' season was looking like, you loved them fiercely. I didn't finish *The Magician* in time, but your love for baseball was always in my head and heart as I wrote, hoping I'd capture what it is that makes fans love the game and the people who play it.

Chapter 1

Patryk Rusek

2019
Outskirts of Donora, Pennsylvania

Ninety feet to go.

Patryk bolted down the tree-lined lane, away from Blue Horizon Retirement Community. He was nearly into the heavier woods. Each bone in his ninety-two-year-old body ached as he puffed air in and out of his chest, right arm pumping, left hand holding tight to the towel wrapped around his waist.

Keep going. Keep going, he coached himself, eyes squinting into the wind. A car buzzed toward him, then slowed. A boy in the back pressed his nose against the window and dropped his jaw as a gust of wind opened Patryk's towel.

"Sorry 'bout that." He raised his hand to emphasize the apology, but as he did, he lost grip of the towel and it fell away. *Shit.* He stopped and reached back for it, but seeing the brake lights on the car, he knew this sweet family coming to visit their half-dead relative would try to do good and get him back to the facility. Luckily the lane was narrow and the giant Suburban wouldn't easily turn around.

Keep going.

Deep breath, both arms pumping, he dug into his run, focused on the white post of the missing picket fence, half-hidden by a cluster of oaks. Just a little farther. They wouldn't follow him into the woods. Not if he moved fast enough.

Forty-five feet.

Toughen up, he told himself. *Owen gave you new Nikes.* Putting on the shoes the first time had made Patryk feel like he'd sprouted wings on his heels as he walked around the halls of Blue Horizon. But now, running fast as he could over the gravel lane, weaving around potholes, the shoes seemed to have lost their springiness. But no matter. He'd rehearsed it all. His clothes were waiting at the tree behind the post. A jug of water, some crazy cardboard-tasting oatmeal bar, and a cell phone his great-grandson called a burner. Though leaving during shower time wasn't ideal, it was the only moment he and Owen had discerned as "right" to spring him loose.

Patryk clasped his chest and turned back to see the family who'd driven past him milling outside their car, pointing toward him. A teenage girl was holding something, looking disgusted. The towel he'd dropped. She held it by one corner, pushing it toward her mother.

Focus.

Patryk reoriented toward the fencepost. *Just get there and you'll be safe.*

He took off again, each stride lengthening longer than the last. He would've sworn in court he was running toward his youth, breaking some sort of time barrier. Air and energy filled him, swirled around him. And just as he reached the post and saw his things exactly where Owen said they'd be waiting, a shadow passed in front of him.

Then another and another and another.

"Dammit." His shoulders slumped.

The family from the car.

The skinny, scowling mom plugged her fists on her hips. "It *is* you. Grandfather, what in the hell are you doing?"

Patryk squinted into the woman's face. He pushed his hand through his hair, trying to recover his dignity. The husband held the towel open, lifting it toward Patryk's nether regions. "Now don't be alarmed. I'm just going to slip this riiiight back into place," he said.

Patryk jerked back and forth as the husband tucked a corner of the towel at his hip.

Lucy. He shook his head. No, no. Not Lucy. This was her sister. The bossy one. The one Lucy constantly bickered with on the phone. How long had it been since he'd seen Laura and her husband? Was Patryk losing his mind, like they seemed to suggest he was? No. He wouldn't accept that.

He realized what was going to happen next. And the surge of inspiration that had gripped him just seconds before dissolved. His shoulders drooped, and it was all he could do to keep from bursting into tears.

∗∗

That was it. Patryk had had enough. He'd thought she was on his side.

Yet, no. Lucy had abandoned him, too. Had she? After the time they'd spent together? Where was she? Probably floating around the ocean on vacation somewhere while she sent Laura to deal with the old man. Had Lucy had enough of him?

The stench of antiseptic swelled as Nurse Vera bent near while a sewage odor from the guy next to him competed for real estate in the room and won.

A nurse jammed Patryk's sleeve up past his elbow, her rubber glove catching on his arm hairs. "Dammit. Abuse. That's what this is."

"Stop wiggling, *please*," Nurse Vera said with a sigh. The nurses were always sighing around him.

His life had long been emptied of people who loved him, but when Lucy and Owen showed up earlier in the summer, he thought perhaps that had all changed.

The rubber tubing pinched and squeezed. Nurse Vera wiped alcohol squares over the veins that poked through his skin like arched bridges.

There she goes. Poke, pull out, poke… got it in? He glanced at his arm as Nurse Vera grimaced and pulled the needle out.

"Ach. There's no gold in these veins. No use looking fer it. Just Iron City beer. Maybe a shot o' whiskey."

"Cute." Nurse Vera pulled the needle out and held it into the light. She tapped the syringe and came at him again.

He pulled away. "I want a new nurse."

She smiled.

He held his arm up. "Could drive a Mack truck through these beautiful veins, but ya can't get that tiny needle in?"

She held the syringe up and studied it again. "Off day, I guess."

Lucy wouldn't stand for this treatment of him. The thought of his granddaughter's name made his heart pause. A nurse herself, Lucy had watched over much of his care since he'd had some health trouble. And he'd thought she was different. He thought Owen, her son, was different too.

The two of them had conned him into visiting an old friend and then left him to fend for himself in the blasted old folks' home. A farm for adults. Put out to pasture, to prod and lasso him toward death. There was no life here, just the undercurrent of it.

Nurse Vera lifted his arm and turned it so she could go at his veins again. He wiggled out of her grip. "We're done here." He pushed to standing, got his bearings, and waltzed past her as forcefully as he could.

"Like I can't find you, Mr. Rusek. I'm going to exchange this for a smaller needle, and I'll be right down to draw your blood."

He waved her off. "You'd like to jab me again, ya old vampire. Wouldn't ya?"

"Just turned twenty-six yesterday," the nurse said, her voice fading as he drew farther away. "Told you that twice today."

He grunted, fully feeling the disappointment of the failed escape, at knowing Lucy and Owen weren't coming back. The other residents had warned him but he hadn't believed. He neared his room, dressed, Nikes back on his feet, expecting an orderly or another nurse to guide him to the Sunshine Center, as they called it. It was really just a black-death center. Every soul who left the Blue Horizon Retirement Community seemed to exit via that center writhing under a sheet, grasping their chests, gasping for air—or quiet as a stoned mouse, stone dead.

Soon he'd be gone and they'd all… miss him? No. Obviously that wasn't the case. They didn't care what he wanted. Not one bit. And at ninety-two years old, after his thwarted, naked run, he'd finally reached the point where he didn't care either. Perhaps his next goal should be to execute one of those hushed, still, final exits. Like every time it happened, fellow residents would peek through their curtains at him, or barely look up from their bridge game as EMTs compressed his chest and put an oxygen mask over his face. An awful thought, but at least it would be almost over.

In his room, he curled onto his bed and replayed the plan he and Owen had made. He would have made it to freedom if Laura and her nebby-nose family hadn't arrived when they did. He pulled the velvety throw blanket Owen had given him, up to his chin. Perhaps Patryk had been suffering auditory hallucinations and he and Owen *hadn't* made the plan for him to run. He closed his eyes and listened for disembodied voices or any sign that he was losing his mental faculties. He sat up and looked at his feet. The light-as-air Nikes certainly weren't imaginary. Those were part of the plan for sure. He wasn't crazy.

People talking down the hallway drew Patryk's attention, and he wished he'd shut his door. The woman sounded just like Lucy. Laura. One of the other Rusek girls who had spent the last year trying to lock him up must have either convinced Lucy to let her take over or she'd elbowed her younger, sweeter sister aside, staging a coup.

He pushed the blanket away, steeling himself, jaw clenched, waiting for the attack, trying to appear as alive and "with it" as he could. The conversation grew clearer as the people drew closer, and before long Laura and her entourage entered his room without even pretending to ask for permission. It was as though he were a toddler, if he could remember that far back. The age when people just scooped a person up and set him down somewhere else without any thought for his desires.

Laura plopped her purse on his dresser, nearly knocking family photos off. "Grandfather."

He looked over one shoulder, then the other. "Wrong room. Grandfather? *Pfft.* I'm Gramps to my family."

Laura leaned on one hip, resting a hand on the opposite one as though this was the posture she depended upon anytime she stopped moving.

She drummed her fingers on her hip. "Lucy wasn't exaggerating."

He didn't know how to respond, seeing as he had no idea what aspect of him Laura was referring to.

"So yinz guys are partners in crime? Or." He shook his finger. "You staged a rebellion against yer sister."

Laura's husband extended his hand and moved toward Patryk. "You're just like I remember."

"Hrumph." Patryk took his hand but looked away. He couldn't recall the man's name. Or maybe he just chose to forget unimportant people who never visited until he became a burden.

"Danny, sir. And if I had to characterize today's maneuver, I'd say hostile takeover, without a doubt."

Patryk's gaze snapped to Danny's. He appreciated the man's strong handshake, his candor, though if he was married to Laura, he couldn't be trusted.

Danny lifted the getaway bag containing Patryk's clothes, snacks, and burner phone. "Looks like you'd worked out quite a plan." He tossed the phone into the air and caught it. "This wouldn't have helped much."

Patryk leaned in to see it closer. "My burner. Owen set me up nice."

Laura and Danny appeared confused. Danny flipped the phone open and showed it to Laura with a shrug.

Laura's shoulders slouched. Her face softened, and she sat beside Patryk. But instead of feeling her presence as kind and warm, Patryk had to resist pushing her off the edge.

Laura gestured to her son, who handed her the fat book that Patryk had been reading with Owen and Lucy, the book that Patryk's wife and sister had made over the years, filled with illustrations, stories, articles, and facts about friends and family from Donora, Pennsylvania.

"I hear you're Donora's favorite casual historian." She ran her hand over the cover, petting it, and Patryk saw that she was genuinely drawn to the book. This just made him remember Lucy and Owen, the two he'd come to think of as allies until they abandoned him.

"Where's Owen? Lucy? They lied."

Laura opened the dusty book and pointed to a page. She was lost in the illustrations the way everyone became when they looked at his memories. He knew she wasn't feigning interest, but he had no desire to entertain.

"Lucy and Owen told me you were going to tell them about this section of the book—about Stan Musial… right here. The Magician. You and your friends knew him?"

Patryk pursed his lips, looking at the splayed book. His eyes burned. He wanted Lucy and Owen, not these people. Knowing how much Owen had come to enjoy the stories broke his heart. Where was he? "When're Lucy an' Owen gettin' me outta here?"

Another side glance between husband and wife and Patryk knew he was about to hear another lie.

"Now, Grandfath—*Gramps*. As soon as Lucy phones I'll tell you, but I'd really like to hear about the Magician. How good *was* he? Did he work the country-club circuit? Make people disappear? *Oooh*. An illusionist. Stan Musial…" She looked at the ceiling and shook her head.

Danny rubbed his forehead and connected with Patryk's gaze, sharing an exasperated expression. "Babe. You're joking, right?"

"Joking? I love magicians. Remember the one who made a dollar bill appear on our ceiling? Madison," she gestured toward their daughter, "went nuts over him."

Danny put his hand on Laura's shoulder. "Sweetie, Stan Musial's a baseball player."

"Best ever," Patryk said.

The boy sat on the other side of Patryk, looking at the book. "I've heard of him."

Laura poked at the page. "It says the Magician."

The boy scooched so close to Patryk that he could smell the pancakes and syrup the kid must have eaten for breakfast. Patryk strained to remember the boy's name. He'd never been good at names, especially of those he'd only met a couple times. But this time not remembering felt different, as though it was a sign of decline.

"I know about him," the boy said. "My teacher said he was— "

Laura exhaled. "Why don't you men enjoy the story about this baseball magician? Madison will help me with phone calls. We can't have Gramps running around nude anymore or they'll throw him out of here."

"Yinz can toss me out with the rubbish," Patryk said.

Danny gave his wife a nod and sat beside Patryk. "Look at this book. Newspaper clippings. Tickets from the 1944 World Series? Stan Musial met President Kennedy?"

Patryk found better humor for Danny and the boy than for Laura. The daughter was all right. Kids couldn't help who their parents were. Husbands sometimes made bad choices and kept vows in spite of it. The lure to talk about Stan and the book grew stronger. Patryk's mind began to light the sections of his memory that held Danny and the boy in them. He had met them a couple times. Danny always had a smile. The boy was a lively, sweet child, never a back-talker—that he remembered. What was his name?

"Stan sure did meet JFK." Patryk flipped a page. "Imagine. A skinny, poor kid who once stammered and ate nothin' but cabbage, jumbo bologna, pierogi, and bread ended up chattin' up the president."

"Wow," the boy said.

Patryk looked up. "Thinkin' of it, I'll bet Kennedy chatted Stan up. Everyone loved Stan." This story was meant to be shared with Owen.

Danny elbowed Patryk. "You all right?"

Patryk closed the book, an ache in his heart dampening his desire to talk. Could Owen and Lucy really have just left him without word? "Nope. Not all right. Where's Owen? This is where we left off, and I won't share a bit of it until he shows up."

The kid reached for the book. "Please? Can I just look at some of it? Please?"

Patryk looked down at the boy's big brown eyes.

"My teacher'll freak if he knows I met someone who met Stan Musial. Freak. He'll freakin' freak."

Patryk groaned. It wasn't as though the pages would disappear if he looked through them before Owen returned. It was a link to everything important to him after all and maybe if he cooperated, Laura would see he was sane, reasonable. It just might be his path back into his Donora home. He brushed his fingers along the rough edges and opened the book. "Fine. A little bit. But don't get too comfortable because I don't like kids."

Patryk studied his great-grandson, expecting to see a pout, but the boy grinned instead. Danny beamed as well. Perhaps he could tolerate them.

"What's yer name anyway? I don't think we've met."

"Harrison. And I don't remember meeting you either. Parents say we did, but…"

"First name's Harrison? What're ya? A Cement City kid?"

Harrison squinted and shook his head, obviously confused.

"We're in the same boat with yer parents telling us what we should remember," Patryk said.

"Mm-hmm."

"Not sure Harrison's a good first name, but I suppose I'll use it until I think up another fer ya."

Harrison's eyes went wide.

"Everyone from Donora has a nickname or three. You shouldn't be an exception."

"But I—"

"Oh yes, yer from Donora. Whether yer mum told ya so or not."

Harrison looked pleased and slid even closer to Patryk, already starting to read.

Chapter 2

Mary

February 1920
Donora, Pennsylvania

Donora exhaled its sulfuric air twenty-four hours a day. Spewing, hiccupping, belching. Each iron-and-steel body created hot-red, black or white breath—a mix of raw earthen materials their feed. Three sister mills filled out three miles of the curved banks, hugged by the Monongahela River. Hulking, grinding machinery—Donora's organs and skeletal system—provided shape and purpose, as though natural outgrowths between steep, craggy valley walls. Every bit of steel and each finishing element for wire and fencing was made right there, beginning to end. The products simultaneously fueled and responded to the country's growth even as the flu epidemic had ravaged it, carried by men returning from war to settle back in with loving families.

Donora suffered the epidemic like all towns. School closures, mass cancellations, gathering restrictions, prayers, novenas, candles lit—all to keep the flu from stealing more lives than it already had. It was in this environment that Mary Musial had found herself repeatedly pregnant, giving birth, and wanting to be pregnant again. Children were the embodiment of hope, and the desire for Lukasz and Mary to have a boy after four girls was strong.

On one particularly cold, heavy-aired afternoon, Mary turned up the hill on Sixth Street from Thompson Avenue. Arms laden with groceries, head down so her mouth fit behind her turned-up coat collar as a makeshift mask shielding her from the waning but still lingering flu epidemic, she dodged neighbors, nodding hello to friends running errands or heading back to work after lunch. The Musial home wasn't all that different from others in Donora, given that most were cobbled together little by little when families got their hands on materials to add more rooms and floors. Theirs was white-turned-sooty clapboard with blue-turned-gray shutters and front door.

Mary and Lukasz rented the small home, number 465. It wasn't what they'd dreamed about—they were renting after all—but it gave them the shelter they needed to continue to dream about buying one day.

Mary entered and released her parcels onto the bench. The cabbage scent wafting from the kitchen didn't make her heart sing. But she and Lukasz had filled the space to bursting with four baby girls in six years. And being a mother was what she'd been made to do.

The silence jarred Mary. No crying? No six-year-old Ida rushing to greet her with baby Rose on her hip, Helen and Vicki trailing behind?

A note from Matka lay on the kitchen table. Her writing was hard to decipher as she had just started to seriously learn to read and write in the past few years.

> *Mary, don't tell Papa I helped with yer laundry so ya could hire yerself aht. He's ignorin me 'cause I haven't… Well, good luk fer it all. Lukasz sez the infuzons are in the boot-room near the door…*

Lukasz must have convinced Matka to take the children up to the Lancos house on Marelda so the two could focus on their task. Mary let the paper flutter onto the kitchen table, onto the Polish newspaper that Lukasz read in addition to the *Donora American* or the *Evening Herald*. She was grateful Matka and Luksaz got on so well, that she had taken the children that day, but Mary didn't need to read the rest of the note to know what it said. Matka would remind her that Papa was not ready to accept Lukasz even after nearly six years of Mary being married to him, that Papa thought Lukasz should show more respect. Mary agreed, but telling Lukasz that yielded nothing. He considered Papa stubborn and cruel and unable to see his own shortcomings. Papa didn't see Lukasz's work ethic, not understanding that a couple injuries had put him out of the mill and into work as a hotel porter, or whatever he could find. Nothing Lukasz did was good enough for Papa. The two men had even competed on who would get American citizenship papers first. It had taken Papa decades to even try.

Mary's heart still seized at the thought of gentler girlhood moments they had shared, rowing him to and from work across the river. And it swelled at the love she felt for Lukasz despite all their current troubles. How could two men who claimed to love her not care a lick for each other? They were unable to socialize without it ending with roaring, circling each another, grappling with enormous bear paws, Lukasz's belying his shortness. The two would crash to the floor like iron ingots, rolling, grunting, red-faced until one bested the other and the loser stormed away, sucking the oxygen and the happiness out of the day. Still, Matka was always willing to help. Hardscrabble as she was, Mary had finally come to accept Matka's actions as showing the love her words never would.

The kitchen clock ticked, the eerie emptiness giving Mary a chill. She reached for the coal shovel, and her elbow broke through the worn wool coat sleeve. It would have to wait to be mended. Coal in place, she lit fires in the stove and in the fireplace in the front room. In the boot-room, she pulled the sliver of soap

Mrs. Hanlon had given her out of her pocket and shook out the coat, hanging it on a peg.

At the basin in the kitchen, she dragged a soapy rag over her face and neck, up and down her arms, then under them, feeling better with just that much grooming. She smoothed her hair, wanting to be as pretty as possible after a day's work in another woman's home.

The front door whined open. Mary tossed the cloth into the water and moved to where she could see Lukasz entering. He stepped inside and removed his hat, then held his arms wide.

"Już czas."

She nodded. "Yes. Yes." Her insides tumbled, excited.

"Weź napoje?"

She waved him toward her as she backed toward the boot-room. "In here." By the back door, there were two jars, one labeled with Lukasz's name, another with Mary's.

Each unscrewed the lid. "I'm not sure I can get this down," she said. "Who knew nettles and oat straw and raspberry leaf could taste like mill spit?"

He lifted his jar toward her. "Ginseng and saw palmetto— no better. But better than that grippe drink Mrs. Mazur gave us last year."

Mary met Lukasz's gaze. "Troubles and lost dreams be damned."

"Be damned." He winked.

Suddenly she was a young girl again, seeing her shy Pole for the first time as he tossed wire bundles into the back of a train car at the mill. His attention on her never failed to stoke desire, to remind her that he was a good man despite his flaws. The love he bestowed on her made her feel worthy of it in the first place.

He lifted his jar in their ceremonial toast.

Not ready to swig the drink, she pulled hers into her chest. "Wait. We have the date right, yes?"

He nodded.

"The moon's in a male sign. The return of the sun and moon cycle…" She shook her head. "Or whatever Mrs. Mazur said." She shrugged. "We better get moving if we want—"

"Our boy. It's time for us to make our heir."

That always made Mary smile. Their heir. The idea that Lukasz still thought that someday they'd build enough savings that it would even matter to their children, that he would have something to leave behind and someone to look up to him, like sons looked up to fathers, always made her ache and smile at the same time.

He leaned into Mary, tinked his jar to hers, his gaze falling to her lips, his free hand releasing the pins that held her hair at the nape of her neck. He kissed her hard, then soft, his lips whispering over her cheekbone, biting her ear playfully, sending chills through her, their drinks pressed between them. "*Moja miłość*, my love, my love. I turned the bed to face north. It's all set."

When he pulled away, they chugged their twiggy brown infusions, the ones specially mixed by a gifted midwife, the drinks they'd barely been able to keep down earlier that week. But this time, instead of ending their drink by holding back the threatening release of the mixture and marching back to work, they tripped up the stairs to their bedroom, giggling, excited, full of hope.

Clothes flew in this direction and that. Mary and Lukasz fell onto the bed, fingers pushing through hair, limbs entwined, speaking their shared, wordless language, expressed with the brush of fingertips over bellies and inside thighs and the backs of knees. Breaths caught against the slope of necks, and the connection instantly filled their pitted marriage like a flash flood in saturated streets.

The easing of tension never failed to remind Mary of the vows they'd made nearly six years before. It was all they had of value. It was all they had to keep their original dreams alive. Though she'd thought it silly to enact these fertility rituals, that a good confession and friends and relatives saying novenas was a much more sensible approach to ensure the Musials finally conceived a boy, in those moments, each wrapped in the other's arms, she was quite sure they'd made their son.

Lukasz fell asleep immediately, his even breaths and his soft slumbering expression the only time he ever seemed at peace these days. Mary tucked her head into his shoulder, the scent of work filling her nose. She kissed his shoulder, his skin transferring salt to her lips. She crossed herself and said her prayers to Mother Mary for a son this time.

Unable to sleep, Mary traced each of three scars on Lukasz's shoulder, collarbone, and chest. Each one earned in a mill accident, wild wires having escaped their bundles, the ends slicing through his clothing, putting him in bed to heal, having to wait his turn to hire back into his job, turning him miserable. She outlined the third scar—circular, pink-and-white mottled tissue over his breastbone. She closed her eyes and sorted through her prayer list. How many times she'd prayed for Lukasz over the years. She wondered how many prayers she'd said over the course of her life.

Hands.

She wove her fingers into his, stroking his skin with her thumb. He'd always been gentle with his hands, firm, protective, electrifying. Over the years Lukasz's dreams took unbidden, loopy paths that tangled before lashing out. Like those wild loose wires sprung from tight coils, life laid down scarring damage, shading Lukasz's general reticence with darker, moodier tones.

Please, God, let Lukasz hire back into the mill. Give him back the job that makes him whole, that uses his strength and leaves him in good humor. Make him look past the bar, past the Polish Falcons after work, and just bring him home to me. A son would do that without me even having to pray for it. That would change everything. Even his hotel work would be bearable with a son at home. So please make us a boy. Make us what Lukasz needs us to be.

Chapter 3

Mary

November 20, 1920

The sulfurous air turned Mary's stomach. Nothing unusual for late pregnancy mixed with Donora's mill fumes to set her a little queasy in the morning. She stepped up her pace to get to work, to get inside a home where the air was free of smoke and soot and scented with all manner of delicate food aromas and flowery fragrances. Grateful to have arrived, Mary entered the cloakroom and was greeted by the missus waving a chore list. The gentle rose perfume wafting off Mrs. Hanlon's wrist grew sharp and made Mary wretch. Mrs. Hanlon's eyes widened at the sight of Mary clamping her hand over her mouth. But when Mary didn't leap back outside to throw up, the woman continued with her day's demands, waving Mary on to follow her into the kitchen.

The scent of butter and onions dizzied her. She gripped the countertop near the sink and nodded, indicating she was listening to Mrs. Hanlon's list, that she wasn't missing a thing. This sensation would pass quickly, just as it had the first few months of pregnancy. But when Mary's beloved lemon water and cleaning oils sent her racing to the servants' washroom to vomit, Mary knew the baby would be coming sometime soon.

Steady contractions followed, but they rose and fell miles apart, and so she continued to work. If she moved slowly, she'd be fine, and the pay for a day's work would help significantly as she recovered from giving birth. That day her biggest assignment was to scrub the twelve-inch baseboard molding that belted each room on the first floor.

Mary's belly was large but low. Her nearly six-foot height always camouflaged how far along she was and made it easy for everyone to forget that she should be taking things easy by then. Busy with four girls under the age of seven, a home to keep, and her work, she luckily found this fifth pregnancy the easiest so far. Though she wanted Doc Bonaroti at the birth just to be sure the baby was born safe and healthy as he suggested, she was glad Mrs. Mazur would also be there and Mary wondered if the woman's fertility drink had been partly responsible for the easy pregnancy.

On her knees, scrubbing Mrs. Hanlon's mahogany woodwork, Mary scooted along in the children's dining area. She dug at the crumbs and morsels of food with a wire brush, preparing the area for when the men came to refinish the expensive wood.

Mrs. Hanlon wasn't the type of housewife who'd allow for workmen to think she didn't keep her home nicely—meaning that her help better be up to standards for the wife of a mill manager. The fact that the Hanlon boys ran the town like pack animals, that they left food debris, bodily fluids, and whatever it was that boys tended to leave behind in the home didn't bother her a bit. As long as Mary's help got it all up before company took note.

Mary's belly contracted. She stopped mid-scrub and breathed through the pain, focusing on the one dried piece of banana that stuck to the wood like industrial glue. She drew deep breaths, assessing whether she had enough time between contractions to keep working. Plenty. She reached in her apron and ran her thumb over the rosary beads Lukasz had given her that morning. Lukasz had presented it with his lopsided, shy smile, showing his pride at having found it after it had been missing for months. Mary had gone breathless, speechless, feeling as though a piece of her had been returned.

"In the corner behind the bed. I know you like to dust back there but haven't moved the bed due to…" He'd looked at her belly. He'd told her not to worry that it went missing. He teased, reminding her that an endless string of prayers and trips to church hadn't produced a boy for them the first four times.

Lukasz coming to her with the found rosary, with his bashful gaze, reminded her of when he used to make gifts for her, gifts that had meant so much that she hid them away behind loose fireplace bricks so her papa wouldn't sell them for the mortgage. But when they moved into their Sixth Street home, a box of her treasured items including the wedding rings Lukasz had made went missing.

With various mill injuries and wear from twelve-hour shifts, Lukasz's fingers no longer moved easily or pain free, capable of shaping thin wire into angels and mermaids and rings. So when he'd found the rosary that their friend Zofia had given Mary before moving away, she felt loved, cherished, like he used to make her feel every day.

Mary clutched the rosary to her chest, recalling Lukasz's sweetness that morning as he caressed the back of her neck and pulled her in for a kiss, gentle as their first one, his love for her clear and precious as a Donora sunny day.

The contraction subsided. She exhaled and went back at the dried banana. Things would be different; Lukasz would be loving all the time, gentler, like he was that morning, if they had a boy. Mary was sure Lukasz would be happier to come home after a long day's work, that the screeching child voices wouldn't bother him if one voice came with the ability to carry on the Musial name. "Boys are easy," Lukasz had told her many times. He loved the girls, but there was just something missing for him without a son.

"Girls keep families together," she would remind him.

He'd wave his hand. "No." Lukasz would hold her gaze. She always knew what words would come next. "You left your family for me."

Mary was tired of explaining the intricacies and subtleties of the female influence on the family unit. Yes, her father had disowned her for marrying Lukasz and thereby she had been taken out of the equation that allowed for the idea females kept families together.

"You know my sisters and Matka are taking care of stubborn Papa just fine." Though it still crushed her that she and her father were estranged.

Lukasz shrugged. "Need a boy in this house. Only girls? Then I'm a failure. Mrs. Mazur's infusions must work. She promised, or I don't pay. Case shut."

Mary saw both sides of the gender equation. Lukasz obviously didn't know the abuse boys introduced to a home, via something as small but labor intensive as removing dried banana from dining room baseboards. Boys messed things up. Girls set them right. Thankless, tiring, boring. Still, she had to admit she had a soft spot for boys and their games, their baseball and football and foot-racing, fishing, river swimming, and loud laughing, and now that she was a woman, their dancing, their arms, their kisses and caresses.

Mary had played her share of games under the streetlights at the park. Heck, she was still the first and last spectator to enter and exit the ball field each season to watch the Donora Zincs beat Monessen. It was she who dragged Lukasz to games, even though she'd given up hope that he might fall in love with baseball like she had, like all of America had.

Once while sitting on the porch, after the children fell asleep, he'd confided, "I go to watch *you* watch the game. Seeing you smile, laugh, heckle those boys. It fills me." He'd patted his heart when he explained this. "I fell in love with you when I saw you at a baseball game that first time."

"I thought you fell in love with me at a dance?"

He'd lit a cigarette and shook out the match, squinting through smoke. "I fell in love with you thirty-three times. At least. Love folded over and over on itself to fit into my tiny heart, as you tell me I have."

The way he described his layered feelings always surprised her then cabled her tighter to him, tethering their souls closer than she thought possible.

"My tiny black heart traps my love for you inside. Not much room for others."

He remembered her harsh words, unearthing them from time to time. She'd said them during an argument about why he seemed so indifferent to his own daughters, that it was his little black heart that let them scream with tear-drenched cheeks, little arms reaching up to be held, Ida opening and closing her hands as though the very movement would cause her father's heart to pump open and make room to tuck her inside.

That image had been seared into Mary's mind. And Mary's angry words were branded on Lukasz's heart. Sometimes she repeated them in a teasing way, with her back to him as she stirred cabbage soup, swallowing tears, wanting the joking to soften the original words, to temper him. Instead, he'd found another way to think of it.

"My feelings unfurl inside me, and then I fold them back up. No room for others than you. No escape from loving you. No retreat for me. Unless I have a boy. That would change everything. A boy would grow my heart."

Another contraction pulled at Mary's abdomen, causing a sharp inhalation. She leaned on one hand, eyes squeezed shut. Could he really not feel love for their daughters? She hadn't expected him to be overly involved with them at their ages—that was normal; the men in Donora were charged with work, work, and more work. But in those desperate moments when she needed his help around the house, when the girls needed held or changed or fed, he easily tuned them out, his indifference surprising Mary as much as his declarations of love.

Their daughters were just now starting to be individual people with ideas of their own. She had thought this would be interesting to him, that he would speak more English as they learned it, that it would allow him to practice and loosen up on his mandate to speak Polish at home. But the girls' demands and bickering in Polish or English fell hard on his ears, grating his nerves, darkening his moods and sending him to the Falcons or fleeing to the Bucket of Blood bar for peace and comradery.

The contractions came closer. Mrs. Mazur's calculations had predicted a baby born by the end of the week, but Mary's body said different. When her belly relaxed, she breathed again, moved along, and pulled the bucket of lemon water behind her, rubbing down the wood as she finished scraping each section.

Mary completed Mrs. Hanlon's chore list, dropped the ironing she'd done up for Mrs. Matthews, and stopped at the grocer to place the monthly order so she wouldn't have to do it after giving birth. She arrived home in time to instruct Ida to fetch Mrs. Mazur, to leave word for Doc Bonaroti at his office, and also for Lukasz at the Irondale Hotel.

This was it. The boy was about to arrive.

Chapter 4

Mary

Mary called for Helen to bring the extra sheets to cover the mattress, and the two of them pulled the tarp from under the bed. It was clean but stained from the girls' births. Mary flung the canvas tarp over the bed, then bent forward, breathing through spreading pain as Helen patted the small of her back.

Mrs. Mazur zipped into the room with her bags, waving some burning herbs around the room as she barked at Helen to fetch extra coal for the stove to boil water. "Told Doc no need for him to come. Another bill for someone doing the same job as me is unnecessary. He said he'd stop up to check just the same."

Mary nodded. Maybe the midwife was right.

Mrs. Mazur laid newspaper over the dresser top near the window and spread her instruments and glass bottles containing liquid ergot, castor oil, Mercurochrome, tea-tree oil, and eucalyptus, the soft clinking of the bottles followed by a cocktail of medicinal scents that made Mary begin to retch. Mrs. Mazur leapt toward the bed, bucket in hand, ready for Mary to throw up. She wiped Mary's mouth and face, easing Mary fully into the birthing process. "All right. All's well."

Mary finally released the tension she'd been holding, no longer needing to push away fear that labor might move too quickly or be unsafe if she didn't get home. In her bedroom, she let it all go and allowed her body to do what it needed.

Mrs. Mazur's methods, her choreographed comforting touch calmed. She smoothed Mary's hair back, tying it in a knot on the top of her head so she could lean back comfortably.

Mary tensed.

"Your body knows what to do. You are well prepared." Mrs. Mazur patted Mary's shoulder.

Helen, looking stricken, edged closer. Mary caught her daughter's fingertips and squeezed, forcing a smile, hoping to prune back her worry.

Mrs. Mazur shuffled the girl away. "*Odejść.* Let me settle Mama. Fetch Ida. Then I'll tell you what to do next. *Dzieci.*" The midwife murmured about Helen being too young to help, but Mary couldn't decipher the rest of her words as a rising wave of pain submerged her. Sweat poured down her face, dripping onto the sheets, Mrs. Mazur's firm, soothing touch losing its power.

Mary fell back on to the pillows and flicked her fingers toward her discarded apron. "My rosary. Pocket."

Mrs. Mazur dug it out and handed it over. Mary sighed. With the smooth beads pressed in her palm, she knew she could handle anything.

**

Hours passed. Ida returned from making sure her father had been told about Mary's labor. She reported that Lukasz should be up the hill in no time. He hadn't attended his daughters' births or even been home within hours of them arriving. A man couldn't rush out of the mill upon hearing his wife was in labor. But this time, with Lukasz working at the Irondale just blocks away, he'd been able to find a man, Herb Rancroft, willing to exchange hours. This would mean Lukasz could see the baby fairly soon after being born. In fact, this time, with all they'd done to encourage the birth of a boy, Lukasz had been insistent he wanted to be there.

"Lukasz?" Mary asked at some point deep in the night.

Ida and Mrs. Mazur shook their heads. Perhaps Herb had changed his mind about helping out. But something made her worry that Lukasz's absence meant he doubted the chance this one would be male. He'd taken the news of Rose's birth, a little over a year before, with a shrug. He'd used the excuse of celebrating with friends, not wanting to bring flu back home, as reason for staying out for two days after her birth. Mary had actually been grateful for that at the time. But now he'd promised to be there waiting.

Eventually Mary stopped asking for Lukasz, and she tuned completely into herself, into the waves of pain working to move the baby out. Eyes closed, she imagined how it would feel to hold him, and she was filled with calm. Her entire body tightening, she felt as though she were the only one in the room. Ida's and Mrs. Mazur's voices faded away, and an incredible sense of one life readying to start his own way outside of another fell over Mary. *Hail Mary, full of grace*, she repeated the beginning of the prayer, lips moving but keeping the words inside, drawing even breaths, letting the constant waves soundlessly spill through her.

Mrs. Mazur draped Mary's forehead and wrists in cold cloths, then checked her progress again. She smiled then pressed Mary's abdomen with firm hands. "Ripe and open. Time for pushing."

Doc Bonaroti appeared just as the baby was entering the world.

A son.

"A very vigorous boy," Doc Bonaroti said. When he was assured everything was fine, he made some notes and left the women to finish.

Ida, with tears in her eyes, laid a cool cloth over her mother's head again. She cooed at her new brother, brushing his slick hair back. Mother and daughter nuzzled the baby, counting fingers and toes. Mrs. Mazur went to the bowl of water they'd placed on the dresser under the window. She moved the curtain back to check the night sky and plunged the cloth into clean water. The scent of eucalyptus filled the room. "Look at *that*," she said, Ida going to her.

"See how the clouds shifted." Mrs. Mazur moved her attention to the bowl of water.

Mary nestled the baby against her breast, glancing at the midwife.

"The moon's reflection captured here in miniature." Mrs. Mazur backed away. "Never seen such a thing."

"It's pink," Ida said.

Mrs. Mazur ran her finger through the liquid, saying the reflection looked like a painting she'd seen once in a museum with a child she'd nannied for. But she'd never seen it in person. She slowly lifted her gaze. "Look at that sky. Like sapphire jewels of every shade."

She gasped and turned back to Mary. "Look."

Ida and Mary followed the midwife's gaze. Ida crept closer to the window.

"Oh my. The moon." She gestured, "Mom... can you see it?"

Mary shook her head. "Just the light coming through."

Mrs. Mazur pointed at the water again, then back at the sky.

"And there, see." She angled Ida's body toward the left and drew a line with her finger, making an invisible arch up from the horizon. "Jupiter's rising. The moon. It's pink. Oh my goodness. There's Sirius, too."

"Pink moon?" Mary said, straining to see but unable. Yet the soft moonglow, washing over midwife and Ida, was as obvious as the baby she'd just birthed.

Mrs. Mazur added some oils to the water, dragged the cloth through it, wrung it out, and glided toward mother and baby. She draped the infant in a dry sheet and moved it as she cleaned him. "Yinz got a very lucky boy."

Mary shook her head, confused, her belly cramping as it finished the birthing process.

Ida looked over her shoulder from the window as Mrs. Mazur shifted.

"Clouds moved, moon's gone. In the sky and the bowl." Ida dragged the corner of a cloth over the surface of the water.

Mrs. Mazur swaddled the quiet boy, studying him. "Gentle soul. Ain't he?"

Mary nodded. The midwife had Mary sit up to wipe her back and arms down.

Ida was still mesmerized by the scene outside the window. "Back to normal, no stars, no pink moon, just smoky clouds."

"Bring me another wet cloth for your mother's cleaning."

Ida wrung one out, the water droplets accompanying the baby's soft breath.

"Like it was never there," Ida said. "Everything's the same again."

Mrs. Mazur took the cloth from Ida and gently ran it along the nape of Mary's neck. "But we did see it. And this soul, born under a lucky star, will make everything different all at once."

The cool water sent a chill over Mary and she chuckled. "Boys'll do that. Get ready for a ruckus, Ida. This muted child won't be that for long."

Mrs. Mazur traded her spent cloth for a newly moistened one. "Ahh, well, he'll change more than that, sweet Mary. Luck like this, laid down in his birth moments will unfold in life over and over again."

Mary nuzzled her boy, unsure of what Mrs. Mazur meant, but not needing to know anything more than her baby was safe and warm against her.

**

Ida, Victoria and Helen snuggled onto the bed, Rose fast asleep in Ida's lap. They inched closer to Mary, in awe of the baby and every tiny sound and movement he made. Mrs. Mazur quietly bundled the sheets, tucked her instruments and medicines into her bag, and slipped away. After soaking and boiling the linens as her birthing ritual demanded, they would be returned.

Mary adjusted her nightdress to give the baby room to nurse. "Pop back yet?"

Victoria leaned in and caressed her brother's head.

Ida shook her head. "No."

Mary's heart beat fast, and even as she rested her eyes and encouraged the baby to nurse, she couldn't wait for Lukasz to see their son, to name him, for the baby's presence to breathe open his heart just a little more.

But Lukasz didn't return until after noon that day. Mary knew he'd made it home when she heard a whoop and the sound of thundering feet up the stairs. The door swung open, smacking the wall. He practically dove into bed with her, unwrapping their son and marveling at every bit of him.

"Oh, Mary. A boy? A boy." He wrapped the baby tight and sank onto the pillows, the baby between them.

"Why are you so surprised? You're the one who hired Mrs. Mazur to usher a boy into—"

"Shush." He put his finger on her lips. "Let me look at you, my beautiful wife. We did it." He laid his head against hers, stale booze filling her nose.

"Why didn't you come earlier?"

He hesitated to speak, brushing hair back from her face. "You're so beautiful, my Mary, my love."

She turned on her side a little more. "But why didn't you—"

"Afraid of disappointment. I didn't want you disappointed in me."

"Lukasz, no. I'd never—where'd you go?"

He laid his palm over the baby's chest, and Mary watched it rise and fall. Lukasz didn't answer that question, but she knew anyway.

"Wpadł do tawerny," he always said. "I stumbled into a bar…" as though it was the beginning of a joke. And then he fell into a bottle just like half of all the other fellas in town.

His breath evened out as the often sharp-angled features softened. Mary laid her hand over Lukasz's chest, wanting to feel her husband's heart expand and sense its reawakening, the shaking off of its sooty, protective covering as he promised would happen with the birth of a boy. The sensation of blood flashing through Lukasz's chest warmed her palm. Perhaps he'd been right all along. Perhaps Mrs. Mazur was, too. This little one would change everything. She didn't like separating her aspirations for her children into before and after the boy was born, but she couldn't deny something had shifted upon this birth, as though Jupiter's rising dragged the little one's spirit up with it. Something they all tried to reason out, and never could, but knew right then. Something was absolutely different.

**

Mary was back on her feet tending the family within days of giving birth. Matka had splurged on fresh chicken, new flannel diapers and safety pins, and lavender infused diaper cream made special by Mrs. Mazur as a gift. So even with normal soiled diapers, the lavender filled Mary with fresh scent while soothing the boy's hind end. With the baby in one arm, Mary stirred a broth with her free hand. Ida sliced vegetables and Vicki sorted them into piles. The steady chop of the knife kept the rhythm of their life that evening.

Lukasz should have been home by then. Mary's stomach clenched at the thought of his tips from the hotel going down his throat just as the front door flew open. She spun toward the commotion, unable to see who'd entered around the corner. The baby tensed in her arm and let out a disgruntled squawk. She bounced him, shushing him. She felt Ida's and Helen's eyes on her as she edged toward the doorway, seeing Lukasz. He cussed in Polish, hung his coat, and knocked the girls' coats from the rack. He plugged the heel of one boot into the bootjack and yanked a foot out.

"Ahhh," he groaned. "Oh, that's good." Mary let out a held breath. The next boot brought the same pleased sigh. She backed into the kitchen. Silence followed. Mary waited to see what his mood was.

He entered the kitchen, arms spread wide. "I've done it, my Mary. *Moja słodka* Mary." He covered the space in four strides and clasped Mary and the baby into his arms, drawing laughter from his girls. Mary inhaled, her nose searching for the scent of booze. Nothing. Sober. Where had he been?

"I've decided," he whispered against her ear, sending thrills up her spine. Mary knew what he meant. But she wasn't sure what to expect. She leaned into him, savoring Lukasz calling her his sweet Mary, the warmth in him that evening. He pulled her tighter.

"Watch, watch, baby's asleep." Mary wiggled away but kept smiling at her husband.

He kissed his son's forehead, then Mary's, running the back of his fingers along her cheekbone.

"You've got the name, Pop?" Ida said, chopping faster and faster.

He shot her a grin. "I've got the name."

He peacocked to the table and popped a coin of carrot into his mouth, making Mary smile wider. It was as though the whole kitchen had exhaled in response to his delight.

"He will be…" He drew his hands overhead like a marquee. "Stanisław Franciszek Musiał." His Polish accent enveloped each name, shaping the letters into distinctly foreign sounds.

Mary was well aware that many an imported-sounding name could be shortened, altered, or outright replaced with a nickname that was as American as hers. She nodded, repeating the name.

"They mean 'achieves glory,' 'free man,' and 'he had to.'" Lukasz said the words with force, this time his broken English as clear as Mary had ever heard it.

"You selected very special names," Mary said.

He nodded. "They are set, they are powerful, they are great like he will be. I imagine him a line boss in the wire mill, great strength." Lukasz held up his hands. "Like me. He'll be just like me."

Mary grinned.

"Mrs. Mazur said he was born under a lucky star, a special moon. I could not give him a plain name like John or Joe or…" His voice was tightening and his neck tensed, a tendon straining against the skin.

Mary saw the impact his son had on him, feeling the birth in ways he hadn't seemed to with the girls. "How did you pick the names?"

"Library. Stopped after work. Miss Tennyson helped me with meaning."

This pleased Mary more than anything she could have imagined. She reached for Lukasz, who came to her again and held her tight. "Those are lovely names. Lovely." She felt him swell with pride against her. Lukasz took Stanislaw, kissed him, handed him to Ida, then reached for Mary. She took his hand, and he drew her close, humming a tune, moving her delicately around the kitchen, making the girls giggle at the sight of them dancing, at the lightness of it all.

"Our future is bright, my daughters. You will see. Our path is clear and again and…" He buried his face in Mary's neck. "I love you, Mary. I love you more every day."

She hugged him tight as he guided her around the kitchen, feeling weightless in his arms. His selection of names made sense. Lukasz, like many men who emigrated to America, saw their American Dream transformed from simple desires to wanting the spoils that came with greatness. "I lay groundwork. I till soil. I build a home…" He looked up and around, and Mary knew the fact that they were renting the home, not owning it, stung him.

"With a pretty blue door though," Ida chirped. "You promised Mom that, and we have a blue door."

"Just so." He cleared his throat and formed words carefully. "This good luck birth of our boy surely means we will soon own a home, and Stanisław Franciszek Musiał will take all that I leave for him and spin it into gold. Like fairy story."

Like she let herself be swept and spun into the dance, Mary let herself be carried off by Lukasz's dream once again. She scrubbed the kernel of doubt away like she had scrubbed that dried banana at Mrs. Hanlon's a few days before. With Lukasz's history of getting injured on the job, she found it hard to imagine them ever owning a home. That was partly what kept Papa from forgiving her and Lukasz for marrying. The idea that Papa, an immigrant himself, owned his own home, while the man who had taken his daughter gave her less than she deserved, could not be set aside.

Lukasz disappeared into the boot-room and returned with a pail of beers. He set it down and selected one bottle. Mary was hoping he wouldn't have alcohol at all. He lit a cigarette then pried the lid off with an opener. "Why you look sad? The name?"

She shook her head. She thought she'd veiled her worry. "I love the name."

He sipped the beer then looked at it. "No worry. Alexander always tell me 'drink at home and you'll never drink too much.'"

Mary wanted that to be true.

"Stanislaw will speak Polish like his sisters."

Mary's breath caught. She flinched, thinking that Lukasz's goals for their son's greatness, his fairy tale, would be hampered by not speaking English from his first word. That she couldn't be excited about. But the path to telling Lukasz no to anything, even small things, was always winding and steep. She rarely—no, she never told him no. Sometimes she worked around his opposition to inviting friends to dinner or having her mother to Sunday breakfast by surprising him with an extra-special meal. Or she simply did whatever it was that he disagreed with when he was working. But, still recovering from childbirth, back at keeping her home to the standard she liked, she didn't have the energy to think of a workaround for not starting their son on English immediately.

"Both," Mary said, not wanting to argue, but not wanting to agree. Not about something so important. "English, too," she whispered as she turned her back to him to stir a vegetable broth.

"It's all I have to give him right now." Lukasz's voice was strained. She recognized its tenor, that it was often a hint at growing irritation that could snap to anger in a second. She forced a smile and turned to placate him.

He set his cigarette on the ashtray. "I give him Polish language and an important Polish name."

Mary laid the spoon aside and took Stanislaw from Ida. She stepped closer to her husband, holding the baby so Lukasz could see his face. "He has the shape of your eyes and your coloring and… you've already given him everything he needs. Remember that."

Lukasz drew back, a look of surprise coming over him. "Yes."

Mary knew his worry about leaving something behind was rooted in them not yet buying a home. She ran her fingers through his hair and trailed down to the nape of his neck. "We've hit a rough patch with our savings. That's all. That will change. You'll have something to leave behind. You will. You have all of us. That *is* something."

He took a swig of beer.

He hadn't always been like this. She believed he could go back to being the man she married. "You're my husband, and we'll have everything we've ever wanted." She would make it so herself if she had to.

He smiled. She could see it was forced. But it gave her hope that he was trying, that this boy had in fact made things different for them. November 21, 1920, had indeed changed everything.

He brushed a lock of Mary's hair behind her ear. "You're a mountain. Unmovable. You always believe for both of us, when I can't even believe for me."

She may have been unmovable like a mountain, but even shale and granite could crumble or be shaped by rivers coursing past, running through them. She ran her hand down Lukasz's arm and sat at the kitchen table snuggling Stanislaw. "Stir the soup, Ida."

Lukasz popped another carrot into his mouth.

"Stan," Mary said. "We'll call him that."

Lukasz shook his head and pointed his beer at her. "Stashu. If you must shorten his name, it is to that. Not Stan, as though he was born to Irish parents."

She chuckled. "No Irishman would name his son—" She bit back her teasing words.

His features hardened. "I know. I know exactly that."

"Well," she said, wanting to change the topic. "Baptism."

He took a drag on the cigarette. "No."

She drew back. "No? What… I plan to ask Julia to be his godmother and…" She'd become adept at questioning him in a way that didn't emasculate him or call his limitations to mind, as Matka used to do to Papa. But Mary was tired, and he knew that her faith was everything to her. "It's important to—"

He pulled another beer bottle out of the pail and opened it with the lip of the kitchen table, the cap flipping along the wooden surface, landing in the center of the carrots.

"We will wait."

"But his soul. We can't just *wait* as though—"

"I pay for one baptism after the next boy is born."

Mary's eyes widened. Next boy? One out of five children was a boy. She couldn't fathom having another five just to get one more boy. "Lukasz, please. Be reasonable."

He winked.

"Please."

"We'll have another boy, and we will baptize both. One price for two."

Mary looked away. You couldn't just let a child float around the world unprotected, unbaptized.

"Look into your arms, Mary."

She did.

"I'll pay Mrs. Mazur double for another."

Mary tried not to scowl. Was he insane? Did he really believe that consuming all those putrid infusions, turning the bed, and so many things did more than her rosary and confessions?

He lifted her chin and gently kissed her. "You're tired—your thoughts are stretched or…" She could see he was searching for English words. "Rest your faith with me again. I promise another boy."

And with that, she leaned into him, her head on his shoulder, hoping the next one, boy or girl, was still years away from coming, hoping that somehow their first son would not end up soaring around in Limbo for eternity if harm came to him before baptism. The worry was too painful to let it settle in. The image of nature's elements shaping a mountain returned. Anxiety over Limbo threatened to nick away at her strength.

She couldn't let that happen. She'd protect their son and make their life peaceful, happy, prosperous. And she could do it by being exactly the kind of wife a man like Lukasz needed. Even if it meant giving in to him, even if being a good wife meant outwardly accepting his decisions when she knew they weren't quite right. She'd chosen this life with him, and she would not belabor the idea that she may have picked wrong. No. She loved Lukasz. For all his shortcomings, he was the one she had been meant for.

But with the health and protection of Stan's soul in mind, she stole into St. Mary's one afternoon in early December, dipped her fingers into the holy water font at the back of the church, and baptized him in the name of the Father, Son, and Holy Spirit. Though the formal ritual with oils and godparents and paperwork signed by a priest would still be required, what she'd done, in this crisis moment, would allow her to put away the most immediate worry on the matter of baptism. It was done. And the mountain walls that gave her strength and protection went unblemished.

Chapter 5

Mary

Christmas Eve 1920

Standing on their porch, Mary pulled Lukasz's collar closed, pushing the top button through and brushing her hands over his shoulders in an impotent attempt to rid the wool of lint and dust. With one hand tamping down his hat, he leaned in and kissed her, and squeezed her tight. "I'll bring the tree," he said.

"The girls are so excited to decorate."

"I will find a nice fat one," he said then disappeared into the trail of the Donorans heading down Sixth Street to work. Pleased with Lukasz's enthusiasm for the tree, she wrapped herself in her arms and stared skyward.

Christmas Eve dawn approached, but the Donora morning was coming heavier, murkier than its usual darkness. Charcoal sky hung low, lit with metal dust flecks caught in weak streetlight glimmer and hiding lingering starshine or even the sense that the sun was soon rising.

"Merry Christmas, Mar," a voice startled Mary.

The person drew closer. Julia Haluch.

"Hang on… let me grab the basket," Mary said.

She reached inside the house hoping that the contents would be helpful as the Lamberts had been sick for ten days. Mary went down the steps to Julia. "Merry Christmas, friend."

Julia handed the platter of pierogi to Mary so she could slide the basket handles over her arm.

Mary handed the platter back. "There's some hard salami, cheese, jellies, soup. For tomorrow. They feeling any better?"

"Lou went to work, but no. No one's feeling any better."

"Oh boy. I wish we could do more."

"You're a good soul," Julia said.

"You are."

"Lukasz get the tree?"

"After work."

Julia nodded. "See you at mass," she said, starting to move on.

"See you then," Mary said, excited that midnight mass was waiting to end one day and usher in another.

She crossed herself, saying a prayer for the Lamberts, hoping Lou was all right to take his shift. Not that he had a choice. The monotonous relentless mill production had a way of keeping everything and everyone in its predictable grip, entire families submitting to its demanding shifts and patterns, needing the rewards that came with doing so.

Back inside the Musial home, even with the darkness outside, Mary felt a spark of light, a transformation underway. The scent of Christmas helped. Pine boughs stuffed on the mantel framed a crudely carved-from-scrap-pine gathering of Mary, Joseph, Jesus, and the wisemen. Mac Schultheis, the head of one household Mary did laundry for, had given her the figurines in trade. Mrs. Schultheis had died the year before. Mac had been fired from the blast furnace for showing up to his shift drunk. Mary continued to wash for his family, free of charge. With their finances strangled, Mary wouldn't take food out of the Schultheis children's mouths.

Since she had an employed husband, Mary could find ways to stretch their dollars to pay for the most important parts of Christmas. With its own meager decorations, the Musial family did its best to ready the home to celebrate the birth of Jesus. Mary and the girls found pine in the gully and laid it on everything that didn't move and even gathered sprigs of pine and holly into tiny bundles they could pin to their coats for Christmas mass.

They hummed Christmas carols as they readied for Wigilia. Though Mary's ancestry was Hungarian and Czech, not Polish like Lukasz's, their Christmas Eve traditions blended nicely. She was happy to take on the more complicated, formal Wigilia meal to make Lukasz feel loved. It also reminded them each year of the night the two had admitted how completely they loved each other, both surprised with the intensity of the other's feelings and the risks they were willing to take.

Weeks of procuring food items and preparing them as demanded by Polish and Czech tradition had put all the Musials in a happy mood. Even Lukasz sprang out of bed with a smile. He returned from work without any stops at taverns, and Mary thought the birth of their son had indeed changed everything, had lifted them all.

The kitchen was alive with scents of beetroot soup, cep-and-onion dumplings, potatoes, sauerkraut, carp, herring prepared with cream, sour apples, and onions, pierogi, and cabbage rolls. And one of Mary's favorites—kutia—wheat grains, poppy seed, fruits, honey, and nuts soaked in red wine. The girls' mouths watered as they prepared the gingerbread, fruit compote, and poppy seed cake. It was a king's banquet compared to their typical food allowance.

Ida and Vicki did their best to busy their little hands, keeping watch over three-year-old Helen and one-year-old Rose, bouncing handmade knitted balls, readying them to hang on the tree when Lukasz brought it home.

Mary admired the dinner table they were setting for Wigilia. They had scattered straw on the wood top to recall Jesus's birth in a barn. Then Mary had spread the special linens that Zofia

Kowalk had given her and Lukasz for their first Christmas as a married couple. Mary's heart was full with the sounds of daughters chattering and Stashu's soft cooing.

Scant flu cases had signaled what Donora's health board considered the end of the Spanish flu pandemic. This lent additional excitement and gratefulness to a season that Mary adored even without a new baby boy or a shift toward better healthy days. She had pulled an extra chair to the table and set extra dinnerware. "Why'd you add that one?" Ida asked, tugging Mary's sleeve as she chopped mushrooms they'd foraged and stored for Wigilia.

"In case an unexpected visitor arrives."

Ida smiled. "Like when *you* were the unexpected guest."

Mary smiled. "That's right. In 1913, the Kowalks took me in for a meal when I was running errands for Father Kroupal. Icy rain and…" Mary stopped, overwhelmed by the memory.

"And you and Pop fell in love."

"Fell in *full* love; we were in love long before we admitted it that night."

"Maybe Grandma Lancos will be our surprise guest?"

Mary shrugged and went back to chopping. "She's still afraid of the flu. Auntie Rose is delicate. Not sure they're going out even for mass."

If only she and Lukasz could have Mary's sisters, brothers, and parents to celebrate with dinner and mass. But it had been since that Christmas Eve of 1913 that she'd spent any part of it with them. Mary had been forced to flee due to a preying boarder who Papa decided she ought to marry rather than clobber with her umbrella to stave off his advances. In love with Lukasz, and angry and hurt at Papa's idea, she'd fled. Through a series of fortuitous events, Mary had ended up at Wigilia dinner at the Kowalks'. Zofia had noticed Mary's bent umbrella and invited her in because there was a man at dinner who could fix it. Lukasz. Mary's love.

That night was the first the two spent together and each declared their love to the other—a miracle. Mary had given up her family for Lukasz, but he had saved her, and so her choice was correct, and she revisited the tender moments of that Christmas Eve regularly. Lukasz loved her like no one ever had, and for that she would forever keep her vows. Forsaking all others, including her own family when it came down to it, even when it hurt so much it forced her breath away.

Mary crossed herself and considered the idea that maybe Stashu's birth would not only give Lukasz what he needed to be truly happy, but perhaps it would change things between Papa and Lukasz. Maybe they'd see each other differently as fathers of sons. A blessed birth. The midwife had said as much. Lucky Jupiter with Sirius alongside it, and an unusual pink moon. Mrs. Mazur had never witnessed one before. But Mary had. A pink moon had brought Lukasz and her together, shining down the first time he saved her.

She stirred the mushroom soup, little Stashu bundled in her free arm, light as a feather, just days past a month old. She hummed carols, the girls' sweet, high voices joined in, with Vicki making up verses, causing them all to giggle. Midnight mass and the Christmas tree were Mary's favorite traditions. Lukasz loved the oplatki—the wafer they'd break before eating, making their wish for the new year. Mary had traded Father Kroupal for some unblessed wafer by helping Matka do up the Christmas linens for the church. Stirring the soup, Mary whisked away any lingering resentment that had formed when Lukasz had lost the higher-paying mill job. They could not both afford to blacken their hearts.

Things were changing. They had to.

His getting canned that summer had been notable, but she only sporadically let the rumor that he'd been to the tavern on lunch break that day sink in. She pushed away the truth because there was no use in marinating in it. It was said his boozy meal led to him and Buddy Bratcher getting the wireworks shut down twice in one shift, resulting in Lukasz's last injury as well.

Mary told herself that wasn't the full story. He'd been exhausted after barely sleeping through the sultry, humid heat of the summer. Further drained from pulling two double shifts, all in the attempt to save enough money for the down payment on the pie-slice of land he'd had his eye on since they first met. The truth was Mary accepted her part in his dismissal. She had excitedly showed him the wad of cash they'd saved, how they were just a hair from being able to buy the property. If they'd just had a little more before summer's end, they could have done it. And so he started taking every money-making opportunity that passed his way—including the extra shifts. When the firing came, Lukasz's black mood had expanded, mushrooming like smoke pushed back into a home by a closed flue.

Stashu stirred and let out a high-pitched cry. Rose imitated her brother, her tired eyes revealing growing discontent. Mary sat at the table and nursed while the girls pulled out the box of paper snowflakes for the tree. Mary gestured toward the decorations. "Girls, that box. Dig through there."

Ida and Helen knelt down and started sorting. Vicki tried to soothe Rose with a steady stream of soft ornaments that little hands wouldn't break.

"In the middle there... gently, Ida. Grab that," Mary said. Rose toddled toward Mary, reaching up with both hands. Mary scooped Rose onto her lap and she was asleep in moments.

Ida's eyes went wide. "The angel?"

Mary nodded. "Your father made it one Christmas. He was so very good with his hands."

"But now his hands hurt." Ida held up her own hands, making claws to show how Lukasz's fingers were sometimes bent after working.

Toiling in the wire mill had eroded Lukasz's dexterity. Though he was still strong as an ox, his fingers had been caught between hundred-pound wire bundles too many times, blunting their nimbleness.

"But we have the ornament," Mary said.

"The angel," Vicki echoed. "Like Rose and now Stashu."

"Like all of you."

Ida grinned.

"Sometimes I can't believe we still have it after…"

"After what, Mom?" Ida stopped and squinted at her mother.

Mary's breath caught. She wouldn't go into all of that. "The years. After all these years."

Ida pushed aside graying cut snowflakes and pulled the enameled angel up into the light of the room.

Vicki kissed Rose's head then petted Stashu looking at her mother. "Sweet baby boy."

Mary nodded. "The sweetest." In fact, he'd been easy, this fifth baby. A good sleeper, especially when he fell asleep in bed after nursing. Like honey dripped and swirled into hot tea, Stashu permeated their lives. His presence lifted everyone's mood, most especially Lukasz's. A gift. If there had been an appropriate word for gift in Polish to use as a name, she might have suggested that for him. But that was not her place to suggest such things. Lukasz was the man of the house. He would make decisions about the boy, and she would defer to him when he paid enough attention to push an issue in that regard. It was the way things were. And it was a small price to pay for Mary having her own passel of children, a family where she was its center.

The boy. He worked like a magnet, drawing Lukasz home after each shift, luring him past the taverns, the Falcons. Their new baby boy eased Lukasz's need to drink in order to clear the sulfurous debris that came with setting up house in a town like Donora, its people who lived, breathed, and choked along with the mills that lined everyone's pockets.

And so, Mary nestled into their small home surrounded by the children who gave her life as she'd given it to them, and invited contentment. Finally, unafraid that it would dissolve with a turn of bad luck, peace washed over her. Seven years since the fateful Wigilia that had shifted Mary's world, filling it with unrecognizable but unquenchable wants and needs. After all those years, everything finally seemed to have its proper place.

Chapter 6

Mary

Noon came and went. The sun wouldn't wait for Lukasz to begin its setting. Mary opened the front door, stuck her head out for the twenty-third time that day. The sky was thick with stippled shades of gunmetal and elephant, tinged with Prussian blue. Combined with the heavy zinc mill smoke, Mary doubted the girls would be able to identify the first star of the night, the signal that Wigilia dinner would begin.

Lukasz was late. Forced to the countryside to cut his own tree with some of the men he worked with? Herb late to relieve Lukasz again? Mary busied herself with the girls, bathing them, brushing hair, wiping down shoes, even pairs that didn't fit them, making them as shiny as possible.

She resisted the urge to jump to the conclusion that Lukasz had gotten a Christmas bonus or earned extra tips and was drinking them away. No, she preferred to imagine him arriving home, dragging the tree, his pocket full of coins or a few dollar bills from generous travelers, ready to present to Mary more money for the property, their American Dream.

It's what she would have done. In fact, it's exactly what she had done. Mrs. Hanlon had given Mary a five-dollar Christmas and baby bonus. It was an enormous sum, and though Mary could think of a thousand ways to spend it on presents and clothing and shoes—pretty shoes for Ida and Vicki—well, once she started spending the money in her mind, it was gone in a snap, and there was never enough. So she rolled the dollar bills and wrapped each in red paper like cigarettes, bundling and tying them with twine, tucking a sprig of holly with three berries into the bunch for a festive look.

She'd bought some elderberry wine from Mrs. Mazur. She had it all planned, envisioning the children asleep, she and Lukasz in front of the fire sipping wine and exchanging gifts, thereby re-establishing their dreams, making progress toward them concrete. It was ridiculous to get excited about five dollars when a down payment would be upward of five hundred unless they could get the property owner to give them a break. Still, the unexpected bonus felt like a million, and just thinking of Lukasz's smile when he opened the bills filled her with joy.

A fresh start. So Mary continued to cook and bake and prep the foods, hoping that maybe despite worries about the flu and Papa's disapproval, Matka, her sister, Victoria, or Rose might appear out of the smoke and fog. She knew better than to wish for Papa to stop by, for he'd not forgiven Mary for marrying Lukasz and putting an end to his American Dream for her.

She eyed the table and adjusted the runner down the center where they would place all the platters and chuckled. How strange that she'd yearn for Matka after seeing her as so harsh, so angry and discontented all the time when she was growing up. Yet it was she who had hidden behind the confessional at Mary and Lukasz's wedding. It was Matka who Mary glimpsed dropping baskets on the porch stuffed with bread and cabbage stew—the stew Mary had sworn she'd never have in her house due to its pervasive odor. Yet having her mother drop it off was precious.

"Mom." Ida yanked on Mary's sleeve. She held up her coat. "Time for the first star of the night."

Mary slipped coats over arms and buttoned the girls up and then went into the yard to begin their Wigilia, their Christmas Eve. Mary sat on the top step while the girls frolicked.

"There!"

"No, there!"

Their voices rang in the darkness, arms thrown to the sky as they searched. The sun never shone golden that day, but Mary could sense its position in the sky. And as it fell below the hills, the churning, firing, blasting, and smelting narrated her story, her fears. The mill sounds pulsed in her veins. A barge groaned a low, long song, mirroring how Mary felt with Lukasz's absence on such a special night.

"*There* it is!" The girls went silent, and that drew Mary to her feet to see.

Their little faces upturned, tiny fingers pointing.

Mary looked up. "Well, there it is. I didn't think…" She draped her free arm around the girls, pulling them in close. The hushing of their voices, their still bodies, the awe inspired by a single star that seemed revealed just for them was a treasure. Suddenly her prayers, their carols, their decorating, the anticipation, the comfort of tradition seemed as valuable as anything she could think of. It was all for the girls. They would remember this, Mary told herself.

Back inside, they gathered at the table, retelling Lancos and Musial holiday lore.

Helen's face shone like Mary had never seen it as she seemed to grasp the idea of Christmas, the religion and the presents. And so Mary dug out bits of the day's happiness like she'd done with coal from the seam in her childhood backyard. Ida would take Lukasz's place in breaking the oplatki with Mary. His favorite part.

God, he could have fallen in a ditch on his way up the hill. His stomach had been queasy that morning. His long hours dealing with the public. But something in her gut told her his lateness was due to none of those things. Looking at her chapped hands, the mounds of linens she prepared for the church so he could have his oplatki—no.

She wouldn't wait anymore. No tree. No word. No oplatki for Lukasz. She forced her mood to lift as the children enjoyed the mushroom soup in the first course down to the poppy seed cake in the twelfth. And when the meal ended, the girls insisted they lay all the tree decorations on the table, ready for when their father returned with the fat, beautiful tree he'd promised. Their eagerness stung Mary as she could taste the disappointment that would probably follow. But she let Ida have her expectation that all they planned would unfold the way they'd imagined. She didn't need to tell her not to get her hopes up after Mary had collaborated with Lukasz to raise them.

All was different now. Wasn't it? Wasn't it? She had believed it so.

They headed to mass, stuffed into layers of sweaters to keep drafts from spreading coat seams with sharp winter air, each girl with her own teeny holly-and-pine bouquet pinned to her lapel. Under the smoky night sky, Mary's longing for her Lancos family expanded like the orange blast-furnace flames firing down below. Lukasz filled the Lancoses' absence for Mary most of the time. But now, on this night, with their beautiful new son, her husband was absent, too. And that was nearly too much.

Squashed into a pew, Mary waited for the predictable Latin words and carols. But for the first time in her life, instead of being swept into the dependable rhythms of her beloved Catholic Christmas mass, Mary said her own prayers, asking God to somehow make it possible that Lukasz had been given an extra shift at the hotel, that he'd not forgotten the tree on purpose or out of carelessness. Not after everything had changed. Not after believing it could.

**

Mary wasn't the only woman in Donora to attend mass without her husband. The mills knew nothing of holidays or sacred religious celebrations. Triplet tyrants—the steel, wire, and zinc works provided the undergirding for America and promised men and their families prosperity. But the mills took back just as much as they gave. A cooperative arrangement the workers agreed to and even craved, but the exchange meant that no one, no thing, not even God interfered with production.

Mary lingered in the hugs of friends a little longer than she normally would have. Perplexed expressions slid over the friends' faces, followed by understanding nods as mothers were pulled away by children eager to return home. Not even Julia asked for details of why Mary Musial seemed to need conversation that night, why she seemed to yearn for something unspoken. She simply held Mary's gaze longer, knowing without even asking—she'd experienced it, too.

So with churchgoers scattering to their homes like ants up and across hills to a picnic, Mary, with baby Stashu in her arms and the girls skipping along, alert for icy patches, trekked through town on Thompson Avenue toward home. Vicki waved her hands above her head and pranced along. "The tree, the tree, the tree! The Christmas elves will have come!"

Ida scooped up Rose to keep up the pace, and she smiled at her mother. With that one gesture, picking up Rose without being told to, Mary saw herself in Ida, the caretaker of siblings, the one who filled in all the gaps without a second thought. Mary patted Ida's back, and the girl joined in giggling with her sisters, making up rhymes, causing Mary's belly to clench as she filed through her mind for just the right words to excuse their father's failure to deliver on his promise. There would be no tree. He would have appeared with it hours before if there was going to be one.

As they approached Sixth Street and turned up the hill, Mary had begun to grease the wheel of apologies. "Now, girls. Remember your father may have pulled another shift, and if so, the elves might be a little—"

Mary slowed. Was it possible? The streetlamps spit out enough light to see the shape of a man and a tree at the front door of their home. Mary's breath caught. The girls squealed and rushed forth. Mary paused. Like a boilermaker drink, a shot and beer set on fire, two distinct conditions flamed inside her. Relief and resentment.

She walked on, assessing the scene from afar. Lukasz's cigarette hung from his mouth, the orange glow tracing his animated movements. That was good. At least there was that. A joyfulness. He was singing "Joy to the World," her favorite carol. She exhaled. He was safe. He had brought a tree. She drew nearer. His legs looked wobbly. He barely kept the tree upright. Closer still, the scent of beer and whiskey came through the settling fog, past the potent pine scent.

"Mary! My sweet Mary, on her favorite day of the year!" He reached for her. "My boy." He took his cigarette from his mouth and flicked it away, then bent in to nuzzle Stashu. Mary eyed the tree.

Lukasz drew a deep breath. "Scotch pine." It jiggled in his outstretched arm, the boughs whispering up and down.

"It's beautiful, Pop!" Vicki clapped her hands over her mouth.

Lukasz pulled her into a hug. "*Chudy*. Not as fat as we wanted."

"Fat enough!" Vicki laughed.

"*Nie jest idealny.*"

"It *is* perfect," Helen said.

"Like us. *Niedoskonały.*"

Perfectly imperfect described them exactly, Mary supposed. She gestured to Ida, who set Rose down. Mary kissed Ida's forehead, lifting Stashu toward her open arms. "Careful with his neck. Put him in the basket." Ida nodded, and Mary reached around her to open the door.

The girls trailed inside first. Mary reached through the branches to the trunk, ignoring the spiked bark, and started to drag the tree inside.

Lukasz stepped in front of her. "Ahh, you're not mad? No. Not tonight. Not…"

Mary studied him for a second, his eyes carrying some happiness behind the boozy haze. She nuzzled into him for a moment. "I'm just glad you're home."

"Home is everything," he said.

The two lugged the tree toward the door, Lukasz lifting it by the bottom of the trunk. It scraped along the doorjamb, pine needles dropping onto the wood floor sounding like icy rain. It must have been sitting on a tree lot for days without water.

"Ooooh, our tree," Helen said, hands clasping her cheeks. The girls were not bothered at all that it was a terrible specimen. Mary wanted to focus on its hidden beauty same as they did.

Lukasz dragged it to the corner spot they'd designated the day before, a trail of needles dribbling behind. Ida followed along with dustpan and brush.

With it balanced in the stand, Lukasz turned. "Merry Christmas, my lovely daughters," he said, scooping each one into his arms for a hug before moving to the next. They giggled into his neck, and this made Mary smile—his attention on the first four of his children.

"And my beautiful, wonderful wife…"

Tears burned Mary's eyes. Happy he was home, sad that she didn't need to ask why he was late because he would report the same story he had countless times. She didn't ask about tips or bonuses. The answer would hurt too much.

Lukasz dashed outside and returned, a parcel in his arms. He set the package in the middle of the table with all the decorations that were waiting to be hung on the tree. He ripped into the paper, and one soft orb after another rolled onto the table with muffled thuds.

The girls squealed again, grabbing oranges, holding them to their noses.

"And for you…" Lukasz ran outside again and returned with another package. He handed it to Mary. She looked inside and pulled out one of what must have been a dozen lemons.

Lukasz held her close, the scent of booze tinging her relief.

"I promised you a lemon-scented life, and I've…" His voice cracked.

She held a lemon to her nose, wanting that to be what she smelled, not the alcohol.

"Mary, Mary, Mary," he said against her ear.

She glanced over her shoulder at the girls excitedly dressing the spindly tree in handmade ornaments.

"I… money go up and down, and I get ahead, then…" His words, still hobbled by a thick accent, sank into her.

"It's stupid that I bring you lemons for Christmas, but I wanted to say…"

She leaned her forehead against his, appreciating the thought behind it. "It's not stupid, Lukasz. I hadn't thought of it in years—the lemon-scented house. It's not what really matters. But you… *you* remembered."

He looped his arm around her waist, pulling her into him, the familiar angles of his body pressing into hers. He grazed his lips over hers, then kissed her fully. And in that moment, with the lie that she'd told between them, that the dream didn't matter to her, her world was righted. Even if just for a moment. For better or worse.

They held each other. Lukasz hummed "Silent Night," and the two swayed in a half-executed slow waltz. As they circled toward the tree, the flowerpot on the shelf near the window caught her eye. She'd hidden the gift-wrapped dollar bills inside. Beside it was the bottle of homemade wine. Perhaps they could still enjoy it?

Happy squeals from the girls drew Lukasz to them. Vicki held the angel up and Helen took it, cradling it.

Lukasz knelt and looked at the girls directly. "The angel. Back when my hands worked well, I made this for your mother. Added enamel and all."

"We know! We know!" Ida said.

"You made so many beautiful things." Vicki put her hands against her father's cheeks.

He blushed and took Victoria's chin. "The most beautiful of all is you girls."

Mary's eyes watered. She swiped away a falling tear, surprised at how quickly this one sentence dissolved the resentment.

"Mary?" Lukasz stood and reached for her.

"Yes, yes." She took his hand and climbed the step stool. He gave her the angel then gripped her hips, steadying her. She stretched to her toes, holding her breath, and placed the angel onto the top branch, sending a shower of needles to the floor.

"There," she said.

The girls clapped.

Lukasz gently tugged her, and she fell back into his arms where he spun her, making her laugh, bringing squeaks of delight from the girls. "Me! Swing us! My turn!" they sang. And Lukasz did. Mary made cocoa and readied the cut-out sugar cookies on a plate. With everyone under one roof, Mary deemed her world secure again, as she'd felt earlier, even if not exactly the way she'd thought it would be on that first Christmas Eve when her life's path had been set.

**

Mary and the girls swept up loose pine needles and finished the tree by tucking the flannel skirt under it. They had cider and cocoa with real cream. Lukasz trundled off to bed before they'd finished their drinks.

Mary nursed Stashu and tucked the girls into their shared bed, encouraging them to say their prayers and think of baby Jesus instead of only sending repeated wishes to God for Santa's arrival. She pressed a kiss on each girl's forehead and cheeks making them giggle. Ida grabbed Mary's hand and held it to her chest. "It hurts, Mom."

Mary sat on the edge of the bed. "You're sick?" She thought of the flu-induced pneumonia that had killed so many. Had she been careless in listening to the board of health about the illness having run its course?

"Not sick."

Mary leaned down and put her ear to Ida's chest. Perfectly clear, her heartbeat strong, no cough, no fever. She slid closer to Ida and tucked a lock of hair behind her ear. "Then what?"

"Inside. My heart. It hurts… and it's empty at the same time."

Mary shook her head, not understanding.

"I don't know why. When Pop came home, he seemed happy at first, but not happy. He was laughing, but not really laughing, and he couldn't hold the tree… I don't know." Her voice came cracked, quiet, as though hiding her words from her sisters. They'd already dropped into sleep, their breaths even and soft.

Suddenly Mary knew. "Scootch over." She snuggled in, pulling Ida close. She'd felt the exact same way as a girl. The sense of unnamed sadness that came like a gasp, hit like a train, then liquified, seeping through the body like maple syrup, all without warning. Once the sensation was recognized, it never really left, just receded, until something caused it to suddenly intensify. Mary held Ida tight, wanting to absorb the strange sadness and remove it from her for good.

She'd tried so hard to keep the girls from ever feeling that, seeing their father stumble, catching the scent of sadness that could be every bit as powerful as the scent of Christmas. Mary had kept her vow never to humiliate Lukasz the way her mother had Papa. And in doing so, she thought she'd managed to hide anything that would cause melancholy to take hold. Mary could name a hundred women in Donora who felt the exact same way as she did, as her daughter now did. But she didn't say any of that. She just waited for Ida's sniffles to dissolve into deep, peaceful breaths, and then she slipped out of the room, sure of what she needed to do next.

**

With the house quiet as could be, with Stashu sound asleep, Mary padded off to the closet where she'd hidden away five packages. She pulled them out and finished each with a red ribbon she'd traded a week's worth of bread for with Mrs. Michaels, the owner of Tweed's Dress and Hat Boutique.

Two shirts for Lukasz—half-sewn by Mary and finished by Mrs. Michaels.

One pair of used boots, shined to perfection, fresh laces zigzagging up the leather, the insides scrubbed and powdered so Ida would feel like they were new. One new dress in trade for a month's laundry service.

One dress for Vicki, remade with a looser waistline from when it was given to Ida two years before, but a growth spurt had made it impossible to wear more than a few times. A new shirtwaist in crisp white cotton.

Two shirtwaists, remade for Helen with new sky-blue ribbons to tie at the collar, and a skirt.

Two dresses for Rose, remade from one of Mary's, as all the sisters' hand-me-downs had worn to see-through.

And two baseballs for Stashu. Mary made them from played-out rag scraps sewn tight as anything around wine corks, then wrapped with black electrical tape. Mary traded a new white shirt to Paul Navotny who pilfered the tape from the mill.

In the peaceful moments of preparing the Christmas presents, Stashu fussed. Mary fed and changed him, humming "Joy to the World." He kicked his feet, mewling. She ridiculously showed him one ball before wrapping it. "Look at this, Stashu, a ball. All boys should have a pile of them." She put it near his hands, and he gripped it, startling her. His eyes went wide, as if he realized his hands had just done something.

"Oh my. Oh my goodness." She couldn't stop smiling. "You like it."

With everything under the tree, Mary exhaled, pleased. But now with idle hands, she was swept by the same sensation Ida had described earlier. She gripped the back of the chair. The ache. How it hurt to be surrounded by people yet feel alone. This wasn't how it was supposed to be. She'd given up everything for Lukasz because she loved and trusted him. Because once they'd found each other, the awful aloneness disappeared. In an instant, his love wrapped her like skin, shielding her from hurt and disappointment. And now… Ida. Mary had been ignoring the slow yawning reopening of that space inside her for… how long? She didn't want to pinpoint when her marriage stopped being a magic fairy tale.

Mary glanced at the flowerpot hiding the money, wrapped and ready. She stared at it for what felt like an hour, and then she did it.

One by one she unwrapped each bill, not wanting to later have to be reminded of the gift she would never give, the reasons she could not trust Lukasz not to spend it.

She stowed the money in a coffee can in the pantry, behind the lye and old butter churn, choking on what she was doing. She'd never kept anything big from Lukasz. She may have maneuvered around him, tried to convince him to change his mind about this or that, but she'd never hidden things like money from him.

Would he catch her? Did he search for things she may have secreted away? When he met her, he knew she tucked treasures away from her family, that she'd been desperate to start her grown-up life with "important" things, special items every young woman should take into marriage. Things her parents would have rather seen go to fund their mortgage or taxes.

The realization struck her. Perhaps he'd worried all along that she might keep things from him, and she wondered if she'd be able to keep this up—compensating for what he couldn't reliably contribute to the family.

Her breath caught. Here she was, rationalizing lying. The thought chilled her. Was she sullying their marriage by saving money Lukasz wasn't aware of?

She sank into a chair at the table. Was she hurting her husband? She shook her head. No, she had no choice. She loved Lukasz despite his slow unraveling over the years. She was saving them. Taking on the responsibility of keeping the family whole *was* the right thing. She could hide the money, build stability, hopefully ensuring their future involved buying a home, that this would give Lukasz what he needed to feel more American, accomplished. Or she could give Lukasz the money now, and it would vanish like the glimmering metal bits that flickered outside right in front of her eyes before disappearing in the wind, as though they'd never been there. Much as she wanted it to be true, not even a baby boy could change things the way she'd imagined he might. And so she hid the cash away knowing it wouldn't be the last time she tried to keep it all together, all by herself.

**

Early Christmas morning, the sound of scratching at the back door startled Mary. She squinted and moved toward it with a stutter step. Was someone there? Closer. A hand waved at the window. She stopped and gripped her chest. A face drew toward the glass, and she saw.

She opened the door and stepped aside to let the person in.

"Matka? Matka."

Her arms were full. She stepped inside, smiling like Mary couldn't remember. She looked past her mother.

"By myself," Matka said.

Mary took some of the packages, her heart soaring at the sight. "What on earth?"

Matka set the rest of the things down. "Somethin' little for each. Hats. Gloves. Saw yinz the other day, and with the wind and snow n'at. Well, the girls…"

Mary knew what Matka was getting at. "Thank you, Matka. Thank you." She hugged her tight, but as usual, her mother only slightly softened to the affection, letting Mary hold her more than she held her back.

"Oh…" Matka wiggled away, reached inside her coat, and pulled out a large white candle decorated with greens. "Fer the new one. The boy. Needs his thunder candle and figured if yinz hadn't bought mittens fer the girls, then…"

Then Mary certainly hadn't splurged on a candle for her newborn son, much as it was a tradition in their family.

"Matka, do you think maybe that you could… you and Papa and Victoria and Rose and George could… come for supper tomorrow? I mean today. It's already today. Nothing fancy, but— "

Matka held up her hand. "No. And Papa don't approve of me giving yinz these things. I was gonna leave 'em on the porch, but I saw ya in the lamplight and…"

They looked at each other. Mary's throat felt tight. How many soft moments had she shared with Matka in her life? Ten? There must have been more. And yet this felt like a first. She wanted to beg Matka to push Papa to accept Lukasz, to love Mary again, like he used to when she rowed him across the Monongahela every blessed day. But she knew better. This moment with Matka would have to be enough.

"Well," Matka said. She lifted her shoulders and dropped them.

"Yes," Mary said.

Stashu stretched and gurgled in his basket.

Matka's gaze went to him.

Mary lifted him from the basket, nuzzling him. Matka had been by a couple of times when Papa went to work, but she was never one to demand to hold a newborn.

"He wants his grandma," Mary said with a wink, moving closer.

Matka bent in, studying Stashu. He opened his eyes and mewled. Matka's face lit up, and she took him, swaying gently, the way all mothers did when someone handed them a child. She stroked his cheek with the back of her fingers. "Sure is sweet, this one. Ain't he? My, oh my, just somethin' 'bout him."

Mary crossed her arms and smiled. "Mrs. Mazur said the same thing the day he was born."

Matka raised her eyebrows at Mary, then turned her attention back to Stashu. She patted his belly and pulled the ball out of his blanket, holding it into the light. "Shoulda known you'd make a ball fer his first Christmas. Think of John and George. They wouldn't a had a moment's playtime if not fer all the toys ya cobbled up fer 'em."

Mary nodded.

"Wish Papa and I could give yinz a house, some money fer the first payment. Not just some hats and... That's what we wanted fer yinz. Something solid."

Mary took Matka by the shoulder, thinking of the money she'd just unwrapped and hidden away. "It's all right. We'll get our home. Like you and Papa. Promise. Lukasz works so hard and…"

They each grimaced, knowing Mary's defense of Lukasz wasn't needed. Neither could honestly say Lukasz worked as hard as he needed to, at least not enough to compensate for the money that went missing between work and home. No point in discussing it because Matka understood the circumstance exactly.

Matka kissed Stashu's forehead, suddenly awkward holding him. She shoved him into Mary's arms and backed away, wiping her hands on her coat as though she'd just finished cleaning fireplace ashes.

"Stay," Mary said. "Sit with me. Just for a while."

Matka shook her head. "Lots to do up at the house. And…"

Mary nodded, the dull ache that Ida now felt, reasserting itself in Mary again.

"Yer a *good* mother," Matka said, her voice a whisper blanketing Mary. "Grand. Like them ladies ya work fer."

"Please," Mary said. "Stay."

But Matka was already reaching for the doorknob, a silent exit her response as she faded into early morning fog. Mary listened to her footfalls until she couldn't hear a single step. She shut the door, wanting to trap those magic moments inside.

Never before. Never so soft, as though an angel had visited in the form of her mother. And in the final tranquil moments of night's transition to morning, Mary rearranged the gifts, then slept until Stashu woke for his feeding.

Chapter 7

Patryk

2019

Patryk stirred. He stretched, unfurling his limbs an inch at a time, stiff joints popping, betraying each of his ninety-two years. He coughed and gulped, trying to introduce moisture to his mouth. Without looking, he groped for his eye drops on the bedside table. His fingertips hit something boxy and mechanical—not his clock, not his eye drops, not his table. He struggled to his forearms, blurred vision revealing, even if hazy, that the Blue Horizon ogres had slid him over to the medical wing. He writhed through the fog. Were they drugging him? Had they done it to him like they'd done to Walter Sneed? Everyone knew.

Walter's pain had demanded something strong as his urethra was too small for an adult-sized catheter. It took two days of the man's agony for the doctor to finally purchase pediatric-sized instruments and give the man some relief. Patryk reached for his groin for a catheter check. Nothing. Thank God. He was fine. Other than stiffness, he didn't have pain. Were they drugging him for fun?

His eyes adjusted as Owen strolled into the room. *Was* it Owen? Or had Patryk died and gone to hell? No. Owen was much too young to be dead, way too innocent to have been sentenced to hell.

Patryk pushed upward, struggling. "That really you?"

Owen's face lit up, and he dashed to the bed supporting Patryk, adjusting his pillows so he could fully sit. Owen poured water into a cup of ice and held it to his great-grandfather's lips. "It's me."

When Patryk had drunk the entire cup down, he collapsed back, the pillows swelling around his shoulders. "What are they doin' to me? I'm high on somethin'," he grumbled, tensing every muscle in his body, his words fat and clumsy in his mouth.

"Shhh, Gramps. Take it easy. If you get riled up, they'll shoot you up with that horse tranquilizer all over again."

Patryk forced himself to take deep, even breaths. "Git me outta here."

Owen's face fell as he poured more water into the cup, causing the ice to crack and pop. "Enough with the water. Gimme an Iron City. I'll live another forty-two years if I let 'em turn me into a health nut." He was tired of living if it meant being at Blue Horizon.

Owen looked over his shoulder and then slid a bag from under the chair. He lowered his voice. "I brought two Iron Cities, but you can't tell Mum, and we have to hide them from the doctors. And you need the water. If you don't keep alive, you'll never see my major-league debut."

Patryk winked at Owen. He'd forgotten about Owen's baseball dreams. Something for both of them to think about. "A shot of Old Granddad *with* water, then."

Owen screwed off one bottle cap. "Don't push it, Gramps." He offered the beer to Patryk, who nearly fell out of bed to spring for it. "Wait." Owen pressed Patryk's shoulder back and held the beer away. "Only if you catch me up on the book."

"Book?"

"Don't play dumb. Harrison said you read about Stan Musial to him, and I said that's not possible. Gramps would not betray me like that, his co-conspirator."

Harrison. Patryk smacked his hand against his forehead, remembering for the first time, through his muddled mind, that his escape had been thwarted by Laura and her gang. He straightened and tossed his hand at Owen. "Just where in hell were ya? My God, that *Laura*. Forgot what a battle-axe she is. And her husband, that Danny, who, well, he's tolerable. Harrison's fine. But your aunt Laura... *Where the hell were you?* I reached the pickup point."

Owen pulled the chair closer, forearms resting on his thighs. His shoulders slumped, and he seemed to have to fight to maintain eye contact.

Patryk could see he was embarrassed. "Go on."

"When we planned the escape we forgot to take into account I'm not in charge of my life." Owen finally kept his gaze steady on Patryk's. "Mum had no idea what we'd cooked up, and she had me on a plane headed back to Grosse Pointe before I knew it. I thought it was just for two days to collect my things for the summer, but my father interfered and changed the flight and... I figured when I missed our pre-escape 'briefing' that you wouldn't... I mean, the nurse said she gave you my message."

Patryk squeezed his eyes shut, trying to recall a message from Owen.

"I told the nurse to tell you: *The eagle cannot take off. The eagle has a bum wing. The eagle will not land.* She swore she told—"

"Oh... oh." Patryk's brain fog began to dissipate.

"Oh what?"

He scratched his chin. Now *he* was embarrassed. "I thought she was talking about the actual eagles nesting up the river 'cross from the house n'at..."

"The Webster eagles?"

"Oh man," Patryk said. "What an idiot." Now he was fearing for his cognitive abilities.

"I'm so sorry." Owen shifted in his seat. "I should have said it more clearly, but—"

"We set up the cancel phrase. My fault, not yours."

Owen looked down.

Patryk tapped his shoulder. "Still. Bet you didn't think I'd make it to the post." He ran one hand through the air like a knife. "A thing of beauty. A blur of speed and ambition. Wings on my feet. Just like you said."

Owen raised his eyes without lifting his head. "A white-ass naked blur."

Patryk's mouth dropped open. They'd tattled on him. A rumble of laughter worked through Patryk and he leaned toward his grandson. "I panicked. Thought I was late. And so I put on those shoes, wrapped my ass in a towel, and just…" He pushed his hand through the air again, whistling.

Owen covered his mouth. His shoulders began quaking.

"Ran like the dickens. I think I clocked the first forty yards at 5.1."

Owen laughed so hard he wheezed. "Oh, that's fast for an old man."

"Bet your ass it was fast."

"So you lost the towel and…"

Patryk reimagined that part of the scenario for the first time. The image made low, rumbled laughter turn thunderous, and the two sniggered for a good few minutes, the release feeling better than anything he could have imagined besides freedom itself.

"Oooooh, boy it felt good to get out and stretch the hamhocks and just… be free, to move…"

"Well, I got a taste of freedom, too."

"Flying away from me? That's your freedom run?"

"No way. They dragged me to some hearing, and I stood up and demanded to spend my summer with my abrasive, beer-swilling gramps."

Patryk cocked his head. Did he hear that right?

"That's right," Owen said.

Was the kid serious? Patryk was swamped by a mix of bashful satisfaction and disbelief. "What about yer mum? Summer ball?"

Owen lifted his shoulders and dropped them.

Patryk didn't want the kid to waste a summer without playing ball, even though he was touched that the boy had chosen him over the game. "Can't sit on your dupa all summer swilling beer with me." Much as that's exactly what Patryk would like.

Owen pulled out his phone and started stabbing at it as he talked. "Turns out the baseball academy down the road could squeeze me in with their pitching guru." He turned the screen toward Patryk. Fast-moving images flew across the small screen as Patryk's eyes struggled to track everything happening. He pulled it closer, and Owen released it.

"Submitted a highlight reel from spring, and they took me—modified schedule, modified price. Told my dad that's what I was doing this summer. Spending it with you."

Patryk slid his gaze to his great-grandson. Could it be true? Owen looked as though he was going to cry.

Patryk felt as though he'd cry, too. He knew Owen's parents' divorce had been bad, that the boy might want to escape all that turmoil. But he couldn't believe someone was choosing him. Someone was sneaking him beers. Someone wanted to hear more about Donora and Stan Musial.

"Judge said I could. So here I am."

"Well, I'll be a monkey's bastard uncle."

Owen smiled. "One thing though."

Patryk set the phone on his legs and lifted his eyebrows.

"My mum'll be with us. Judge said no way to me staying at your place alone."

Patryk wasn't surprised in this day and age. Kids were lucky if parents allowed them to be alone in the bathroom. He could live with Lucy being around. "Gimme that beer."

"Tell me more of the Donora story. About the Musials."

"Grab the book."

Owen did that and handed Patryk the beer. He pulled a rolling bedside table toward them and set towels up behind the book so they both could look at it like it was a movie screen of sorts.

"So catch me up," Owen said. "I read the part about Mary and Lukasz Musial having all the daughters, living on Sixth Street, having Stan, who was to only speak Polish at home, according to his dad."

Patryk leaned toward the book. "Yes, yes. And don't you know it, but Lukasz nailed it about having a second son? Called it exactly right. Two years after Stan was born, another boy arrived, and the two of them, Stan waddling along and Mary carrying Edward, got their baptism in St. Mary's, the two of them at the cost of one. Just like Lukasz promised."

Owen puffed out his air. "They drank all that midwife infusion stuff again? Those disgusting recipes?"

Patryk shook his head slowly as he stared at the book as though he could see into the pages, as though there was more written and drawn there than was obvious to Owen. "Who knows. No petri dish baby stuff or injections or…" He shrugged. "People did what they could back then. Mrs. Mazur was who and what they had."

"Hmm," Owen said.

Patryk dug a finger between two pages and flipped one, revealing the next page. "Well. I haven't thought of this in… who even knows how long?"

Patryk felt himself falling down the winding rabbit warrens, lit with images, having to attach words to the silent films that guided him back in time.

"What's wrong?" Owen stood. "I'll get the nurse."

Patryk grabbed Owen's wrist. "No. I just remembered all of a sudden."

"Remembered what?"

"Looking at that page in the book. The years I wasted."

"This page?"

"Yes. I spent a few years after high school in single-A ball."

"What?" Owen's eyes went wide.

"I thought I could buy success with hard work. Turns out luck is required and no, no… not just luck. It's *magic*." He shook his head. "It's somethin' more. Somethin' that can't be taught or worked for or given or… I should've realized long before I did."

Owen cocked his head and collapsed back into the chair. He pushed his hand through his hair. "You mean I may not be good enough? No matter how hard I work?"

Patryk met his gaze. Owen's expression had turned worried. His vulnerability made Patryk uncomfortable. He'd never been good with any sort of ambiguity. "How the hell would I know if yer any good? Ain't never seen you play."

Owen flinched. Patryk thought the boy was going to cry for the second time that morning.

But instead, Owen straightened and lifted his chin. "Well. We'll change that this summer."

Now it was Patryk's eyes that went wide. Summer ball?

"But if you're dead, you can't go so…" Owen filled and handed Patryk a fresh cup of water. "Drink up, Gramps."

And with that, Patryk was struck with glee and sadness at the same time. Like the elderberry wine his aunt used to make. The sweetness was always infused with a dankness from the attic it was made in, from the smoky, sulfurous essence of Donora itself. Yes, Patryk was thrilled at Owen's companionship, but he was suddenly paralyzed at the idea of him having so little time left to live. Why couldn't they have discovered each other years ago? Why did life work just like that? Bitter and sweet. Lost and found and lost again. Maybe there *was* more life to live.

Chapter 8

Stashu

Almost five years old
1925

Company arrived. The chirping dragged Stashu out of sleep.

Down the hall, Mom shuffled through her drawer, utensils smacking against each other. The can tapper. The popping puncture sound.

He sat up.

Stashu's brother, sharing the bed, was curled on his side, covers over his head.

The scent of bread made Stashu's stomach growl.

Laughter. Mom's ladies and Stashu's sisters were in the kitchen.

Saturday morning. Bread Saturday. The moms had been up since the crack of day. Never went to sleep. They'd say all this over and over while they drank their hot coffee.

Another puncture to the milk lid. Stashu popped out of bed, pulling on his trousers, shirt, and too-big sweater with braided cables that ran down the front.

Sweet milk. He could already taste it, the thickness coating his tongue. He rubbed his belly.

Drawn downstairs, yawning, Stashu entered the kitchen.

Grandma Lancos's head snapped toward him. He'd forgotten how this went. How could he forget? The milk. His mind had been on that. Grandma clamped his arm and yanked him into her. "You'll catch double the flies with your trap open like that. Oh good, we can have *hors d'oeuvres* tonight with all those fancy flies you'll catch." She said that every time she caught him yawning. Never explained what *hors d'oeuvres* were, but he took it they weren't something he would want to have with a name like that.

He tensed under her grip. She dragged Stashu to the pan near the dry sink, dipped a rag in the water, and wiped his face, pulling his lips this way and that. She let him go to re-dip the rag and wring it out. He bolted. But Grandma was fast. She snatched him up again, this time splashing water all over his face, the rough cloth scraping his forehead, neck. And then—he knew it was coming. He braced, gripping the countertop. He considered running again, but she would just smack his backside hard when she caught him for making her scramble after him. She covered her finger with the cloth, squeezed his cheeks with one hand and dug into his mouth, her finger scrubbing over his teeth, his tongue, the roof of his mouth, making him gag. "Comes like a stray cat, Mary."

Mom turned with the can tapper in her hand. "He lives here, Matka. Gave birth to him myself."

Grandma tossed the cloth into the water and stood with hands on hips, breathing heavy. Stashu scooted to the far side of the kitchen table where Ida was sitting, kneading dough. She brushed her hand over his arm where Grandma had gripped it. He eyed the dough. She tore a piece off and gave it to him.

"Could waken him out of a fever sleep with the first hole in the milk lid," Grandma Lancos said.

Mom winked at Stashu and wiped the sharp end of the milk tool with a rag. "A little milk for the boy doesn't come up to an economic calamity."

"Sure does in my book." Matka glared at Stashu. "Every lost penny..."

Stashu swallowed the dough, and his gaze went to the can set on the table. His mouth watered. Musials didn't have funds to support kids swilling sweet milk. It was for coffee, recipes, not Stashu. The words rang in his head as he watched everyone's movements.

All the ladies at the table squawking, Grandma pushed the can to Mom. She tipped it, a drip into her coffee, just sometimes, she always said. Normally took it black as the Donora night sky. Mom pulled Stashu close. "Just a plop of milk landing like a little full moon." She kissed the top of his head.

Even with Grandma Lancos's rough handling, Stashu loved these mornings. With Pop at work, the mood in the house went bright and filled with female voices, ringing happy and loose, words no longer pressed through tight lips. The women softened, stopped barking orders to keep hushed. They started their yakking, laughing the morning away.

Except when Aunt Rose passed from the flu. Not the big flu, but the one that came after, surprising them. Stashu remembered that. The moms and their tears. Their hands that shook and grabbed tighter, but not for angry reasons. Stashu didn't like that, the sad softness in them when their faces crinkled and tears dropped like someone pumped a well behind their eyes in order to keep them coming. He felt lost when the moms went sad-soft instead of laughing-soft. Even plain hard was better than the sad-soft.

Most bread days brought Grandma Lancos with her rolling deep laugh, the one she only let out once in a while since she was mad almost all her life. Even her sads came out like her mads. Mrs. Henderson with her high, squealy laugh. The squeals climbed up like the craggy hillsides Stashu played on near the woodsy hollow. And Mom, her loud, loose laugh spread easy, her face so pretty, as though she was two different people—the one who laughed and the one who didn't. The children would take to laughing along with her, even if they had no idea what was so stinking funny. Mom's laughter filled them all with their own, and that was good as the sweet milk itself.

The can landed to Ida's left, right in front of Stashu's nose. He eyed the moms and sisters. Not one of them barked at him, warned him, said no, don't drink that or smacked his hand. It was right there. They must be saying yes. He snaked his fingers onto the table and worked the can to the edge, tilting it toward his mouth, better than he remembered, the sweet milky yum. He righted the can. The moms were too busy with their stories to notice Stashu's theft. He exhaled and smacked his tongue off the top of his mouth. More?

The moms were discussing yet again how Grandma Lancos had snuck away from Grandpa Lancos (who did not favor his Musial grandchildren at all, and Stashu wasn't sure why, but it had something to do with his pop), brought extra eggs, and thought she had extra time for coffee that morning. Mrs. Henderson, who always entered the Musial house by poking her head, scanning for what, Stashu wasn't sure, but she'd enter with one body part at a time as though she feared someone would stop her and she wanted to have fewer body parts to pull back out when they said no, she couldn't come in.

She came between cleaning up from breakfast and starting her baking and dinner. She motioned for the milk, and Ida passed it away from Stashu, to Helen and so on until it was in Mrs. Henderson's paw. She liked it as much as Stashu, and it was she that Stashu had to keep an eye on, watching her pour that sugary, thick liquid into her coffee by the ton. He licked his lips, the white magic rushing into her mug.

Helen got up for the coffeepot to serve the moms and make more.

Mrs. Henderson moved Vicki's hands, teaching her how to make her stitches smaller when darning socks. "Put the work in right once. You'll be happier for it," she said, making Vicki smile.

Stashu stared at the milk can until Ida asked for it to be passed to her, as she'd recently been permitted to add it to tea. Stashu questioned her position as adult and therefore eligible for sweet milk, but she did do lots of mom work, so he didn't complain.

Hands.

Mrs. Henderson's smelled of cabbage and garlic as she took Stashu by the cheeks and kissed his forehead. Grandma Lancos's were red and sandpapery, like the gritty soap she used to remove grease and such that embedded in her skin. And Mom's. Hers were chapped, too, but she tried to soften them up with some lemon-scented lotion she and the sisters were endlessly trying to get "right," stirring it in an old pot they didn't cook with, and oh boy, don't ever bring the lotion pot when Helen calls for the cook pot. They were always trying to get it to be the perfect mix of thick but not greasy with a hint of perfect citrus.

And so Stashu swiped sip after sip, eyeing up the moms to be sure they weren't watching. Grandma Lancos shook her head. "Old Ms. Hannity's boarding so many men she had to file papers as a hotel down at borough council. She's liable to end up in the clink if she doesn't keep a lid on it."

Why that made the ladies all buckle with hilarity, Stashu didn't know. The sisters didn't seem to know either as they passed glances with raised eyebrows and shoulder shrugs.

Another tip of the milk can. Heaven. Stashu's sisters were supposed to monitor him when there was condensed milk out in the open. They weren't paying him any mind. Another sip.

"Well," Mom said, "Mrs. Robert's going to put me in an early grave if something doesn't change at the house."

Grandma Lancos sipped her coffee. "That house? Not as big as some. What's so bad?"

"She keeps house like a rat."

"Rats are neat, organized," Matka said.

"Not this rat. Everything everywhere. Even leaves piles of frayed thread pieces. Doesn't clean a lick between when I come and go. And I never get to the woodwork or the chandelier, seeing how I'm busy scraping food dried to the point of cement on every blessed plate and bowl piled in the sink. Never saw a thing like it. Mrs. Hanlon was a breeze compared to her."

Stashu figured it was time for him to swipe another sip.

"Heard that baby of hers is still in a diaper," Mrs. Henderson said.

"Stashu was pot-trained at eleven months," Mom said.

Hearing his name made him freeze. He eyed the women.

"Well, she refuses to give the tyke meat juice. Kid probably doesn't have much to expel."

Mom sighed. "Eats like a bird. Caught him digging through the garden seed bin, nibbling on sunflower seeds, of all things. His waste was black and beady, like scat..."

Stashu exhaled and focused on his mission. Once the moms started in on diaper waste and baby feeding, he could escape their attention. The sisters were equally taken with their handiwork, whether with needles or dough. He walked his fingers toward the can, but this time as he neared the target, his little brother, nicknamed Honey by a neighbor who loved his sweet laugh, shoved Stashu out of the way and grabbed for it. Stashu gripped it hard, and the two of them crashed to the floor, milk splashing as they wrestled.

Hands. Punishing and loving. Stashu learned early that sometimes both were the same.

Grandma Lancos yanked Stashu by the arm and wheeled to smack his back end with that hard chapped hand.

Mom swooped in and rescued Stashu. "Matka. No."

"Goddamn it, Mary. Yer spoilin' 'im."

Mom eased her grip, and Stashu dove under the table, balling up in the center of the space. Grandma Lancos reached underneath, grappling for him. He lurched back against a set of legs. Ida's? Mrs. Henderson's? Helen's?

Hands patted his shoulder. Mom. He snaked his hand up and latched on to hers.

"The boy needs discipline!" Grandma Lancos said. "You girls were supposed to be watchin' 'im."

Ida and Vicki began to bicker, their legs getting jumpy as one accused the other. Even Rose caught a piece of the blame for Stashu's infraction.

Grandma Lancos got on her knees, scaring the breath out of him. He'd been caught in her clutches plenty of times and wasn't going to submit without a struggle. Grandma Lancos's face creased in anger. "Come out right now, Stashu."

Mom's warm hands pressed to his shoulders and reassured him.

"He's doin' it, Mary," Grandma Lancos spit, eyes growing wide. "Holdin' his breath. Face's beet red." She crawled under, closer to Stashu. He refused to let air in or out. He couldn't help it. He didn't want it to happen. But there were times his breath just stuck right inside him, like cement. The sisters' voices rose with continued bickering. Stashu pushed farther back against Mom's legs, her one arm across his chest, the other giving him firm smacks between the shoulder blades to start him breathing again. Stashu hated the noise, the arguing; it roared in his ears.

"Breathe, Stashu." Mom had come under the table, too.

"He can breathe, dammit, just choosin' not to… Stubborn… just like…" Grandma Lancos lunged for him. "Let me handle 'im, and he'll never hold his breath again."

Even Mrs. Henderson was under the table, siding more with Mom, begging him to breathe. But then the clash of voices was cut in half. The girls hushed. Mrs. Henderson poked her head out from under the table and froze. Her movement provided enough of a view that Stashu finally understood what had ushered in the shift in mood, what had silenced them, one after the other as each caught sight of him.

Pop. Lukasz Musial. Stashu had a clear view of his feet through the space made by Mrs. Henderson backing out from under the table.

Her voice was quivery, like paper lanterns in the wind. "Oh." She stood and backed away. "Lukasz. So nice to see you. I just stopped by for…"

Grandma Lancos got out from under the table, and Mom pulled Stashu against her chest. Warm, strong hands. She patted his back and kissed the top of his head. Then she took a deep breath and Stashu remembered that moment because there was something in her taking that breath that told Stashu she might be as put off by the appearance of Pop as the children were. The laughter, the softness of the morning disappeared like sweet milk down his throat.

"Lukasz." Mom's voice came next as she stood, leaving Stashu on the floor. "Lunch. You must be starving. Matka brought fresh eggs, and I'm boiling some—"

Pop squatted down and glared. It was then Stashu noticed the empty sweet milk can near his foot. Pop did, too. His tight lips and hard gaze fixed square on Stashu. "What in hell? You get out here right now."

Stashu pushed back against Ida's legs. Tears streamed down his cheeks. Fear tasted bitter, solid on his tongue.

Lukasz clenched his teeth. "The boy's crying. Tears? What's he got to cry about? I said no more milk for him. The money tree out back dropped its fruit. Where's my milk? There better be another can."

Stashu squinted through closed eyes, bracing for rough handling. But instead, Pop stood and Stashu watched his feet head for the boot-room, where they kept some canned goods. Before Stashu could form the thought, he was up and running for the front door, Honey close on his heels.

They huddled on the front porch, shivering in their shirtsleeves. Snowflakes fell. Stashu drew an arm around his brother. It wasn't often Pop paid attention to the children, but when he did, Stashu felt it like the heavy dresser that fell on him once when he opened the drawers and climbed to the top like stairs. But it was that day that Stashu realized how the appearance of his father shifted their existence like… well, it was like the switch that made train cars go this way or that, everything jerked away from where it had been going, everyone stopped, hushed up, and skulked away if possible. From that moment, Stashu decided his goal was to go unnoticed by Pop. Because garnering his attention was never good. No. Right then, a clear thought formed in Stashu's child mind—quiet as a mouse who understood his place in the world: stay out of Pop's sight, off his mind. And that was what Stashu did.

Chapter 9

Mary

December 23, 1928

It was done. Prayed over, finished, buried. Though her father's body hadn't been there, the scent of death filled the front room of 465 Sixth Street, and Mary was left to soak in the sorrow. Everyone had gone about their saying goodbye business in quiet ways, pushing down any pain or regret that came with it. Mary had, too, until that moment when she was finally alone. She sank into the chair near the fireplace, still as Papa's dead heart. She squeezed her eyes shut, trying to imagine what it felt like when one's heart went stony, when life ended.

It happened December 20, 1928, and all the daughter-papa hurt, sadness, anger, and resentment had funneled into her heart at once, now fluid and coursing through her as regret and loss. After all these years of mutual acts of looking the other way, he was truly gone. No more chances to make things right. Papa had not forgiven her for marrying Lukasz, for leaving the way she had, and Mary had managed to live with it, busy with her own children, occupied with keeping Lukasz content, keeping their household up and running.

Being shunned by Papa since 1914 had left Mary with clotted points of pain that marked the years in lost holidays, birthdays, and sometimes even hours. The sudden puncture wound brought by his death liquified the rotten clots, sending shocking pulses of emotion through her all at once. She'd thought she'd done a better job of hiding the markers of pain away like she used to hide treasures.

Images of their father-daughter life flooded her; laughing together as she rowed him to and from work across the Mon, her mediation role between Matka and him when he spent rent money in pubs in Webster, when his bad lungs made working impossible at times, when… She sighed, staring at the flames as they receded to embers, like the pain had done inside her for so many years.

"Mary."

She spun in her seat. She hadn't heard Matka enter. But there she was, head covered with a scarf tied under her chin, arms crossed over her wool coat that was worn even at the chest and belly. No. Papa's coat. Her face conveyed a fragileness Mary couldn't remember ever seeing.

Mary rose and turned fully toward her.

"Yinz'll move up to Marelda Avenue with me now that…" She jerked her head in the direction of the street where Mary spent her childhood.

She flinched. She couldn't handle an argument right then. Not with Papa's death, with Christmas Eve one day away, and so much to ready for the Wigilia.

Matka stared at Mary, stroking her thumb against the wool sleeve, the only part of her that moved, appearing unsettled even though motionless.

"Don't make that face, Mary. I talked to Lukasz. It's settled."

Mary grabbed the chairback for support. Talked to Lukasz. That couldn't have gone smoothly. She was afraid to ask for the details of that conversation.

"He took a stab at his usual stubbornness. I reminded 'im of the house and property he dreamed of. If yinz guys move in, I can stay in the house, and there will be money for you to save."

Always practical, even within hours of burying Papa, Matka was sorting coins, assigning where they'd go.

Mary finally found words. "You just told him that, and he said all right? Just like that?"

"Fished 'im outta the Bucket of Blood. He was easy. Didn't even make me walk on eggshells fer it. Didn't even raise my voice."

A memory of Matka dragging Papa out of a bar in Webster, humiliating him in front of his friends flashed to mind. She hoped to God Matka hadn't treated Lukasz like that. None of this rang true.

"Don't fret. I was polite. He was polite." She brushed her hands together. "Papa wanted it. Said so years back. Deal made. Said it again just before he dropped in the street on the way to the doc. Last words. And ya know I have a way with Lukasz. He likes me. Even if he fakes not."

Mary sank into the chair. That was all true. Was this Papa's way of admitting he forgave her without saying it aloud? Relief. Could moving to Matka's be the exact right thing to do? Though she believed Matka's story about Lukasz's response, she wondered if his acceptance of the offer would stick. But maybe he thought this was exactly what they needed to begin again.

Maybe even he'd had enough with the outhouse. Rustic as it was, her parents had put in plumbing, and except for them still digging away at that coal seam in the backyard, they were living with more ease than the Musials of Sixth Street. Still, Lukasz's moods came in waves of dark and light. Though there were patterns to them, there was the occasional unexpected torrent. She hoped that upon the beer wearing off he'd be just as agreeable to the idea as he apparently was when Matka snatched him out of the bar.

So many reasons for moving back to 1139 Marelda Avenue. Could the best reason be true? Yes. She decided she would accept it as fact. Papa wanted it. Being back there would mean she was finally in his good graces again. Gone as he was, as sad as she was about that, this released her from the sins that had broken them apart so many years ago, connecting them as tightly as before the falling out. His forgiveness filled her, sending tears of quiet closure.

Matka sat in the chair across from Mary, watching her.

Mary shifted farther into the chair, molding against the cushion. "Yes. This is the right thing." She said it aloud as though it needed to be released with the regret, feeling a little bit of herself repaired, healed, contented.

"It is," Matka said. "It is."

Chapter 10

Stashu

Spring 1929

This was it. He kicked the mound. Dirt mushroomed up as he dug out just the right groove for his foot, for just the right leverage to give his heater just a bit more speed. Blinding speed. That's what they all said. He'd practiced it forever. He'd achieved so much. But this was what he'd been dreaming about. Bottom of the ninth, three men on, two outs, seventh game of the World Series. It was up to Musial. He eyed the man on third, drilling him with his gaze. Nobody stole home, but he wasn't going to let Lazzeri consider it for a second. Hargreaves signaled for the slowball.

Stashu shook him off. Not the junk. The big man would know it was coming, and it would be game over. Fastball. Chump could never hit Stashu's heater. Never. He wouldn't abandon his bread and butter, not when the team needed him most. He breathed deep, drew back for his windup. Wind whipped dirt into his eyes. Thirty thousand voices blended to an indistinguishable roar, a mash of sound like the crushing mill noise. He was used to it. Now or never.

A voice cut through the cheers. A single voice calling his name. A woman. A fan. He shook it off. This was too important.

He hesitated, reset, then restarted his pitch.

"Stashu Musial. Now."

Yes, now. He was about to be the hero.

"Now!"

He startled and his grip slipped, causing the ball to roll off his fingers. No. It dribbled off like a slow spigot and hit the grass with a thunk, bouncing, not a bit of heat on it.

A dead duck in the World Series? Batter walked, run scored. Tie game.

"*Stanislaw Franciszek Musial!* Right this minute."

He scooped up his handmade ball and dashed toward the back door. "Coming."

Mom waited inside the boot-room, hands on hips. She looked over her shoulder and lowered her voice. "Take and get the laundry down to Mrs. Miller. Go now, and maybe we can get some ball in. And remind her I need the deposit in order to buy the wallpaper she wants me to put up."

Stashu looked back outside. Plenty of daylight.

"Temp's dropping like an anvil. Snow's coming." She tossed him his coat.

He put it on and picked up the basket. "Can't snow. Opening day's over."

"Mother Nature doesn't follow the baseball schedule." She jerked her head. "Get a move on if you want to throw before your pop gets home."

Stashu forgot Pop had the day off and did some work clear-cutting a field for extra money. He'd be home right around dark that night.

Stashu clutched the basket tight against his belly and bolted for Mrs. Zelinsky's. This little errand gave him a chance to practice his speed and agility all at once, hurdling a fence, fast feet in between pitted holes in the dirt road. It all would lead to his goal. Stashu may have been eight years old, but he was sure of what he would be. Daydreaming, sleep-dreaming, praying, imagining in clear pictures. Starting lefty for the Pirates. Half the fellas in town had the same dream, but he was different from them, and he knew it in his bones.

Scrap paper covered in scores, batting averages, RBIs, every detail reported by papers and broadcasters—he filled the pages with baseball. Then Mom taught him to use her sharpest needles to sew the pages together. But his pages contained way more information than the newspapers. He sketched his favorite players, Lefty Grove throwing different pitches and third baseman Pie Traynor stretched out to nab a line drive. He sketched baseballs with fingers wrapped around them, showing how to throw a fastball, a curveball, a slider. When games were broadcast, he took notes, recording pitching patterns of winning and losing players, noting details of hitters—not just their home runs but their fails, trying to figure out how to avoid the pitfalls that led to poor hitting. And for a lefty, there were many. Every baseball detail his mind could snatch out of the broadcasting soundwaves he added to his paper and studied over the winter months when there were no games, not even a whisper of the season to come.

**

Soft hands and eggshells.

Heading back home after dropping the laundry, with the coins in his pocket for Mom, Stashu's eyes swept the roads and grass and walkways, searching for round objects that could be used as balls when he and the fellas were in a pinch.

Stashu had written that at the top of every page of his notebook one year. A broadcaster said Lefty Grove grew up on a farm and had his friend throw eggs at him, thinking if he could manage to catch eggs with soft hands, he could train himself, right down to his fingertips, to perfect pitch delivery, to feel it all differently, in ways that would set him apart from others. Until he'd heard that story, Stashu only thought of eggs in terms of food and the beautifully decorated ones Mom created to be blessed at the church before Easter.

But after hearing the story, Stashu and Honey tried Lefty's egg technique themselves. Once. But as Stashu had been perfecting his feel for pitch delivery, Pop came home. Stashu would never forget the roar, Pop's face drawn in sharp anger, like a mountain had sprouted arms and legs and come to life in front of their eyes. The boys had scaled the only tree in the backyard, escaping their father's rage. He'd stood under that tree reaching for them. "I earned those eggs. And you're tossing them like we can afford to lose food. A game! Go make a ball of slag and twigs or throw rocks at each other, but don't you dare…"

Stashu had nearly opened his mouth to tell his story about Lefty Grove. But he knew better. Stashu's body had shrunk in the face of his father's anger. He hadn't meant to make him upset. He hadn't thought anything of it after he heard about it on the radio. But he should have known better. He knew his parents fought over money more than anything else. His father's raging had spiraled into all Polish. But the boys didn't need to understand every word of the language to know what he was saying, to understand how angry he had been.

Like the toddler kid who visited with Mrs. Henderson too close to naptime, Pop's temper tantrum had exhausted him, forcing him to coil to the ground, flop on his back, hand over his forehead, mumbling until he passed into a deep sleep. Still, the boys had stayed in the tree.

Mom had come home from work just after sundown. The girls who'd watched it all from the bedroom windows came into the yard with her.

"Eggs? Stashu? *Eggs?*" Mom had said. The sisters must have already reported the entire thing. Her voice hadn't been angry like Pop's. It had been more full of questions, the way Stashu's voice sometimes was when he didn't understand something at school.

"We walk on eggs enough around here, Stashu. We don't need to break them, too."

He and Honey had jumped out of the tree. Mom had stared at one, then the other, then settled her gaze back on Stashu.

"Now don't go thinking your pop's any different than the rest of the men in this town."

Stashu had stared down at his father, who looked more peaceful than he'd ever seen him, his face soft again, unworried, like Honey's looked when he slept.

"No," Mom had said. "That's not true. Your father *is* different than other men. That's why I married him. This…" She'd looked down. "This is just…" She'd shrugged. "He doesn't mean to drink so much. But sometimes with the work and worry about everything. Well…"

Honey had nodded. "I seen plenty of dads flat out."

The sisters had agreed.

"Well. Your pop overcame a lot to get to America, to find me, to…"

Pop had stirred.

"Let's get him up to bed."

And so the entire Musial family had helped Pop into bed, into a deep slumber that somehow managed to erase any memory he had of coming home and catching Stashu and Honey playing catch with eggs.

But the other part, walking on eggs around Pop, keeping them from breaking, that part hadn't changed.

Neither had the business about hands. Like Lefty Grove had figured out, a ballplayer's hands felt things differently. Stashu had known that even before he heard about Lefty's eggs. He'd seen other kids fumbling catches, stoving fingers. Honey was a good player, though younger than Stashu, so his hands didn't work quite right yet.

In baseball, there were batters with fast hands and quick-snapping wrists, fielders with soft, snatching hands, and pitchers with sneaky hands that hid grease and came over the top with camouflaged curving pitches that only the best batters could hit, usually by accident. He didn't need broadcasters to tell him any of this. He'd felt it himself. Games anytime and anywhere he and Honey could play, they did.

Except during school hours, Stashu had a ball in hand, tossing it against walls, into the air, back and forth with friends. His hands felt full that way, purposeful, even if the ball was handmade by Mom instead of a bright white regulation type that he and the kids were only sometimes able to play with.

The boys' methods for getting a "real" ball involved waiting for the men playing for the Industrial League to hit one over the fence, so the boys could disappear with it before they were caught. Not the most reliable way to ensure a full load of good balls.

Back home from running the laundry, Stashu gave Mom her coins.

"Not sure when your pop'll be back, so let's get some throws in before."

They took their places, one at each end of the yard. Stashu set the pile of balls his mother had made him over the years in a pile at his feet and loosened up his shoulders.

Mom smacked her hands together. "Let's go, Stashu. It's nearly dark and…" She held her hand out, palm up. "Snow's comin'."

Stashu was starting to agree with her. It was freezing.

Mom rubbed her palms together. Her hands weren't like other mothers'. Yes, Stashu's mom baked bread loaves by the dozen in the oven near the back hill. She mended clothes and cleaned scrapes and sewed dresses and did the girls' hair with pins and barrettes. But she also threw and caught baseballs and could smack a homer with half a picket from a broken fence. Being a lady, she wasn't officially a ballplayer, but Stashu couldn't help thinking his mother had been waiting for a boy as excitedly as Pop had just so she could teach somebody to play.

Stashu nodded, drew back deep, and imitated the pitcher he'd seen playing for the Zincs. He'd studied Mike McQueen, his long, lean back, the lift of the leg, the lever arm movement when he released the ball. Stashu did the same, sending it whistling toward Mom.

She caught it. "Heat on that one. But throw some easy, warm up a little, or you'll end up with that hanging arm like Mick Woods. Can't even throw garbage into the can these days."

Stashu nodded. He wouldn't argue. With Honey up at Charlie Graham's house, the girls doing homework, Pop at work and also generally unwilling to play games, and all his friends doing homework, Mom was his only hope for a few minutes of baseball happiness.

She whipped the ball back, and he caught it barehanded, swinging his hands back to soften the catch.

"Looking to find you a glove this year," she shouted.

Stashu stopped mid-throw. "Really?"

"'Course. Promised you last year."

Stashu threw the ball back, a smile lifting his lips. "Gee, thanks, Mom. But—"

Mom tossed the ball into the palm of her hand a few times. "I won't hear of it. I've been saving up, and I can hire out for extra ironing—"

Stashu ran to her and smothered her with a hug, his arms circling her waist, the scent of soap lifting from her apron filling his nose. She squeezed him hard, then pushed him away.

"Back. Don't have much time before dark."

Stashu looked up into his mother's smiling face. Fat snowflakes fell between the two.

"Look at that." Mom put her palm out to catch some.

"You were right," Stashu said.

"Even a broken clock's right twice a day, Stashu. Now go on, let's catch while we can."

Stashu sprinted back to his position and waited for the ball to come whizzing his way. He knew how lucky he was to have a mother who knew way more about baseball than any other mother in town—and more than some men, especially his own father.

He smacked his fist into his palm. Mom fussed with her apron.

Stashu bounced from foot to foot. "Let 'er rip, Mom," he said.

And she did. This time, even with the darkening sky, even between the snow falling heavy and fat, Stashu knew something was different about the ball Mom had just thrown as soon as it left her hand. But it wasn't until he caught it that he fully understood. Everything—its weight, perfect shape and regulation size, little islands of smoothness between the laces, so different than the beloved handmade balls Mom had produced over the years.

He stared at the ball, rubbing his thumbs over the faces sectioned off by red laces. He couldn't speak. A real ball.

"Now don't you go cryin' over it. It's just a ball."

He looked up at her. Her smile. They both knew it wasn't "just a ball." He sucked back the tears best he could, knowing the way his mom wanted thanks was for him to get back to throwing.

"Thanks, Mom." He wiped his eyes with his forearm and whipped the ball back, the sound of it hitting her mitt-less hands echoing in the hush of the snow falling over them.

She threw it back. The feel of it hitting his hands was just right, just as it should be.

"You're welcome, Stashu."

"Now I can do it." He threw it back. "I can be a Pirate for sure."

She caught the ball and flinched. She blew on the palm of her hand. "Can *and* will."

She threw the hardest one so far but bounced it in order to give him fielding practice.

He caught it, spun around, and threw as fiercely as possible, imagining making a close out from the mound to first base. It felt so good to throw a real ball.

She threw it back.

Next one, he wound up good and let it rip.

Mom caught it, but she doubled over, dropping to her knees.

"Mom!" Stashu bolted to her, getting on the ground.

"Woo-wee that was a brutal throw." She held one arm against her stomach and pushed the words out with uneven breaths.

"I'm sorry. I didn't mean to hurt you."

"Just my belly. Plenty of padding." She started to stand.

He helped her up and brushed off her stocking knees. "I'm so sorry, I really just…"

She took his chin and shook her head, breathing normally again. "You got an arm."

Something was different in how she stated that, something in the way she looked at him made him understand.

He jumped up and down. "So you believe it, right? I can play pro?"

She patted her belly then tossed the ball into the air and caught it. "Well. I'm not the one who has to believe."

She threw it to him. He caught it with soft hands. "But you do believe, right?"

She stared at him then smiled. *She believed.* He chucked the ball off the back wall of the house and caught it. When he turned back, she was still staring.

She walked toward him, rubbing her stomach. "You'll knock out one of those lights on the house, and your pop'll knock you silly."

He knew it was too dark to keep catching. Since they'd missed paying the electricity bill that month, they used candle and lantern light at night until they could scrape enough money together to pay it off.

She scooped the homemade balls into her apron and slung her free arm around Stashu as they walked toward the back door.

"But you believe, right? I was born under a lucky star. And just now I saw the way you looked at me. I mean I didn't want to peg you in the belly but—"

She nodded. "Jupiter. A planet and Sirius, the brightest star in the sky."

He looked up into her face. "And that moon…"

"Pink moon."

"Like the moon the night Pop rescued you from the river after you rowed across for Gramps, who wasn't there, and—"

The back door opened just as they stepped onto the porch. Pop stood in the light, outlined by the lantern glow as he lifted it high.

The warmth Stashu had felt as Mom retold one of their family stories dissolved with Pop's appearance. He stepped into the yard, arms crossed. He didn't have to say a word for Stashu to feel the air being sucked away, as though Pop had packed it all up and away for himself. "Games with your son instead of dinner for your husband."

Stashu glanced at Mom. She straightened, made herself tall and big as possible.

"No food for me, no baseball for Stashu," Pop said. "He could be working on that land I cleared today. Old enough to earn. I was asleep on barn floors at his age. Money in the land of the free. That is why I come." Pop brushed his thumb over his fingers to symbolize cash in hand.

Why didn't Pop see how much Stashu loved baseball, how good he was at it? All the dads in town noticed. Mom noticed. But not Pop. The man Mom described in her story—the one with big, gentle hands, his delicate handling of her, sweeping her up the winding, icy streets of Donora under a weird pink moon, after she fell into the winter river—was not the man Stashu knew. And that made him consider that if she'd made the fairy tale up about his father, perhaps she'd made the whole thing up about Stashu and his lucky star as well.

And so as Mom made herself big as she could, Stashu made himself small, ducking into a shadow to avoid Pop's gaze. When the door slammed, he exhaled.

But then he thought of how Mom had brought him this ball, a real baseball, and he tucked it up into his long sleeve so Pop wouldn't see. Without being told, Stashu knew his mom must have traded something big to get this ball, and if Pop knew she'd done that instead of putting the lights back on, well, it wouldn't go in a good direction.

Stashu didn't like when the electricity had to be put out every once in a while, but Pop wore it as a shroud of shame. And for that, Stashu would hide away the ball somewhere safe, not even showing Honey until the Musials had a chance to light their world with electricity again.

Chapter 11

Stashu

It had been an eggshell morning. Without even leaving the bedroom to see their pop, Stashu and Honey could feel the tension radiating from the kitchen, up the stairs to their room, penetrating the wood door. They'd slept a little later than usual, and so they hadn't yet gathered the coal.

"Gotta go out the window and get it," Honey said, opening the curtains and positioning a chair to use as a stool.

Stashu agreed. They dressed in a flash with Pop's voice rising enough that it sent another wave of tension their way. When Pop got that way, he'd tick through what Mom referred to as his "list of disgruntlements," not the least of which was that eight-year-old Stashu ought to have a job, like the girls.

Stashu could hear when Mom responded to Pop, but not what she said. She was using her quiet words to attempt to soothe and distract. Other things on the disgruntlement list that morning: that Grandma Lancos gave him orders he didn't want to follow, that he would not get the coal after pulling the night shift at the mill, that the girls were out scrubbing floors for several women on Thompson and the boys were tucked into a warm bed.

So Honey and Stashu climbed out a window onto the back porch roof and dropped down into the grass. They tiptoed along the house and retrieved the buckets from the back porch. Stashu held the pail up in the window so Mom could see that he and Honey were on the job, that Pop didn't have to fetch the coal. It was the same seam that Mom had worked as a child, and now that the Musials were living with Grandma Lancos, that job had fallen to them. Stashu didn't mind doing it. Not having to buy as much fuel as they'd needed at the Sixth Street house helped them put away savings. And that was something Stashu knew was important to keeping things smooth and steady in the house.

So Stashu and Honey filled the buckets, stealing quietly, gingerly over those eggshells, not breaking a one. Finally Pop disappeared into the bedroom to sleep off his shift.

**

The girls returned from cleaning houses and joined their brothers for toast, canned peaches, and coffee before heading off a couple miles across town to St. Joseph's Hall, the indoor gym where the Polish Falcons of America Nest 247 held training sessions. The Falcons allowed adults and children to preserve Polish culture through physical competitions and social activities even while immersing themselves into American life.

Stashu's belly, stuffed with bread, still growled as he, Honey, and their sisters schlepped toward Second Street. Fourteen-year-old Ida, along with Vicki, Helen, and Rose were charged with ushering their brothers to practice on time. When Stashu and Honey slowed to pluck stones out of the brush along Thompson Avenue, tossing them back and forth, Ida grabbed Stashu by the back of his collar. Vicki snatched Honey up, and they forced the boys to keep pace.

"Geeze, Ida. Your nails are scrapin'," Stashu said.

"Pop'll give us all a lickin' if we're late," Vicki said. "And I'm way too old for a lickin'."

"A sound mind in a sound body," Ida recited the Polish Falcon ideal as she always did when frustrated with keeping her brothers in line.

"Pop expects us to live that—especially at training," Helen said. "And I certainly don't want my hind end reddened either, not on account of you two."

Stashu shuffled along and comforted himself with the thought that Pop was fast asleep and wouldn't show up that morning at the Falcons despite how important he thought it was that his children competed in gymnastics and track and field, that the Musials kept traditional Polish standards at the center of their American life.

At St. Joseph's, the coaches moved the boys and girls into separate groups, rotating them among stations that taught and tested strength, flexibility, and agility. Some of the exercises were specifically performed on competition equipment like the horse and rings, double bars, and horizontal bar. But other drills featured calisthenics that built strength for track and field as well as gymnastics.

The Musial sisters were always at the top of the track and field team, but Stashu only paid specific attention to their tasks when the coaches cheered them after besting other girls in competition. Stashu concentrated on his own work, absorbed in every new movement and test of strength being taught.

At eight years old, his handstands were straighter and held longer than any teenager. Coach Sura, the big one in charge of everything, rubbed one shoulder (always that same one) and scowled as the other coaches praised Stashu, patting him on the back.

The comradery there, between the kids and the adults, made him feel as though it were a second home. Yes, the coaches were tough, wanting the best for and from the kids, but boy, they came with the praise in ways that made Stashu feel light, airy, and good like nothing else did. This particular day, several coaches huddled, heads bowed, talking one moment, and then they'd unfurl and point at Stashu, bark an order for him to tumble and land in a handstand, then they'd close back into their jumble, conferencing, loud enough for everyone to hear.

"Small and wiry," Coach Sura growled. "'Course he holds a handstand. Doesn't have anything to hold up, yet."

Coach Hokaj gestured. "Strong as an ox. Wiry, yes. That's good, not bad."

Coach Sura held his hands up. "Look at the kid's mitts. Tiny."

"Yet. Holds a handstand for years. It's time," Coach Hokaj said. "He will be top of the group on the horse and rings and double bars. There's no end to his potential. He is what we are about."

Coach Sura scratched both cheeks and drew his gaze up and down Stashu's body as though determining if pig iron was ready to move to the next stage of steelmaking.

Stashu's supporters continued to argue with the big coach, their hands whipping around, emphasizing, making their points in Polish, the home language for all the kids who belonged to Nest 247. Finally Coach Sura threw his hands in the air, surrendering. The other coaches collapsed around Stashu, jostling him and tousling his hair.

Hands. His coaches, with bear paws like Pop's, encouraged Stashu with cheers, smacking him between the shoulder blades, shouting praise, filling him with pride again. Stashu wished there was a way to can what he felt when he performed at practice or in competition, like Mom canned summer peaches to enjoy in dark winter months.

"You're moving into twelves-and-thirteens group." Coach Hokaj grabbed Stashu's shoulder. There it was again, swelling inside him, the pride, the sense of accomplishment, solid but soft, like the coal he'd mined that morning in the backyard seam. Coach Hokaj moved toward his fellow coaches, guiding Stashu with him.

Honey.

Stashu stopped and turned. "My brother." They were so similar in skill; surely he was supposed to move up as well. He lifted his hand to get Honey's attention, but his brother was spinning in circles. A weighted ball rolled into the back of Honey's legs and he sat on it, his lips moving as though he were telling himself his own private story, lost in his own head, as Grandma Lancos always said. "Honey." Stashu reached toward his brother again.

Coach Hokaj smacked Stashu's hand down and nudged him. "Just you."

The thrill at being singled out was now singed at the edges. Honey came up to him, and Coach started to pull Stashu away again.

"You stay there," Coach said to Honey. The boy's face fell, and he looked confused. Stashu didn't know what to say or why they wouldn't have pulled Honey into the older group, too.

"Stushy—this way. Watch this group for a minute."

Coach Sura yelled for Honey, who hesitated, then finally followed in the direction his name was called. Stashu couldn't remember a time outside of school that he and Honey weren't together.

"Pay attention, Stushy. This is where you belong."

Without Honey? That didn't sound right.

Coach Hokaj stood behind Stashu and pointed over his shoulder. "Right there, watch Abe Gurski." Coach Hokaj moved toward the older kids and directed them through their workout. Suddenly self-conscious, Stashu lowered his head, raising his eyes enough to soak in every word and study every move. Watching the older boys, Stashu felt as though his body was moving along with them as they flipped and rotated through the air, as though he'd already learned everything.

Stashu grew antsy just watching. His body jerked back and forth as he mirrored the boys throwing themselves into a flip, mentally following every swing on the bars and rings, the mount onto the bars, feeling how it would be to balance on each other's bodies to give his own flight a chance.

Coach Hokaj signaled the teen group to rest and called one boy aside to explain the next trick he wanted him to do. Stashu could no longer contain what he'd just processed. A glance at

Honey was the last bit he could take as the little boys had started their push-ups and sit-ups and balancing practice that all built toward using the equipment. Stashu stood there like a broomstick without a hand to push it. What was the point of all this waiting around?

When the older girls went to the water jugs, a large section of the mat cleared. Stashu looked over his shoulder—all the coaches were occupied. Without really telling himself to, Stashu's body just started moving, playing out what he'd just seen. He drew a deep breath and broke into a mad run, arms and legs churning, and just before he reached the edge of the mat, he threw his body up and forward into the air, spinning to land facing the opposite direction, arms circling. But he was upright, knees slightly bent, pushing hands overhead, like he'd seen the older boys do. His breath wheezed in his ears, blocking out everything else.

He'd flown like a bird, first forcing his body into the air, then with invisible wings budding right out of his body he effortlessly elevated another couple feet, time slowing, making it easy to complete the twisting trick. He knew he'd never forget that magic of sailing through the air that first time. Finally, sure of his balance, he straightened fully, then lowered his hands. The gymnasium erupted. Hand clapping like thunder. He turned slowly, wondering what he'd missed.

Hands blurred in front of his face. The entire mass approached. The applause was for him. Coaches lumbered toward him, some faces screwed into grim frowns, everyone screaming in Polish. Most were thrilled at what they'd just witnessed, and Stashu sopped up the attention, the joy on the others' faces, so proud it was brought on by him.

Hands.

Tousling his hair, shaking his shoulder, slapping his back. The pride he'd felt in being moved to the older group was dwarfed by this development. He smiled and accepted the praise.

"Great trick. A real acrobat…" They went on and on. But as the crowd began to quiet and disperse, the thinning group revealed a familiar figure lurking—arms crossed, face carved from hillside stone.

"Pop," Stashu said and lowered his gaze. He could never seem to find the right words around his father. And so he did his best to stay out of sight and mind. When his father didn't react, Stashu raised his gaze and searched Pop's face for evidence of what he was thinking. Angry? Worried that Stashu may have hurt himself? Mad that his son hadn't followed directions and just took off tumbling without permission?

The longer his father's face stayed hard, the more uneasy Stashu became, glancing at Pop then away, then back. Pop rubbed his palms together, slowly nodded his head, and finally a smile drew his lips across his face.

Stashu trundled toward Pop, gaze still downcast. All his time spent staying out of his father's sight and now this smile from him. He wanted to be sure his father knew everyone had been clapping for him. He *wanted* to be seen by his pop. "Did ya see?" Stashu glanced up.

Pop's smile snapped away, but he nodded. Stashu scanned his face. Pop was pleased. Not thrilled like the others, but definitely pleased. He cuffed Stashu by the neck and pulled him into his chest, the familiar scent of drink and work filling Stashu's nose.

"Beat me."

Stashu was confused. He squinted up at Pop.

"Let's see."

Did his father really want to compete with his son in the gym?

Pop released Stashu and backed away, gesturing. "Come on, come on, Stashu. Win against me. Against boys, you do well. But what about me? What do you say?"

Stashu surveyed the gym. "I… All… riii… ght." The words stretched like accordion bellows, the middles lodged in his throat. The kids and adults closed in, circling around him and Pop. Ida's eyes were wide, mirroring Stashu's surprise. But Vicki, Helen, and

Rose grinned, cheering their brother on. Honey stood off to the side, arms crossed, his jaw clenched like Pop's had been.

"Come on, Stashu." His father smiled, bouncing from one foot to the other, tossing his chin. His liveliness made Stashu feel lighter, too. Coach Sura took Stashu's shoulder, squeezing. He looked right into Stashu's eyes, his gaze, his proximity, comforting.

"Thunderous clapping for you, Stashu?" Pop bounced closer, hands up like he was preparing to box. "Your own coach? My paid dues give you training." Lukasz pointed to his chest. "Let's see if your practice makes you stronger than me." Pop's eyes lit up, and he suddenly looked like one of Stashu's friends rather than the lumbering, moody, unsmiling man he knew.

"Come on, little man," Pop said. "Your handstand against mine."

Stashu finally recognized his father's invitation as an offer to play. And that excited him, again stealing his words away. Pop wasn't the type for recreation. But now here he was inviting him. Coach Sura nudged Stashu forward.

Finally he nodded.

A roar went up, the reverberations filling his chest like parade drums. Stashu could not have imagined something as simple as his gymnastic ability, his strength, could draw such attention, not to this degree. Yet here it was, the thrill, as though this were a meet and everyone had been waiting for this match their entire lives. Stashu rubbed one hand and then the other, trying to even out his breathing.

"Ready for feet up," Coach Hokaj said, glancing between his watch and the two Musials. "Ready! Set! Up!"

Stashu flipped to a handstand.

Cheering commenced, mostly for Stashu. His friends got onto the floor, looking into his face, screaming. Minutes flew by. Stashu's mind tumbled and turned as he kept his body as still as he could. Pop moved around the floor, bending and straightening his arms, showing off his strength. Now the entire gym seemed to be cheering Stashu on.

"Three minutes," Coach Sura called and got onto the floor. "Stay strong, little Stashu."

"Old man can't do it anymore," one of the coaches said from the crowd.

The next minutes went by, the energy in the gym compressing. The cheering continued, but layers of enthusiasm had peeled away. Stashu walked on his hands in a circle to get a look at his father. His face was fire red, his breath choppy, his fingers curling up. It was as though everyone saw the signs of Pop weakening at the same moment, and the exuberance returned, the rooting for Stashu growing louder and louder.

Pop met Stashu's gaze, and the desperation in it whooshed past him like a spring gust. Since he could remember, Stashu had worked hard to stay out of his father's sight, and in that moment he realized that was impossible. Confusion distracted him, unsure about how the contest should end. If he'd been competing against boys he'd stay up forever; he would win without a doubt.

He drew several more breaths. But suddenly his mind spun forward in time, imagining Pop's reaction to losing to Stashu. Pop's labored breathing caused a vein to enlarge in his neck. He gritted his teeth, appearing pained and surprised at the same time.

Stashu's thoughts were no longer muddled. He dropped to his knees. Pop stayed up a few more seconds, fell into a squat, and sprang up, arms raised in victory.

Stashu studied Pop from his knees, breathing heavily. The joy on Pop's face was like nothing Stashu had ever witnessed in his father. After a victory round with some of the coaches who'd been watching the two Musials, Pop pulled Stashu up, roped his arm around his neck, and pulled him close. "You don't realize your strength yet. You fell out of that handstand, but you're strong enough to hold it for an hour, a whole day, if your life depended on it."

Stashu was torn between being gratified that his father whispered these particular words in his ear, that he understood his strength, and petrified that he was no longer invisible. He didn't know what to say, so he nodded.

"I won my way to America with a handstand. Don't ever underestimate the power of your own body, that it can feed you, it can buy your liberty. You're my son, you're Polish, you're as strong and flexible as the Donora wire strung across the country, holding up all of America. But you lost. You don't have strong instinct to win. You are nice, not a fighter. You let someone beat you."

Pop yanked Stashu so hard and close that he sputtered out his air.

"Someday you might win. But you are afraid of it, the pain in it," Pop said, releasing his son, backing away into a group of coaches, replaying his victory. "Winning means separating from the rest. You like the herd around you, the comfort."

Stashu didn't grasp exactly what Pop meant. But he exhaled, relieved, understanding that losing to his father ensured he could most likely go back to being invisible to him. But the others, the kids and the coaches, they were still cheering and marveling at his tight flips, rotations, and his standing on hands. *That.* The applause and excited voices, the way it all aimed at him and made warmth spin in his belly, then fill every inch of him, satiating his hunger like a full day's meals. That, he wanted again.

Though Stashu would not say it aloud, Pop was only partly right. Stashu *was* afraid of beating his father. It would have created a mess. And it was true that Stashu felt bad to leave Honey behind. Leaving people behind, risking Pop's pride? Was the exchange for cheers and slaps on the back worth that?

Yes. Winning, the attention felt too good. He would simply tell Honey if he wanted to move up with the big boys, with Stashu, he just needed to stop his daydreaming. And though he wanted to tell Pop to be happy his son could actually beat him, he wouldn't do that.

In eight years, he'd learned to tightrope-walk around and through and over Pop's expectations, upholding them as much as possible. But Pop was wrong about Stashu being afraid to win in general. In fact, there was nothing in the world he liked better. As sure as he stood there, peppered with celebratory smacks from friends and coaches, Stashu knew winning was simply part of who he was. And if Pop didn't recognize that Stashu had fallen out of his handstand on purpose, then all the better. He would find a way to draw adulation from coaches and friends and stay out of Pop's sight. It couldn't really be that hard.

Chapter 12

Stan

Autumn 1931

When Stanislaw Franciszek Musial had started at Castner Elementary, his name was formally shortened to Stanley, and casually to Stan. Pop threw a fit, but his Polish tirade did nothing to sway the teachers and principal from making their case that it was important for Stan to use his Americanized name and to leave Polish words for home and church activities. By fifth grade, Stan had been thinking, speaking, and reading in English for years. Writing was another matter. And getting high marks on grade reports? School did not come easily.

Hands.

Miss McKechnie's worked their sorcery. "Round, round, ready touch, two, three, four." Her singsong voice mirrored her fingers sweeping the chalk over the blackboard in graceful swirls and lines, knitting letters into words, sentences into paragraphs. Stan bit his bottom lip and did his best to make his hand follow what she'd created so easily. He forced his pencil across the paper.

As he made progress with the first sentence, he liked what he saw. Not so bad.

He dove back in to write the next sentence. A shadow fell over his paper. He froze in the middle of the word *celebration*, realizing Miss McKechnie was looming over him, her gaze heavy and sharp. His mind raced. What was she doing? He held his breath, willing her to move on and check some other kid's work. But she stepped closer.

His hand shook. Hands. That was it. That's why she hovered, casting her smothering shadow. He'd forgotten about the problem with his hand. He'd been writing with the left one, the *wrong* one.

She ripped the pencil from his grip and slammed it into his right hand. "Right hand, right mind," she said.

He exhaled quickly and held his breath again. How could he have forgotten? Every teacher attempted to force him to write right-handed, but none had been so persistent as Miss McKechnie. It was as though she thought his soul might fly off into Limbo if it weren't tethered to his paper through renderings made only by his right hand.

Go away. Go back to the board. Leave me alone. But she stayed. He glanced up at the blackboard to remind himself what word came next, gripping the pencil so hard it snapped. The top half flew across the room, whizzing past Sarah Stein's ear, her hand covering her head, making the already silent room go quieter with the scratch of thirty kids' pencils halting, thirty heads turning toward him.

Miss McKechnie balled her fingers around the ruler on his desk but didn't tell him to pick up the flown top pencil half or retrieve it herself. She didn't give him a new pencil. She nodded at his hand, signaling him to continue writing with the dwarfed implement.

Why did she bother? He was a terrible student, cursed with left-handedness. Why didn't she just leave him to rot in his academic coal pit? Stan's eyes burned. He started forming the next word. *Saturday.* His right hand trembled, and the pencil stammered across the page. Humiliation. She regripped the ruler with bony fingers. He stared at the paper, eyes filling.

Smack. Miss McKechnie's ruler snapped onto the desktop. Stan jumped, and the motion caused a tear to leap from his eye onto the paper, magnifying the *C* in the word *celebration*. Miss McKechnie bent down to make eye contact.

She tapped the ruler in rhythm with her words. "Pay attention, Mr. Musial. Dreams of baseball and gymnastic tricks won't provide a home for the half-dozen kids you'll have someday. Young men don't cry."

Stan's throat went dry. He knew what was expected next. But he couldn't get the words out. He could feel classmates' gazes on his neck, pecking at his chest, stabbing, suffocating.

Hands.

The scent lifting off her chalk-dusted fingers filled his nose, the white powder etched into the cracks in her skin, and he wondered if it was painful, if that was what caused her to be flaming mean.

He stared at her hand strangling the ruler. That hand appeared papery delicate from afar, drawing letters and words and sentences with pretty flourishes that brought to mind summer butterflies so clearly that Stashu often waited for her letters to lift right off the blackboard and flap out the window.

He certainly wished he could sprout wings like he did at Nest 247, that he could rise up, flipping and twisting right out the classroom window, never to return.

Say the words. He pressed each one out, slow, molding each like a tool formed in the mill die shop. "I'm to use my right haaaaand for my rigggght miiiind."

She smacked the desk again and slammed a new pencil onto his desk. She thundered back to the board, her dress billowing behind her. She stopped and sighed with her whole body before drawing herself back up and poising her chalk-bearing hand above her head. "Now let's practice our Os." She circled her hand in the air and laid the chalk to the surface, where butterfly-winged letters flowed like the Monongahela, the gentleness belying her harshness, providing false evidence that she might be kind and nurturing.

"I can't hear you, class."

When he was sure that his classmates had refocused on their work, the chorus of "Round, round, ready touch…" filling the room, Stan mopped at his wet cheeks with the heel of his hand, finally finding easy breaths.

A hanky flopped onto his desk. Stan stared at it. No one ever acknowledged when Miss McKechnie humiliated someone. It was the unwritten kid pact. Yet someone was noting his shame. He stared at the hanky, finally turning to see who'd tossed it before touching it. Andrew Morrison. He sat one desk behind to the left and lived a few doors up on Marelda. He was normally seen wandering town with face turned up at the sky, mapping stars, and noting smoke and cloud patterns, lost somewhere none of the other boys, certainly not Stan and Honey, cared to go. Andrew nodded and eyed the hanky, emphasizing that he was the lender. Stan scrutinized him. Was Andrew making fun of Stan's scholastic failures?

This kid was first in class in every subject. He came with questions about electricity, the sun, and suggestions in regard to something he called germ theory, things that caused teachers' faces to fold in confusion, then stammer in a way that rivaled Stan's. Then they'd burst into smiles and pleasure that a student's mind was so curious, so *spongy*, they always said, excited that he equaled their own knowledge.

Andrew never talked to Stan or played ball or tag, explored the hollow, or went swimming in the pond with the fellas. Stan assumed the kid might be afraid his lack of intelligence was contagious as flu or tuberculosis. This was a kid girded to his armpits in smarts, the kind of fella who'd not want his intellectual shine dulled. Even without having seen Andrew's actual semester reports, Stan knew Andrew's grades were always straight As. Everyone knew.

In the classroom, Andrew executed like Stan did on the field and in the gym. When Andrew wasn't asking questions teachers didn't have answers to, they mooned over him like Coach Hokaj did over Stan. Andrew spun butterflied words out of his mouth so easily Stan could only imagine what his papers looked like. He glanced at the kid's work now, noting his neat writing, the entire paragraph completely copied. No, *more* than that. He'd filled the entire front side, but the teacher hadn't even written a full side's worth. What on earth could that kid have written so fast? What kind of kid thoughts even warranted being written down like that?

Andrew jerked his head toward the hanky. His eyes were generous as the gesture itself. Stan nodded in thanks, then wiped his face with the fresh-smelling pure white cloth and started back on his writing, strangling the pencil with his right hand, wondering how it was possible that he couldn't make his right hand work like the left. But it wasn't just the hand, it was his brain. Something he didn't struggle with in any other area of life. Surely the left hand that threw a baseball seven different ways, landing it exactly where he wanted it, attached to a body that he tossed and tumbled as though he wore wings himself, couldn't be completely unable to write simple words with the right hand.

How could this same body trap half-pronounced words inside him, embarrassing him over and over? Just a set of simple words. If only Miss McKechnie and the rest of the faculty thought wielding his body and baseballs like she did a pencil was a great achievement. His life would be much easier if they all just saw it that way.

Chapter 13

Mary

Summer 1932

Mary tapped her notebook with a dull pencil. The only thing to ever mold mill activity instead of the reverse was when the country sunk into a deep, wide depression, eliminating the need for every single thing that Donora was responsible for making. Once, Donora provided the fuel and product that fed and shaped America, but now Donora was stuck. No growth, no shoring up infrastructure or putting a shine on America's glittery surfaces.

No anything except housewives stretching dollars so thin they fell apart in hand while husbands circled round and round to inquire after the same dried-up job opportunities. Nothing. No significant money was paid or earned. Just flour sack dresses and old sweaters made into socks, and community gardens guarded by out of work steelmen.

The depression years staggered on, leaving the mills shut down just shy of a dead heat. With little steel, wire, and zinc fabrication, the skies were clearer, but pocketbooks were plumped with nothing but lint and only if the holes were patched fast enough to contain it. Income was counted in pennies and moods grew dark as the spew that once signaled a chance at the American Dream.

Mary bit the end of her pencil, hesitating to make her list, sitting in the corpse-still kitchen, sweat springing up at her brow. The June sun rose, blasting through the front windows, a head start on roasting the rooms to the point of unbearable, making Mary yearn for days when constant heavy smoke interfered with the direct rays. She recorded her list for the grocer only slightly changing amounts with each biweekly order:

Zero meat and milk.

Nine pounds of coffee. (Could only afford six pounds for five all-day coffee drinkers last time—just not enough.)

Twenty-five pounds of sugar.

Fifty pounds of potatoes.

One hundred pounds of flour.

Two cartons of salt (Matka was using too much!).

Six. Days the above lasted.

Thud. One thing hitting the front door. Newspaper, probably.

She dropped her pencil and dashed to investigate. She opened the door. Matka stepped onto the porch holding two mugs. Mary retrieved the newspaper at her feet.

"Paperboy nearly took my noggin off. On purpose, I'm sure. Workin' for that highfalutin asshole William Watson and his *Herald-American.* Look at that." Matka lifted one coffee mug toward the hollow and handed the other to Mary. "Sky's clear enough to see across the Mon to Webster."

Steam rose off the black liquid. "Coffee," Mary exhaled the word. "Mrs. Adamchek?"

Matka nodded. "All she had in trade today. Coffee for the two of us."

Mary and Matka slumped into seats at the kitchen table, sipping.

"Oh, that's wonderful," Matka said.

The sharp flavor woke Mary's mouth. "Better than anything."

"Mrs. Adamchek said she likes how you do up her linens. Two weeks' time, she'll need you again."

Mary nodded, smiling as she opened the newspaper. Nothing had ever tasted so good. She had to find a way to keep some coffee back to make it last longer. So much to do that day, grocery day. She kept adding to her page, numbers that described the Musials spilling onto the paper…

Nine. Mouths to feed in the Musial home.

Eleven. School years Ida completed before quitting.

Eight. School years Helen finished before quitting.

Four. Years since the Musials moved to Marelda Avenue.

Two hundred seventy-seven. Number of workers out of fourteen-thousand citizens in Donora holding regular jobs due to Hoover's depressed economy.

One. She underlined that word with heavy scratches—*once in a while* fit better—the number of days per week Lukasz worked. And he was one of the fortunate souls pulled into the wireworks for miscellaneous tasks. Less than four dollars for a day's work once in a while meant Mary took on as much work as she could. But really no one was paying, just trading for things to survive. She had landed a position cleaning the Harris movie theater, but most of her laundry jobs paid barely five cents. Even most of the foremens' wives shuttled their household chores to their daughters or did it themselves. *Once in a while.* That was the best descriptor for adults to describe their work lives at that time.

"That damn Watson's editorial 'bout the depression's all wrong, acting like it's nothin'. This *is* a slow, drawn-out panic. A gaping valley of despair's what it is. A way to get rid of excesses? Said too much gov'ment spendin's making us all poor. What spendin'? While he sits on a mountain of gold?" Matka crossed her arms and set her jaw.

Lukasz's feet hit the floor in the room above. Mary and Matka eyed the doorway he'd be coming through soon.

Mary sipped her coffee. "Lukasz's hired on for a shift in the wireworks. Maybe they'll keep him for the week."

Matka rolled her eyes. "Mm-hmm. No one's buying anything, Mary. Nowhere in this entire country. Least of all not steel and wire. Nothing to build. No one to pay."

Mary ignored her mother's irritation. She shared it and then some. Plenty of *that* to go around. "Well, St. Philip's got their soup kitchen up today. I'll make cabbage soup for Lukasz's belly. Got to keep him working if possible."

Matka leaned forward, cupping her coffee mug. "Still gonna run that lunch bucket down the mill like a schoolgirl?" She pursed her lips and held Mary's gaze, the connection tangible.

"Yes, Matka. You ask me that every blessed time I do it. I've errands to do on the way back anyhow."

Matka shook her head slowly. Lukasz flushed the toilet down the hall. "I'll never understand the way ya love 'im. Never. Knowing you coulda skedaddled with the Dunns, not that I liked the missus at all, but how they were gonna school ya and introduce ya to Gary society and that… but you stayed."

Mary looked away. All those things had stopped mattering the second Mary had given them up. "Mrs. Dunn taught me so much before she left. And all that is still mine, in me. Can't take it away, even though they moved and I didn't. Plenty of society here and… *You* love Lukasz. Why do you say these things?"

Matka drank her coffee, silent.

Mary was too tired to go through her list of wonderful things in life. "But I do, too. I love Lukasz in a way you'll never know."

"Even after he never got yer house, that lemon-scented life…"

"Matka. Please. We're not dead yet." Mary was fine with knowing her truth, but that didn't mean she had to unearth it and roll around in it on a regular basis. Besides, most of the world was half-starved. Lukasz's failure to keep a job or buy a home wasn't unique. "I mean it. Why're you saying all this? You like Lukasz. You couldn't stand me liking the Dunns."

"Half-starved and cranky's why."

Stan entered the kitchen, surprising them both.

Had he heard their conversation?

He kissed Mary on the cheek and attempted to avoid Matka as he headed for the sink. But Matka snatched his arm and pulled him close, giving him a squeeze. "Get yer gram some water. Gotta stretch this coffee long as I can."

Stan smiled as he often did, lighting up the kitchen brighter than that now unobstructed sun.

"And coal," Mary said. "Gotta start your father's soup."

"Cabbage soup?"

"You can take your supper at St. Philip's. Father Ronconi's got the kitchen up and running. Donations came in from farmers and the women's club and…"

Stan's shoulders sank. "I know we're lucky to have cabbage for soup."

Mary didn't remind him that she'd be baking bread ten loaves at a time later, that she was doing her best.

He stood behind her and put his arms around her neck, hugging her. "Thank you, Mom. I appreciate it so much."

She patted his hands.

"We're picking teams for summer ball today." He went to the sink.

Mary watched him top off Matka's cup with water. "Pick your teams and practice, but I need you berry picking today— elder, black, and blue."

Stan nodded. "Ida and Helen'll never come help. Ida's got a date or something."

"Take Vicki, Rose, and Honey, then. Or drag your gang along. But I need those berries. If not today, tomorrow for sure."

Stan kissed Mary's cheek before bounding away for the coal. His pants were heading well above his ankles. But he was so thin that the trousers fit him everywhere else.

"Stan."

He turned, eyebrows raised.

"Are all your trousers that short?"

He lifted his foot and looked down. "Suppose so."

"I'll do them up later."

He looked confused.

"I'll add material to the waist, and no one'll see that I've lengthened them."

"Always a wizard with hiding secrets," Matka said.

"Can't have my son running around town looking like he hasn't gotten new trousers in years."

"Right. That's what I said," Matka said.

Honey entered the kitchen. Matka pointed at Honey's feet. "Him too. Can't have 'im lookin' like a beggar neither." Her tone was mocking. "Important to play ball lookin' smart."

Lukasz entered, eyes narrowed. He'd be irritated his boys looked downtrodden and that they'd be playing baseball.

"Jobs. They need jobs. Like the girls."

"Grown men can't get hired on," Matka said with a sneer.

Lukasz glared. "Don't poke at me, Matka." Lukasz blew out his chest. "Found some work."

Matka pressed her chest out, too. "Good. Got me some laundry to do, too."

Stan returned with the coal bucket. "Seam's getting thin out there."

Lukasz stared at Stan, rubbing the back of his neck and circling his shoulders.

Mary shoved the mug half-full of her precious coffee toward Lukasz. "Drink up. Long day ahead."

He took a sip.

Thank goodness he actually had a shift to work, a miracle.

He lifted Mary's hand and tugged it, a mischievous look in his eyes, taking her back in time, to when the gesture signaled her to spin toward him, to dance. Mary couldn't have been more shocked. Matka, Stan, and Honey's mouths gaped. Lukasz set the mug down, pulling her tighter, steps synched like a heart and its blood, the pair three-stepping around the kitchen in a slow polka, cheek-to-cheek, minds locked in earlier days when music had narrated their dancing and held their secrets.

Mary exhaled into Lukasz, gravity falling away. If only world economics hadn't ripped everything apart. That's all it would have taken to ensure he would drink less. She ignored any evidence to the contrary. It was easier to breathe that way. Ahh, yes. If only this great depression, as Hoover had called it, hadn't gripped the country, Lukasz would find steady work and this… this affection that drew her to him again and again would be what they experienced every blessed day. If only.

Matka's exaggerated clapping put an end to the dance. Mary smoothed her hair back, her cheeks flooded with heat. She looked around to see that the boys had escaped and she hadn't even told Stan about the trade she'd made with Mrs. Morrison. The trade that required Stan's participation to make it work.

Chapter 14

Stan

First Day of Summer

School was out. Nothing felt better than summer. Long hot baseball days, cooling off in the pond on the flat above Heslep coal mine, dark nights playing kick the can and ghost in the graveyard, and no more fighting his left-handedness. He was free to be who he was.

June. Early for humid, hot, hazy weather, yet here it was. With chores complete and Pop stuffed inside the smoldering wireworks, one mill away from where the boys stood on Americo Field, the Musials waited for the others. Though not as dark and smoky as usual, down by the river the air was smoggy enough to shroud the sun and turn it a mercury shade of silver. Sulfur tucked inside thick humidity, folded around his bare arms, heating his cheeks. It looked like it did every other day, but it *felt* different. With no school to attend, a sense of freedom came with the hot weather. Even swamped behind fat clouds, the late morning sun burned the back of Stan's neck as it oversaw the boys' first day of summer ball.

Honey studied the line of bats he and Stan had set out and then added a broomstick.

Stan pointed. "Broom handle belongs before the picket."

Honey moved it.

Their weapons of choice: a Spalding All Star Model 1 and a Black Diamond—both at least eight years older than the boys, an old broom handle they'd found in Grandma Lancos's cellar, two homemade, badly shaped pine bats, and a fence picket.

Honey stared at the display, hands on hips. "Nah. Picket's better than the broom." He switched the "bats."

They always disagreed on the next-best bat to the real thing. "We'll wait to see what the fellas bring."

They should have enough kids to make five or so teams, but due to few bats, gloves, and balls, there would be times they had to make do with whatever might pass as "real" equipment.

Honey went toward the river. "I'm looking for that ball we lost last weekend."

"Stan!"

He turned.

Honey also turned but kept moving away. "What's he doing here?"

Stan shrugged and adjusted his hat, squinting at the kid jogging toward him, knapsack strapped over his shoulders just like always, whether at school or out in the neighborhood.

Andrew Morrison.

Had something happened up on their street? Andrew had always been nice to Stan. *Round, round, ready touch...* When Stan saw him, his mind would fly back to the handkerchief incident, and no matter what other kids thought of him, Stan always liked Andrew. How could he not? They just never had cause to spend any time together outside of school.

"What's wrong?" Stan asked.

When Andrew reached him, huffing and puffing, he leaned forward, hands on knees. "Looks like rain. Probably lightning storm. An hour away, maybe."

Stan looked into the sky, unsure why the kid would be reporting the weather. "Always looks like rain." Andrew came all this way to tell Stan the sky was cloudy?

Andrew straightened and adjusted his knapsack straps, thumbs under them. "Well, yes. I thought you'd like to know before we put in all the time and effort of choosing up and finding something for a bat and—well, no. Sky's *smoky* all the time, but the clouds change like those are—"

Stan put up his hand. "What are you talking about 'before we put time and effort' *into what*?"

Andrew screwed up his face in confusion.

Stan lifted his shoulders. "What?"

"Our mothers… um…" A sense of awareness seemed to sweep over Andrew's face even as Stan remained muddled.

"Oh."

"Oh what?"

"Oh boy." Andrew pushed his hand through his hair and blew out air from puffed cheeks. "Our moms traded for… My mom gave your mom some material to make dresses for your sisters in exchange for you teaching me…"

Stan's eyes went wide. He had heard Mom talking about dress material and flour sacks, but she hadn't mentioned a trade with the Morrisons. Could Mom have really done this to him?

"You're to teach me to play ball. Apparently a pitcher is what my old man's ordered up for me." Andrew mimed throwing.

Stan grimaced. The biggest, most athletic fellas played pitcher, not *Andrew*. What the hell? It would be like Stan offering to take physics class. Mom knew that. Pitcher?

Andrew shifted his feet, face flooding red. He shrugged and looked away. "I assumed… I… They didn't tell you?"

Round, round, ready touch. Stan felt bad about Andrew's embarrassment, again picturing his kind gesture when Stan was mortified in handwriting class. "Nope." Stan had left the house before his parents had finished spinning their polka through the house. Mom had mentioned needing to discuss something with him the night before. This must have been it.

"Oh, I…" Andrew said. "Maybe I heard wrong when your mother was at my house this morning around breakfast time."

Round, round, ready touch. Andrew held Stan's gaze and that handwriting chant filled Stan's mind like a clanging gong, the memory making his right hand cramp up and feel clumsy right there on the field. Andrew's kindness remained with Stan, even if he hadn't thought about it daily.

Andrew shrugged.

Stan didn't have time to play teacher. Baseball was every man for himself.

He turned and walked away.

Round, round… That damn chant. It put a seed of pain in Stan's chest. What was he doing? He stopped. He owed this kid. Didn't matter that they barely said hello on the street. This kid had done something for Stan he'd never forget, and this was how he was treating him? He sighed and turned. Andrew was heading the other direction. "No, hey, Andrew. That's fine. That's… I just didn't know. No problem." Stan swept one arm toward home plate as six kids were coming across the field from Meldon Avenue, hurling stones at each other's feet laughing.

"I never knew you wanted to play. I woulda asked you to join up years back if I'd known."

Andrew's face lit up.

"Sure, yeah. Come on. You want to play, you should play."

They walked toward the six kids, Stan wondering how much Andrew knew or didn't know about playing ball.

"Well." Andrew shook the knapsack off of one shoulder, letting it swing from his other. "I *don't* want to play. The old man wants me to, and he goes hunting and fishing with Joe Barbao, and he got to telling my old man you're the fella who can make a player out of me on account of how good you are and all and—"

Stan thrust his hand into Andrew's chest, stopping him. "Wait. He said I'm good?"

"Well, sure, I mean… everyone says so."

Stan knew he was good, but to have someone of Joe's stature declare a ballplayer good? That wasn't nothing. "Joe said that out loud? To your pop? You're sure Joe Barbao said that, not your old man, but Joe?"

"Yes." Andrew made a face. "Joe told the old man, who told me. The two of them ended up at the same squirrel tree and started yakking away. Next thing I know, I'm smack dab in the middle of an exchange between the Morrisons and the Musials."

Stan was thrilled at the thought a pro like Joe Barbao—semi-pro—would say such a thing publicly about Stan Musial.

"Anyway," Andrew said, "I just want to collect my weather data and get ahead in math for fall. But they think a fella should be able to at least throw a ball properly, as though I'm going to make a living out of that and they just remembered last week that I better learn."

Stan was so proud of what Joe said he couldn't deny this favor, even if the trade didn't quite make sense. "I'll definitely do it."

Andrew grabbed Stan's arm. "Just teach me a little something so I can go home and show my old man that I didn't waste my day, as he always says, as though studying the stars and moon and weather and conducting experiments on soil samples is a waste of time. I dunno. You know what I mean?"

Stan picked up the pace and looked at Andrew as he tried to keep up. Lukasz Musial would never have suggested such a thing and often blew his stack over Stan and Honey playing baseball instead of scraping out fireplaces around town for a penny. "You're not afraid my intelligence'll rub off on ya?" Stan asked.

Andrew stopped. "Wait."

Stan turned.

"You're *not* unintelligent, Stanley. And being left-handed doesn't make you dumb."

Stan took his hat off and put it on again, studying Andrew. "You're just being nice. I'm not a mental heavyweight."

"I'm not a baseball heavyweight." Andrew shrugged. "We're even."

Stan shifted his feet. Something about Andrew, something in that very moment, the exchange, the ease, it was as though the two had been friends forever and Stan had just forgotten until that moment. He wouldn't forget again.

"Well, we better hoof it if you're gonna learn something today."

"Yeah, that rain's coming, the sky... Right there over the river, the zinc works smoke is blowing back—"

"Same sky as yesterday, cloudy and—"

"Smoky. Yesterday was smoky and hazy, but not cloudy and—"

"Cool it down, Andrew. This crew'll kick your ass right off the field if you lean away from talking ball. Rule number one. Just talk ball. And by the way, I have no idea how to teach baseball. I just play it."

"Oh boy."

"You can figure it out like every other kid who shows up. I'm positive the lot of us will rub some of your smarts right off of you if you hang around long enough. End of summer, you won't even remember why you love school so much."

This made Andrew laugh.

"Well, good then. You're happy," Stan said.

And so they had just enough time to toss the ball around a bit and start to pick teams for the season with the sixty-seven kids who had gathered at the field.

"Hey, fellas," Andrew said. "Storm's coming." He held up his arm. "Hair's standing up. Smoke's blowing back over Donora. We should get home."

Only Stan gave a cursory gaze at Andrew's hairy arm. "Shush. This determines our chances for the season. Three more picks. I don't even know half the kids who're left."

Stan and Honey selected a boy named Smokestack and another called Melonhead. Their final team member was Blue Louise, a girl, of all damn things. With that last pick, rumbling thunder turned sharp and tore the sky right open, swirling clouds. But still no rain. Half the boys scattered, running from the thick black cloud advancing from over the river. They bolted toward the homes that lined Meldon.

"This way," Cheeks Carvelli said, waving to the fellas on his team—Stan and Honey's team. "Hurry. My house is right over there."

At first they ignored Cheeks. Sauntering along. But when lightning cut through low swirling clouds, striking Mrs. Prentice's front porch with a three-pronged bolt, they scrambled. Halfway to the street, a searing zip of electricity made Stan and the team stop and turn back toward the river. There, moving horizontally as though God himself was snapping glowing horse reins, were horizontal lightning bolts.

"Whoa." Cheeks removed his hat and looked at the hair on his arms now standing up. Another rip of thunder came, vibrating inside Stan's chest. Cheeks took off, his stumpy legs wheeling. They all tore after him. All but Andrew.

Out of the corner of his eye Stan saw the kid skid to a stop, opening his knapsack, pulling out notebooks and pencils as though he'd just witnessed Lefty Grove fan his twenty-third batter in a row and wanted to make note of it.

What the hell? Stan chugged back to Andrew and dragged him toward the safety of Cheeks's front porch, Stan circling back several times to rescue loose papers, being picked up by wind gusts and set back down. On the porch they heaved relieved breaths. Hair raised on all of them, they patted each others' heads, their skin tingling as they laughed hysterically, feeling as though they'd borrowed a day. Thirteen of them stuffed on that porch with the thick humidity not releasing its grip even as dumping rains plunked onto the metal porch roof.

Mrs. Carvelli served them spaghetti. Their nervous laughter connected them like carbon to iron. And though the group only boasted a handful of good players, there was something about that day. The team squished onto that porch, Smokestack sharing cigarettes he'd lifted out of his father's smoking box when he passed out from his sixth boilermaker after a double shift at the blast furnace—something right then anchored the lot of them together.

Smoking away, hiding the Chesterfields when Mrs. Carvelli checked on them, their skin and hair finally coming back to earth, they were mesmerized as Andrew explained all there was to know about weather. And with his prediction for the lightning storm nearly on the nose, they dubbed him "The Weatherman." He talked on and on about how with the mills nearly shut down he was able to see the stars nearly every night, that he'd been mapping them, hoping to get a telescope for his birthday that year. "A good one."

Stan and the rest couldn't imagine wanting such a thing. They'd all prefer a "good bat" or a "nice glove" to a good telescope, whatever that was. But that single stormy afternoon had melded the hodgepodge team together.

And as the talk turned toward Babe Ruth and Pie Traynor, Andrew withdrew from the conversation. But he did so smiling, big as the bridge that spanned the Monongahela River. "The Weatherman." He nodded, jotting something into his notebook.

And Stan realized Andrew had never been given a nickname before. This was the first gang of friends Andrew ever had at all.

Chapter 15

Patryk

Patryk shifted in the passenger seat and unlocked the seat belt, the restraint sliding across his chest, releasing the tightness that came with wearing it.

"Gramps. No." Lucy steered the wheel with one hand and one eye on the road as she yanked the belt back across his chest, locking it into place as though she'd trained her whole life to do just that. Maybe her nursing career lent itself to such things.

"Are there any rules you manage to follow?"

"There're seat belt rules?"

Lucy sighed. "Laws. They're called laws."

"I guess I missed that set of rules, seein' as I took my last driver's test fifty years back or so."

"And that's exactly why I'm driving."

Patryk scoffed. "How much farther? Time fer me to nap 'fore the game?"

She fussed with the radio buttons, attempting to locate a clear station. "Plenty of time. Nap away."

**

When they arrived at the ballpark, Patryk shuffled through the parking lot, surveying the area. Had he napped for a decade? "The kid got drafted? Who took him? Pirates? Like he wanted?"

Lucy slipped her arm around his waist to keep him moving in the right direction. "This is where they play their games. They're all high school kids."

"Boys?"

Lucy looked at him with narrowed eyes. "What?"

Was his hearing going too? "This stadium. For pros."

She giggled. "Things have changed a lot since you played."

"Sure as shit has. Unbelievable. For kids? Really?" He turned slowly, taking everything in.

They entered the ballpark, emerging from the dark concession area to the bright field little by little, sunlight hitting his eyes, the field coming into view, expanding, welcoming him into another universe. He slipped his baseball cap off and clasped it to his chest. Entering at the middle of the seats, half of them stepping down toward the field and half stretching to the heavens, he felt his mouth drop open. Electric-green grass. He put his hat back on, the sun making his eyes water. Brown dirt so smooth he was sure if he got on his knees and dug around there wouldn't even be a pebble. He felt as though he'd been lifted into heaven itself. "Would you *look* at this yard. For kids."

Lucy squeezed him with one hand and pointed with her other. "There he is. In the dugout."

"My great-grandson." His eyes burned and filled all over again, and as Lucy led him to their seats right behind the dugout, gentle summer baseball breezes cooled and dried the tears he didn't even bother to wipe away.

**

Back at Blue Horizon, Patryk, Owen, and Lucy gathered in the recreation room with sandwiches from Corner Deli. Lucy tipped Owen's hat, reminding him to remove it for their meal. Patryk tried to go along like a good boy would. But he couldn't help it. He scowled at his sandwich, studying the crust and lettuce. "What on earth're yinz tryin' to do with these seeds and weeds?"

Owen plopped the last bit of his second sandwich into his mouth. "It's good for you. Ruffage."

"Give me white Town Talk bread with jumbo, mayo, and Velveeta."

"You probably still have some of that stuck in your intestines, Gramps," Owen said, opening a bag of chips.

He looked at the crust again. "Damn seeds'll sprout right inside me. Then what? Seeds on crust."

"Sandwiches aside, you enjoyed your day, right?"

Patryk nibbled around the crust. The blend of turkey with lettuce was surprisingly good. He looked at Owen, feeling his irritation melt away. "Oh, I loved it."

Owen's face lit up. "Next time I get to start."

"Well, your hitting's not shabby. Not fantastic either. Overall team comradery, two out of ten—"

"I went four for four! I'm mainly a pitcher. That's gold-medal stuff."

Patryk put his sandwich down. "Gold medal? I, I, I."

"Yes, I. I'm the one who sacrificed all these years, and I'm the one who went to training at four A.M. for the last four years, and I'm the one who did extra chores and babysat, of all damn things, to pay for a hitting coach and now a pitching coach in addition to… Yes. I've done a lot of work."

"Yer on a team, Owen. Until you heard the crack of a bat, ya didn't even look up to see what your teammate was doing in the batter's box. No chatter, no smiles, no laughter. I don't think I heard one laugh outta yer bench all game."

"I was focused on what I needed to do next. I was getting behind the count every time. And… you know that team isn't going to get me drafted. My own play will."

"Well then, you're missing out on the best part of it all."

"What? I just joined this club. Everyone's nice. Yeah, we're not best friends, but it's not like that. It's not Little League."

"That tubby pitcher-first baseman. Whatchacallit?"

"Mason?"

"Mason? Like a bricklayer? That's his nickname? Mason?"

Owen exhaled and unwrapped a third sandwich. "No. Mason Turnquist the third."

"What's his real name? The name he earned over years on the ball field?"

Owen's eyes went wide. "Pretty sure MT-three is his real name. Emphasis on *the third*. I just joined this club a month ago. New guys are in and out all the time."

Patryk plucked a chip from Owen's bag, exasperated.

Lucy poured Iron City into a paper cup for her grandfather. "It's different now. His team back home is full of kids he knew well or that he knew from tournament ball—"

"So this kid, Mason the third. No nickname?"

"Gramps? Who cares?"

"*Who cares?* I grew up with some of the greatest names in the world. That's how you cement your team. I mean, look at this." He signaled for Lucy to hand over the book. "Look at these wonderful… Look." He jabbed at a list of names. "Scouting report here."

1. Pitcher—Stan Musial—Stushy—The Magician, Donora Greyhound, and more—Pitcher, first base, outfield—everything.
2. Catcher—Matthew Youngblood—Smokestack—because he never stops smoking. Lives with his sister, Hazel Youngblood, who's part-time healer and part-time undertaker.
3. First Base—Louis Smith Jr.—Melonhead—head's so large his mom adds extra fabric into the back just to fit him into an adult-size hat.
4. Second Base—Ed Musial—Honey—Stushy's brother—good at every position.
5. Third Base—Harry Carvelli—Cheeks—because he's got cheeks that appear stuffed with meatballs, his favorite. His uncle's a bookie, and Cheeks is pickup guy for numbers.
6. Short Stop—Nicky Christmas—Santa—because he always delivers the goods. Mother's a seamstress, father fixes cars and anything mechanical—parents revered elders in the Quinn Chapel, A.M.E.—first church built in Donora.

7. Left Field—Christopher Rollins—Tank—because he's the size and shape of a full-grown man—brother is a boxer, almost-famous fella but was only able to stay at certain hotels when he's on the road to box due to being black. Attends church with Nicky Christmas.

8. Center—Larry Harris—Moonshine—because his grandfather makes elderberry wine, etc., and uses it to trade for any services and items he needs to buy.

9. Right Field—Danny Fitzsimmons—Skunk—because the scent of garlic seeps from his skin when he sweats.

10. Scrub who only plays in dire emergencies—Jerry Smith—Monocle—mostly the batboy—forced to wear a monocle because full glasses are too expensive for his family to buy.

11. Left Field—Melvin Fitzsimmons—Yellow Melvin—Danny's younger brother by eleven months—jaundiced kid—gets sick every six weeks or so.

12. Position Undetermined—Andrew Morrison—The Weatherman—predicts the weather—if not for Mrs. Musial's deal with his mother, he wouldn't be good enough to be last picked on any of the town teams.

13. Throws Batting Practice—Louise Orleans—Blue Louise—because of her moody demeanor—Patryk's older cousin.

"You might scoff at these eleven-year-olds and their names," Patryk said. "But they were important. Nicknames marked people as yours. And while Stan's best-known moniker "the Man" is the one known to all, the names of the rest of that crew probably stuck with 'em their whole lives."

"I get it, I get it," Owen said, moving closer to his great-grandfather. "My team needs some nicknames."

Lucy set some cookies in front of Patryk and Owen. "So Andrew stuck around to play that season, huh?"

Patryk smiled and took a sip of beer. "Old man insisted. He wasn't exactly impressed with his son's *Weatherman* nickname. He'd been hoping Andrew had some dormant baseball gift that had been lying in wait, just waiting for a spark provided by breathing the same air as Stushy Musial, that Andrew would return from his first practice being called Hammerin' Andrew or something along the lines of the great hitters of the game."

"But no," Owen said.

Patryk rubbed his stubbly chin, reaching back in his memory. Weatherman… What did happen with him? Like a good childhood recollection of a boy who idolized older kids, hearing their stories as much as being present for them, Patryk's eye caught a drawing in the book of a boy staring into a night sky and a day sky, book bag at his feet. "I believe Andrew spent most of his time at the field keeping the books, organizing betting sheets by address so Cheeks could quickly drop them off and pick up in between games. And the rest of the time Andrew studied cloud patterns at each baseball field and drew them into his book, warning teams when they needed to pick up the pitch pace in order to make it through a game before a hollow-rusher hit."

"And Stan still had to tutor The Weatherman?"

"Mary Musial made sure he followed through on teaching Andrew. She knew something about that friendship was important, that Stan might be the one to benefit from having a friend like Andrew, someone with educated parents."

"What about the other players?"

Patryk leaned back in his seat and crossed his arms. "Speaking of others… Bricklayer."

Owen drew back.

Lucy wiped crumbs from the table into her hand. "What?"

"Mason *the third*. That's the name for him. Came in for the save, retired three batters in a row. Laid 'em down like bricks. Then three more for the save. Bricklayer fits."

A wide grin covered Owen's face. "Bricklayer. I like it."

"'Course you do."

"What was your nickname?" Owen asked.

"Hands."

Lucy shook her finger at him. "That's right. Grandma always hated that name for you."

"Grandma loved my hands, I promise you that."

"Stop." Owen slammed his hat on his head, pulling the brim over his eyes. "Stick to the baseball stories. Please."

Patryk pulled Owen's hat back off, looking him in the eyes. The sight of him, dirt shading one cheek and the other jowl, his dark eyes and shaggy brown hair, fresh dirt field cologne rising off his skin, Patryk felt the sense of his own childhood alive and well. His own eyes gazed right back at him. Three generations down the pike, there were his own peepers on another boy. He wasn't the kind to be effusive. His words caught in his throat. He reminded himself he was ninety-two going on dead, so what was he waiting for? "You *are* good, you know."

"Good, like going-to-the-pros good?"

Patryk drew back with a sigh. So many things determined whether a guy got to the pros, things beyond his control. But what if… "Well. What do *you* think?"

Owen set his hat down. "I think I can."

"Think? That enough?"

Owen looked confused and didn't push the conversation further. Right there, Patryk had seen it clear as day—a seed of doubt, the teeniest kernel of mistrust, possibly enough to keep his great-grandson from making it. Good hands, fast bat, pitcher with a full toolbox—that kernel of doubt wouldn't do at all.

But that was something the kid had to figure out on his own. He knew Owen wanted him to gush over him, to tell him he'd make it. But that was not how things worked. And Patryk would need a few more games to see exactly what Owen had in the way of baseball gifts—the mental game. So for right then, they'd just drop back into the book and live through the eyes and ears and history of a time, place, and people who no longer resembled their stories.

"All right." He slapped Owen's back. "As you know, hands're everything. And I had a good set. But this isn't about me. I was much younger than Stan and this crew. But they knew it, too. Hands're everything."

Owen looked at his own, turning them back and forth. They were giant, ropy. Perhaps they'd been dusted with the gods' outfield dust. Perhaps they contained everything needed to be one of them to get called up to be part of the greatest game on earth.

Chapter 16

Stan

1932

Stan's little team had melded on Cheeks's porch. From the perspective of their personalities anyhow. But it still left the problem of their actual *playing* as a team. They certainly were trying. After one practice, Stan stalked the perimeter of the field, glove tucked under his arm, kicking along the weeds, scanning for two balls that had gone missing. The balls might be a problem, but for the first time Stan and Honey had a glove to bring and share.

Earlier that morning, someone dropped off a beatup 1920 Bill Doak baseball glove on the Musials' porch. No note about who'd done it or whether it was for Stan or Honey. So they'd share it. Mom had repaired the loose leather webbing between the thumb and first finger. A lefty glove. Stan chose to believe that somehow, somewhere, Lefty Grove knew there were two ballplayer brothers in Donora, Pennsylvania, who needed a lefty glove and he made it happen. When Mom walked into the kitchen with it, laid it on the table between Stan and Honey and their

elderberry jam slathered toast, it took Stan's breath away. The
boys and Mom leaned over it, cooing, wiping it down, gently
turning it this way and that.

Grandma Lancos had groaned between sips of coffee,
shaking a hand at them, her crooked fingers and swollen joints
painful just to see. "Holee Peter and Paul," she'd said, "you'd
think someone dropped the newborn baby Jesus on the porch the
way yer fussin' over that dirty piece of leather." She spit the word
fussing out like it was poison.

"Ahhh, Gram, this is…" Stan slipped the glove on and
cradled it against his belly. "It's a miracle. A summer baseball
miracle."

Gram had harumphed and looked away, but not before Stan
caught a pleased smile coming to her even if she clearly hadn't
wanted it to.

Kicking around the field, starting to lose hope of finding
errant balls, Stan's foot made contact. One ball recovered. He
flung it up into the shimmery sunrays, disappearing into the glare
of the smoke-covered sun, higher and higher before plummeting
back into sight. With that blessed glove, he practiced catching
behind his back, one handed, leaning forward on one foot. The
glove changed everything. He jammed his hands in the air,
cheering himself, when the sight of a misshapen, worn-out ball
hidden in the brush caught his eye. He ran his finger over the
ripped threads, thinking he'd restitch the laces at home.

Honey sprinted past Stan, swiping the ball away with his slick
pick he used so often to pluck a ball off the field. "Everyone's
gone. Let's go. Starving." Honey dashed ahead, disappearing onto
Meldon.

Stan sighed and followed along, realizing just how hungry he
was, too. One Pirates ballgame broadcast Stan had listened to
clued him in to looking at ballplayers' hands, how they worked.
Hearing that, he realized he'd been paying attention to hands his
whole life.

Cheeks's, with short fingers, had lightning-fast reactions, his
fingertips blackened with newsprint and ink from collecting

betting slips each day, sleight-of-hand required when collecting right in front of an angry wife. Honey's were large like Pop's and nearly always found the ball that flew in an unexpected direction after bouncing off an infield rock, but he somehow never seemed to feel his skill, the sense of "I'm good at this."

Nicky Christmas's shortstop hands were soft and reliable, turning double plays so fast that Smokestack could no longer justify smoking while catching since he'd gotten three flaming cigs knocked right out of his mouth on account of him not expecting Nicky's speed coming with a ball toward home plate when most would have just let the runner score. Nicky was the one who took baseball as seriously as Stan, always with a ball and something for a bat in tow, ready to play when someone let him into their game, even if just for an inning or two. He had hands that needed to play to keep them out of mischief.

Tank, playing left field, had man hands, but they were supple and easy despite being so thick; it was a wonder he could manipulate his fingers like was required of the position.

Blue Louise, the half sister of the third cousin of Mr. Donner, who co-founded the town of Donora, had pretty pale fingers but a rocket arm and often threw batting practice, giving the lesser players extra practice. Inherited money had bypassed the family tree branch that her particular parents came from, so she skipped girly tea parties and chose to play ball morning, noon, and night instead.

And so on and so on. Most of them had some skill that could be counted on in a game or for practice in one way or another. Even Yellow Melvin caught a ball by accident from time to time, on a day when the sunshine helped turn his jaundiced skin to the pinky blush his brother Danny exuded every single day.

Then there was Andrew. Monkey-large hands and fingers turned calloused from too much scribbling in notebooks. Cement mitts. His arms were unnaturally long, and so he should have had a great advantage at snatching a ball out of the air or smacking a sweet one out of the park. But he stank. Even Monocle, with half a set of glasses, caught and threw better than Andrew. It was as though Andrew's hands had some sort of outerspace forcefield that kept them from catching any ball, not *one ball*. His long fingers wrapped around too far, leading him to hold a bat like it was a toothpick.

"My mother plays better than you," Stan said once in awe when Andrew was practicing at second base, caught a ball, and by the time he got his foot on the garbage can lid masquerading as the bag, the ball was gone. Gone! He'd somehow dropped it, not even noticing until he tagged Cheeks with nothing in his hand. They'd all just stared at the ball sitting in the gap, mocking poor Andrew. The words were out before Stan realized he'd said them.

Andrew laughed. "Your mom? Listen, that's an insult in general, but *your* mom? I happen to have it on authority of having seen her with you in your backyard that she can play. So I'm not insulted."

"She's not *that* good, Andrew."

"Not bad either," Cheeks had said. "You're worse than my ma though. She can't even catch the flu!"

＊＊

For two weeks, Stan and the team tried to remedy Andrew's baseball problem. They threw hundreds of balls at him, coaching him up, Stan taking responsibility well into dark nights, but though Andrew always seemed to get to the ball, he never got the sense of cradling a catch so it didn't whack like a rock against metal plating.

At the end of the second week of baseball, Stan and Andrew trekked up Marelda, past Stan's house to Andrew's to give a training report to Mr. Morrison.

"Old man's gonna have my head for my lack of progress, Stan. I just can't seem to get the hang of it."

Stan's hands grew jittery at the thought of facing Mr. Morrison with fatal news. He knew from Pop that any setback in life, anything that wasted time or money, was met with a bellow or a fast hand if Mom couldn't put a calming move on him first.

Stan prayed that Mrs. Morrison was home to stem the impending tirade. He meant no disrespect to Andrew's father, it was just how dads were. Stan didn't want to be witness to Andrew's humiliation, yet he was the bearer of it.

Just entering the home, Stan's mouth went dry, his words knotting tight. He envisioned which ones he would manage to loosen and then stretch into the stammer that mortified him, rehearsing their proper rhythms to allow for smooth delivery. Inside the Morrisons' clapboard home, Stan was greeted with a fresh cleanliness that reminded him of the first time every spring when Mom opened every window in the house, letting fresh baseball-season air inside. In Andrew's front parlor, there was a record playing jazzy swing, and Mrs. Morrison floated into the room with a smile, a crisp white apron, and a tray of lemonade like the back page advertisement on *Ladies' Home Journal* had come to life right there in Donora.

She set the tray aside. "Hello, boys."

Stan nodded.

She pulled Andrew into a hug and removed his hat. "Not in the house." And then she kissed him on the forehead. "Have a drink. I think I got the sweet and sour correct this time. You know lemonade is not my forte."

Stan took the hint and removed his hat, as his mom often told him to but usually forgot. He tried to slow down his chugging of lemonade best he could, but he'd never tasted anything so delectable. As Mrs. Morrison was pouring their third glasses and plunking ice cubes into the liquid—imagine, ice cubes on a sweltering summer day—Stan nearly forgot why they'd gone there.

"Thank you so much," he said.

Mrs. Morrison patted Stan's shoulder. "Anytime."

Then Andrew's father sauntered in, cigar in mouth, doing a three-step to the swing music with an invisible partner, a smile and a glint in his eyes that Stan wasn't sure he'd ever seen on an adult's face, let alone a *dad* of all things. This was the *old man*? Mr. Morrison removed his cigar and reached for his wife. She did a pirouette toward him, and with joined hands he spun her right into his chest. And they swayed, back and forth, her back nestled into his chest, his cheek against hers, both of them with closed eyes.

Stan had seen his parents take a twirl around the kitchen from time to time, but this was different. This seemed to be how they spent every single day of their lives. Stan's mouth dropped open, and he looked at Andrew, bracing himself for being the one responsible for wrecking this high, happy mood with news of Andrew's horrible progress.

"Dad," Andrew said. He looked at his feet.

Stan was magnetized by these parents.

"Dad. Please." Andrew gestured at Stan, who was basking in the glow of this family. "This is Stan Musial."

"Good afternoon, Stanley." Mr. Morrison opened his eyes and twirled Mrs. Morrison away from him like spooling silk off a bobbin. "Oh say, hey, Andrew, my boy. Your sisters are at Grandpa and Grandma's for the day, so it's just us." He tousled Andrew's hair, then reached for Stan's hand and shook it hard, making Stan flinch. Stan smiled but didn't keep eye contact for long, the man's presence like the lightning that had lifted Stan's hair off his body the day they had chosen baseball teams. "So great to meet you, Stanley. Joe Barbao can't say enough about you. Your intensity, your hitting, your pitching… total package."

Stan's face flamed. He clutched his hat to his belly but stared at his feet before forcing his eyes up. "Thaaaank you, sir." He cleared his throat. "Thank you." He should just lie and tell him his son was the next Babe Ruth or a right-handed Lefty Grove.

Mr. Morrison took Andrew by the neck and jostled him a little. "Your cheeks are sunburnt. You've lost that grayish pall you'd worked up spending all your time in the library." He rubbed his palms together. "So how'd it go today?"

He looked at Stan, who was struck dumb.

Andrew shrugged.

Stan could feel the tirade brewing, invisible but there. Or if not a tirade, a shuddering undercurrent of shame and mockery would certainly seep into the room once Mr. Morrison heard the facts. Stan cleared his throat, dragging his gaze to meet Mr. Morrison's. The man was shaped like a baseball bat standing on its fat end, his tiny head and slim shoulders giving a human shape Stan had never seen before, tall, but gelatinous. Good humored, he seemed, though, there was that.

Still, Stan kept his guard up. Skunk and Yellow Melvin's dad had once swatted Moonshine for supposed back talk, right across the jaw after inquiring how their day had gone, and all he'd answered was "fine." Apparently the single word had been filled with something invisible, something worth smacking him for.

Stan didn't trust whatever this sunny mood was in the Morrison home. This utter lightness and joy, the very sense of it generating right out of their bodies. Stan had never seen happiness like this, for no reason—for a birthday or Christmas, yes—but for just because? Not until standing in that house, watching Andrew's parents float on clouds of peace and joy.

"So? Hit me with the report. Details." Mr. Morrison stuck a cigar in his mouth and raised his eyebrows.

Stan's words thickened in his mouth as he grew nervous at ruining this wonderful day for this fantastic father. Stan shouldn't have been nervous—the man was far too nice to be worrying. But seeing that didn't help Stan's cause at all. Knowing he was going to stammer only made the promise of it stronger.

Andrew glanced at Stan. He knew it was his responsibility as coach, as being deemed a good player by Joe Barbao, in trade for the dress material. It was up to Stan to tell it.

Stan pulled Andrew's right hand into view, and his words lurched and kicked like balls smacking off Andrew's lead palms. Sweat sprang from Stan's hairline, tickling him. When his nervousness dissolved everything he'd prepared to say, he resorted to the shortest words he could get out.

"He stiiinks." Stan looked down and just pushed the words out. "He simply stinks."

Stan dropped Andrew's hand and stepped back, bracing for a fast-moving smack. Mr. Morrison raised his hand. Stan flinched.

But instead of angry movements, Mr. Morrison rubbed his chin, his fingers against thick whiskers making a sandpapery sound, his eyes narrowing, appearing like teachers did when Andrew stumped them with an unanswerable question about the universe.

Finally Mr. Morrison moved toward the boys and took Andrew's hand, gently pressing the swollen, black-and-blue pads of his palms. "Why, you surely had a day of it, son."

Stan forced himself to breathe, to get his words out before Mr. Morrison let his anger out. "Please. Please go easy on Andrew. His stink… his being bad is my faaaail, my fail not his." Stan cleared his throat, regretting his honesty. He should have just said Andrew was coming along. Now he felt even more responsible. "I won't give up on him."

Mr. Morrison smiled. "I suspected you wouldn't. And Andrew is nothing if not hardworking. We appreciate you helping, Stanley. Why don't you stay for dinner? I'd like to hear more."

Stan winced. Wanted to hear more?

Mr. Morrison nodded. "Sound good?"

The tension that always bound Stan's words flooded out of him, replaced with relief and confusion as Andrew led him to wash up in the area under the stairs that Mrs. Morrison called her powder room. Stan eyed Andrew as they entered the tiny space with a delicate, wavy-edged sink and sparkling toilet. The garden-green walls made it feel like it was a room to entertain in. What had Andrew been so nervous about? His father clearly wanted him to be a ballplayer, but he sure didn't respond the way Stan had expected.

Andrew plunged his hands under the tap water.

"That's it?" Stan asked. "That's your old man?"

"That's it? What?" Andrew soaped his hands then his face and neck.

Stan followed Andrew's lead, washing face and hands to the elbow with fresh-smelling soap. Andrew handed Stan a tiny brush to scrub under his nails. "Your *old man*? He wasn't mad at all. What were you so nervous about? He's the nicest fella I've ever met."

"Oh. He's disappointed, trust me."

Stan dug under his nails with the brush, thinking Mom would love one of these at the house. He hadn't taken Mr. Morrison's response as bad at all.

"Didn't you see how he looked like you nailed him in the belly with a line drive when you told him the truth? He nearly vomited right there." Andrew unfurled a small pink towel with flowers stitched into it. "Hand towel."

Stan watched Andrew bury his face in a second one.

Andrew looked up, drying his neck. "Oh, for any part that's wet. Not just hands."

Stan's face flooded red, embarrassed he'd assumed it was literally for just hands so he covered his face with the fresh-smelling fabric, drying his arms last.

"I'm starving," Andrew said. "Hope it's not too early for you."

Eating a full meal before the mill whistle was odd for Stan, but Andrew's dad was home, his family not a slave to the mill rhythms, even though Stan wasn't sure exactly what Mr. Morrison did for a living. Whatever his job was didn't send him home filthy, teeming with stories of cruel managers and injured limbs. Stan had entered one of the universes Andrew talked about, far, far away, where people had powder rooms painted pretty and decorated with clean, flowery towels and rose arrangements on the side of the sink.

During dinner, Stan noticed Honey peeking in the dining room windows, the wind gently wringing and releasing the see-through curtains, revealing his brother's face as the fabric danced. Stan could practically see drool gathering at the corners of Honey's mouth as the aroma of flank steak, mashed potatoes and gravy wafted out the window.

"Hey!" Andrew leaned forward and gestured at Honey to come in.

But when the Morrisons looked, Honey was gone. Humiliation crept into Stan's belly.

"We have people knock at the door all the time, what with the lack of food and…" Mrs. Morrison said.

Stan's face heated, glad Andrew hadn't revealed it had been Honey. Sweat beaded at his brow. It wasn't unusual for people to knock at doors, looking to trade for a meal. "Happens to us, too. Mom always has something at the ready when needed."

Stan didn't reveal that what she had at the ready was often just an end of a bread loaf and the last remains of cabbage stew, better called watery cabbage with a double helping of salt and pepper.

Honey peeked again, and Stan caught his angry scowl before he ducked away. Stan suspected he'd stop doing that and put himself out of the torture of watching his brother consume a king's meal. Steak, potatoes, green beans, and chocolate cake. Stan had eaten so quickly that he agreed to seconds before he realized it was probably rude to have done so. His hunger had never been met with such delicious meat.

Stan was patting his fork over the cake crumbs, putting every last bit into his mouth, the sweetness like Christmas morning, the only time the food at the Musials' approached what he had just eaten.

Meat drunk, he thought at first he hadn't heard right. But then it came again. Mom was bellowing, her shouts for the Musial kids carrying through the Morrisons' open dining room windows. The see-through curtains ballooned and deflated as evening breezes rose and fell with the rhythm of Mom's voice.

"Honey, Helen, Vicki, Rose, Stanley!"

Stan shouldn't have cringed at hearing this because, as if set to harmony, a bucket load of other mothers all up and down Marelda Avenue and Eleventh and Twelfth Streets leaned out their doors and started with their calling, too, each voice distinct as a birdcall. *Bobby! Herman! Viktor! Donny! Angelo! Francy! Becky!* Forty-seven different names shouted one evening was the record. Stan and Honey had counted the summer before.

"I love that. The evening chorus," Mrs. Morrison said.

"My wife grew up on a farm with neighbors miles away."

She reached for Mr. Morrison's hand and held it on the tabletop. "It's what makes Donora wonderful. All these children. All these friends."

Stan squinted at the Morrisons, marveling yet again at their ease with each other, with their world, so easy that they sat there contemplating it like priests and their homilies. Though wanting to stay, and stuffed to the gills, he knew better than to be late once Mom hollered for them. Mrs. Morrison seemed to have already anticipated that and was standing up, ushering Stan outside.

"Wait," Andrew said. He pulled a book from a neat stack of books in the room between the dining room and front parlor. It was lined with shelves, stuffed with books and pots and statues. "You'll like this."

Stan drew back, squinting at the book in Andrew's hand. It was creamy white with a baseball player on the front, mid-catch. *Making the Nine* was etched in gold lettering. "It's about baseball. A story about a fella who plays. You might like it. As a thank-you."

Stan stared at it. A book as a thank-you? He didn't know what to say or if he wanted it. But he knew Andrew's family had already paid for Stan's services. "Our moms traded. That's enough."

Andrew started to say something more. His father put his hand against his son's chest as though to gently stop him from pushing the matter.

"See you tomorrow, then," Andrew said, appearing confused.

"Thanks for the hard work, Stan," Mr. Morrison said as he lit another cigar, circling it in the air, smiling, leaning against the doorjamb to the dining room, the three Morrisons looking as pleasant as a slow-winding summer stream.

Stan lifted his hand and left, feeling simultaneously comforted and edgy, unsure what to make of what he'd experienced. What he did know was that he wanted exactly that for himself.

Chapter 17

Mary

Everyone was at the table except Stan. Mary slid a second pot of cabbage stew onto the stovetop, practically knocking the baked beans off. Earlier that day, she'd discovered two sections of siding hanging off the back of the house. Irritation. So much hard work yielding so little. Never getting ahead on bills, never socking away enough. Like acid, frustration rusted the ungalvanized façade she'd laid down, layers of their life curling back their edges like the fancy chocolate Mrs. Dunn used to put on cakes. These raw moments forced her to experience dinner aromas as both familiar and new.

The scent of sad was how she thought of cabbage stew. She had deemed it so as a young woman and, when she let herself admit, still did. Evidence of lost promises to herself and between husband and wife. She'd imagined having a home perfumed with fresh lemon cleaning oil and beefy meals served by hired "girls," the kind of help she used to offer neighborhood households and still did. She imagined Lukasz promoted in the mill, having an easier time of it by then. Hard work should have made it all possible. She lifted the lid from the pot and fumbled it, chasing it through the air as it bounced off her fingertips, crashing against the floor, the noise reverberating up her spine.

"Arggh," Lukasz said. "Head's aching like forty hammers smacking it." His voice came muffled through the kitchen wall. "Quiet meal's too much?"

Mary swallowed hard and shook out her aching hands. She'd been moving slowly and should have anticipated his mood after another day of failed job hunting. Her full day at Mrs. McDuff's papering crooked walls with a paisley pattern that the woman wanted matched perfectly, to give the illusion of flush walls, plus finishing off a basketful of mending had left Mary's fingers cramped and clumsy.

"I'll get it, Mom." Ida rushed in and dished the remaining baked beans onto the ninth dinner plate. "Can't have him pitchin' a fit like a toddler."

Stan burst through the back door.

"You're late," she said.

"Sorry." He kissed her cheek. "I was at the Morrisons'. You know. Coaching up Andrew."

Mary glanced at Stan, then slid the empty bean pot off the flame. Ida took the last two plates into the dining room, and Mary picked up the platter of jumbo bologna lunch meat. "Grab the bread," she said, jerking her head toward the large basket on the worktable.

He picked up the bread and stood at the doorway. Mary knew he was sizing up where he'd have to sit. "Stan," she said.

He looked over his shoulder. His pink cheeks and nose told her he'd played ball that day.

"Your hat."

He cradled the breadbasket in one arm and tossed his hat across the kitchen, landing it on the top of the coat rack near the boot-room.

Lukasz's grumbling voice made Mary's stomach clench. "Still no work."

Stan blew out his air. "Father Filipek said only 277 men in this whole town have work at the mills right now. Pop's not the only one. Does he have to take it out on us?"

"Men need to feel useful and provide. Pop sees his value in his work, his hands, his strength…" Stan said the words with her.

Mary sighed. Spoken a thousand times over the years, she realized her attempts to tenderize Lukasz's edges so her children would understand the way he was now wasn't how he'd always been, had failed. It wasn't who he was deep inside. Donora suffered like every town in America, maybe more so since its very existence was due to three miles of mills that now barely squeezed out a bit of product. They had nothing else to rely on. Lukasz's dreams, *their* dreams, had been shredded over the past few years. If only he could see himself as more than some strongman tossing wire bales into shipping cars, he might not let his temper fly so easily, he might not hold anger so deep and long that its only escape was eventually with an outburst.

The family uncomfortably quiet, Mary nudged Stan toward the only seat available, right next to his father. The girls got up to help serve. Lukasz, at the head of the table, drummed his fingers. Matka anchored the other end. Mary forked some lunch meat onto Matka's plate, hoping she'd be eating before she remembered to scold Lukasz for tracking soot and mud into the house. "Watch your salt, Matka. Your pressure—"

"Pressure's fine long as yinz guys wipe yer feet 'fore traipsin' in. Pass the salt, Honey." She signaled to him to send it her way. Mary's papa had had many faults, but the one item Matka had trained him properly on was removing his boots before slogging inside.

Lukasz and Matka eyed one another, then looked away, the tension tightening like coiled wire ready for transport.

Mary served Lukasz then forked a piece of meat for Stan's plate. The sight of her son's hands made her stop. "Your fingernails." She eyed his face and set the plate down. "Clean as a whistle." She took Stan's chin in hand, lifting his face, turning it back and forth. "Clean as a… clean." She drew back, then bent in and inhaled deeply. "Smell like a meadow. What the…?"

"People generally wash up before enjoying a steak dinner," Honey said from down the table. Matka's eyes went wide. Everyone's did. The word *steak* must have been mumbled twenty-three different times.

"What's that mean, steak dinner?" Ida finished ladling the stew. Mary continued to serve but kept her eyes on Stan.

He shifted in his seat, the chair leg screeching against the wood floor. "I… well, I weeeent…"

Mary ached about Stan's stammering, wishing he could be comfortable enough when questioned to just answer. "Mr. Morrison wanted to thank me for helping Andrew."

"So he had a big fat juicy steak with 'em," Honey said.

Stan leaned in and glared at Honey. Mary glanced at Lukasz, who'd dug into his stew.

"I mean," Honey scoffed. "Thanked for what? Kid hasn't made one catch or hit one ball."

Stan clenched his jaw, anger flashing to his eyes.

Mary tapped Honey on the shoulder with the back of her hand. "Enough." They didn't need an argument at the table.

Mary moved to Ida.

Stan leaned back, tapping his plate with his fork. "They're just being nice. Mr. Morrison wanted a report. And Andrew offered me a book, of all things. You want a book, Honey? About baseball. Some kid plays… I dunno."

Honey flinched.

"Didn't think so," Stan said. "I reminded the Morrisons that the trade of my help for the material for the girls' summer dresses was plenty."

"A baseball book?" Mary asked, even though she should have stifled the conversation, not encouraged it.

Lukasz grumbled as he shoveled lunch meat into his mouth.

Stan slid his jumbo bologna off his plate and onto his father's. "Yeah. White cover with this fella falling back for a fly ball. Called *Making the Nine*."

"Nine," Mary said at the same time as Stan. She knew the book.

Stan looked surprised and smiled. "Yeah. The Morrisons have a whole room with books."

"A library. In that house?" Matka said.

"House's bigger than it looks. And not a library like the school, just a room with tables and books top to bottom. And puzzles and games and… How'd you know which book, Mom?"

Mary smiled, basking in the memory of when she was a teenager, staying overnight at the Dunns' home while babysitting, the bedroom with the bathroom attached, the giant bed, the books near the flaming fireplace, and the night she spent there reading *Making the Nine* by the fire, sunk into a soft chaise lounge, cozy blanket pulled up to her chin. "The Dunns. They had that book."

"For the love of Pete and almighty God," Matka said.

Lukasz groaned.

Mary snapped back to the present.

"Criminy," Matka said.

"What, Grandma?" Ida asked.

Matka surveyed each face, then pointed to her fork. "Don't put your mother's mind back at that Irish house with that Irish woman and—"

"She was Czech." Mary set the platter aside. Matka was turning her half-starved crankiness back on Mrs. Dunn where she normally laid it. "She's like you, Matka. You know that."

"Husband's Irish," Matka said. "She fergot her people."

Lukasz swallowed his bread, grimacing. His stomach had been giving him fits. Drinking after work didn't help.

"That's not true, Matka. You know that. Mrs. Dunn's the one who gave me all that dye to make kraslice eggs for Easter and let me make baskets for church blessing."

Lukasz set his forearms on the table and leaned forward. "Enough with that fresh-lemon house story. Disrespect in my own house…"

Mary ignored her husband, not drawing attention to the fact that it was Matka's home and, as much as the Musials paid in rent and labor to share it with her, it wasn't theirs. Not in the way Lukasz wanted it to be. To lessen his irritation at hearing the Dunns mentioned, she patted her husband's back, hoping it would remind him that no matter what she'd been treated to at the Dunns', it was him she'd chosen.

"What's this about material and dresses?" Lukasz said, piling lunch meat onto his bread.

Mary had hoped he missed that mention. She squeezed his hand. "The trade means we don't have to purchase new. And I can use the flour sack material for their everyday dresses. The material's far more costly than the exchange for Stan teaching Andrew to play baseball." She forked beans from her plate onto Lukasz's, wanting him to get distracted with eating.

He grimaced and rubbed his belly, flinching, but not pained enough to keep his rising anger to himself. "You're telling me that hoity-toity professor man paid my son with material for you to make the girls' dresses—paid to have *his* son learn a game? Why not just send him over to Joe Barbao, like our Stashu goes?"

"I go too," Honey said.

Mary wished she could reverse the course of the meal and stifle Honey. "We don't pay Joe." She measured her words as though baking a soufflé. "He sees talent in Stan—"

"And Honey," Stan said.

Mary nodded. "And Honey."

Lukasz tore his bread in half. "Next time a fella wants Stan to teach his kid to play a game, make 'im pay. Cash. Could've put that money toward our down payment." Lukasz turned his attention to Stan. The boy drew back, tension coming off Lukasz in waves. "And steak. *Niech to szlag.* My eleven-year-old son was devouring steak while his father eats—" He slapped his sandwich onto his plate and rubbed his stomach. *"Bzdury."*

Mary's heart clenched. "It's not crap. It's more than most… Do you know what I did to make sure we had this on the table?" Mary's exhaustion had loosened her filter, dampened her inclination to always put everything in the best light for Lukasz, to calm and soothe. "And I'm happy people like Daniel Morrison and Joe Barbao see so much good in our son. I'm so proud—"

Lukasz glowered.

Matka scoffed, and Mary knew the woman was recalling that her relationship with Mrs. Dunn had maddened Matka. Much as she wanted to hear more about Stan and the Morrisons, she didn't want Lukasz's irritation to catch fire like a boilermaker. One flammable liquid inside another, lit to flame before guzzling.

Lukasz turned to Mary. "How much money's in the can?"

She racked her mind for the number. "I…"

He leaned toward her. Nerves tender, she reminded herself she hadn't done anything wrong. She wouldn't embarrass him by reminding that they paid out half their savings for the accident he'd caused in Herky's car the month before.

"Tucking away a bit every week. Haven't taken accounting lately, but I can."

"Don't keep things back, Mary." He wagged his finger. "No hiding from me."

Mary knew he was recalling the treasured items she'd hidden away before they were married. This included things he'd made for her, like the angel Christmas ornaments, and the rings they sold when they were short on rent one month. Matka was probably thinking it, too. If only there was more money in the world, the anger and the tension would dissolve like snow in spring rains. And Matka and Lukasz could let go of the disgruntlements they kept close.

"There's a piece of land on the hill…" Lukasz went on and on about the sliver of property the two of them had been so excited about purchasing two decades before, before they had Ida, before something took their savings every time they'd raised a decent amount to put down on it. Nearly twenty years since they'd pronounced their dream to build a home together. She refused to bury that dream, but instead just slipped it into the back of her mind, where she rarely had to consider it. The kids were silent, letting Lukasz brood, everyone just wanting the meal to end so they could blow back outside until the town's curfew siren blew.

Lukasz brushed his hand over Stan's shoulder, then latched on, shaking him. Mary held her breath as Stan stared at his plate. She hated that Lukasz was hard on the outside. She knew he wasn't on the inside.

"Let's see someone buy a house with a baseball, my son," Lukasz said. "That's the man who can teach my sons something. Waste of time, these games. Stashu should be working, nearly old enough for the mill."

Mary shook her head. If only Lukasz had been raised by a man who loved and adored him. Then he'd be that way with his children. But his father had abandoned him after his mother died, and this was what remained, the shelled insides created by a lost mother and a father too wounded to love anymore. The idea that an eleven-year-old boy should work in the mill was ridiculous.

With the depression settling in deeper, there were barely enough jobs for grown men in the mills. No way was Stan or any other boy going to be hired on. She glanced around the table to see everyone focusing on his or her plate. Except for Ida. She was already rising to clear dishes.

"I'll take on more ironing," Mary said. "St. Mary's needs some linens done up, and Stan and Honey can dig extra coal from the seam. Someone'll buy it."

Lukasz scoffed and took a giant bite of sandwich. Mary watched Stan lift his eyes, though he kept his head down, watching his father like a scientist deciding the meaning behind experimental results. And she knew what had happened without Stan saying a word.

She felt it. His realization that nothing in the Musial house was as it should be. The disappointment, the yearning that would live in her son perhaps for a lifetime. It had happened to her when the Dunns treated her like family, and she'd come to understand and want better things than those that mere survival offered.

Stan had just eaten steak in a home that had a room for books and puzzles, with a family who scrubbed up with fragrant soaps before dinner, and whatever else he'd seen over there. She didn't know for sure, but it was obvious he'd witnessed what was possible when people weren't just scraping by. She was quite sure he'd beheld Mr. Morrison's gentle ways with his wife, with his children. And she could only hope Stan would achieve such things, that his experiencing what was possible wouldn't stop with simply bearing witness, as it had with her.

She passed the breadbasket to Vicki and Rose, then to Honey, offering him the last of her meat, hoping he wouldn't hold the steak dinner against his brother for long.

And then she noticed. Matka was staring at her. But the anger that came when the Dunns were mentioned was gone. Instead, her mother's face, creased and furrowed with age, was also shrouded in a mix of curiosity, questioning, as though she'd just realized Mary was now in the same fix as she'd been so long ago.

What did one do when she realized her children had dreams far beyond what might be possible? Mary smiled and nodded at Matka. She didn't let the question bother her for long. No. Stan was different from Mary. Primarily because he was a boy. He was special and had been since Mrs. Mazur pointed out his lucky star and pink moon. And everything in the whole world was truly up for his nimble little hands to grab and keep for himself. And though it had been a long time since she'd thought about Stan's lucky beginnings, she felt the grip of them right there in that ordinary room, eating an ordinary meal, on the most ordinary of depression days. He was different. And his life would be, too.

"Well." Lukasz shot to his feet, causing the table to jiggle all the mismatched plates and glasses. "I've had enough of being told I'm not a good enough father. I got my citizenship. I made you an American."

Mary thought back to how her marriage to Lukasz before he'd been naturalized had immediately transferred her American citizenship to his mother country. "Wait, what are—"

He stomped out of the room and then careened back in, steadying himself by holding on to the doorjambs. Mary turned back to the table, not wanting to watch Lukasz's undoing.

"This country promised me greatness. I saw it on a postcard with a big house and white fence and the greenest grass rolling down to the street, right out from the front of the door, but I arrive and people look down over me. And now us Musials… I'm stuck with nothing, and the foremen have everything. Gated Cement City, fat and happy and…"

His choppy breath and disconnected words filled the silence. Everyone sat wooden, staring at his or her plate. Finally Mary faced Lukasz. When she looked at him, her mind replaced his angry angles and scowl with his face twenty years before, his youth, his crooked smile and soft eyes, and she felt his strength wrap around her. She wanted to hold him, to remind him all the things they'd wanted were possible for their children. And he helped create that. She stood, but before she could take a step, he was gone, the kitchen door slamming.

Mary couldn't breathe.

Lukasz didn't need to tell Mary who he meant by people who looked down on him. All it took was the name of that baseball book to be said aloud for him to submerge further into his black mood. That's all it took to remind him of their dreams, of the life she could have had if she'd gone with the Dunns to Indiana to be their nanny, if she'd never let Lukasz rescue her at the riverside under the strange pink moon.

Matka mumbled something about the evils of booze, Matka's worn, familiar words regarding men who drank too much, a ribbon threaded through their family lore. But Lukasz was different from Papa. Mary knew Matka saw it when Lukasz brought a bag of lemons for Mary's signature cleaning mixtures, when he would somehow earn extra money that made it home before getting lost in a tavern, when he took Mary into his arms and spun her around the kitchen, laughing. But Matka's anger ran too deep, having long ago crusted over her heart, so thick Mary sometimes wondered how it even kept beating.

With Lukasz out the door, the girls leapt up, clearing dishes. Ida began the scrubbing, gently stacking the mismatched pieces to be dried. Mary fished dry towels from a drawer and again, as she had so many times in her life, hid the seed of desperation from the sunlight of her thoughts, keeping it from sprouting, from taking over.

She drew a deep breath, picked up a plate, and dried it, slowly circling the towel around its face. She would remind Lukasz later that she didn't long for another life, that she didn't see the Musials as lacking much, even though they had little. Very few families had extra to share. She would promise Lukasz that people liked him, respected him, saw that he worked hard for his family.

She could already envision how it would go, how she'd take his hand and gently spool him into her, wash him up for sleep, and fold herself into him, their entwined limbs the conduit for their synchronized breath, their shared life. It was all she ever really needed, even if she had wanted so much more.

Lost in her thoughts, she didn't notice Stan and Honey slip outside. The girls had begun chattering, light, fun topics, replacing sharp, aggressive dinner conversation. And it wasn't until Ida's words shocked Mary back into her body that she realized so much of her upbringing had been brought into her own family life.

"I'm going with the girls to a dance, Mom. And when I can, I'm moving out. I want my own place and…"

Mary set the plate on the counter and studied her daughter. Ida, who'd been washing floors for a nickel since she was eight, had grown up wanting out, just like Mary when she had been the oldest of six. And that realization made it harder to entomb that seed of desperation. In fact, the awareness lit it with a year's worth of sun, freeing it to unfurl and strangle anything it came into contact with.

"Girls, please. You have to understand—" She stopped herself. "Things are hard. I know, and I'm sorry they aren't different. I am so sorry."

"You have three jobs, Mom. Three," Ida said. She set another wet dish on the pile, holding Mary's gaze. "*I'm* sorry for *that*," Ida said. And Mary felt as though someone saw her efforts. Someone understood.

She couldn't argue that night or rebuild the façade. She didn't want Ida to move out, but she knew it was coming, and there was no stopping it.

Chapter 18

Stan

Stan wiped his brow with his forearm, then bent forward, one hand braced on his knee, the other with the glove pressed against his chest, absorbing each heartbeat. Pressure. Under a swelling blanket of hot, humid air, Stan finally breathed again. He pushed his forefinger through a tear in the denim, brushing a half-formed scab on his knee, making him cringe. Sliding into third. That's when he'd ripped the trousers. Called safe. Then scored on Honey's line drive through the gap between second and first. He straightened against the weight and strain—the pain it created.

It suddenly sank in. Andrew and all his rambling in between innings about cell bodies and how some types could explode and others had protective membranes that contained anything swelling against them. Stan felt what all that meant right inside his own house.

Some cells, like cork, were joined but still clearly separate. Wasn't that what Andrew said the other day when he pushed his microscope under Stan's nose to examine a sliver of cork, revealing a world only partially visible to the naked eye? Stan was beginning to see his home life like the cork, the stuff he and Mom packed into homemade depression balls.

A resilient material, not steel-strong with combined earthen elements that had been heated, cooled, molded, and galvanized down below Marelda Street. But cork was giving, pliable, better? Each Musial cell member was joined by marriage or birth, still his own man but forced to swell or shrink depending what news or mood was introduced into the household.

Stan decided he was the type of cell that could fill and fill, tension rising and spreading, and still he didn't burst or harden his heart. But the burn of resisting the strain, the grip that came with his pop's moods that stood up like mountain walls despite the man's small size, had been nearly too much that night.

The mountain had come to life and thundered out of the house, one of the family cells disconnected, the exit inviting light back inside. Stan exhaled. The bloat released. He was free to move about.

What had Andrew called that type of cell? The free-to-move-alone type?

A nudge on the arm startled Stan.

Honey.

He tossed a ball.

Stan caught it and ran his fingers along the thick stitching. Peace offering? "Sorry 'bout the steak, Honey."

Honey held Stan's gaze, looking like he had a fight on his mind, but then he just shrugged. "Good as it smelled?"

Their arguments rarely left permanent footprints between them. Most disappeared with a stiff wind, a good rain, or the toss of a ball. Stan looped his arm around his brother's neck. "*Man*, it was... Melted in my mouth."

Honey narrowed his eyes. "Like braunschweiger?"

Stan shook his head. "No, no. Not mushy or grainy. Next time someone gives me steak, I'm going to eat slower. But the sense of it, I'll never forget as long as I live. One bite, juices exploding, salty, peppery, and I don't even know what flavors. Heaven."

Honey nodded. "Smelled rosemary through the window—that stuff Smokestack's sister made as a rub for the bat."

Stan sat on the curb, setting the glove beside him. "Yeah, that's it. Rosemary. Mrs. Morrison shouted for you, you know."

"Didn't hear."

"I'm sorry."

"Won't be the last time I get left in your dust. Been happening since birth, since you toddled down the aisle at St. Mary's ahead of me for our christening. Since your gymnastic feats and your pitching and…"

Stan turned to his brother. "Just practice more."

"It's not practice, Stan. It's something else."

Stan wouldn't argue after just getting relief from the slow-moving, moody anger at dinner. "I woulda stuffed some steak in my pocket for you if the Morrisons wouldn't have noticed. But they notice everything. Everything. The way they were with each other. So *nice*."

"Mom said that about them, too. Got some moony look in her eyes when she said it."

Stan laid back, putting the glove under his head, the hot sidewalk warming through his undershirt. With the mills barely running, there were plenty of clear sky patches, and he imagined Andrew with his parents in their backyard studying constellations once it was dark. "You know how when you catch a ball just right, even one screamin' in and you just know it's gonna sting, but you soften the catch by pulling back a smidgeon, just right, and it feels like cotton balls? That's how these people treat each other. Every throw gets a soft catch."

"I know." Honey lay beside Stan.

Stan shoved the glove toward Honey for him to pillow his head. "Someday when we're playin' for the Pirates and we come off a road trip, we'll stop at the butcher and buy Mom steaks and cook 'em up good."

"Baseball and steak. Salt, pepper, rosemary. We'll even bring Pop a couple cuts."

Honey chuckled. "Yeah."

"Imagine his face if our baseball salaries buy him steak. He'd be proud… I think. I just want him to see us like Mr. Morrison sees Andrew."

"I dunno."

They didn't discuss the family moods often. Stan didn't push. "Well, I can't think of another thing we'd need besides steak and baseball in the whole wide world."

Honey chuckled again. "Maybe tender steak makes tender families. Maybe that's why those Morrisons are so damn nice."

Stan shrugged. "Maybe. Their pop doesn't get injured at work or lose his job when half the country has none. It all just comes together to make this pure, quiet, happy. I could smell it over there. Strong as cabbage stew. But sweet, not—"

"Like the mill itself. That sulfur. The cabbage. Our insides must be made of it."

"Oh man, I know," Stan said. "I'm never eatin' cabbage again once I—"

"Yeah." Honey chuckled. "Me neither, brother. Steak. Yeah. That will be *it*."

**

The sound of a baseball smacking into leather made Stan and Honey leap to standing. Honey stuffed his hand into the glove. Up Marelda Avenue a ways, Joe Barbao and his buddy, Manny, were playing catch. Stan nudged Honey. "Go get the balls."

Honey returned with a canvas bag, and without interrupting the semi-pro players, the Musials took their places alongside them, nebbing into their strategy talk about the next Donora Zincs game. That summer Joe was coaching and playing for the team in between guarding the community gardens that had been planted at Palmer Park. With all three mills' production down to a thin cotton thread, there was plenty of extra time for baseball.

Stan and Honey traded their glove back and forth. Joe skittered balls along the street, making them take odd skips to give

Manny a chance to practice the unexpected. Stan and Honey followed suit.

A burst of mill siren noise came loud, startling them and causing Honey to misplay a bad hop. The ball hit his bare hands awkwardly. He folded over, grasping his hand to his belly. "Ow. Damn. Ow."

Stan, Joe and Manny collapsed around Honey, checking his hand.

Joe shrugged. "Stoved, is all."

Honey continued to groan, and Stan patted his brother's back.

"Take him to my house," Joe told Manny. "Kate put that wrap I was using the other day in the boot-room. That should help stabilize it. Joe Jr.'s sleeping though, so be quiet."

Manny led Honey up the street. "Let's steal these last few flickers of daylight before they're gone." Joe motioned for Stan to come closer as he threw a high fly. The smack of the ball, a real ball, into his glove made Stan feel as though he'd been born with a leather mitt for a hand.

"You getting the feel for your changeup?"

Stan tossed the ball back and shook out his arm. "Aiming for that slower speed but still catching myself unleashing the heat."

"Intentionality, Stan. Letting it rip will catch most batters on your team lookin', but you have an arm and a gift. Don't let the gift sit unopened."

When the last gasp of sunlight passed, Joe jerked his head toward the hillside where they often sat and talked baseball. With the mills working at a fraction, the trains running less with fewer loads, there was a stillness that was peaceful and disquieting since the relative stillness and clear skies meant no money was being made. Only the moan of barges plugging down the Mon came through clear and sad, like a song for the country itself.

At the far north side of Donora, orange blasts still periodically came and went. Below Marelda Avenue, the zinc mill belched white waste; despite lack of money, the business district was peopled with courting couples going to shows when they squeezed an extra dime out of a nearly empty pocket. Those looking to dance went to Palmer Park for big-band swing. Strains of music from the park filtered over and up the hillside as though carried on the fog that had started rising from the hollow.

Stan tossed the ball into his glove. "Did you leave this glove for Honey and me?"

Joe studied it. "It's an old one. Still good. Broken in. Sounds like something I'd do."

Stan nodded, still not sure whether it was Joe or not. "Well, thanks."

Joe smiled. "Show me your changeup grip."

Stan made an okay sign and set the wide part of the seams against the circled finger and thumb, his other fingers extending around the ball over one row of stitching.

"That's it," Joe said. "All right. So think about your speed, your rotation."

"Don't light the flame." Stan repeated what Joe had said before, practicing the motion.

"That's right. Cool it off, let them reach for it, shock 'em with the off-speed at the plate."

Stan felt good that he and Joe understood one another, that there was never awkward stammering when he was with him. They talked as easily as brothers. "Lefty Grove's headed for MVP again," Stan said.

Joe Barbao looked at Stan with a furrowed brow. "You think?"

"Burnin' it up. Twelve wins so far. Still has half the season to go and—"

"What about the Bambino?"

Stan shook his head.

"Iron Horse, then?"

Stan shrugged. "Aww, he's something else. But I think Lefty can win again. He's earning $20,000. Can you imagine? Pop earns eleven dollars every two weeks—when he has a job, if he's lucky. Now it's down to…" Joe knew the Musials' situation. Same as everyone else's. Neither needed to say it aloud.

Joe pulled his knees up and rested his forearms on them, brushing soot from his elbow. "Gehrig's making twenty-five."

Stan let out a whistle. "That's so much money." Stan retied the laces on the glove. "Could live on that for years." He imagined the steaks he and Honey would buy.

"Ruth's making seventy-five."

"Nooo wayyy." Stan gripped his head and fell back into the dirt, sprigs of grass tickling his ears.

Joe laughed. "Yep. Buddy of mine scouts for the Yankees. Told me the other day."

"Wow." Stan sat up and tossed his ball hand to hand again.

"Could be you."

Stan squinted at Joe. Had he heard Stan and Honey talking? Joe's understanding of who Stan was from the inside out gave him the confidence to reveal his dream. "I'm playing pro. I know that. But $75,000 a year? That's not even necessary. I'd play for…" Stan ran his fingers over the red laces on the one real baseball he owned. "Steak dinners. That's all a man needs, right?"

Joe wrenched his black pipe, tobacco and lighter from his pocket. "Not a bad start. But Kate and the baby need more than that."

Stan hadn't been thinking about having a family. He watched Joe pack the pipe, the open pouch releasing whiffs of sweet tobacco. He lit the bowl, let it go out then lit it again, drawing the smoke into his mouth, then exhaling it, looking as though the process was relaxing him.

With the pipe in his mouth, Joe flicked the lighter lid back and hit the striking wheel with his thumb. The flame burst up from the wick, a miniature blast from its tiny furnace. "Aim higher, Stan. I'm not kiddin' around. Every summer, your arm gets stronger and you catch like a cat—if cats could catch. Ball comes and you snatch your glove out at the last second, and your hitting. Man, oh man. You have everything a ballplayer can't be taught."

"Thank you."

Joe ran his thumb over the lighter wheel again, the flame jumping to life on demand. "You know how many parts make up a little lighter like this?"

Stan studied it, eyes always going to the flame. "Four? Five?"

"Twenty-one parts make up this little bugger. And that's not including the nice leather wrapping the outside."

"Wow."

Joe closed the lid and handed it to Stan. He turned it back and forth, then brushed his thumb along the wheel, smiling at the bouncing flame the simple movement produced.

Joe puffed on his pipe, the tobacco glowing bright against the darkness. "Most of the lighter parts are hidden away. Met this fella at the Spanish Club who's in sales for a fella making a new kind of lighter. Says it'll even work in the rain. So he got to dismantling the sample lighter, showing me its insides. There's some flint, fuel, a fuel chamber, a wind hood, a chamber wick… On and on the fella went about it like he was recapping a baseball game."

He took the lighter back from Stan, who was confused.

"Point is, if any of those twenty-one parts don't work right or are made from the wrong material or tilted just the wrong way," Joe snapped his fingers, "thing won't work. It's just a bunch of parts that don't do anything spectacular, least of all light a flame in the rain. The flame. It's all anyone notices, but, without the hidden stuff, none of it works."

Stan felt as though Joe had just laid something important down on him, but he couldn't quite grasp it.

"Understand?"

Stan was inclined to lie to avoid embarrassment when it came to matters of the mind. But Joe had a way of circling back to topics days later, and Stan needed to be able to discuss this.

"I'll tell you." Joe slung his arm around Stan, flicking the wheel. "You've got all the components that make for a pro ballplayer—if you were a lighter, you'd have all twenty-one parts perfectly placed, ready to deliver a nice flame every time someone spins that wheel. Others round here have half those parts or maybe more in some cases. Honey has plenty of parts. But you're different. And you're just—how old're you again?"

"Eleven."

Joe let out a whistle. "For the love of—*eleven*. Good God, Stan. So much time to fine-tune it all. Can't believe I'm saying it at your age." He shrugged. "Maybe I'm wrong."

"No! You're right. I just know it." Stan didn't want to think Honey might not join him on the Pirates someday. He just needed to practice more. But for Joe to sit him down for a serious conversation about the insides of lighters and ballplayers who had what it took and… Stan was one of them.

"Future's as bright as a blast furnace for you, Stan."

He smiled, plumped up like a fat steak. It felt for a moment like Joe was his father, the kind of father Mr. Morrison was. And in that huddle at the top of the hill overlooking town, Stan sent a little prayer to God in thanks for giving him Joe. This thought was immediately followed by guilt as he reprimanded himself. His father just needed to learn more about baseball and see that Babe Ruth wasn't the only player worth knowing. "Wait till I tell Pop about the Bambino's salary. He likes him. Only one Bambino, he says. But I could be next. Pop'll see."

Joe drew on his pipe then blew smoke rings. "Just focus on what you can control. You've got incredible talent but still a lot to learn. You're tentative sometimes. And, well, convincing people of things they don't want to know is same as banging your head against a wall. Your pop may never see baseball as a good job for you. Lots of folks wouldn't."

"But if Pop knew—"

Joe nodded, staring off into the distance. "Maybe. People change. Right about that."

"Pop said my hands are too small to play like the men. Thinks the Musial men ought to be shuttled off to the mill."

Joe bit on his pipe and examined Stan's hands, pressing them, turning them back and forth, making Stan laugh. He pointed his pipe at Stan. "Most times I'd agree with your pop. But one, you're just eleven. And two, you have hands that know what to do without you tellin' 'em. Good as most men I play with. Dunno, maybe he's right."

Stan turned fully to Joe. "No. No. *You're* right. I'm right. Mom's right."

Joe studied his pipe letting the embers go out. He looked off as though remembering something good, something that put a smile on his face. "Well, all right then. It's settled." Then he launched into his stories about when he played pro ball, how every single day he got paid to play was like winning the number.

Sitting there with Joe, night falling darker by the second, the mills firing once a week or so, rotating work among a handful of men, but still molding and grinding out their material, the searing blasts and the lit-up buildings below, hearing these stories, Stan felt as though he belonged, was wanted, had a purpose. Like the lighter. All the parts were there.

Joe's stories, while full of mischief and mayhem, as he was often the player pitchers went after with a little chin music, and he was the one who pilfered signs, there was nothing childish about how he described it all. It was as though the game of baseball was the most important endeavor God had ever gifted mankind. And Stan needed to be a part of that, same as he needed to breathe.

Chapter 19

Mary

Church, faith, kids, work. Lack of permanent jobs for Lukasz. Ordinary life. Mary clamped the clothes basket to her hip, making rounds through the house collecting socks, stockings, underthings, and shirts for washday. Curfew had sounded an hour before, and the girls were already in bed, positioning themselves where they could best catch a cross breeze.

Mary approached the room at the end of the hall where the boys slept, where she used to sleep with her sisters. The door was open enough for her to see into the room. She paused, surprised the boys were saying their nightly prayers aloud like when she'd gathered them to learn the Our Father and Hail Mary all those years ago. She'd just assumed they'd have started praying silently by now. They didn't notice her listening.

She was proud that Stan never missed mass. He seemed to take comfort in the weekly rituals and rhythms of the up-and-down and kneeling and the priest's Latin. More and more, Honey would slip away from the family pew to assist old Mrs. Lizinski to her seat or Mr. Sawa, after having his foot crushed by a crane. Honey would then declare that his charitable actions caused him to be "late" and sat in the back. But Mary suspected him of wandering the streets, slinking back into the sanctuary in the nick of time for Communion, to give her a wink as he trailed down the aisle, hands clasped at his waist with the last of the parishioners, putting on his best angel face. But his pink cheeks and windblown hair always gave him away.

Mary leaned against the doorjamb listening.

"… and please heal my jammed finger so I can play well tomorrow," Honey said. Stan started to interrupt, but Honey cut him off.

"'Cause you see, Lord Jesus, Prince of Peace, if we've got to shuffle ballplayers too much, we'll end up with only Monocle to take first if I can't slide over for Melonhead since he's gonna have to haul ass to the field on account of his pap's funeral lunch and— "

"Honey," Stan cut his brother off. "God isn't going to—"

"I asked Jesus, not God—"

"You think Jesus cares about baseball?"

"I think Jesus can see the short end of having a fella with only one working glasses lens that only stays attached to 'im if he maintains the perfect level of squint, and I think Jesus wants us to do our level best in every game, and yes, Jesus would be a ballplayer if ever given an up."

Mary covered her mouth to stifle a laugh.

Stan dropped his head on the bed, then righted himself. The boys knelt on opposite bedsides, their elbows resting on the mattress, hands clasped under their chins.

"Welp," Stan said, "I'm asking God and Jesus to provide work for all the pops in Donora, for Pop to come home without passing through the Falcons Nest for a refreshment first. To have him come home happy and maybe even play a little ball with us."

Honey coughed. "Never gonna play ball with us. Hates it. But I'd like that, too. I'll clip it to my list of prayers. At the end. In case God gets bored and stops listening."

A wave of sadness worked through Mary.

"Welp, Pop doesn't have to play ball, but maybe he can say something nice about us playing it, seeing how it's gonna be our life's work and all."

"Never gonna happen. Pray for something else."

"I pray for Pop to be proud of us. Me. Please, God, let him be proud of me."

"Whole world's proud of you, Stushy," Honey said. "You really need Pop to be proud, too?"

Stan ignored Honey. "And for him to be nicer and… well, be a little bit, just a little like Mr. Morrison or Joe. Please, God."

Hearing Mr. Morrison and Joe Barbao named in a prayer stopped Mary's breath. She understood as she too caught herself thinking of those two men—envious of how Daniel Morrison treated his wife and how Joe treated her sons. Earlier that night, she'd gone up the street to drop stew at the Minskys'. She'd caught a glimpse of Joe and Stan sitting on the hill overlooking town. She couldn't hear their words, but their laughter had curled up to her, their bodies, leaning into each other as they looked at something, then the flash of a lighter and Joe's pipe glowing as Stan looked up at him. She didn't know what words of wisdom their neighbor was dealing right then, but whatever it was, it enraptured Stan and made her ache for how Lukasz never even tried to take that kind of time with his boys.

She crossed herself, asking forgiveness from God for betraying her husband, even if it was only in her mind. Lukasz was like most men. Mr. Morrison and Joe were not. It wasn't fair to hold Lukasz to the standard of the elite, the unusual, the ones who carried wonder and wisdom with them same as her husband carried resentment.

It wasn't fair. She pushed into the bedroom and stabbed the round button that lit the light above the bed. "I don't want to hear that again, Stanley Musial."

The boys jerked toward her, mouths gaping.

"Your father works hard for us, and yes, sometimes he takes a path through the Falcons." Mary breathed deep. Something in Stan's tone reminded her of Matka, how she had repeatedly embarrassed Papa in public, pulling him out of bars, humiliating him in front of friends. She had never respected the work Papa did, and Mary swore she'd never do that to her husband. And she hadn't, but she was mortified that her sons saw what she often looked away from in order to keep her promise.

Like with Ida, she'd mistakenly thought she had managed to hide some of Lukasz's shortcomings—at least provide a buffer for them. "When the mills are open, your father's lungs are fat with soot and smoke when he gets off a shift. Every stinkin' man in there clears his throat with a shot and a beer, and your father has it worse. Since I've known him, his belly's been a bit… troubled. Yet he gets up and goes to work. So I take him his lunch rather than expect him to eat in a bar or slurp cold soup. It's my fault if he's stopping into the Falcons for a sandwich after his shift. Or after no work at all. You know Mitch Watson's father hasn't worked one day this year. Not one single day. That eats at a man. And that's why they gather at places for a bit of relief. Just a bit. We've had hard years, but this one… it's got a clamp-grip on us. Right around the throat."

"He's not nice to you either, Mom, not like—"

Mary's face flooded with heat. She shook her finger at Stan. She didn't want him to name Mr. Morrison or Joe, to let that out into the air of their home. "*Everyone* is mean, Stan, even Mr. Morrison—even Joe. Just because you don't see it, even if their anger only visits once in a while…" She thought of the boy she used to like before she fell in love with Lukasz and how his father's awfulness was easily hidden behind enormous wealth and a large, well-appointed home.

"But he treats you so—"

"He loves me."

Oh, how she wanted him to treat her as he had when they first met, as he still did when the right stars aligned.

"But the Morrisons were dancing together and laughing it up and…"

Mary's eyes teared, remembering that dancing was her and Lukasz's first shared language, their bodies pressed, the safeness she felt in his arms, his agile feet, that even though he drank too much and lost their money in the bottle, that he'd rescued her, he'd given her the family she dreamed of, if not the house. He had saved her.

"You've seen us dance to the *Big Swing* show on the radio a million times, dances at Palmer Park, at the church. I've told you how we met." She shook her head.

Stan straightened. "I know you two dance. I've seen you, but then it's like all that falls away and Pop is mad again. It looked different at the Morrisons' is all. Here it's always so—"

Mary got on her knees beside Stan and clasped her hands together. "Your father is a good man in a very difficult position. Someday I'll tell you all of it. He produced you two good souls after all. A bad man couldn't do that."

Stan flinched.

"What?" Mary asked.

Stan hesitated.

"Tell me."

Stan clasped his hands tight under his chin, squeezing his eyes shut. "I don't think Pop knows that he's a good man, Mom."

Stan hit it right with that one. Right out of the ballpark. She fought to find her breath and steady her voice. "Sometimes people don't see their own strengths. Can't *feel* them. He's been through so much. His life in Poland was… He was alone and starving. Really starving. For everything, for love, for food, for opportunity. That creates a different kind of person than someone born here like you, with the family you have. If he would tell you the stories, how long it took for him to get here—"

"I know," Stan said, sliding his gaze to meet Mary's. "And we have you."

Mary nodded. "He's not easily understood, it's true, but I'm his wife, and so that should tell you all you need to know. The two of us finding each other was like…" She shook her head. "We were meant to be together. It might not seem clear why. And sometimes I wonder, too, but then I think of what I have with him, in him choosing me, that we have your sisters and you two and… it was meant to be. He saved me. And so I am the wife that a man who saves a woman deserves."

A little smile came to Stan's face, and he patted Mary between the shoulder blades as though he were comforting her. And the gesture did just that. She studied him, his lopsided grin like Lukasz's, his soulful eyes his father's too, though darker like infield dirt instead of gray Donora sky. Stan understood something about her, that her words dripped with resignation as much as with faith in the man she had married. Somewhere inside, perhaps he understood that the two things were the same.

She brushed Stan's hair back and made eye contact with Honey. "Honey's right about asking God to change Pop. God's got to rescue starving children and motherless babies and has wars to stave off. You two have everything you need."

She planted a kiss on top of each boy's head and shuffled them into bed, lying flat on their backs, limbs stretched out. She wrenched open the windows higher and spread the curtains as far as they'd go to let the breeze in. She snatched up stinky socks and shirts and drawers one by one, revealing balls that she kicked into a pile by the dresser.

She shook out Stan's trousers, sticking her finger through a hole in the knee. She looked back at the boys, sorry about what she just demanded—that they shouldn't pray for what they thought they needed, that perhaps what they saw, the dark, broody mood Lukasz brought with him most of the time, should be excused by them as she excused it every single day.

She backed halfway out of the room. "Pray for what you need, but be sure of what you're asking for before you want God to go changing people up just because you think it ought to be done. Some people feel empty and awful their entire lives, and they act awful on account of it."

"Okay," Stan whispered.

"Pray for a person's relief from the black grip on their soul so they can be free to be nice and kind and all the things you think other people are. *That*, God might grant someday."

"Okay, Mom. I will," Stan said. Honey responded with a snore. Twenty years of steady love should have softened Lukasz Musial, should have filled his emptiness a little bit. Maybe it had, and they just hadn't noticed. In comparison to Mr. Morrison or Joe Barbao, measuring up was impossible. Thinking that was a betrayal of sorts in itself.

Her words sent out to mold her boys' perception of their father had really been to maintain the shape of her own. It was the only way to keep on with any semblance of contentment or satisfaction. She poked the switch to turn out the light and left the room. She was strong enough to bend her world toward goodness, strong enough until her children learned to do it themselves. And she didn't know when it happened, that wanting to see her children's success had replaced wanting to see her own, but it had and for that she felt a swell of optimism. For them, all the world stretched out in front. No need for any of them to go looking back.

Chapter 20

Stan

Donora's history was braided into Stan's life like thousands of steel wires woven into bridge cable. Founded in 1901, the town had sprung up when miles of fertile Monongahela River shore birthed sprawling, flaming open hearths and wireworks, spurring a community that made the steel that built the country. Like its metal, made of amalgamated earthen materials and hot blasts of oxygen, Donora's population saw titans of industry, learned teachers, shop owners, and immigrant laborers melded, each group strengthened by the other's presence.

Internationally known business and intellectual giants named Donner and Mellon provided the steely seed from which it all sprouted. The world knew them by name, trusted their wizarding industrial wands would mean production and wealth for all. But it was Americans of modest means and anonymous, penniless immigrants who were summoned into town bearing little education but massive stores of strength, force and zeal.

They were the ones who coaxed the seed to fruit, who filled in gaps between machine and nature, sacrificed life and limb and literally built the machinery that built everything else. And as each immigrant reached the shores of Donora via train or wagon or foot, he or she unloaded meager satchels stuffed full of traditions but not much else. Clustering in churches and ethnic clubs built around what they had left behind, Donorans often kept one foot in their comforting old country ways while planting the other on a new path to the American Dream.

At first the foothill land was snatched up for well-appointed homes. Then other, humble homes came, billeted mill-side, scattered up the hillsides, wedged into sandstone and limestone and shale. These meek homes were assembled from scrap, backed into tight bends in the four-hundred-foot sloping valley walls. The frenetic pace at which the steel industry grew resulted in these stretches and cozy enclaves to comprise every nationality, race, and social class.

With so many people bridging old country traditions and new American ways, Donora's early years brought celebrations like St. John's Eve on June 23. With picnic baskets and late-night fires, folks of every nationality prepared beloved foods and drink riverside. Their daughters crafted flowered crowns set alight with candles and sent down the river, hoping the love of their lives would pluck theirs out of the water, cementing a future together.

But things changed around 1915 when that third mile of mills was added. The zinc works—a smelting operation that heated earthen feedstock like sphalerite in order to release zinc stores and create pure zinc ingots. These ingots were then transported on property and to other United States Steel works locations to galvanize products—protect them—ensuring wire, fencing, and more could last a lifetime.

Roasting and sintering, the hot work at the horizontal zinc retorts like a metal beehive, was nearly unbearable. As though the god Vulcan set up housekeeping there, the mill so blistering hot that workers were permitted to pull short shifts, leaving when their work was finished rather than when prescribed hours ended. Even the zinc byproducts—sulfuric acid, lead, and cadmium—were valuable.

The gasses not captured in the baghouse escaped right in front of the retort ovens or out of the stacks, into the bodies of the men at work. White smoke flowed across the river toward Webster, causing lush, fertile hills to go brittle and bare. When it was going to rain, the wind blew the zinc mill smoke back over the river and up the hills of north Donora, making riverside recreation less palatable.

In 1917, the first planned neighborhood came to the south end of Donora, threaded into hills away from the zinc mill smoke that kept lush vegetation from growing on the north end. The new neighborhood was intended for mill foremen and their families as the town's expanding population still struggled with a housing shortage. Cement City's streets, with names like Bertha, Ida, and Helen, ran ladder rungs up the hillsides, connecting to the ladder's side rail streets called Chestnut and Walnut.

Cement City was Thomas Edison's innovation for homebuilding. The impermeable materials would keep soot and smoke from entering and fire from destroying. They were built to last, and each came with a red rosebush and lilacs. And there were maintenance workers to service any needs within the home or neighborhood. It was a modern, clean existence that provided a place for any kid to lay his aspirations for the good life.

By the time Stan was eleven years old, Fourth of July had replaced St. John's Eve as the prominent summer holiday celebration in Donora. Baseball games, parades, and picnics were organized to take the sting out of the depressed days of the 1930s. Stan and his team, who had dubbed themselves North Donora, were set to play against the Cement City team at noon at their field. Later that afternoon, the Industrial League teams, the Zincs and Monongahela, would play at Palmer Park—the big game before fireworks and dancing at the pavilion.

Stan had been up since dawn throwing with Honey. They'd had trouble beating Cement City all of June. Each game, Stan had made errors that he held up as costing them runs and outs and, in the end, wins. He was determined to play up to his ability.

Andrew hadn't answered the door at his house when the Musial brothers went to get him, hoping to take the field early and get a feel for conditions. But the Cement City guard denied them access, saying the North Donora team needed to wait until game time to enter.

Irritated at the rude treatment, Stan and Honey retreated to an empty lot a couple of blocks away to warm up as best they could. They lost two balls down the hill, and the brothers snapped at each other, issuing mutual blame. "Everything isn't always my fault, Stushy."

"Did I say it was?"

"I can *feel* you thinking it." Honey whipped a ball back at his brother. "Here. Take the glove. Take everything."

Stan fitted the old glove onto his hand. He'd let Honey use it the entire time they'd been practicing that morning. What else did he want? Still, not wanting to be distracted, he held his tongue, remembering what Joe Barbao had wondered about Honey—whether he was as good as Stan. He didn't want Honey worked up or nervous for the game, so he just let him run his mouth.

It wasn't long before teammates began to show up and practice alongside them, cutting the tension between the brothers. If Stan could have the game he was capable of, they'd win and he and his brother would be back on the right track.

Cheeks arrived first, pulling a newspaper from his waistband. "Check this out, fellas." He snapped open the paper and held it up in one hand, gesturing to a photo. "Not that we need any more motivation to beat this team, boys, but here. Half their fathers were at *this* very special dinner."

The newspaper photo showed men gathered at a table, cigars, drinks, and a caption that described them eating "fat, luscious oysters straight from the Rappahannock River in Virginia." Another quote from treasury secretary Andrew Mellon claimed the depression was "a godsend to purge the American economy of excesses." The same paper quoted several of Donora's leading citizens agreeing that "the depression was a result of high taxes and excessive government spending."

"Grandma says the fat cats say that all the time," Moonshine said.

Cheeks smacked the paper with the back of his hand. "She's right. Fat cats are mighty generous with the criticism of the people who break their backs working for 'em."

Stan and Honey agreed, having overheard similar conversations since the depression years began.

"My father told me blustery bullshit ain't worth a damn." Cheeks looked from Honey to Stan and back again. He folded the paper back up. "We show our worth on the field today. Their dads might be riverside, sucking back oysters and smoking fine tobacco, but we're gonna kick their boys' asses on the field."

Stan couldn't stop smiling at that. He slapped Cheeks on the back. "We are. I got my game together, and I know I can go four for four. At least."

Cheeks stood between the Musial brothers and put one arm around each of their necks. "Now that's exactly what I wanted to hear. If we can only get the rest of our misfit team to step into line for once."

Stan adjusted his hat and snagged a ball from the pile he and Honey had made. "We're hitting our stride. All of us."

Andrew arrived, hauling his knapsack as usual, staring into the sky, notebook under his arm. "Cirrus clouds—indicates a front could be coming through."

Smokestack came on Andrew's heels, flicked a spent cigarette on the ground, then lit another.

Andrew stomped out the burning stub and opened his notebook, paging through it. "We're ripe for rain. Been calm for days, and this fat humidity…" He looked into the gray sky.

Smokestack dragged off his cigarette. "We'll know the weather when it shows up."

"Sometimes," Andrew said, "knowing what's coming gives an advantage."

Smokestack shrugged. "Okay, Weatherman. If you insist."

Stan changed the subject. "Where were you, Andrew? Wanted to get some throwing in with you, but no one answered at your house."

"Oh." Andrew set his knapsack down and opened it farther. At first no one paid attention to what he pulled out of his bag, assuming it was another notebook or science tome. But out of the corner of his eye Stan saw the unmistakable shape and caught the scent of a genuine leather baseball glove.

"My dad made a supernova deal out of it. Said something about D&M or Lucky Dog... something." Andrew tossed it to Stan as though it were nothing. Stan ran his finger over the logo of the hunting dog and the baseball diamond underneath it. "Store owner said it's from the 1930 product line. It's new, but not from the newest line."

Stan was so excited at the sight of it that he couldn't speak. "It's brand new to us. Lucky Dog."

"Old man said with my black-and-blue hands, I ought to have something to help."

Stan couldn't believe it. "So he just up and bought this?"

Andrew nodded. "Took me this morning. That's where we were when you came knocking. Old man still doesn't realize I barely play and that we share gloves and mitts with the other team." Stan slid his hand into the new leather, wishing he was a righty. He looked over his shoulder at the weathered lefty glove he and Honey shared. This righty was beautiful.

Smokestack tossed his cigarette aside. "Give it here."

Stan did. The other boys crowded in to see what the commotion was.

Stan looked at Andrew, still confused at his fears of Mr. Morrison. Stan could barely recall a single father who wasn't loud and lumbering or smoldering silent when dealing with their families. But Mr. Morrison was the opposite of most of them. Stan smiled, watching the boys taking turns, stuffing their faces into the glove, inhaling the new leather.

Stan would have thought Mr. Morrison would see Andrew's black-and-blue palms as a reason to end the torturous demand that he play baseball. But the "old man" had surprised Stan in many ways. Though he insisted Andrew play, he was somehow soft and gentle as summer rains when it came to encouraging his son, spending spare money on something like a baseball glove. Something Pop would never have purchased on a whim.

Smokestack pounded his fist into it. "Man, oh man. My auntie has an oil we can use to break it in." He stuffed his hand into it and held it up. All the boys ran their hands over it as though they could extract its magic for themselves.

Andrew stepped closer and pulled some laces tight around Smokestack's wrist. "Fella said this lace should help keep it snug even if we aren't grown size yet."

"Tank is."

"Nicky Christmas, too."

"And Melonhead."

They started to bicker about who should get to use the glove when North Donora was fielding. Stan moved away from the argument. It didn't matter for him and Honey, seeing that they were lefties, and he needed to focus on what was ahead. Tank jogged up beside him, handing Stan a bat. "I sanded the handle down a little more. You'll get a better grip," he said out of breath.

Stan swung it, sinking into his stance. Then, imagining the ball roaring toward him, he unleashed a mighty swing and smiled as his imaginary ball cleared the rooftops, the mill stacks, the smog and dunked right into the black river below.

Tank whistled, miming excitement for Stan's pretend home run. "Don't know how you hit the ball like you do with that stance."

Stan exhaled and took a couple half swings. "Don't know how you hit like you do with your stumpy bat."

Tank smiled and reached for it. "Those pitchers see my big behind crowding the plate and they back off."

Stan handed the bat over and adjusted his hat. "Yeah. It's like they're afraid to hit ya."

"Petrified."

"It's a gift."

"Well, you can hit anything in any direction. Bet you could lay one right inside the mouth of that stack down there if you set your mind to it. *That's* the real gift," Tank said. "All I got's power."

Stan nodded. "I'm thinking of making my own bat. But what you did sanding this down feels good."

Tank picked another bat out of the pile by their feet. "That's right, Stan. Make yourself your own wizarding wand."

"Yeah," Melonhead said, rolling up with three extra hand-stitched balls. "A magic wand for the magician."

Stan felt himself get taller, growing with the praise. It made heat creep up his neck to hear the compliments, but he reminded himself athletic grace was all that God seemed to have granted him. He wouldn't brag, but accepting others' kind words? That he could do.

Tank handed Stan the ramshackle, barely round bat, flaying apart as though it had been glued with school paste.

"I can get you an old bat to mess with," Cheeks said. "Fella owes my uncle for unpaid numbers, and he used to play ball for Buffalo. Make yourself a real weapon of choice."

"Your unc will just give it to us?" Stan asked.

"Uncle Dom's world is numbers, and he sees your future value."

Stan drew back. "Okay."

Monocle slipped into the group. "Cement City guard said we can go in."

"The peasants are summoned." Andrew rotated his hand above his head.

"Time for an uprising," Nicky Christmas said. "If they hadn't locked the rest of yinz out, I'd think they didn't like the color of mine and Tank's skin."

Stan put his arm around Nicky. The two marched up the street, the rest of the North Donora pack scattered behind them, "bats" over shoulders, ready for a win, the cluster of them approaching like an accidental army, cresting the hill, ready for victory.

"Whoa." Stan stopped abruptly when the ballfield came into view. His teammates did the same. Honey removed his cap and swiped his brow with it, a smile covering his face. The field was neat, with a few of the players' mothers walking around plucking stones out of the dirt. Other mothers were hanging festive red, white, and blue Fourth of July bunting on the fencing. Jonathan Malkey greeted North Donora, meeting Stan's gaze.

He gestured at the bags set up around the field. "My uncle's been auto camping lately, and he wore his canvas tenting nearly through. My ma made the bases out of it. Real bags."

Stan couldn't believe his eyes.

"Still using a manhole cover for home plate though."

Stan nodded, his words knotting on his tongue. He felt as though they'd been invited to play in the big leagues. He wasn't prepared. There was even relatively thick grass and baselines drawn with chalk.

"Golllleeee," Tank said.

"Will you take a look at all this hullaballoo." Smokestack's cigarette fluttered, nearly falling out of his mouth. "For us?"

"Check out their threads." Monocle angled his head so he could study their opponents' uniforms. *Uniforms.* They'd never seen any team of boys wearing anything even close to uniforms.

Each Cement City player had baseball pants, socks, red shirts, and red hats. And most astonishing—six of them wore leather baseball shoes.

Stan punched at his glove, trying to act natural. He didn't even have leather shoes for church and school. And these kids had leather shoes to play ball in. Like the pros.

"We're gonna get smoked," Monocle said. "We're missing Skunk, Yellow Melvin, Blue Louise, too. Which means we basically have eight players if you consider me and Andrew. Ain't worth a shit for a win. Moonshine's had a few cups of that elderberry wine on account of it being a holiday and all. Smokestack's got some sort of cough he can't shake, what with the number of cigarettes he smokes." Monocle cocked his head so he could see the players better. "Damn. Cement City. Look at 'em. *Fan-cy* pants."

Stan's belly tightened.

"Probably had a stack of pancakes and eggs and bacon for breakfast," Moonshine said, tossing a ball from one hand, then back into the other.

"On silver platters, no doubt," Cheeks said.

"Silver for breakfast. Nah," Andrew said.

"Oh yeah. My ma cleans for one of them fella's mas, and they eat off silver every meal."

North Donora milled around but didn't move toward the field.

Stan adjusted his hat. He was not going to lose. Not that day. The sight of the uniformed team did set his nerves on edge. He knew these fellas' playing habits like he knew Honey would hog the bed, nearly booting Stan off by three A.M. every blessed morning. He told himself that strapping on new shoes and donning matching clothes didn't change their ability to play.

Still.

Nicky Christmas pointed at each player. "No, no, no, yes, yes, yes, no, yes, yes…"

"What's all that?" Andrew said.

"We've got five better players than them. We're good. We can win. Easy." He smacked his hands together.

Stan nodded, glad Nicky didn't point out North Donora also had three guys who couldn't catch and who only tipped a ball when batting every once in a while. "Nicky's right. And we're due." Stan ran his own numbers on their fancy opponent, then eyed up his own team, all with dirty canvas years-old Keds, toes poking through. "Come here, Weatherman. You too, Melonhead," Stan said.

The two approached Stan, Andrew sighing as he licked his finger and paged through his weather log. "Maybe we can work up a rain dance and end this thing quick."

Stan took Andrew's log and bag, set them aside. "No need for rain dances, my boys." He scooped some dirt off the field and smacked Andrew's shirt with it, spreading it over his chest and shoulders and back. He did the same to Melonhead's. "Now *we* have uniforms, too."

The rest of the team followed suit, picking up dirt and smacking it over Andrew's pristine T-shirt, laughing as they did. Andrew broke into giggles and coughs as they worked up dirt plumes rivaling mill spew.

Once they'd had a good laugh, they decided they were a strong match for Cement City no matter their uniform status. Andrew began to scribble down the lineup. Stan watched over his shoulder.

Andrew squinted. "Skunk and Yellow are still missing. Thought they'd show by now. Mr. Lahey in the stands there said Blue Louise went visiting relatives or something."

Stan got into his batting stance, taking pretend swings. "You'll play, all right."

Andrew's face went white. "Batting though. Oh boy."

Stan scratched his nose and considered that in the entire six weeks he'd been teaching Andrew to play baseball, he could only count three hits. Three. Not three home runs or three dozen foul balls, not even in batting practice. It was like Andrew tried to miss the ball. Two of the three hits had been accidental. If an able-bodied toddler wanted to join their team, Stan would've put him into the game. But no. The time had come.

He whispered to Cheeks and Nicky, who took the rest of the team into the infield to warm up. Stan needed a few minutes to put Andrew and Monocle at ease if they were going to be any use at all. He sent Monocle out to field what Stan hit.

"I'll take care of the batting for three of us. We'll be fine. I'm feeling mighty lucky today." Stan jerked his head at the ball lying near the first base bag. "Toss me batting practice."

Andrew looked at the field, where the rest of the team was practicing fielding drills led by Cheeks. Stan eyed the balls near the first base bag. "Never mind the rest of them for now. Just you and me. Monocle in the back."

Andrew picked up a ball like it might snap closed around his fingers.

"Closer," Stan said. Andrew was too weak and unpracticed to throw from a distance.

Andrew edged forward, tripping over his feet.

"Closer." Stan gestured for Andrew to toss him one. "Won't hit ya. Promise."

He adjusted his hat, drew a deep breath, rolled his shoulders, and got into his stance, letting his mind forget everything except for waiting for Andrew to release the ball. These moments let everything but baseball recede from his mind.

Smack, pop, smack. Baseballs slapped into bare hands and leather all over the field. The most beautiful sounds in the world. One particularly hard throw from behind Stan resulted in the pop of a real ball hitting a leather glove. Both teams stopped to look at Cheeks wearing Andrew's glove, grinning ear to ear as he whipped the ball back to Smokestack.

Crack, thunk, crack—balls hitting bats echoed from every direction. A few whistles would come after a long bomb, a whiff and a groan after a miss. Each makeshift and ramshackle bat emitted a slightly different tone depending on whether the ball was an actual store-bought ball or a handmade one, how soft it was. By Fourth of July, Stan could have told you which bat was making which sound and how far a given ball had flown out just by listening.

Most of the Cement City players watched Donora warm up. Schmitty and Hound were particularly chatty, noses in the air as they loudly complimented each other on their uniforms, saying how a win was guaranteed just for having arrived in such elegant garb.

"Ahhh, stuff it," Andrew said as Monocle tossed him the balls he collected from Stan's hits.

Stan shook his head. "Don't get your dander up over them. We talk with our bats and gloves. Well, mostly our hands, but you know what I mean."

Andrew looked down and then sighed before winding up to toss Stan another one.

Whack. The sounds of summer. Stan switched from the heavily taped bat to the one that was barely hanging together. As Andrew wound up, Stan would sink down, adjusting his feet as he came out of his coiled pose to ensure he put the ball where he wanted it.

Andrew's accidental pitches came at Stan. One throw would inadvertently curve out and another would come inside, whisking his belly. But even still, if Stan paid attention in just the right way, once the ball had left Andrew's unskilled hand, he could see where it was going. No. He felt it. The ball screaming toward the plate gave Stan plenty of time to adjust, smacking those horrible pitches far and wide, then inches from Weatherman's waist, making his friend go white.

"For the love of Pete, that was close, Stanley."

Stan shrugged his shoulders to loosen up.

"You doing a dance with that hip wiggle, Musial?" Schmitty said.

Wiggle? Stan ignored him. "I won't hit you, Weatherman. Swear. Keep 'em coming."

And even though Stan prepared for each pitch in the exact same crouched position, once he committed to swinging, he'd already instinctively angled his body this way or that to pepper the field from left to right, making sure he didn't hit so hard it got lost over the hill. "How's that wiggle working for ya now, Schmitty?" Stan said over his shoulder, eager to face him when he took the mound.

"I'll spin the shimmy right outta ya, Musial. Just you see."

"Quit your yippin'." Stan turned back to Andrew and Monocle, and when he'd sprayed the outfield back and forth twice, and desensitized Andrew to balls coming right past him, he waved the two boys in.

He took both by their bony shoulders. "I'll do my best to make sure none of those swanky boys hit a single pitch. But be on alert and—" Stan stopped himself when both appeared frightened. "Just get out there, and you'll be fine." *They'll be fine?* Stan was surprised that lie came off his tongue like a whizzer off Babe Ruth's bat.

Stan considered which of the two terrible players should play left field. Had to be Andrew.

He met Monocle's gaze. "Can't risk you losing the one lens you have, Monocle. And this Cement City squad doesn't have a single lefty. Big mouths, they got." Stan left unsaid that it might be possible for none of the hits to go so far right that Moonshine wouldn't be able to cover from center. Melonhead was quick enough to stop what might zip down the gap between first and second.

Monocle nodded. "Won't let you down."

Stan smiled and sent him to bat with the rest of the team, who were now taking pitches from Honey.

Andrew started to walk away. Stan pulled the back of his shirt. "Okay, Weatherman. Just don't let one ball past you. Not one. We're gonna shut those jerks up."

Andrew looked at his hands, made for glass microscope slides and notebooks depicting weather patterns and diagrams of night skies.

Stan pushed Andrew's hands down. His friend's face looked like Stan's felt when he was called on in class, when words tripped halfway out or snarled completely on his tongue, silencing him, washing him in shame. He thought of how Andrew was always telling him scientific facts and relating stories about ancient men with enormous ideas that couldn't even be contained by gravity or visible moons and suns, how Andrew seemed to make sense of the world that way. He put his arm around him. "Listen. There's a fella, Pepper Martin, better known as the *Wild Hoss of the Osage*."

Andrew squinted at Stan from under the brim of his hat, clearly unaware who the man was.

"He's an outfielder. Like you. Plays for the Cards like a crazed, unbroken horse."

Andrew's brow furrowed more.

"He's a hustler. Like you. You're an academic-type hustler, but same thing." What a line. Stan couldn't believe what was coming out of his mouth. But sometimes miracles did happen.

Andrew scoffed. "Stan. Really. Come on."

Stan stopped and faced Andrew. "Every minute of the game, the wild mustang's mind is sharp, eyes on what's happening, even when he looks undisciplined to fans, and when he can't get a ball in his glove, he stops it with his forearm or knee or his chest or… once he took one in the gullet, then homered the next at bat." Stan raised his eyebrows, the story getting him excited to play. "Understand?"

"I, uh…"

"Just throw yourself in front of any ball comin' your way. Hand, foot, ass if you want. Whatever body part you can use to stop the ball, shove it out there." Stan took Andrew's shoulders, squeezing, looking directly into his eyes. "*Wild Weatherman of Donora.* That's you for today."

Andrew looked at Stan with a smile, his lanky, small body getting taller. He pulled at the neck of his T-shirt. "I *am* a little hot under the collar with those fellas and their rude chatter at you earlier."

"There," Stan said leading Andrew to home plate. "Now you got it. Just pay attention to the game as though you were reading one of those giant chemistry books your father brings home—"

"Physics."

"Science, whatever. You know what I mean."

"I do."

"If the ball goes toward center at all, Moonshine'll snag it up with no trouble. He's got magnets for fingers, and the ball's made of steel when anything's hit his way."

"Okay. I can do it," Andrew said. Stan noted his friend's jumpy nerves and wide eyes and thought no way was Andrew going to stop a single ball. And as the sun shimmered like a

Vaselined tangerine, its rays fought through the thick half-bright haze. North Donora and Cement City gathered to sort out which equipment was in good enough shape to be used.

They studied the balls. The true baseballs were so worn that each of the three had loose stitching to one degree or another. The homemade choices would be used if they lost the real ones, so the outfielders were tasked with not only playing well for each team's benefit, but to ensure that no real ball went missing.

They selected the bats in the best shape, forced into having to use a bat as heavy as the pine tree it must have fallen from, what with layers and layers of tape and tacks holding it together. And the gloves. The teams shared those too, but it was up to each team to decide who got to use a glove and who went barehanded. Andrew gladly gave up the chance to use the glove his father had just bought.

"Maybe it will mean all the balls go to Moonshine, then, right?" He held up his hand.

Stan stared at him, pulling on his game mood like the uniform he wished he had to don. *"Wild Weatherman of Donora."*

As the two teams went to their baselines to get ready to start the game, Andrew dug through his bag. "Almost forgot."

He pulled out a couple of boxes and tossed them to his teammates.

"Dubble Bubble," Cheeks said in awe.

The gasps and excitement around gum were the same as if he'd dropped a pot of gold between them all.

"Wow, haven't had me some of that in *years*."

"Got a good deal on it at the sporting goods store," Andrew said. "Came with the glove."

And as Stan explained the variation on Andrew's nickname and went over simple baseball rules for the benefit of Andrew and Monocle, each player unwrapped, smelled, and jammed the gum into their mouths, bursts of sugary delight bringing smiles. How could they not win with bubble gum and a new baseball glove?

They blew bubbles, one guy's bigger than the next, as Stan and Nicky delivered their lecture.

"Cheeks's brother Meatball's gonna keep score for us. When you bat, take the first pitch no matter what."

"Are you sure I shouldn't at least try to hit if it—" Andrew said.

"Shhhhh," Stan said, drawing his palm slowly through the air. "Don't think too much. Batting's not science." Stan knew asking Andrew not to think was unreasonable and that he had no instincts to act in place of his intellectual gymnastics. "Keep an eye on Meatball. If he sticks the scorecard out, you swing at the pitch. Don't be obvious with it. Just glance over and see if he's got it out."

"Got it," Monocle said.

"When you're on base, same thing. Keep an eye on Meatball so you know if he's telling the batter to take a whack. You'll be ready to run if you at least have an idea of what our guy's about to do."

Andrew nodded. "Yep. Got it."

"Same goes for fielding. Just run through what you're gonna do before the pitch so your body will just do it."

Andrew blew out a puff of air. They all knew Monocle's and Andrew's bodies would never "just do" anything.

"We'll win if we don't beat ourselves."

Andrew nodded, then blew a giant bubble. His eyes grew wider as the pink gum expanded farther and farther. The team gathered around, cheering as the bubble hid his entire face. The meeting was over. The bubble popped, and deflated pink gum flopped over Andrew's face, landing half onto his hair. A cheer went up, and Stan thought in that moment, before a single pitch was thrown, he was the happiest he'd ever been. They were going to win. He knew it in his bones.

**

North Donora clustered around the bats as Cement City took the field. Stan read the lineup. Moonshine was leadoff hitter, then Smokestack, Stan, and Tank. Moonshine busied himself with the bats, and the others either took a seat or talked to fans who'd begun to gather to watch the game. Cheeks, who was slotted to bat seventh, went to talk to his uncle and his friends who'd come because they'd bet on the game. In Donora, people would bet on just about anything. Girls and women passed out red, white, and blue crepe paper flowers and small flags that fans could wave later during the parade and the Zincs game.

"Hey." Honey grabbed Stan's arm. "You moved me out of leadoff?"

Stan shrugged out of his brother's grip, irritated that Honey had gotten to feeling underappreciated. This inevitably would lead to the brothers bickering, and it wasn't worth it. "Relax. We need you in the five hole. It's good."

Honey clenched his jaw. Darkness slid over his face, and in that moment Stan thought he looked so much like their father.

"I oughta be battin' cleanup, if we're honest."

"No. Tank launches a shot to the outfield half the time, and the sight of him alone makes Schmitty's throat close."

"Tank's double my size, but my average is better. And I score more often. You know it."

"Relax. We need ya at five."

Honey poked Stan's chest. "I'm tellin' ya now, I'm not volunteering to be the sacrifice fly guy. Not this game."

Stan pushed Honey's hand away. "Find a way to be the hero in the five slot."

Honey chewed his gum as though he were attempting to kill a piece of still-writhing red meat. "Only one hero on this team."

Stan sighed. This pouty and jealous routine was exhausting. He was going to lecture Honey on his lack of game preparation but knew it would only enflame things. "Don't start this. Not today."

Honey stalked away and sat near Smokestack, who'd put away his cigarettes for the start of the game. Smokestack's auntie Hazel knelt in front of him, pulled a hanky from her sleeve, and wiped her nephew's face before giving him a kiss on the forehead. Smokestack turned all manner of reds and purples, appearing like a five-year-old boy rather than the chain-smoking twelve-year-old he normally was. Next Hazel wiped at Honey's face as though she were his auntie as well. The sight of Honey's scrunched-up face amused Stan. He focused on the game.

First up—Moonshine. A little guy, but he could hold his booze like a thirty-year-old wire-puller and got on base more than any of them except Stan.

"Hey, Moonshine," the hecklers started from the field and the kids in the stands. "Hot one today. Give me a little breeze."

Moonshine ignored the heckling, stepped into the batter's box, drew a line with the bat across home plate, and bent his knees, bouncing just a little as he waited for his pitch.

First pitch, swing, miss.

"Whoo, that's it. Fan me again." Little Sammy Tillman draped himself over the railing of the bleachers, his scratchy voice ringing out.

Cheeks started to return the heckle, but Stan grabbed his arm. "Just think about hitting."

Moonshine repeated his batting ritual, and this time when the pitch came, a thick crack of the bat threaded the ball right outside the reach of Darren Hostettler at shortstop and Freddy McShea at second. Safe at first.

Next—Smokestack. Single into the gap between left and center. Safe.

Batter three. Stan ripped one past Schmitty's cheek, putting him on the ground, the pitcher blocking McShea's line of sight just long enough for Stan to make it safe, easy.

"Come on, Cement City! Put these dogs down."

Batter four.

Cleanup.

Tank.

He used his preferred short bat, crowded the plate, glowering at Schmitty. The crowd roared, fans for both teams standing. Schmitty paced, kicking the wood block they used to mark the pitcher's "mound" forward and rolling it back before surrendering to his work.

"Pull out the jumbo bologna. He's serving it up!" Moonshine's brother said.

This shook Schmitty for some reason, as he stepped out of his windup, eyeing all three runners as if it might be possible for each of them to steal their way home.

"He serves up steak, not jumbo!" someone said.

"North Donora wouldn't know steak if it came butchered to the house with labels."

"See you at the soup kitchen, Mack," Cheeks's uncle said over his shoulder.

Schmitty shook his shoulders, grabbed the back of his neck, and then got back into position to pitch. Stan watched as the kid calmed, a draping of peace and quiet seeming to fall over him. For a second Stan thought their lucky streak might be over. But when Schmitty lurched forward to throw, his ankle turned just enough to mess with his release and the ball went screaming toward Tank, a little outside, a tiny bit high. Stan would swear he saw Tank's smile start before his swing did. He stepped into the pitch and walloped it just like a big fella batting cleanup was supposed to do.

Oh, the feeling. The cheering and the jeering in equal parts from North Donora and Cement City fans. Four batters, four runs, first inning. As North Donora batted around with another run after Honey doubled and stole a base and Nicky Christmas with a sacrifice fly, Monocle and Andrew were easy outs, but not unsettled. That was as big a win as Stan could ask for where those two were concerned.

Stan got the balls and bounced one in his palm, deciding it was the one he wanted to use. It was the ball with the least loose stitching, and the weight was just right. Five runs to start things off. His confidence swelled.

He blew out his air and pitched. A perfect line down the middle. Hound took the strike looking.

Stan got the ball back and turned away from the plate. He jogged over to Andrew. "Remember. Anything that comes to you, you throw yourself in front of it."

"Like a cellular wall. Not letting anything past. Wild Weatherman. I got it, Stanley. I predict a win. Fair skies ahead."

Stan squinted at his friend, amused at his inability to leave science out of it.

Back on the mound, Stan refocused.

"Aw, come on, Hound! Musial's reading you."

"He can't read!" a voice shot from the stands, hitting Stan in the gut. He scanned the stands for who'd said that. But he didn't recognize the voice. He surveyed the faces, and then his gaze tripped like someone had tied his shoes together when he wasn't looking.

Pop, sitting beside Mom, arms crossed, mouth drawn downward, as though he were waiting for a doctor to get at him with a syringe instead of enjoying his sons playing baseball.

"Let's go, Pitch. Need a map to find the plate or what?"

That heckler broke Stan out of his surprise at seeing his parents in the stands. He struck out Hound, but Jerry and Mark got base hits. Tim McClellen stepped up to the plate.

"All right, Timmy. Everyone gets a hit with this kid."

"His play's as poor as he is."

Stan flinched at that, but then exhaled and worked through his delivery. The ball blistered toward the plate, but then lifted at the last second, right over the plate. Beautiful. Tim tipped it and the ball smashed Smokestack in the jaw, knocking him onto his backend. With a time-out to evaluate Smokestack's injury, the fans were first quiet. But when Smokestack sprang back up, rubbing his mouth, shaking it off, the heckling bounced back as well.

Stan continued with a string of pitches that would have pleased him any other day, but these batters kept getting enough on them to zing past Nicky and Cheeks. Bounders smacked Weatherman's chest, then under his chin, and once even stopped a ball with his foot, practically running into Cheeks before tossing it like a little kid.

"Wild Weatherman!" the team shouted, even though they weren't stopping their opponent from scoring.

Second inning left North Donora with no bats. Cement City found a slew of hot ones, crushing hit after hit. Not for home runs, but methodical, surgical hits in tiny gaps. One ball whizzed back to Stan, and he only got his glove up in time to keep the ball from hitting him in the face. The ball tipped and landed between him and Honey.

Honey screamed at Stan for not making the catch. Stan clenched his jaw, the sloppy play turning his blood up. "Bungled that one, Second Base."

"You bungled it," Honey said.

Stan glared at him. "Quit bellyaching."

Honey rolled his eyes.

Stan threw the next pitch. Schmitty cranked it, skimming the field between second and first. Honey dove, caught it, and threw him out. The base runner going from second to third tripped.

"Nice trip, Magellan," Weatherman screamed from left field.

This caused everyone to turn to Andrew, confused.

"Who in hell's Magellan?" a voice came from the stands.

He shrugged. "The explorer. Get it? Nice trip?"

The game fell apart from there. Stan's breath grew shallow as he tried to keep his pitches exactly where he knew each batter couldn't hit. But something was off. Likewise, nearly every North Donora fielder, even the ones they normally counted on, was elbow deep in errors.

"Errors for sale! North Donora's got plenty of stock available."

And from there the team grew rattled. And as it did, Stan withdrew into himself, focusing on every element he could control about his play. And as Stan was busy making sure he delivered what he promised, with his hitting especially, the others were left to cope without Stan's guidance.

Monocle lost his monocle at the plate once and then got dirt in his eye when he was putting it back on. Andrew took a ball in the back as he flinched away from a firecracker pitch. Honey foul-tipped and struck out every other time at bat. And Tank smacked a few more, but not far enough to make up for how slow he ran.

Only Stan had a hot bat. His next three ups were home runs.

His last at bat brought cheers again. "Bring on the blast furnace," a voice caught in his ear, and he delivered. Finding his rhythm, catching the ball with his gaze as it left Schmitty's hand, he caught the speed of rotations—off-speed.

On the final up, Stan hit the ball so hard the leather peeled right off, the loose stitches releasing its string-tied cork center, ripping ahead. He jogged around the bases, watching as the ball's innards unspooled like kite string, sailing toward the mill stacks below. As he stomped on second base, he released all the irritation he'd felt from the game's worth of heckles, especially from Schmitty.

"You thought that loose-wrapped ball was going to give me a blooper, didn't ya?" He pointed at Schmitty. "See that string as it took off like an eagle? Fourth of July screaming eagle, that's what that is." His teammates met him at home plate, surrounding him, smothering him.

Moonshine and Cheeks got a few ugly hits, and Smokestack hit a double. At the bottom of the ninth, Stan actually thought they could pull out the win even with the horrid fielding they'd been turning in.

The first batter hit a single that leapt over Cheeks and hit a hole, trapping it.

"He's got feet for hands," someone shouted at Weatherman. Stan saw his friend's face droop. That play wasn't his fault, but he could have run faster to get the stuck ball.

The next hitter golfed one in between Tank and Honey. Honey threw down the glove he'd been wearing and stalked across the infield, right past Stan.

Stan stared at his brother as he huddled with Cheeks, talking. Stan joined the two to get a grasp of what was going on.

"I'm playing third for this inning. Cheeks'll take second."

"You can't just shift guys around, Honey."

"I can and I will."

Stan put his hand on Honey's shoulder to get his attention, to try to calm him down, but Honey whipped Stan's hand away, his fingers grazing Stan's chin. Fuming, Stan yanked Honey by the back of the shirt, dragging him toward second base. Honey wiggled away, squirming out of his shirt. Stan held the shirt up, a soft breeze blowing it.

"You son of a…" Honey plowed back toward Stan, tackling him. The band members waiting for the start of the Fourth of July parade played chase music to accompany the Musials as they rolled around, punching and grunting, dirt filling Stan's mouth.

Finally Stan pinned his brother with his forearm. Another couple deep breaths and he reached for the shirt and whapped Honey across the chest with it. "Get back to second and shut your yap."

The remainder of the game fell apart like the ball Stan had whacked out of its skin. Honey couldn't catch a thing, and the rest of the fellas were distracted with trying to talk Honey back up to his normal sweet self. The fans smelled the unraveling and let North Donora have it with the chants and heckles and all-out harassment. Before long, the game had shifted from North Donora leading 11-10 to Cement City clinching the win at 15-11.

Stan bent forward, hands on knees, disbelieving how it could have gone bad so fast. He'd hit like the blast furnace fire gods themselves had blessed his swing, and yet they'd lost.

Dusty, sweltering, thirsty. Stan couldn't have imagined after starting the way they had that they might have ended up spanked in front of the whole town on the Fourth of July. And Pop. Stan sighed, afraid to even look to see his reaction. The fight with Honey. Pop would be humiliated. Mom would have her hornet stinger at the ready for sure. But he forced himself to scan the crowd for them, to face them sooner rather than later. But they were gone. And Stan exhaled that part of his discontent away.

Chapter 21

Stan

After the game, Mr. Tuttle, Hound's father, interrupted Cement City's celebration and North Donora's dejection by wheeling a wagon full of Dixie ice cream cups right up to the pitcher's mound. Cement City got theirs first. Stan crossed his arms, glowering. Maybe he wouldn't accept ice cream after such an embarrassing loss. His teammates shrugged off any humiliation they might have felt, whooping with glee when one pared back the lid from the ice cream cup to reveal a circus elephant, then another revealed the trapeze artist drawn in full color. Stan bit the inside of his cheek. They'd already forgotten the horrible game. Like they didn't care at all.

But as he watched his friends spoon creamy white delight into their mouths, he decided passing up free ice cream was ridiculous, as it was a rare treat. Last in line, Stan remembered the cheers that had come as he hit to the right, left, and center fields, the adulation rushing through his veins like blood itself. A miserable loss. But he himself had done all right. And he should at least be proud of that. Shouldn't he?

The thick vanilla cream melted on his tongue, the decadent summer sweetness as good as anything he could have eaten. He watched Cement City given their instructions, as the winning team, to go down to McKean and take their places on the wireworks float for the parade that would end in Palmer Park.

Girls, smiling and laughing, passed out another round of crepe paper flowers and flags. Stan accepted a flag as he finished his ice cream cup. Their loss would be boldly advertised by Cement City as they'd been given the privilege of riding on the float from one end of Donora to the other. Stan and his team started their trek to Palmer Park on foot, where they would watch the Zincs play Charleroi.

Stan, head down, meandered behind his team as they trooped toward the steep steps that stood in for sidewalks in flatter towns. The ice cream provided no shield against sour tears that threatened to drop. Honey stomped ahead with Cheeks and Smokestack, arm in arm, singing like Sunday. This reignited Stan's anger toward Honey. Who was he to make demands about the team when he didn't even care when they lost? To Stan, the loss was like someone reaching inside him and crushing his organs, the pain radiating from the inside out.

A bump on the arm startled Stan. Andrew smiled. "Great hitting today." Andrew looked happy too—Christmas morning when the mills were going full-tilt happy.

It was then Stan turned his thoughts away from himself.

"Thanks for the advice," Andrew said.

Stan realized then, playing back the game, each piece clicking through his mind like a film-reel, Weatherman had taken Stan's words to heart. A dozen balls had gone his way that game. One off his chest, one off his thigh, one off his hands, and the rest stopped by his foot. Frankly, relative to the talent of most of the fellas, Weatherman played the best of them, loss or not, hits or not.

"You did great." Stan patted Andrew's back. "Wild Weatherman of Donora. You did it."

Andrew adjusted his bag over his shoulder and his face flushed, turning the sunburn a deeper shade. "Thanks, Stan. Thanks."

As they approached Thompson Avenue, a voice filtered down, coming from back up behind them.

"Andrew! Fellas! North Donora!"

They all turned.

Mr. Morrison. Hand in the air, waving hysterically. Stan's stomach lurched. He'd failed at teaching this man's son simple basics. He'd never expected Mr. Morrison to come to the game, not with knowing Andrew was horrible.

Stan held his breath, thinking of his pop, the way he grew angry with mistakes and when things weren't as he wanted them to be.

Mr. Morrison raised his hand higher. "Andrew!"

Stan started to follow his friend, ready to take responsibility for not turning the kid into a future All-Star, the player he'd paid for. The Lucky Dog glove. The man had bought that beautiful glove for his son, and he'd played like a two-year-old out there. Yes, relatively speaking, Andrew had been amazing but using his body as a backstop wasn't what his father had traded expensive dress material for. Not even the good players had fielded better when they passed around the beautiful glove, trying to pull some good fortune out of it.

Mr. Morrison descended, face beet red, huffing and puffing. Stan stopped at the sight of the angry father, not wanting to subject himself to a tirade. He thought of Mom's insistence that people eventually showed their true colors if pressure got to be enough. And fathers sometimes felt pressure no one else understood.

Stan wanted to run. He nearly did. But he looked at Andrew, his glum expression, and didn't have a choice. Stan realized right there, Andrew had become his friend. And Stan wouldn't let a friend take a lashing on his own. So Stan edged closer to Weatherman and his father, the team squeezing in from all sides as well.

Mr. Morrison drew back a hand. Stan's breath went out of him. What an embarrassment. Now Andrew would pay. The glove, the coaching. A waste of money for Mr. Morrison.

But instead of hauling off on Andrew, he broke into a huge smile, spread his other arm wide, and Weatherman fell into him. Mr. Morrison threw his head back, laughing aloud, bouncing his son with joy.

Stan inched closer.

"Andrew! You played," Mr. Morrison said. "You scrambled around like a wildcat out there."

Andrew looked up at his father, and though Stan couldn't see Weatherman's face, he saw Mr. Morrison's. He beamed like the sun itself, confusing the heck out of Stan. He'd never seen anything like it.

"The Wild Weatherman of Donora!" Smokestack raised a fist.

"That's your name?"

"Well, for today," Andrew said.

The team chanted, "Wild Weatherman."

"Nice trip, Magellan? You used it!" Mr. Morrison said.

"Who's Magellan again?" Cheeks said.

"Some guy," Tank said.

"A traveler," Honey said.

When their voices died down, Mr. Morrison patted his son's back, plumes of dirt rising off his shirt. "Oh, Andrew. I'm so proud of you."

Andrew looked at his feet and started back into the fold of teammates.

"And the rest of you. You played hard. That's all a man can do."

The boys thanked Mr. Morrison. He gave Stan a wink and thanked him. "Joe was here. He caught half the game." This news caused Stan's mouth to go drier than it had already been. He nodded but couldn't push his words out to say, "You're welcome," his stammer taking hold before he even tried. What would Joe think of his play, of them losing in such an ugly way?

Cement City had punished Stan after a first good inning or two of pitching. Maybe Joe'd left before seeing that. Hopefully Pop and Mom had also. It should have made Stan happy that Joe had been at his game. But this time it didn't.

Mr. Morrison put his hand out toward Andrew. "I'll take your satchel?"

Andrew patted the strap. "I got it."

"Well. Have fun at the Zincs game. We'll see you there," he said, waving as Weatherman, Stan, and the rest crossed over Thompson Avenue and headed down to McKean to join the back of the parade, hoofing it toward Palmer Park.

Stan was quiet. Miserable over their loss. His hitting display hadn't been enough. After the first inning, Tank had hit like he was bat-less. Smokestack had grounded out five times. *Five.* Honey had flown out three times. The fistfight. Stan touched his cheek and wondered if it looked as puffy as it felt. They'd all fielded like they didn't have hands. Mortified, Stan choked back the tears that lumped in his throat. He shouldn't have been embarrassed. He'd played all right compared to the rest, even compared to the winning Cement City team. Yet he choked on the loss.

More than that, it was Mr. Morrison who weighed heavy on him. That enormous grin, the hug and backslapping for a kid who'd been called out as having "feet for hands" during the game. And the guy had been right. Yet the effort, his unvarnished attempts to stop balls and throw, and his fruitless batting was more like swatting at flies. Yet it had been enough for Mr. Morrison. Just to see his son play was enough. Had Pop heard the heckles about Stan being poor? Not being a good student?

The softness between Andrew and his pop slipped into Stan's heart like a knife, so sharp he didn't even realize it hurt until it twisted. Before that day, he couldn't remember the last time his father had attended a game. Even when others shouted Stan's name, like way back when he turned his first aerial tricks at the Falcons. His father hadn't reveled in his son's achievement, he'd wanted to best it. And from that moment Stan had been conflicted about wanting to hide from Pop's gaze and wanting to bask in it, dying to make him proud.

Walking to the park that day, the American Steel and Wire band led the parade. The tuba and drum rhythms bounced in Stan's chest, surprising him with a surge of loneliness growing even while surrounded by a crowd. He rubbed his chest to make the sensation go away.

And as they turned up the drive that led into the park, Weatherman's laugh pulled Stan out of his self-pity. He looked at the kid, fenced into the middle of the rest of the fellas, the worst player he'd ever seen. Yet one of them. Somehow. Finally. Stan had failed at making him a ballplayer, but, with Weatherman taking six weeks of bruising to play along, with one wild day, the other guys had made him theirs. He was a teammate even if not a player. And Stan moved farther into the pack, wanting their closeness. Finally he allowed himself to let the loss go and enjoy his team. With them, he felt the best belonging of his life.

Chapter 22

Stan

Palmer Park was swathed in bunting. The Zincs warmed up and the Charleroi team sat on the bench, their coach going over the lineup. The band sat beside the home stands and played the "Battle Hymn of the Republic" and other patriotic tunes. Little boys and girls marched in front of the musicians waving flags. Mothers fanned themselves and spread picnic blankets. Near the pavilion there were tables being set up with donated food from St. Philip's. Father Ronconi, Sister Anne, and Sister Thomas directed the men who were unloading wagons. Closer to the stands, Mr. Klepin was grilling hotdogs and his wife made lemonade and fried dough. Stan's mouth watered with the scents, but it was the baseball game that drew him.

The teams warmed up. Joe Barbao barked orders at the Zincs, hitting balls to the infielders while the pitcher warmed up with the catcher off to the side.

The walk to Palmer Park had defused Stan's anger at their loss and dulled his embarrassment. He stood at the outfield fence watching the orchestrated movements of men. There weren't any Andrews or Monocles on either of these teams. Yet as the game went on, he saw that Joe benched his best man, Tubby Smith, for two innings because he was harassing his own teammate, scolding and mocking his lazy play.

"We're a team, Smithy! You're on a team, for the love of… Quit bickering with Jonesy. No one cares about your stats. We want a win! Go sit."

In the sunlit columns that shot between clouds, the anger in Joe's eyes, the spittle that left his mouth as he sent their most reliable man to the bench stood out. Stan suddenly felt scolded. Had he done that to Honey—acted like Smith, more concerned with his own stats than the team? Lost his cool with Honey because he was too worried about himself? If they'd had a coach, would he have benched Stan? He thought of Mr. Morrison telling him Joe had been at the game. Had he witnessed the infield wrestling match?

The rest of Stan's team joined him at the fence to watch the game. Stan eyed Honey, who was joking with Smokestack, sneaking a cigarette from him. Stan thought about warning him that their mom would probably show up and rail at him if she saw him taking a puff. But then decided against it.

The game moved quickly, as though everyone wanted to finish and celebrate the Fourth. Cheeks's uncle and his friends had arrived to check up on their bets and bettors. And as the Zincs took up their bats for the last time, a rolling, familiar laugh rang out.

Stan tracked the sound and found her on the far end of the stands, sitting with her friends and Stan's sisters.

Mom.

Sitting with Mrs. Haluch and Mrs. Rochini she seemed like a different person, bending in to listen to a secret before throwing her head back and laughing all over again. She brushed her hair back like always, but the smile never left her face as it did at home. She looked almost like a stranger, so happy. No darkness clouding her eyes, no worried frown. She seemed like a teenager without a care for having to keep house or watch over a gaggle of oftentimes out of sorts loved ones.

The crack of the bat startled Stan, and a high ball took an ever-rising arc toward the outfield. McClelland, the center fielder, kept his eyes forward while backing up and ran smack into a tree, knocking himself out.

Before Stan could process what he was seeing, his mother appeared, over the downed player, gently shaking his arm, rousing him. The Charleroi coach knelt on the other side of McClelland, the two helping him to sit. Not another soul had moved as quickly as Mom, and Stan was struck with yet another fresh view of her. Or perhaps it was just a new circumstance that confirmed who she'd been all along. Sprinting to and comforting someone she didn't even know—a player on the opposing team—made him want to rush over and lay a hug right on her. Stan was filled with pride.

Back on his feet, waving off further help, rubbing his temple, McClelland insisted on finishing the game. With three more runs from the Zincs and the last up for Charleroi, the game was over within forty more minutes. The Zincs won, and Mom leapt up, hands in the air, clapping overhead, her laugh piercing the applause all over again.

The teams shook hands and went their separate ways. Stan watched his mom separate from her friends and approach Joe. The two fell into conversation, Mom helping collect bats and balls, stuffing them into canvas bags. Were they talking about him? Had either one of them seen the whole game? The fight? No. They were laughing. Mom used her hands to talk in between tucking the bats into the bag. Joe shrugged and leaned against the backstop. Mom tossed a ball in the air, catching it repeatedly. Once, Joe snatched it out of the air. He waved Mom closer, and she leaned in. Joe was turning the ball in his hand, showing Mom how his fingers lay along the laces, just like he'd done for Stan when they practiced up on Marelda.

They talked like friends, like when Joe talked to Stan. Stan jogged around the fence, wanting to hear the conversation.

"Hey, Stushy." Mr. Klepin grabbed his arm as he passed the hotdog stand. "Saw ya hittin' today. Wowsa's all I can say. You sprinkled a pinch of magic dust on that bat or somethin', didn't ya?"

Stan's teammates inched closer. He nodded, shyness sweeping over him as he looked at his feet. "Thaaaank. You." He sighed, frustrated that his words got caught.

"Have a hotdog," Mr. Klepin said.

Stan's mouth watered. Now that the Zincs game had ended, he was terribly hungry and hoped to get in line for the food that the church was serving. He cleared his throat. "Thank you, but," he jerked his head toward his teammates, "my friends. The church has food."

Mr. Klepin leaned on the wagon, studying his inventory. He raised his gaze. "Tough game today." He surveyed the entire team. "Other than Stanley's hitting."

Stan hoped Mr. Klepin wasn't offended by Stan declining to eat in front of his friends.

The man finally straightened and spread his arms. "Help yourselves. Either you eat 'em or I haul 'em back. Overshot my estimates. Wasn't expecting Father Ronconi to bring the food they normally serve at the church."

Stan felt a surge of excitement. He waved his team closer, and they trailed to the cart like millworkers streaming toward a tavern for breakfast and a boilermaker.

Mr. Klepin raised his hands, making room for the kids swarming around him. "How about a win next time though, boys?"

They all agreed to that, Stan's growing hunger replacing his curiosity over what Mom and Joe had been talking about.

**

Seated under the tree that McClelland had run into, they passed around the eight bottles of pop they'd been given and devoured the most delicious hotdogs Stan had ever eaten. They were careful not to be too greedy with their sips.

"Ahhh, Coke," Moonshine said. "Best I ever had." He raised a bottle in a toast. "Thanks for making sure we got to share the wealth, Stan. You're a good soul."

"'Course. But I didn't do anything," Stan said, hoping to gobble three hotdogs himself.

"You're first class, Stushy," Melonhead said.

Mrs. Klepin brought them fried bread wrapped in crinkly brown paper. "Some are cold, but they're still so good."

A chorus of gratitude was followed by silence as they stuffed the cinnamon-and-sugar-dusted, buttery fried bread into their mouths. Rolling thunder sounded from somewhere across the river. Heavy clouds blotted out the last of the setting sun.

Smokestack lit a cigarette and laid back. "Hey, Wild Weatherman—I'm gonna call you WW sometimes, all right?"

Andrew nodded. "Sure thing."

Moonshine tapped Andrew. "Hear that soft tumbling thunder coming in. Should we be getting up to run home before the sky opens up? Or no."

Andrew laid back and pointed into the darkening sky. "Those cumulus clouds there aren't thunderheads. Don't think so anyway. See? The other side of them's way lighter. Just shadows and some smoke on the underside is all. Should be safe to see the fireworks."

The rest of them laid back in the grass.

"Maybe some kick the can, later?" Melonhead said. "Mom said she'd love to have the gang up to the house."

"Won't be storming by then?" Honey asked.

"Early morning or later," Andrew said. "We're definitely due." He held up his hands. "I can feel it. Bones are getting heavy."

Stan turned his head. "Feel it?"

"I can."

"Hmm. That explains a lot," Smokestack said. He lit another cigarette. "You sound like my auntie. She feels everything. Bad people about to knock at the door. The plants that will heal this guy's bellyache or that guy's heartache. I don't feel nothin' but a full belly of dogs and fried bread." He patted his stomach. "Auntie Hazel says I'm not evolving properly. I'm all body and no soul. No idea what the hell that means. But shit, she's always feelin' somethin'."

As they lay under the clouds, Stan's eyelids felt as though they'd close and drop him into sleep right there.

"Psst. Guys," a voice came.

Skunk and Yellow Melvin stood above them.

The team sat up and peppered them with questions as to where they'd been all day, recounting the game.

Skunk knelt, the closeness revealing bruises on his face.

Stan looked away.

"It's all right." Skunk touched his cheek and winced.

Yellow Melvin groaned as he lowered himself to the ground, holding his ribs. He laid back and covered his face with his hands. White bandages draped his fingers on one hand.

"Dad got laid off today," Skunk said. "Mills are going down further. So we tried to help out at home with… Well. Our help wasn't wanted."

Stan knew that a family's loss of income could cause them to experience a burst of anger and arguing. Losing one job meant multiple mouths would have no food. The grip on the families in Donora was too tight. The losses too heavy.

Skunk tied his shoe. "Just suggested the Labashes might extend credit. Nice people. Really nice."

"Let's just say Dad didn't agree to asking," Yellow said.

Skunk sat cross-legged and tugged at the grass. As the dusky night settled deeper, shadows played on Skunk's cheeks and eyes. Stan hoped it was the light-play that made the bruises look so bad. His insides coiled, hating to imagine what had happened in the Fitzsimmons house earlier. He looked at Honey, who for the first time since their fistfight made eye contact. They understood the grip of job loss on a household. Honey gave him a little nod, and Stan returned it. That was enough to dissolve the anger behind their fight at the game. The game-interrupting grappling match would soon be relegated to the storytelling trove, retellings fueling gales of laughter, no longer an incendiary event. No matter how much the two of them argued, they understood each other, and that would always be more important than who was in charge on the ball field.

Weatherman blew out his air. "Storm front came through, huh?"

Yellow Melvin uncovered his face and looked at Weatherman with a scowl, making Stan think he might get a punch. He slowly sat up. "Yeah… *storm front*. Like you said that one day when the lightning just cracked everything open."

"Yeah." Skunk's voice came fractured. "Just split right open, the tension finally broke, but…"

Weatherman yanked his book out of his satchel and paged through it, holding it up to show the drawings. "Pressure builds and cold and hot air meet and it just—" He made an exploding sound and pushed his spreading fingers upward.

"Oh yeah," Cheeks said. "Oughta see it when folks neglect paying their debt at Uncle Vince's place. Talk about a dark storm."

Andrew tapped his book. "Some weather hangs around, pleasant. You know. That spring and fall weather."

"When the mills were full-throttle," Nicky said.

Andrew paged through his book. "In summer, or when Donora's losing jobs by the ton, there're hot storms that never cool the air."

"Yeah, my house is hot and sticky all summer—hot with a chance of lightning every day." Moonshine mimed a zigzag lightning bolt, making a whistling sound.

Then they all started referring to their home tension in terms of weather. This made sense to Stan, what he couldn't ever really verbalize, like cell bodies. Andrew explained there were weather cells too, the growing pressure that would hit a household and then just explode—one front meeting the other. Mom always playing the role of Mother Nature, easing back one front from the other.

Stan remembered Joe's coaching earlier in the game, how he managed his players, easing back one fronting player from another. Seeing Joe in action after North Donora's devastating loss sank in deep. Stan sat up. There were things he could have done differently, outside of his great hitting. That hadn't been enough. He rested his arms on his pulled-up knees. "Guys. Rain or shine, practice tomorrow. Get ready for the rematch next week."

"I'll bring the oil for the new glove," Smokestack said.

"I'll bring canteens," Melonhead said.

"We're ready to work, Stan," Moonshine said.

"Need a little fine-tuning," Honey said.

"Like the radio station that isn't coming in just right. Just a tweak," Moonshine said.

Stan laid back again. "We'll get us working right. We will."

The fireworks started with a drizzling of white colors trickling to earth like liquid spider webbing, then growing ever more dense, colorful and loud. Oohs and ahhs filled the air. And Stan looked around at his friends, pleased at their closeness. In that moment, he was as grateful for them as for his family. If he could have stayed out all night just like that, yakking and laughing it up, he would have. He didn't want that night to end. Loss or not, this was his team.

Chapter 23

Mary

At the game's end, Mary started back to serve the next round of food. Joe Barbao was cleaning up bats and balls and he motioned for her to come closer. "Saw some of your boys' game today."

"I saw the beginning," Mary said.

Joe's face had lit up as he repeatedly tossed a ball into the air, catching it, tossing it. "Your Stan's a *special* player. Honey's good, too. Fast as Stan for sure. But Stan's got the stuff you can't teach. Stan is—"

"He's only eleven!" Mary put her hands on her hips. She tempered her expectations but there was no question that Joe's descriptions confirmed what she thought of Stan and Honey— especially the sliver of difference between them.

"You're right." Joe studied Mary in between tossing and catching that ball, his eyes kind and warm. "A lot can change."

Mary snatched the ball away before he caught it again and started tossing it, catching it. "But he's *good*."

"Very." Joe snatched the ball from Mary just before it hit her fingertips. He dug a pipe from his pocket, giving Mary a chance to take the ball again. She backed away, needing to get to the buffet to serve. "Grab something at the pavilion. Make a plate for Kate. Heard Joe Jr.'s got a belly problem this week."

He smiled. "Thanks, Mary. I'll do that."

"Food's going fast."

"Just enough time to swing home before my shift guarding the garden, so that's perfect." He plugged the unlit pipe into his mouth and held up his hand signaling for Mary to throw the ball.

Mary threw it. He caught it one-handed and smiled before looking at it. She knew he was admiring her arm. The two moved closer to each other.

"And thanks for helping McClelland when he ran into that tree. He's a bit of a—"

"Klutz," Mary chuckled. "Obviously. No problem. Anyone would have done it."

"*Anyone* didn't though. I was gonna let him lay there all night."

She chuckled at Joe's competitiveness. She should have gotten moving to the pavilion, but something in the moment made her stay. "Thanks though. I don't think I say that enough to you. For the boys. You know."

He shoved the ball into the bag.

Mary caught the words that would defend Lukasz in his lack of interest in his sons before they left her mouth. Joe understood and she didn't need to explain.

He straightened and pulled the bag strings tight. "It's *all* all right, Mary. All's good."

"Well. Good," she said.

"See ya up on the hill."

"Yep. Up on top of the world," she said.

"Just a bunch of kings and queens lording over the peasants," Joe said.

"Don't I wish," she chuckled before jogging toward the food tables. She caught a glimpse of Stan and Honey and their friends sitting under the tree near the outfield fence. The North Donora team provided so much more than games that really didn't matter. It was an extended family of sorts. She was thrilled at the prospect of their futures. Being males, except for Blue Louise, anything was possible, but friendships were so important, too. She looked back over her shoulder at Joe.

He saw her boys as she did, their promise, not their lack. Admitting such a thing caused a longing to snake through her. She pressed her chest, saddened that she'd allowed it to show itself. It was the same feeling she got when she thought about Mr. Morrison.

And as she helped serve the final round of meals, the sun began to set behind heavy mushroom-shaped clouds. She debated how much she should tell Lukasz about Joe's report on Stan and Honey, if anything. What response would it evoke? Had he found work that day? Had he been to the Falcons? The Bucket of Blood? Was he home waiting for her?

She wanted to live without having to weigh and measure what came out of her mouth. She wanted to capture fleeting moments of mindless fun, like she'd experienced watching the game. If only she could do just that.

**

With her melancholy in tow, Mary headed home, foregoing the fireworks, not believing the rain would hold off. She inventoried her day, what she needed to do next. She'd worked a few early hours for Mrs. Walsh, helping to get her ready for the family she'd be entertaining for the Fourth. The kind woman had remembered that Vicki's birthday had been July first and gave Mary some painted hairpins for a present. "Sweet sixteen. Every girl needs something special from someone she doesn't know very well." Mrs. Walsh always remembered Mary's children with some token, small but monumental when the Musials didn't have an extra penny even to buy sugar for a cake that week. She couldn't wait to see Vicki's face when she opened the present.

Lukasz. Where was he? The last she'd seen of him was when he left the boys' game, saying he was bored and needed to find work. She'd reminded him that she would be volunteering to serve food at the park and he could eat there later. She'd assumed he'd show up, that he wouldn't view it as charity since Mary was working. But he never did. He often avoided baseball games, shunning the idea of a whole town getting excited over adults playing a game.

And, though reading the *Herald-American* was laborious for his mind, which still searched for words to be written in Polish, he seemed to be one of the few in town who understood the newspaper highlighted these games as a means of getting citizens to ignore just how bad things were economically. Mary agreed. But she saw baseball as a wonderful pastime, a positive way to obscure what was going wrong in the world, to get lost in nine innings of play that usually saw the Zincs the winners.

Traipsing home to the tune of rumbling thunder and the spiced air that came before a storm, she felt a little sorry for herself. Every man at that field suffered the same job limitations as Lukasz, yet obstacles sat inside his skin differently, becoming part of who he was instead of something to work around or over or through.

The thought stopped her short just where she crested Marelda and could see their home. Like Joe Barbao did, she wanted her husband to see their sons' opportunities. But more than that, she wanted them to see the goodness in Lukasz. For even with the sad way her relationship with her father had ended, she had fully experienced his love for her, his belief in her, the majesty of a parent's affection for the first sixteen years of her life.

Always short on words, Lukasz now held back everything positive. This awful, depressed America—it was like jamming people into canning jars and asking why they weren't stretching their legs. But he should express what he appreciated, starting with their daughter Ida, who'd brought Mary and Lukasz into marriage in the first place. Why couldn't Lukasz see the seed of good in anything, not even the tiniest corm where he used to see a forest in full bloom? What happened to the man she had fallen in love with? Joe's enthusiasm revealed what Mary could no longer deny.

Lukasz had made his sons, lived with his sons, but did not know them. And they did not know him.

His darkness used to come along with a softness, a curiosity and hope, a hand reaching for Mary, pulling her close in bed or the dance floor, where the two of them sheltered beneath the mood until it slid past. Now when the cloud shrouded him, it isolated him, hardened him. Why hadn't becoming an American citizen changed the way he saw himself? Mary was the only one who knew the vast landscape of his body was like a valley wall masking its valuable coal. Perhaps if he hadn't worked so hard to hide what lay beneath, his goodness would have the light it needed to grow, to be seen by everyone else.

**

Sweltering from the day's heat, Mary entered her home, her sense of smell registering no food cooking, ears ushering in nothing but the tick of the kitchen clock, eyes seeing the laundry basket exactly where she'd left it between work and going to the boys' game, reminding her Matka had gone to Anna's, Mary's sister's, for the holiday. Home alone. She washed her face, hands, and neck and sighed as she dried off with a fresh, clean towel, the stillness a luxury.

A splash of yellow on the table drew her attention. Lemons. Against the grayed walls and brown weathered wood—the kitchen's dullness—it was as though each of the dozen orbs were suns captured and delivered to brighten her world, to also highlight its typical muted shades of earth and smoke. A bag of sugar sat beside it. A piece of paper peeked from between two orbs. She plucked it out, expecting a note from Matka. But it was Lukasz's backward-slanted, hobbled lettering that took her breath away. "Sharp and sweet for my love. Please, some lemonade and cookies? For our Vicki's birthday. Something from both of us— me to bring the parts and you to make them into something special."

Mary covered her mouth. Like the ingredients, the smile behind her hand was sweet and bitter. She let the sensation take hold. The sweetness as Lukasz reintroduced himself as the man she knew and loved should have sent her sailing. It once would have. How quickly he could sway her. How badly she wanted him to.

But this time his intention didn't turn her mind foggy with unexamined belief that he was suddenly someone new, the somebody old she met years back. This wasn't an earth-trembling permanent change, but just a sunny day in Donora, one that would soon give way to typical hazy gray. She'd resigned herself to the ups and downs of married life. But for her daughters and sons to see some softness in their father? She was pleased for that. She checked her feelings. No schoolgirl thrill swept in. What she felt was the evolution of the love that had started their family, a now dampened stirring, but one rooted more deeply than ever.

She went to the fireplace, stood in front of it, hands on hips, remembering. Finally she moved. She ran her fingers over the brick and mortar, wiggled *the* brick, pulling it away, peering inside, reaching into the darkness, soft dirt against her fingertips. Empty. Her father had found it all. She tumbled back in time to that Christmas Eve when her secrets had been discovered and she'd fled the house to take refuge with Lukasz.

Secrets. A bitter lemon taste filled her mouth. A sign from God or her Catholic training telling her the thoughts she'd entertained earlier—measuring Lukasz against Joe and Mr. Morrison—were wrong. The flavor was identical to what she'd experienced when holding Matka up against Mrs. Dunn decades before.

Mary no longer had special presents to stow away so her parents wouldn't use them to pay the taxes on the home. She waggled the brick back into the wall and tucked the judgments about her husband into the back of her mind as though it held brick-covered fireplace compartments waiting to hide her thoughts away. She brushed her hands. Enough of that.

She sorted through the laundry basket, organized the ironing into piles for the next day and inventoried the preserves in the pantry—those for keeping and those for giving away. She would need the kids to go for another round of berry picking just to be sure jam, whole fruit and syrups would last through the following year. Perhaps the tomatoes Matka planted out back had finally plumped and turned red.

With a plan for the next day, her aloneness surprised her yet again, bringing a disquiet. She told herself to revel in the silence everyone always wanted until they had it. Deep breaths and a ticking clock were the only sounds against far-away thunder. Was this what it would be like when she no longer refereed arguments or worried if children were about to disturb Lukasz? Emptiness… she wasn't sure she liked it.

She mixed a large tub of lemonade. Booming and hissing fireworks started in the park. Released from the stillness, she turned on the radio. A band playing patriotic and dance tunes lightened her mood further. Lukasz's note had lifted her in one way. His bringing lemons and sugar meant he must've done some amount of work that day to purchase or trade.

Before long, Mary's home was full of four giggling daughters. They spilled into the kitchen, fanning themselves, their new dresses made from the traded material of crisp white cotton, embroidered with delicate yellow and pink flowers at the neckline or on the pocket or cap sleeves of each dress. She presented Vicki with the hairpins and the sweets that Lukasz had made possible.

"Pop brought you—" Vicki said.

"No—*you*, Vicki. He brought the groceries for you. He must've found work somewhere today. Maybe blacksmithing with Mr. Hostenske or… Haskel's farm? Not sure."

Vicki ran her fingers over the pins from Mrs. Walsh.

Mary took them and slid them into Vicki's hair, shaping the waves along her hairline. "I wish we could do more for your birthday this year."

Vicki held Mary's wrists. "No. This beautiful dress and the lemonade and cookies… and the hairpins from Mrs. Walsh. What a birthday. I can't wait to thank Pop. It's a wonderful surprise."

Mary engulfed Vicki into her arms. Holding her felt so good, reminding her of when her children used to fight to crawl into her lap for snuggling.

Helen, Rose, and Ida whispered to one another.

Mary released Vicki. "What's going on with you three?"

The girls continued to laugh, and now Vicki had joined in.

"What on earth is… You're all walking on air. Stars in your eyes." Mary was pleased they were enjoying their dresses so fully, that Stan's talents had made the trade for the fabric possible. But anything Helen was so excited about struck fear in Mary's heart. She was mischievous.

"So spill. What's going on?"

Helen stuck her chin in the air. "The *boys* walked us home, Mom. And one is especially sweet on Ida. And he's something to see."

Ida's face went tomato red.

"What *boys*? The Sawas?" Mary'd never been so grateful Matka had gone away, not wanting to draw her into such conversations. Mary poured more lemonade, searching Ida's face for a sign of something that might signal her daughter wasn't being chaste.

The thought shocked Mary. Ida had never talked about boys, and though she grumbled about being the eldest daughter and having more responsibility—especially more than the boys, who spent most of their day playing ball—she didn't really complain. Mary had never registered a sense of resentment between her and Ida. Not like Mary and Matka had shared. She certainly never saw Ida as yearning for affection or attention as Mary had. Helen was a different story. She'd quit school in eighth grade, and though was a hard worker cleaning offices and anyone's home who would hire, she reveled in garnering as much attention as possible. "You kept your sisters with you the whole time, right?"

"'Course, Mom," Ida said, her voice lifting like wispy clouds.

Mary quickly calculated Ida's age, matching it to the memory of milestones in her own life. Seventeen—older than Mary when she'd fallen in love with Lukasz. "So what boys?" Oh, the things she and Lukasz had done together. The thought of Ida in the arms of a man… It couldn't be true.

Ida had quit high school in 1930 to work more. Mary's heart began to thump. Had she been as blind as Matka? Was Ida in the midst of leaving them? She was self-sufficient, but she didn't suffer the big dreams that Mary had as a young girl. Mary had been so focused on the boys, keeping Helen in line, and managing Lukasz that she hadn't stopped to really consider Ida's aspirations. "Who're these boys? This *particular* boy?" Mary asked.

Vicki seemed more practical and hadn't gone moon-eyed as her sisters had. And while Ida collapsed into a chair, lost in love and thought, Vicki and Helen provided the narration from the day, listing the names of three boys (Rose was with girlfriends at the time), beginning to end, how they bought the girls sweet tea and ice cream and fried dough. This, the chatter and laughter, was way more precious than the earlier silence.

Mary broke ice apart with the pick, fragments skittering across the countertop, landing in Vicki's outstretched palms. She added some to the poured liquid, the warmth causing the ice to crackle, the sound tantalizing.

"So this Frank Daniels…"

Helen laid the back of her wrist across her forehead. "A dream. If I was a bit older, I'd take him before Ida."

Mary sighed. "Helen. Please." Mary had been teaching them about proper courting behavior, tying it to the church, hoping to ensure her daughters didn't sneak away, toeing the line between like and love the way she had, tumbling over it. But she knew it wasn't lack of knowing proper courting expectations that caused problems. Far more powerful understandings and explorations could lure a girl away before it was time for her to go. And Helen had a lot of Mary's personality. She couldn't deny. Fifteen and loud, big laugh, bold as anything.

Thoughts flew through Mary's mind, taking her back as much as taking her forward, to the point her daughters were talking about boys being dreamy. Matka had never wanted to hear about the boys Mary was interested in. And when Mary introduced Lukasz to the family, Papa hadn't approved of her marrying an immigrant. He couldn't see the hypocrisy in that given he hadn't yet declared for citizenship even though he'd been in America for decades.

His argument had made no sense to Mary, and the marriage caused a rift until the day he died. Why hadn't Papa understood? Lukasz appeared in Mary's life every single time she needed someone, needed *him*. Her insides felt heavy at the remembering, the hope tied to their beginnings, the reality that followed. So much of it was exactly what she wanted. That was where she'd lay her heart for the moment.

And so she took Ida's hand in hers. "Use your head. That's all. Your heart will tell you a million lies, but you are so practical and... Just let me know what you're thinking when you think it. I will help you with whatever you need."

Ida looked confused for a moment, and then she smiled. "Thank you, Mom."

There. Mary had done something right that day.

**

The Musial ladies enjoyed the lightness of that Fourth of July night, and soon Stan and Honey arrived home, covered in a day's dirt, further dusted by hours of kick the can after the fireworks.

As much as Mary enjoyed the story of Ida and her interest in Frank Daniels, it was the rundown on every play of every inning of the Cement City loss that Mary loved most. She shared their disappointment in the result and poured two glasses of lemonade. "You'll get 'em next time. Joe said you barreled it up, Stan."

Honey pushed between Stan and Mary. She took off his hat and brushed his hair back. "And Joe said you found a couple of holes, too."

Honey's face drooped.

Mary kissed his forehead. "Wash up good tonight. Hair and all." Honey rolled his eyes. Mary knew he wanted stronger compliments from Joe Barbao. "Said you're a fine player. Like your brother."

"Like my *brother*." Honey's mouth drew into a pout.

Mary took him by the chin. "Work harder. You and Stan are made from the exact same grit."

"But no one says how I play just—"

"Then work harder."

"That's not it."

"It is," Mary said. "And you're younger. And—"

"Mom—"

She pulled Honey into her and eyed Stan. "And Mrs. Peters came through the food line and said you two had a brawl. Rolling around, grapplin' like a pair of circus monkeys. Front of the whole town."

Stan's cheeks reddened. He only liked some kinds of attention. Mary reached for him and drew him into the hug with Honey, her chin on top of Stan's head as he folded himself into her. "You're brothers. Most important thing there is. No more caterwauling and punching or people'll think I'm keeping a barn instead of a house."

"I'm sorry." Stan squeezed her tight, shouldering Honey out of the way. Honey in turn did the same. And though Mary didn't want the boys to bicker, she didn't mind being at the center of their current battle. She pushed them both toward the table. "Sit."

She arranged more sugar cookies on a plate. Made with one-third of the sugar called for, they still tasted delicious in the face of largely sweet-free years since the country had started its long economic nap.

With her flock gathered around the table, laughing about the day, recounting the magic of the fireworks display, the way the colors hung in the clouds, creating immeasurable variations on basic hues, Mary marked the moment, the contentment, her worries offset like sugar balanced lemon. They reported that no one was injured by the fireworks that year. Contentment provided the undercurrent that evening, but what she felt right then was utter joy. But not the loud, firecracker kind; it was soft and warm and hushed—something to be stored away and re-experienced when the pressures of surviving a world folding in was too much.

Rose, who'd been mostly quiet that night, got up to rinse her glass. Mary noticed the hem had fallen on the right side of her dress. "Hold on." She grabbed her sewing basket and dug out her pincushion. Kneeling, Mary pinned the fabric. Blocked by Rose, pins jutting out from Mary's mouth, she didn't immediately see what had changed, what had caused the laughter to stop, what had sucked the air right out of the kitchen. But when she saw Stan's feet shift under the table and him clasp his hands in his lap, she knew. Lukasz had returned.

"What happened to the dress? New dress? Ruined already? Trading for that material was a waste."

Mary patted Rose's legs and stood. She searched his face for happiness, a sign he had returned to enjoy the cookies and lemonade he'd helped make possible. Vicki flew to her father and flung her arms around him. He patted her back and kissed the top of her head, but his face was stoic. Vicki pulled away, shifting her weight back and forth. "Thank you, Pop." She swung her arm toward the table. "You made my birthday so special. Thank you."

Lukasz nodded and passed Vicki, making eye contact with Mary. He swayed, and his vacant gaze gave away where he'd been. Or at least what he'd been doing. Mary held her breath, confused. He looked at his daughter as though he'd just then remembered what he'd done. "Your birthday."

"Mom made cookies and lemonade for me. Thank you for getting everything and the note."

They all watched Lukasz, feeling the invisible grip he'd brought with him.

He smiled then and pulled Vicki into another hug. "Happy birthday, my girl. Happy, happy birthday."

With his hand around the back of Vicki, Mary saw Lukasz's bleeding knuckles.

She poured a lemonade and set it aside. She approached Lukasz and took his hand. He flinched away. She wanted to ask what the hell he'd been doing but stopped herself. He cradled his hand against his belly. She went to the dry sink, where she pulled out some wrapping and liniment.

"Stan, honey, get up so I can take a look at your father's hand."

"Cut it fixing umbrellas."

This made Mary turn. He'd been quite good at repairing umbrellas when they first met. It was possible if he'd been drinking that he might have injured himself doing that work. But the cuts, trailing along each knuckle, were clearly from fighting. "Well, what you bought with your fees certainly made our night." She eyed the lemonade and cookies.

Lukasz ignored her hint to stay on that subject and glared at his boys. "Heard you lost to Cement City."

Stan grimaced, his lips moving a little as though he was going to say something but couldn't get the words out. This would only add to Lukasz's anger.

"Lukasz, please sit."

"Cement City boys just like their foremen fathers." Lukasz puffed his chest and arms out, mocking. "Just take what they want."

Stan shrank in the presence of his father, but stayed right there. Honey took the tact of sliding behind his sisters, out of sight.

"You're an angry bear with that injured hand," Mary said. "Your sons hit five home runs between them. Can't help the rest of the team, I suppose."

She snapped her fingers at Ida and mouthed for her to pull out bread and lunch meat. They needed to get something heavy into Lukasz's belly. "Stan, grab the cabbage from the icebox."

As Mary unwrapped the bread, Stan started across the room. His foot caught on the braided throw rug.

"Oof." The word stretched like bubble gum.

The whole world slowed, drawn into a blur. Stan hung in the air, face full of surprise. As he was about to hit the floor, he curled his shoulder and somersaulted, springing to his feet with a finishing leap, hands above his head. Mary could see Stan holding his breath, waiting to be yelled at for clumsiness. *Tick, tick, tick.* The clock didn't know to silence itself when Lukasz turned dark. But instead of lashing out, Lukasz released the most beautiful thing Mary had heard in a long time. His low rolling laugh filled the kitchen like the thunder that had hung around all evening.

Stan's shoulders relaxed, and he laughed along. Then Honey, then Ida and Helen and the rest. Mary approached Lukasz, gently pulling his hand into the light. He shook with laughter, making Mary's work difficult. But with the gentle touch of her hand on his, he softened further and she led him to sit. Ida pushed the lemonade to him, and he sucked it all down while Mary cleaned the abrasions and bandaged his hand.

"Pop?" Vicki slid a paper onto the table. "You dropped this."

He looked at it, then at Mary, giving her permission to open it. She unfolded it. Wireworks letterhead. She skimmed it and met her husband's gaze. "They want you on daylight. Tomorrow."

"Well. Good news, then. Hired back."

Mary squinted at him. Though Lukasz could read typewritten and printed English, this handwritten note would have been nearly impossible for him to decipher even when sober. What she didn't say was that the assignment was just for two days. When the news had further transformed his expression, his bearing, his mood, she let half the information stay put—out of sight. He would find out soon enough.

"Turn that music up," Lukasz said. He stood and reached for Mary, big-band tunes filling the room. He pulled her to her feet, drawing her back in time to when Lukasz had fallen for her, when their connection had first formed through dancing, their hands finding each other, providing the path for their hearts to meet. He dipped her dramatically, his face buried in her neck, her head skimming the floor before he whipped her back to standing, the motion releasing her laughter, the shot of hilarity as good as a beer softening a mood.

For those few moments in the kitchen, the kids dancing along as well, all of what the Musials didn't have, the ramifications of what that meant, fell away. Lukasz pulled Mary close, their bodies melding, the music running through them. And though she had resigned to Lukasz never being who he'd wanted to be, who she thought he'd be, that didn't stop her from loving who he was. Exactly who he'd been all along.

Chapter 24

Stan

Hands.
Weather.
Home.

Stan thought of Andrew's connection between the way the weather broke or held tight and how the same thing happened at home with tension building and a mass of something, too much trouble in the form of an opposing force always led to the unleashing of held tempers, the nursing of old grudges, creating a cycle.

Just like Skunk and Yellow Melvin had disclosed how their father tornadoed through the house, each family member taking cover in low, dark places. Unfortunately Skunk had made the fatal error of suggesting his family not only accept charity but seek it out. He hadn't made note of the cold front and approaching bruised skies in time to avoid the storm.

Stan shuddered at the thought of Mr. Fitzsimmons pummeling his son, visualizing the blows bringing pain to his own body. Why would God let that happen? Why would God have let so many men in Donora lose their jobs?

Hands.

Pop's red, swollen paw, Mom's gentle taking of it, rubbing in the liniment, wrapping it up. Stan got to his knees to pray, curious about who his father'd been tussling with to earn his injuries. He didn't believe the story about it happening while repairing umbrellas, but he saw the storm coming and wouldn't be the opposing front to set it off.

Hands.

Mom's—red, raw, damaged. But differently than Pop's. Stan wondered if the slow, daily wounding to her hands hurt more than something fast and unexpected, like the fight that had obviously hurt Pop's. Was there a fella over the age of six who couldn't recognize what caused bleeding knuckles? Stan touched his cheek then looked at his own left fist. He'd landed a punch or two on Honey, but mostly they'd wrestled around, sending dirt plumes down their throats. Thinking of Mom's gentle cleaning of Pop's hand made him wonder if anyone had ever gently taken Mom's hands and soothed them with liniment, softly wrapping them. Had Pop ever returned the favor?

Honey entered the bedroom and plopped to the floor across the bed from Stan, clasping his hands under his chin. Stan eyed the redness on two of Honey's knuckles but didn't mention it. They said their Hail Marys and Our Fathers, and their voices trailed off into specific prayers.

Honey squeezed his eyes closed. "Please, please end this awful time with no jobs and food. Please. And thank you for the umbrella work and Pop's note from the wireworks and Mom's baking and lemonade." Honey shifted. "But please, God, let us win our rematch with Cement City. Please heal Monocle's eyes or give him two monocles or regular glasses or whatever. Please keep Skunk and Yellow safe from storms and heal their bruises and make me field better, make the rest of 'em find a hit next time. Just one. If we all hit something, we don't have to rely on Stan or me or…"

Stan narrowed his gaze on Honey, watching him pray earnestly, and decided perhaps it was none of his business to tell anyone else what to pray about.

He spoke his own prayer aloud, the way Mom had taught them since they were small. "Please, God, let the mills open back up. Please let Pop get his job back permanently." The floor down the hall creaked. Honey met Stan's gaze. "And please forgive me for my impatience with my brother."

Honey tilted his head. "Same from me."

Down the hall, a door clicked shut. Footsteps drew closer. The long, smooth loping indicated it was Mom.

Stan admired her more than he could ever express aloud, but he didn't quite understand how she managed. Pop's mood hung like the thick mill smoke, ever present even when weather clouds went away. Stan's tripping over the rug had broken the tension and his mother had gone to work on the hand, and that was it—storm passed, parents dancing, a gentleness between them that he witnessed when Mom worked her magic. He wasn't quite sure how she maintained the energy to work her own weather system against Pop's, yet she did it constantly. And he'd done the same with the fall. Laughter just might be the cure for everything.

Mom's footsteps closed in on the doorway, but she didn't enter. Stan had been awake the night she gave them permission to pray for what their hearts needed, but he didn't want to upset her. And so he reclasped his hands and blew his air between his palms, thinking of Andrew and the brilliant way he painted a picture of the tension in all their homes as being like storms. "Please, God, keep the weather calm. Let the thunderstorms pass by. Please keep all the floods away. Please keep the warm fronts from crashing into cold and causing storms, and mostly keep the tornadoes away. Please bring soft, gentle summer rains that make us smile and turn our faces toward the sun. Please."

Chapter 25

Mary

Mary stood outside the boys' door listening to them pray. Behind her, Lukasz stumbled in the hall. "Mary," he whispered.

She held her finger up, then put it to her lips before brushing her hand through the air to direct him. He nodded and entered their bedroom. He needed to sleep off the booze so he wouldn't get injured or reprimanded at work the next day. The wire mill was too dangerous for hungover men who couldn't focus. Two days' mill pay was a fortune that summer. There was nothing that added tension faster than losing promised money. The mill situation, the utter devastation from so few men working, shouldn't have caused shame to individuals, but to be offered a shift and ruin it being hungover? That would bring suffocating infamy. Lukasz wouldn't weather that well.

The girls continued to giggle in their room. Ida. A sadness pulled at Mary's insides. A transition. It was coming. Something. But she didn't want Ida to sneak off in the night, to find comfort only in her husband. That was not enough for a woman to depend on. Even if the man was dreamy, as Ida and Helen indicated Frank Daniels was. Mary couldn't imagine a man courting Ida, sitting at a table with Lukasz. Yet it was time. No secret meetings in sheds or lying on marriage certificates. It was time for Mary to tell Ida she would find a way to make courting work out in the open. Lukasz couldn't be predictable. But Mary would make it work.

A drawer slamming in her bedroom brought Mary back to the present. Catching the end of the boys' prayers, she heard Honey's plea for his usual things—baseball success—but Stan, he'd focused an awful lot on the weather. She wondered if all the heat lightning that had been flashing in the sky had scared him. Or maybe it was the news that the Roman boy from Tenth Street had been struck by lightning at the beach the week before while on vacation. No. He hadn't given the weather a second thought when she'd warned them in the morning to skip the fireworks if it looked like storms. Stan wasn't the type to be afraid of the weather. Perhaps he just liked the idea of soft summer rain. Who didn't?

Stan stopped talking, and she heard the bed squeak, so he must have gotten in it.

"Yeah," Honey said. "Gentle summer rain. I'm liable to find a lump of gold under the bed each morning as often as fine weather in Donora."

Mary drew back at the comment.

"Weather's mighty fine three doors up the street now, isn't it?" Stan said.

A thud coming from Mary's bedroom got her moving. Lukasz would require soothing and a deep night's sleep and only Mary could usher that in.

Chapter 26

Stan

Stan, Honey, and Andrew rounded up as many "real" bats as they could for the rematch against Cement City. Stan was ready. He'd noticed how Joe had managed his team on Fourth of July—having several guys try different bats for size and weight. Stan did that himself, but as he saw Joe having to convince some of the fellas to try something different, he thought the kids his age may need to pay more attention to the length, weight, and feel of the bat they chose.

Stan had grown up hitting bottle caps with broom handles and balled-up stockings off the end of a log. Once he even hit twenty-one chiclets off a pencil in a row. There wasn't anything he hadn't put in his hands and used as a bat.

"Remember, Stan. Lighten up a bit on the fellas," Andrew said.

"What? Come on. Let's get to the field. We can at least throw a little."

Andrew pulled out his notebook and gestured for Stan to sit on the stairs beside him. "Look. I've sketched out this calendar. I used blue ink for your name and black for the rest of us and wrote the words *baseball* and *school* to show what we're spending time on." It was easy to see that Stan spent every spare moment on baseball and the others had some balance at least. Andrew was nearly one hundred percent the opposite of Stan with studies and baseball. "You see why you've got to allow for them to learn. Like you do for me."

"Practice, Andrew. That's the difference. Easily fixed." Walking to the field, Stan thought about that and what he'd seen with Joe. He was a dynamite pitcher, but Joe also knew how to get his players to perform.

When they reached the field, Andrew pulled Stan back. "One more thing you need to think about. Aside from you practicing more than the rest of us, you were born with something different that I can't even describe, and for that reason you've got to let these fellas off the hook. You are such a nice person. It's all right that some of us stink. You can let us stink."

That made little sense to Stan, having seen hard work as being the remedy to so many problems. *Round, round, ready touch…*

He stopped and smacked his forehead. "Oh. Oh, okay. I get it."

He thought of Andrew's dedication to baseball that had resulted in little improvement. "But… mostly, hard work works."

"Mostly," Andrew said. "But just something to keep in mind is all."

Stan nodded. Even with understanding overall what Andrew meant, with the game ahead, he wouldn't sort through all the fine lines running through his friend's thinking. He put his mind on the game, and he was determined for it to go their way. "We have a game to win, my friend, so let's go."

⁎⁎

The rest of North Donora arrived at the field, sticks, bats, clubs and balls in hand. They were ready.

Stan could feel the win in his bat, in his glove. Each team organized themselves along the sidelines. The field, the atmosphere was missing the Fourth of July game glamour. Sure, there would be bookies and parents and curious shopkeepers and mill foremen who stopped to catch an inning or two. But there was no pageantry—no girls with crepe paper flowers or flags or parades for winners. But this game was just as important to Stan and his team.

As North Donora was going to take the field, Hound sauntered over, a brand-new Spalding bat in his hand. He swung it like a man on the boulevard with hat and cane. "Say, Stan. Word with ya, please?"

Stan nodded, punching his fist into his mitt. Smokestack's auntie Hazel had fixed it nice by giving Stan a special oil to work into the leather over the past week. Same with the bats. They were poised to win.

Hound removed his hat. "Listen. We've got some players gone to the beach. Don't ask me to comment on parents who'd inflict such punishment on their sons as to make them miss the last game of a season for a trip to Miami and whatnot. But here we are."

Stan surveyed the opposite bench. Seven players. He crossed his arms. "*Here we are* what?"

"To square up. How 'bout you give up two players and we're even, lookin' at who you've got there."

Stan clenched his jaw. This was their chance to whoop 'em good. One outfielder? Or maybe they'd have one fella play third and short. Stan smiled and stole a look at Weatherman, who was staring at Stan, eyes wide. Stan wanted to beat the pants off of Cement City, but not with them at such a disadvantage. What would that prove?

"How 'bout we take Honey and Nicky Christmas?"

"How 'bout you take Honey and Blue Louise?"

"A girl?"

"Hits better than four of your boys over there."

Hound dug his bat into the ground, rotating it, making a hole. "With her eyes shut."

"Oh, all right. Fine."

Honey rushed Stan and punched him in the shoulder.

Stan rubbed it. "What the hell, Honey?"

"You put me on their team?"

Stan drew deep breaths. It almost felt like his words might get caught, but he reminded himself this was his brother. "They picked you, Honey. Doesn't that make your day?"

Honey flinched and swiped a glove off the ground. He stuck it on his right hand and pointed it at Stan. "They think you'll go easy on me. Don't think you're gettin' any favors from me. We're enemies for this game. Bitter, hateful enemies. You could have said no."

"But then you wouldn't have the chance to beat me good now, would you?"

Honey stuck his chin out the way he did when he was angry or trying to be big or bold. He was the picture of their mother right then, and Stan knew he'd done the right thing. Honey needed a chance to beat Stan as much as Stan needed to beat Cement City.

And so they played.

Cement City stuck Honey in center field, which was a good spot for him. It didn't take anyone's infield position away, but Honey could play from anywhere. He was good, and Stan wanted his brother to make a good showing.

Honey found himself with three base hits, but then Stan struck him out. Honey spat and swore and broke the bat that had been taped and tacked together all summer. This caused both teams to scream at him. Honey didn't notice. And while Stan was hitting well, getting on base three out of four times so far, by the fifth inning the score was even at five. Both teams were hitting well, one fielding as bad as the other.

Stan's next up felt good. He rolled his shoulders and sank into his corkscrew, crouchy stance, peeking at Schmitty over his shoulder. Schmitty made Stan wait, kicking at the wood that marked the pitcher's mound.

"Catch him thinkin', Pitch," Honey screamed from the outfield, even as he was backing up, knowing Stan could crank it into the river if he wanted.

Stan stepped out of the batter's box and took a few swings, pointing the bat at Honey.

"Hey, Pitcher! He's gonna take you so deep you'll need your granddad's mining headlamp to find the ball," Smokestack said.

Honey shouted, "Inside, near his belly. Set him back a step. He can't take the nerves. Not at school, not on the field."

Stan glared at Honey, then drew deep breaths before settling back into his stance. Schmitty wound up and stopped halfway through, throwing the ball to first base, scaring Smokestack back off his lead.

Stan exhaled and stepped away. Schmitty went through his pre-pitch rigamarole, with the fans and teams heckling batter and pitcher. Stan blocked it all out and got into position, waiting, letting it all unfold, keeping his breath even, ignoring even Honey's taunting. This time Schmitty pitched the ball, and as soon as it was out of his hand Stan knew it was his filthy fastball. It did some fancy sinking just before it reached the plate, but Stan got a chunk of it.

The crack echoed, the bat vibrating in Stan's hands. Far from a perfect hit, but it left his bat hard. He immediately knew it wouldn't be high enough to clear the fence, but if he ran tight around the bases, he could at least earn a triple.

Moonshine stood near home plate, windmilling his arm, telling Stan to keep going. He didn't even look to see how close Honey was to throwing him out. His team met him at home plate, euphoria lifting him high.

But when the boys pulled away from Stan and stopped patting his head and back, he saw Cement City pointing to the outfield. North Donora and the fans grew quiet.

"What? What? No way he caught that," Cheeks said. He stomped into the outfield to investigate.

Stan agreed. He hit it hard but flat. Even a great fielder like Honey couldn't have caught it on the fly.

"Under the fence!" someone in the stands said.

Cheeks nodded, clomping back, yelling something over his shoulder at Honey as he did.

Cement City went crazy.

"Automatic! Take! Your! Base!" the fans chanted.

Automatic double. Stan hated his run being called back due to the ball grounding out before leaving the field of play. *Automatic double.* If not for thinking he'd scored, for running like the devil for nothing, he might have been satisfied with that.

Still gasping for air, Stan took his place at second base.

"Honey's sweet, my ass," Cheeks said as he rolled past. "Just called me *paczki*. What the hell is a *poonchki?*"

Stan was too angry to explain.

"Polish donut," Moonshine shouted.

"I'm Italian!" Cheeks threw both arms in the air. Honey's laughter carried from the outfield.

"Paczki are stuffed with jelly and creams. Great donuts but bigger than my head," Second baseman, Marty Turner, said punching his glove.

"Better than some old donuts," Stan said shaking his head, irritated at the world.

Cheeks pressed his belly. "I'm not that round!"

Stan kicked at the bag. The automatic double gave Cement City a bolt of energy and sucked it out of North Donora. The inning ended with Yellow Melvin flying out and Skunk thrown out at second. Stan drew deep breaths, trying to regain his focus.

As he got to the mound, Honey passed him, whispering something.

"What'd you say?" Stan asked.

Honey sauntered back, smirking. "Beat ya outta your home run."

"What?"

"You heard me loud and clear."

"You did *not*—"

"Kicked it right under the fence," Honey said. "A double stinks after that mad dash all the way home, doesn't it?"

Stan couldn't speak.

Honey's smirk hardened further as he walked backward. "Shoulda fought for me to stay on the team." And he jogged the rest of the way to the bench.

Stan's body tensed, anger bursting through him. He resisted the urge to tackle his brother and rub his face in the dirt. He paced. No. No. Tackling Honey was not the right thing to do. Joe. Yes, Joe Barbao exploded at games, got tossed out plenty of times for fighting with players and arguing with umps. But Stan had promised Mom no more fighting.

Stan drew deep breaths forcing himself to focus on pitching. And so with the first two batters, Stan channeled all that anger and cleaned them out quick with the help of Tank, Melonhead, and Nicky Christmas. Even Monocle scooped one up, tossing it to first just in time.

"That's it, that's it." Stan jogged to pat Monocle on the back. "That's how you do it." He felt good. Their weakened team didn't matter. Only positive thoughts and words. That was it. Next up: Honey.

Stan eyed his brother.

Betrayed.

Stan bit his lip. He'd promised. No more scrabbling. So instead of throwing punches and rubbing Honey's nose in the infield, Stan focused. He threw his first pitch. Inside, a little high. Enough to rattle Honey, who didn't fluster easily. Pitch number two. Stan threw it exactly where Honey couldn't ignore it, exactly where he wouldn't forget it. Hard as he could, the ball released just right, and Honey's eyes widened a bit as he realized what was happening. He spun his right shoulder toward the catcher to avoid being hit in the chest, but exposed his back. Stan landed the pitch right between the shoulder blades.

The thud of the ball hitting Honey brought a collective gasp from the crowd, Stan adjusted his cap, tracing his brother's path to first base. *There you go, Honey. Try kicking my ball under the fence again.*

"Hot one up," Smokestack said, snatching the ball from the ground and throwing it back to Stan.

Honey took his base, face purple as he glared at Stan, trying to hide the pain. No one else knew it for sure, but Stan did. He'd knocked the air right out of his brother and shut him up once and for all. And from there the game turned for North Donora. They won 18–6, fully erasing the weight of the loss on Fourth of July.

**

After the game, Stan and his teammates, including Honey and Blue Louise, walked arm in arm back to Heslep Avenue to St. Philips's to have a meal at the soup kitchen. Honey refused to look at Stan, as he always did when he was angry. Stan was excited about the victory, and he was going to enjoy it. When they reached the church, Melonhead and Andrew slipped out of line and walked away.

"Hey!" Stan yelled, waving for them to return. "Where ya goin'?"

Andrew shrugged and dug through his backpack. "We just…"

"What?" Smokestack asked. "Thought we were gonna practice batting after we eat."

Andrew slung his backpack over his shoulder. "I'm going to eat at home. Melonhead's mom's expecting him, too."

"We'll meet you after. Up the lot, right?" Melonhead said.

Moonshine stepped closer. "Too good for the soup kitchen?"

Andrew and Melonhead glanced at each other. "No." They looked away.

"What gives?" Smokestack said.

They didn't respond.

Tank waved them off. "Knew it."

Andrew stepped forward. "No, guys. Look." For the first time ever, Stan saw Andrew struggling with his words.

Stan's mind sorted through what he knew about Andrew. "Hey, guys. Weatherman and Melonhead are doing the rest of us a favor—saving two meals for other fellas. We oughta thank them."

Melonhead adjusted his cap. "Trying to help out is all."

Stan nodded. "Yeah."

Smokestack grumbled, then finally nodded. "Makes sense. If you don't need it, don't take it."

Andrew and Melonhead looked embarrassed at having too much, uneasy in a way Stan had only seen Andrew appear when it came to baseball. Pop wouldn't know what to make of these two boys embarrassed about not needing charity, seeing as he was against taking aid for his own family, even when they had nothing. Stan had never imagined before what Pop would be like if he was the one to have abundance when everyone else didn't.

"We don't mean anything by it," Andrew said.

Stan thought of the steak dinner he'd enjoyed at Andrew's, and his mouth started to water. "Guys, come on. I'd do the same if it were me. We'll see ya at the lot. Hurry back." His ease made the rest of the team visibly dissolve their humiliation-fueled resentment.

Truthfully, families like Melonhead's and Andrew's should've been living in areas like Cement City with perfect landscaping, a gated community, and special holiday affairs, extra ones that the mill gifted them beyond the normal ones for the full town. But their families stayed with the mixed people, the raw, earthy material to Cement City's finished steel, the folks who did all the mill work for little pay when they were running at record capacity and lost it all when they weren't. Yet the two families stayed put, content to have everything they needed just where they were.

**

Honey held his anger at Stan and the loss with Cement City between tight-lined lips. And after getting a meal, he pouted all through their practice. Stalking home, Stan and Honey reached Heslep before Stan tried to soften things between them.

The streetlights flicked on as they crossed the raised sidewalk. "How long you gonna be mad?"

Honey scoffed.

Stan shook his head and sped up. "Forget it, then."

"Yeah, why not?"

Stan stopped and turned, Honey crashing into his chest. Honey was two years younger, but not much smaller, and Stan didn't want to fight with his brother but fair was fair. "Why not what?"

"You get everything, Stan. Everything. And I'm sick of it."

"Oh no. You're not going to put this on me. You brought it on yourself."

"You should have fought for me."

"I let you be picked. If they would have picked Nicky Christmas or Moonshine, you would've cried like a baby that no one ever picks you. They picked you because you were the next best guy."

"After you, right?"

Stan sighed. "I'm older, Honey. Baseball's everything to me. All I think about. You go fishing with the Mauros and creek walking and crayfish hunting with the Knabels while I hit peas off of straws all day."

"I'm tired of you getting all the attention."

"Which is exactly why I let Cement City take you. I never thought we'd win without ya. I was glad they snatched you up. I was proud of you."

"Bullshit."

Stan waved him off and started toward Tenth Street.

"It's not fair."

Stan ignored him and kept walking.

A blow to the back, right between the shoulder blades, knocked Stan forward a few steps. He turned, seething, balling his fist.

Honey pursed his lips, breathing heavy. "Now you know how it feels."

Stan wiggled his shoulders, trying to work the smarting out of his muscles. "How *what* feels?"

"When your brother stabs you in the back."

Stan rubbed the back of his neck. "You mean the pitch?"

"Yes, that knife in the back in the seventh inning. That one."

"You kicked my ball under the fence. You admitted it. You—"

"No, *you*! It's always you. Stan this, Stan that. Born under a lucky star. First boy. On and on." Spittle flew from Honey's mouth.

Stan's insides hurt. His brother was angry that Stan had something good. And it immediately made him think of their father. "You're just like Pop." Stan started up Tenth.

Honey followed, stepping on the back of Stan's heel, pulling his shoe off.

"Can you get off my ass for a second?" Stan bent down and fixed his flat tire.

"What's that mean?" Honey said. "What you said?"

Stan started up the hill again, Honey beside him, yanking on his arm.

Stan didn't want to say it.

"What did you mean?"

Stan stopped, facing Honey. "You can't be happy that I'm good at something. Just like Pop. You think it hurts what others think of you because they think I'm good."

"I'm just as good."

"Sure."

"I will be someday."

"I know."

"But I'm not like Pop. I just want to be better than you at something. Something."

Stan's heart clenched. He didn't want Honey feeling jealous. Not about this. He started back up the hill. There was no way around the truth at the center of Honey's disgruntlement. "Take up violin or science or—"

"*You* hate that I'm good, *too*. You cry when we lose. I see you. And you hate that I'm younger but almost as good."

"I don't hate that, Honey. But baseball is all I'm good at. And I won't let you win or pretend you're better than me right now. Just pick something else if you don't like me winning. Because I'm never going to be anything but this. It's exactly who I am. It's everything I am."

Stan stopped. He looked at his feet, the torn canvas shoes with holes where his dirty socks poked through. Flashes of him sitting in school came to mind.

"It's the *only* thing I am." The words he'd just spoken came with a fully formed understanding he hadn't really felt before. In his mind, being a ballplayer had been a thing far off in the future. But having said what he had, he already knew—baseball was who he was already. Eleven years old. He knew others thought it was silly to say he'd play baseball for a job, but he knew it would happen.

Honey knew Stan was right, too, and that's why it hurt so bad. Because though Honey was a good player even for how young he was, something was different. And it wasn't something obvious in how he hit or caught or ran. Something like the innards of a lighter Joe had mentioned. Something missing in others that Stan felt present inside himself. Like Andrew had said, too. And there was nothing Stan could do to change that for his brother. Nothing at all. "Just keep working hard. That's all we can do. Like Mom always says. We'll both play pro."

"We," Honey said.

Stan met Honey's gaze. It was like looking in a mirror covered with condensation, obviously related, their features slightly different. Honey's eyes watered. He stretched out his hand. Stan took it, and they shook. "Yes. We. *Us*."

"We're even?"

Stan was confused.

"The pitch in the back for the ball under the fence."

And the win. Stan wasn't sure he'd be so forgiving if North Donora hadn't walloped Cement City. "Even Steven." Stan yanked Honey into him, arm around his neck, and they trudged the rest of the way home just like that.

"Steak and baseball. Right, Stan?"

And the air between them cleared.

"Definitely."

Stan wasn't sure what Honey took from any of the day's events, but like Stan, he strove for blue skies on the home front. And for that moment, they had just that.

Chapter 27

Mary

November 1932

August had brought a slight upswing in mill activity. More often, sparks flew at the open hearths, firing, spitting, and churning, doing their work turning earth and scrap into hard-wearing steel. Lukasz was one of the lucky few who'd been lassoed into a work cycle that allowed for fifteen to twenty hours per week. This eased Mary's worries to some degree as Matka brought in much less laundry and sewing due to her high blood pressure, labored breathing, and a constant stomachache. The stomachache was just another thread that tied her to Lukasz as they commiserated over foods that either eased or inflamed belly pain.

Mary gathered her bag, put her wallet inside, and double-checked her list: cabbage, flour, potatoes, sugar.

"Coffee, Mary, I love that coffee soup you made me the other day. Only thing I can keep down," Matka said, her slippers making a sandpapery sound as she entered the kitchen.

"You liked it with the thick cut bread?"

"Yes, that. That batch was perfect."

Mary smiled, glad something was soothing for her digestive system. In having the chance to care for Matka this way, Mary felt as though she was righting a wrong and forging a new relationship with the person who knew Mary the longest in the world.

"Apples, if they got 'em. The green."

Mary studied Matka, noting that her long powerful gait had turned shuffling, her overall build suddenly stooped, brittle, her stout limbs gone twiggy like trees in the almost-winter landscape, at the mercy of even the gentlest winds. "I won't forget." She pulled a chair out for Matka, and when she got close enough, she pulled her into a hug.

"Oh, Mary. Enough. Enough."

Mary would have thought Matka would grow more affectionate with age, but she hadn't.

Matka groaned as she sat then swept crumbs into a pile on the tabletop. "Tell Ida to mop up the table." She scraped at something with her thumbnail.

Mary set her bag down and poured Matka's coffee. "She's gone. Working two houses today."

"She's still in the room. I seen her when I come down."

Mary flinched. That didn't make sense. She started toward the hallway to verify that when the front door swung open; daylight flooded in before a shadow darkened the space again. The door slammed. Lukasz appeared, his eyes carrying a lost, searching look.

Drunk. Mary's heart seized. She put her hand to her temple. What day was it? Was he off already? The men were sharing shifts, three guys to twelve hours.

He pressed his fists onto the table. The scent of whiskey filled Mary's nose. She was careful to keep her expression neutral, not wanting to set him off. He straightened and flung his hat toward the coat rack. It landed on the stove, the flames catching it. Mary dashed over and smacked the hat against her leg, putting out the fire. "What on earth's going on?"

"I quit."

She must have heard wrong. She set the hat aside. "You what?"

"That's right." He poked his finger into the air.

"No."

"I did."

Matka's hands shook as she set down the coffee mug, sloshing liquid onto the table.

"That meat-slob burgess Mr. William Hamilton Watson—no! *Chief* Burgess, the asshole man corrected my foreman. 'Chief,' he said *three* miserable times just to be sure we gave a *gówno*."

Mary couldn't breathe. "Lukasz—" The family couldn't handle another stressor. Lukasz couldn't see that?

"So Chief Burgess and some reporter start in on how we all need to vote Republican because if we don't, then none of us will come back to work. He'll fire us all. Just strolls into the mill, poking around. Spouting off numbers: 270,000 lost manufacturing jobs in Pennsylvania. Only 277 men had jobs in Donora last year. Now about 1,500, he says. And then he starts in on how lucky we are. And since we aren't the lazy ones, but others are, that we owe our votes for the chance to work, to him, to the Republicans, to Hoover. We owe them all."

Mary forced herself to breathe. She squeezed the edge of the table, not sure she wanted to hear the rest, but needing to. Why couldn't Lukasz just let things be? "Who cares what he says? Votes are private."

Lukasz narrowed his eyes on Mary as though she was the one causing him trouble. "He comes right to me and pokes me in the chest. 'Lucky Polish man,' he said. Still the finger in my bone." Lukasz poked himself. "So I stick my finger in his chest. '*Get your finger off my sternum*,' he said, and I couldn't hold it in, Mary. I just started laughing and laughing, and I said, '*I'm* American, and I vote for man I choose.'"

"Oh, Lukasz." She certainly agreed with him, but it was his job at stake. His English tripped over the Polish that still came more naturally especially when drinking. But Mary understood what he meant and was sure the men at the mill had, too.

"So he motions to Mr. Yantz, who comes lickety-split like a starving dog to steak. Next you know he agrees with Chief asshole and says I'm fired."

"Oh Christ," Matka said, guzzling her coffee.

"I tell Yantz he can't fire me for my vote."

"Oh boy."

"So he said he fired me because I'm an asshole."

"Sweet Peter and Paul," Matka said.

"So I said I quit instead. Then Yantz called me stupid. And I give him this finger."

Mary sighed and pushed Lukasz's middle finger down. This couldn't be the end of it. "Will Yantz give it back? When Watson cools off?"

"He tried."

Mary put her fist in the air. "Yes. Thank God."

"No," Lukasz said.

"No what?"

"I say no. I reject."

"Oh my God." Mary collapsed in the chair, her mind flying through her list of things to buy and how she'd shift the money to make up for Lukasz's firing. She could get on the list at the Red Cross for free flour. She'd been asked to clean more hours at the movie theater. The soup kitchens still received food from time to time, but donations were dwindling. Mary's heart raced. Sweat broke out on her brow. She wiped it away with her apron hem.

"So I drank away my heartbreak at Bucket of Blood, weeping in my beer that some man would try to buy my vote in the *United States of America*. The land of the free. And Vincent Tambelinni says I can work in his kitchen."

"Thank God!" Mary crossed herself. She exhaled to her toes.

"Oh sweet Jesus," Matka said. "What luck!"

"No."

"No?" Mary and Matka said simultaneously.

"Alfred Harrison says I may work in his haberdashery sewing hems on extra pants he's taking in."

Matka grinned. "Oh good."

"I don't take it. I reject both."

Mary felt as though she'd just come into the house after running the town end to end three times with a laundry sack in tow. "*Why?*"

Lukasz held his hands up, then rubbed a shoulder. "My pride, *siła*, comes from working with my hands. My strength." He reached around to the small of his back. "I break my spine for family, for mill, for Donora. Double the work in half the time. It is what I am known for. It is what I do. Who I am. I will not fry potatoes or stitch pantaloons like a woman."

Mary was wordless, her energy sapped, disbelieving what Lukasz had revealed. And even as he continued to ramble on, Mary's mind was three miles away, on the south end of town, putting a pin in Labash's Grocery where she would stop first to see if they'd extend her credit for bologna and cheese. She'd heard they'd been kind to anyone who asked. Being far from Marelda and the path Lukasz wore through the north end of town each day, he would have no reason to stop there, to ever know she took credit, that she asked for it. Matka glared into her coffee cup. Lukasz stalked around the kitchen flinging his arms in the air, ranting about freedom and citizenship.

A quiet voice cut into the chaos. "I guess this is as good a time as any to ruin your day. Since it's already ruined." Ida stepped into the room.

All eyes went to her. Lukasz froze.

Mary ticked off a list of things that would cause her to enter the kitchen, tentative, white faced, frightened looking.

"I'm marrying Frank Daniels."

Mary froze, flooded with emotion, with memories, with her own pronouncement when she'd declared to Papa and Matka that she and Lukasz would marry. Her first baby. Her little girl. She eyed the kitchen door, expecting Frank Daniels to arrive and claim his bride, as Lukasz had done. "We'll live in Pittsburgh."

Mary nodded, but was still paralyzed, her emotions flattened. With Lukasz's mood, his drunkenness, what would he say? Mary was ready to leap in between him and Ida if it turned to screaming and yelling in dissent. She would not let her daughter leave feeling as though her family had kicked her out, as Mary had felt nearly two decades before.

But of all surprises Mary got that day, none astounded her more than Lukasz bounding across the kitchen, sweeping Ida into his arms, rocking her tight against him, brushing the back of her hair. *"Moja dziewczynka. Bardzo cię kocham."*

Matka raised her mug. "Well, yinz guys could knock me over with a toothpick with all this news. I might start drinking myself. He's *actually* happy fer his girl."

Mary reached for Matka's free hand. Sadness rose up amidst the bloom of happy feelings. Ida was leaving. Matka was weak and sick. Lukasz never quite seemed to know how to use the advantages that came with American citizenship. But he was happy for his daughter. And that was all Mary could have wished for in that moment. She stood and opened her arms. As Lukasz released his firstborn child, Mary pulled her close. "You will be such a good wife, Ida. That I know like I know the day you were born. Frank Daniels is one lucky man."

Chapter 28

Owen

2019

Owen's teammate Zeke dropped him off at Blue Horizon, where he would meet his mum and they'd have dinner with Gramps and try to get him moved back home now that he seemed to be doing better. Owen was always excited to see Gramps, found himself completely at home with him, secure with him. Yet that day he would have preferred just going to Gramps's house in Donora, climbing the stairs to his room on the second floor, and dropping into a long, deep sleep.

He knocked at Gramps's door.

"Enter at your own risk."

Owen took his hat off and approached Gramps, who was sitting in an overstuffed chair beside the bed, shuffling cards on a small table set in front of him. He studied Owen, squinting. He pulled on his glasses.

"Whatcha blubberin' 'bout?" Gramps said.

Owen looked away. He had been crying, but he'd stopped his tears for the entire drive to Blue Horizon.

"Ya got tear trails cut through the infield dirt on your face. Clear as day."

The backs of Owen's eyes burned. He held his breath and tried to fight away a rising sob.

"Stanley F. Musial used to shed a tear or two over a lost game."

"Really?" Owen squeaked the word out.

"Oh Jesus. Lie down. Tell Gramps all about it."

Owen crumbled onto Gramps's bed.

"So you lost a game. It's the natural cycle of things."

"I lost my arm, my bat."

Gramps set the cards on the countertop and pulled his book onto the table. "I read you all about Stan weeping after a particularly hard loss."

"It's not just that."

"Yer pop?"

"It's always something with him, but no."

"Can't find the plate?"

He shook his head. "They stuck me in center anyhow. Some hotshot from Ohio's coming in to train, and they slotted him in to pitch. I like center. I was off today though."

"All right. One bad day—"

"I lost my girlfriend." Owen couldn't breathe. His throat closed tighter with every breath. Sharp needle-poke pain stabbed his heart. The hurt radiated to the tips of his fingers and toes.

"The girl with the legs?"

"They all have legs, Gramps."

"The girl you showed me on that computer of yours? With the *nice* legs. Long and—"

"*She's* nice. All of her." Owen pulled the pillow over his head. "She dumped me because…"

"'Cause what?"

"'Cause I'm here."

"Well, Christ, then who cares? She ain't the one fer ya."

"But I can't breathe. I can't—"

"If she can't even let ya be for a couple a summer months, how's that gonna allow fer ya to play a full major-league season?"

Owen had to agree with that.

"Still. It hurts. My heart throbs, like a cartoon or something. I can literally feel the outlines of an organ in my body that I can't even see. Now I know how Mum felt when…"

Gramps reached for Owen's hand and squeezed it. "Ya ain't the only ballplayer to experience heartbreak. But yer too young to feel like this. Christ. Better to get this outta the road before ya get down to real business."

A sob squeaked out of Owen, ignoring his attempt to hold it back.

"For the love of… Here. Let's take a look at the book. If I remember correctly, we're about to see when the love of Stan Musial's life waltzes into things. All his friends, Nicky Christmas and Honey and—" Gramps squeezed Owen's hand again. "Enough blubbering. Please now. I can't take it. It's like yer sending the pain right through me. I'm too old to feel like this. Not part of our bargain."

Waves of pain continued rolling through Owen, but he obeyed, letting the emotion work up and out a little quieter.

A knock at the door startled the two. A man entered wearing a doctor's coat.

Gramps looked at the clock, the movement of turning his neck so quickly making him gasp and grab it. "Not time yet."

The man held up his hands. "No, no. I'm interrupting, yes. I'm Dr. Lewis." He met Owen's gaze and drew back, realizing Owen was in a vulnerable spot. He politely turned his attention back to Gramps while Owen wiped his face.

"We met once when they hauled you back after your escape attempt. But… I'm sorry. I overheard you from the hall. You said… *Did* you say the name Nicky Christmas?"

"Sure did." Gramps tapped a page in his book.

"Can't be." Dr. Lewis leaned back against the doorjamb. "Haven't heard that name in years."

"Who's he to ya?" Gramps said.

"If it's my Nicky Christmas, it's my grandfather."

Owen and Gramps drew back.

"Ya don't say. The ballplayer?" Gramps said.

Dr. Lewis eyed the book. Gramps pulled it closer, as though protecting it from a thief.

Owen sat up and smoothed the bedspread. "Would you like to see?"

Dr. Lewis lit up—his bright eyes making him appear more little boy than accomplished physician. Owen studied his face, wondering how much of Nicky Christmas was present in his features. It was as though the book had come to life.

Owen made room for the doctor to sit. Gramps turned the book.

"What *is* this?" Dr. Lewis said.

"My book. 'Bout Donora and my family and friends. I was the town historian for a few years even."

Dr. Lewis pointed. "Stan Musial."

"'Course."

"And the Griffeys—son, grandfather, grandson, right?"

"'Course."

"Well, I'll be." Dr. Lewis set his files and clipboard aside and leaned into the book. "My grandfather died fifteen years back. But his stories… His family left Donora for farmland over in Ohio, but Donora never left him. He talked about Stan as though they were great friends."

"They were."

"But then…"

"Then?" Owen asked.

The doctor sighed. "If my grandpa told it right, Donora was in some ways like every other town dealing with race in the '30s and '40s. But in other ways race didn't matter a lick. The boys played ball together. Most of Donora was mixed racially. His family lived in a clinger right beside—"

"Clinger?" Owen asked.

Gramps laughed. "Yeah, the houses that went up willy-nilly during Donora's founding years. One house clung to the valley wall in this direction, and the house next to it clung, turned half the other direction. Miracle they all held, but they did."

"My grandpa said the schools were mixed. And except for some situations and places, they lived in this incredible bubble. That's what he called it. Grandpa's father couldn't join an ethnic club, but neither could a Pole join the Croatian Club. Or an Italian join the Russian Club. But the boys. They played together as though there wasn't a bit of difference between 'em."

Gramps paged through the book, stopping where a heading said *1936*. "That's exactly right, as I remember it, too."

Owen poked the date at the top of the page. "Was everyone still poor from the depression?"

Gramps grumbled. "Compared to what? Your mum's short every month on account of divorce, but yer waltzing around with a computer in your hand. Yes. Entire middle-class families had less in their whole house than you do now right in your hand. In '36, Donora still had soup kitchens, even though the mills were starting to build for the war, for what the Brits and others needed. But it took a long time before mums weren't sewing dresses from flour sacks and patching hand-me-down trousers. And I'm not sure the Musials ever had much. Their nothin' was less than most."

"But the mills were up again," Owen said.

"They were producing more. Wire for the Golden Gate Bridge. Union organizers sneaking in and getting kicked out by the Chief Burgess." Gramps slapped his hand against his forehead. "Oh yeah. Like when Lukasz got fired for speaking his mind. Oh man, were the higher-ups bent when Roosevelt won in 1932. Whole town lit lanterns and danced down McKean singing 'Happy Days Are Here Again.' Scared the pants off of the powerful folk. And for a while they did their best to keep the unions out. There were some scrapes that year—1936. But unions came, and men finally got pay and benefits worth their toil."

Gramps turned the page.

"Whoa, look at that clipping." Dr. Lewis pointed to a faded, browned article.

A *Herald-American* writer said, *"At an age when a youngster is all legs, he [Musial] is a clever ball handler and good shot. Provided he put on a little weight and height, his name should find its way into the headlines within a year or two."*

"And that's my grandfather with Stan. In the picture."

Owen looked at the blurry photo and back to the doctor. They looked alike. "You have the same smile."

"You think?" Dr. Lewis said, putting his hand to his lips.

Owen nodded.

Gramps pointed at an article about Stan's basketball playing prowess. "Kid could've played college basketball for sure."

Dr. Lewis slid to the edge of the bed and shook his finger. "Now that we're talking about this, I think my grandpa said the summer of '36 was one of the best years of his life, just hanging out with his boys, playing ball. Said he really learned a lot about humanity that summer."

"Really?"

"Yeah. He never really explained it all. But just said Stan was special. I was never a decent athlete, and so the Musial stories—other than the fact that my grandfather proclaimed him one of the kindest souls he ever met, even as a boy—I can't remember everything exactly. I wish I could have that time with him again. Ask more questions."

"Well, settle in, then, Doc. This might fill in some gaps and spark your memory."

And Dr. Lewis did just that.

Chapter 29

Stan

Summer 1936

Summer rushed in hot and fast, but not too fast for Stan and the boys looking to fill their days with baseball and any part-time work they could scrape up. Over a hundred boys gathered at Americo Field that first day of summer break. Eight Donora Junior City League teams were formed. Stan and Honey were on the Heslep All-Stars—named for the street in North Donora where most of the team lived.

After a few days of working the kinks out, a practice game schedule was set up. The first team Heslep would play was the Cement City Cardinals. When Heslep took the field to practice, Stan couldn't help but smile. Their team was nearly the same as it had been the year when Stan was eleven, the day of the infamous home run turned automatic double that Stan had hit. This was going to be a great season. And this time he and Honey would be the best of teammates. If Stan had something to say about it. After Stan had played in older age groups for a few summers, his normal age group caught up. All the older boys he'd been playing with moved on to semi-pro in the mill leagues or gave it up all together.

Stan surveyed his team. They didn't have a formally named captain, but everyone knew he was. He'd learned so much from playing with better, older kids that he thought he could be a natural leader, if not a demanding one. He would simply be a good player and a good person, and that was what would make a difference. Monocle now sported a full set of spectacles and served as a decent utility man, filling in wherever and whenever called upon. Andrew had hung up his bat and donated his beautiful glove to the team after one more year on Honey's team when Stan had gone with the older kids. Still the Weatherman to Stan and the others when they were at games, they even sometimes pulled out the Wild Weatherman name if they needed a particularly strange heckle or for him to sacrifice his body in left field. But generally, with his head in the clouds, he happily committed to keeping score, taking notes on the game, and predicting the weather.

It didn't take long to see the Cardinals would be stiff competition. A new fella named Benjamin Hicks, son of a boss at the blast furnace, strutted around like he'd grown up in Donora all along and had been crowned king on Memorial Day. He wore baseball pants, like high school kids and pros, even for practice, had blond hair that held its neat shape even after removing his cap; he had clean hands and bright blue eyes that all the girls who'd been hanging around couldn't shut up about. He was the kind of guy Pop and Matka were always complaining about at the wireworks. Tall and thick for a fifteen-year-old, Benjamin possessed man-sized confidence that came with being born into a family with everything. He sneered at Stan, which caused his shoulders to slump for a second. Nervous that he was out of his league with this guy, Stan's hands shook and butterflies spun around his belly.

What the hell? Stan adjusted his hat. He'd just played three summers with older boys, and though Pop didn't have what Benjamin's pop did, this wasn't an office in the wireworks, and

Benjamin was not Stan's boss. So Stan picked up a bat, swung it a couple of times, and approached Benjamin, who'd just finished reading the lineup to his team.

Stan spun the bat in his hands. "I'm Stan."

Benjamin smirked. "I know you. Throw some heat and hit like you've got a magic bat."

Stan smiled. "Well. We share bats and gloves, and we're short on balls, so anything we can find for a game…"

"Sorry state of affairs," Benjamin said, leaning on his new Louisville Slugger, one foot crossed over the other ankle. Stan could easily envision how this kid won the state debate championship with his old school, his fancy airs accompanying him wherever he went. Well. This was a baseball field, not a debate stage.

Stan walked back to the Heslep bench.

"You're cleanup," Weatherman said.

Stan nodded.

"Deep breaths, Stushy."

He turned.

"Benjamin Hicks is a jackass. Kids like him need your oxygen to get fired up. Don't give it to him."

"How do ya know he's a jackass?"

"My dad knows his dad from back in Braddock… and we went to a dinner soiree at his little abode the other night."

Stan lifted his eyebrows.

"We toured their renovated home on Prospect—four bathrooms, *two* ovens *inside*. I mean, since when do people give a tour of their kitchen? And the trophies. Debate, baseball, football, father-son golf tournaments, on and on. They had a five-piece band set up in their foyer. Playing all the stuff we hear at the dances. Even my favorite, 'Did I Remember?' You know that one by Shep Fields?"

"Oh, yeah, good song. But dancing at their dinner party? Their house?"

Andrew nodded.

"Girls?"

"They weren't my type."

Stan squinted.

"Too good lookin.' I need someone who likes books more than hair curlers. To find both in a woman would be great, but… I know my limitations."

Stan rubbed his forehead, more agitated.

"Anyway, then we had shrimp cocktail, crab hoetzel, steak— "

Heat climbed up Stan's neck, making him sweat, a drip curling into his ear. "Andrew." He stuck his hand out. "Why're you telling me all this?"

"'Cause Benjamin's got all that stuff. That opportunity. And it gives him this swaggering John Wayne kinda I-might-decide-to-be-a-cowboy-or-a-physicist-or-president, for land sakes—"

Stan's nerves vibrated. "Shit, Weatherman—how's this helpful?"

Weatherman finally met Stan's gaze. "He's got all that. But he's nothing like you on the field or in here." Weatherman put his thumb against his chest. "He doesn't have heart because he hasn't needed it. And it's too late for him to develop it. No dirt under those nails, no heart in that chest, no magic touch. Get him out of your head. He's no better than Monocle against you."

Stan exhaled and nodded. Weatherman was right. This Benjamin was no different than the rest of the guys on the field. And so with Heslep the home team, Stan took the pitcher's mound. Tank was now their catcher. Honey played center or pitched when Stan had off days. Melonhead still took first. Nicky was the fastest shortstop on both sides of the Mon. Cheeks took third, still heckled as a Polish donut despite growing right out of his chunky childhood physique, appearing more cinnamon stick than *paczki*. Smokestack and Buddy Griffey took turns at right and second, and Yellow Melvin's hobbled liver left him too weak to play anymore. So Moonshine and Skunk rotated around as needed. Blue Louise had graduated to daintier hobbies but threw batting practice in a pinch.

Stan held his glove to his chest, shook his head, and wiggled his shoulders, trying to concentrate. Benjamin was leadoff, sauntering up to the plate like *Baseball Magazine* had named him the next Babe Ruth. Stan wound up and let his fastball fly. It rose out of the strike zone, making Tank shoot up to catch the ball flying over his head, but he missed it, the ball finally stopping with a *thunk* against scrap wood they'd nailed together to create a backstop.

Benjamin stepped out of the batter's box and threw his head back, laughing, satisfied he hadn't swung at the high wild pitch. "Winter's been rough on ya, Stushy? Maybe basketball's your game. Saw lots of articles about you in some scrapbook up at the school."

Tank whipped the ball back to Stan with a scowl. He pushed his hands down, indicating Stan should take it easy. He squatted and gave Stan the sign for his wicked slowball. Stan chomped on his gum, strangling the ball, three fingers over the seam and thumb below. He spun the ball in his mitt, getting just the right grip. He wanted to throw another fastball, thinking Tank was wrong, that Benjamin would be expecting his slow pitch, that even if it started out looking like his fastball, Benjamin would ignore that and wait for the ball to slow and come in with its slight break. This Benjamin wouldn't be fooled like others.

Stan exhaled, regripping, splitting two fingers for his fastball, then pulling them closer together, trying to find the right feel to better control his ball. He stepped off the mound and paced.

"Aw, come on," someone yelled from the stands. "It's a practice game. Can we get a little practice in?"

"Waiting for the servants to bring afternoon tea, Musial?" Benjamin got set in his stance, smiling as if he could read Stan's mind. This caused Stan's heart to race, and he gripped the ball so tight his fingers went numb.

Frustrated, he lost track of what he did best—let his body lead.

"Hey ya, hey ya, Stushy, serve it up, why don't ya," Benjamin said, his grin ever widening. Jackass was exactly right.

Stan remembered the last pitch he'd thrown the year before. The batter had known the slow ball was coming, and he'd sent it into the Mon, cackling as he rounded the bases, fist in the air. This kid didn't know Stan's tendencies. Yet.

Stan drew another deep breath. Who was he kidding? Benjamin even knew Stan's basketball background. No way was he going to give him what he expected, so he sent his fastball flying.

Stan's eye registered the ball coming back at him just in time to duck, the ball screaming right past his head. With a mouthful of dirt, he got to his knees to see the ball lift just enough to clear Honey's head in center, soaring right over the fence.

"Plop!" a fan screamed. "Right into the Mon."

Stan leapt to his feet. Humiliation stabbed, shocking him. He couldn't remember feeling like this when it came to a sport—ever. His eyes burned with dust and tears he was trying to hold back. Benjamin trotted toward first base, giving Melonhead a little bow topped off with his screen-actor smile. He rounded second and passed through Stan's sightline before his gaze retraced the path the ball had taken.

"Like that clothesline I hung up there, Stushy?" Benjamin said. "You can use it later if you can reach it."

Stan kicked the dirt, angry for not listening to Tank. Stan paced toward first and tripped over his feet. Melonhead gave Stan the same "calm down" gesture that Tank had.

"Mama could hang six days' laundry on that one," Benjamin said as he took the straightaway to third. "Maybe Cinderella's night at the ball's finally over."

Stan paced back to the mound, hands on hips. He wouldn't respond, but he felt the taunts like a branding iron. "Dammit. Shit, dammit."

Tank joined him. "What's wrong with you?"

Honey had rescued the ball from over the fence and ran it back, shoving it into Stan's glove. "Sorry 'bout that, Stushy. Shoulda had it."

Stan kicked at the mound, releasing dirt clouds, making his teammates cough. "Nah. Never should have…" Stan's words caught in his throat—something that normally only happened in school or around adults. He exhaled. "Shouldn't have made it anywhere near you, Honey. And sorry, Tank. Thought I had 'im."

"You're taking me for granted, Stushy Musial. Don't do that," Tank said, sauntering back to the plate.

Stan struggled through most of the inning, finally getting the last few in the lineup out easily, as they weren't savvy like Benjamin or the others up early. Any hits the bottom of the lineup got were easily dealt with by Nicky, Cheeks, and Melonhead.

Stan hit cleanup that day, struggling with hitting as well. He'd heard Rosey Rowswell on his broadcast going on and on about the Pirates' Gus Suhr and how he seemed to be hitting strangely in spring training—too hunched over. Rowswell raved about how Suhr fixed his stance and his average shot up. Stan focused on not stooping, straightening his back to the point that he was losing sight of the ball. Added to that, he fell for every bit of bait that Benjamin slid on his fishing hook. Stan followed Benjamin's motion from his set to his release. But all it did was dismantle whatever hitting prowess Stan used to have. *Cinderella.* That may have been the most accurate statement of all that day.

Second-guessing the fastballs and sinkers, Stan practically golfed a ball to Murphy, the second baseman. With every decision he made, he grew more tense, nipping the top of the ball with the end of the bat, grounding out with bleeders and bloopers he hadn't hit since he was eight years old. He held the bat tighter, choking up, every pitch bringing a worse result.

When the game ended, practice or not, Stan was mortified in a way he'd never been in his life. He stalked home, separating from the group, not accepting their encouraging words, confused as to how he had finished junior high playing basketball and baseball with high school kids, and now this?

He couldn't begin to process his performance, but it laid heavy inside him, like soot that clung and settled into pitted brick. He worried he wouldn't be able to scrub this failure off his skin.

Stan reached Marelda Street and took the hill, his appetite gone, even though he'd yet to have lunch. As he neared his home, he saw the outline of Joe Barbao and his brother near Thirteenth Street, throwing catch.

"Stan!" Joe said. "Come here." Joe's brother disappeared down Thirteenth as Stan caught up.

Stan wanted to bury himself in the coal cave in the backyard, shaken not only by his terrible performance, but by his inability to mentally remedy any part of his poor play.

Joe headed down the street toward Stan, and so he couldn't avoid him. "Hey, hey, bad game today?"

Stan drew back, his neck and face flooding with heat.

Joe jerked his head toward the hill and Stan followed him to the woodsy crest where the two normally sat, looking over town, talking everything baseball. There was no avoiding this conversation even though the last person Stan wanted to disappoint was Joe.

They sat on the ever-thinning grass, the zinc smoke causing the hillside to go patchy like a middle-aged man's balding head. They plucked stones from between blades of grass and chucked them into the hollow. The zinc works belched its smoky funk, most of the particles blowing over the Monongahela, settling on the Webster side of the river. Still, enough of the exhalation blanketed the Donora side to hamper vegetation growth near that mill, so bad this year that Grandma's tomatoes were barely plumping past walnut size. And when a storm was brewing, the wind blew all the waste back up the hill to Marelda. It was the one weather pattern that everyone, not just Andrew, recognized.

Joe lit his pipe. "Give it to me. What happened? Caught a little bit of the game after my shift."

Stan plucked grass and blew it off his hand like people did when wishing on a fallen eyelash. He hadn't even noticed Joe at the field.

Joe pulled his knees up and rested his wrists on them, the pipe tobacco glowing. "Listen, Stan. I've never seen a talent like you. No one like you. I've seen power hitters who launch a pea over a fence every stinkin' time at bat. And wailing fastballer launchers and fellas who can come up with the most unbelievable groundballs. But you, you can do all of it and better than any of them guys."

Stan didn't feel deserving of such praise but for the first time in his life, Joe's words felt heavy, weighed down by a twin current that actually undercut the compliment.

Joe dragged on his cigarette, then pointed it at Stan. "You want to make a career of this game, you're gonna have to start to critique your own play. Have to start measuring and recording, *noticing*, concentrating. Like Andrew and his weather book and bag of science experiments. You're gonna meet up with better and better players now."

Stan felt attacked. His throat tightened, and tears threatened to fall. The one person he'd come to depend on to encourage his dream of pro baseball was clearly unimpressed with his play.

"Rusty as hell a-a-after winter, suppose." Stan hated hearing the excuses, repeating what Benjamin had suggested. Reaching for words to describe his bad play was foreign, unsettling. Stammering in the presence of Joe was a first.

Joe pulled the baseball out of his glove and held it up. "You haven't had your growth spurt. Benjamin Hicks's a man out there right now. But he's done growing, Stan. His talent right now is his peak. And today he outshined you in every phase of the game. And that shit-eatin' grin of his… He enjoyed it, and I wanted to smack him. I mean, kid'll run the mill someday—probably be my shittin' boss for the love of…" Joe shifted, looking directly at Stan. "Right now he thinks he's gonna round the bases through the pros 'fore he takes his spot down the hill. But you see that grizzle on his chin? He's done growing. You'll see. You. It's all still developing."

Stan thought of his pop's height. Stan was already as tall as him. And though Mom was nearly six feet tall, Stan wasn't so sure he'd be lucky enough to get her height. Maybe Joe was wrong. Maybe it was him who was done growing. Maybe Stan had peaked the year before.

Joe set his pipe beside him and held up the ball. "Never seen you pacing and… My God, you trip over words, but never your feet. Ever." Joe nudged Stan's shoulder playfully. "I only tease you because your talent's so big I finally found some fault with your play. All at once, all in one game. Be open to it. Never be too big to listen, to laugh at yourself. But be careful who you listen to."

"You?"

"Always me. I see the best in you. But I see what's wrong, too."

Stan looked at Joe, his sincerity expanding inside Stan.

"I've tripped over my own feet, too. Maybe after a beer or two, but happens to everyone. Now you know you're human."

Stan nodded, surprised he didn't feel stung by Joe's observations, that Joe had spoken them aloud. He trusted him more than anyone besides Mom and Andrew.

"Show me your fastball grip." Joe had spent years working with Stan and his pitching.

Stan held the ball as though he were going to pitch and then showed Joe.

"Okay. The rest of you might not have grown yet, but your fingers are longer. You've lost your placement." Joe took the ball and split his fore and middle fingers over the seams, the horseshoe seam against his ring finger. "Look. Thumb's at the center of the horseshoe. You need to be sure you, well, don't strangle it. You need a gap between the ball and your hand."

Stan held the ball and memorized the feel of the placement.

Joe put his hands on his knees. "Now. Show me your off-speed."

Stan held up the ball, his claw grip exactly what Joe had helped him with a couple years back.

Joe shook his head. "Nope. You've slid the ball a little…" He turned Stan's hand and wiggled the ball so that it wasn't jammed back in his palm. "Loosen up. Just tight enough that you don't drop the thing."

Stan released and gripped the ball again.

Joe studied Stan then held one hand, palm up. "Think of those Czech Easter eggs your mom makes with the food dye and vegetable oil? Kate goes nuts for them—can't make them to save her life, but don't tell her I said that. But those eggs your mom gives us every Easter? Well. Would you jam those beautiful, fragile eggs into the back of your hand like you've got that ball wedged in there? Squeeze like that?"

Stan chuckled. "I'd catch hell if I did."

"For good reason. Same deal with your grip. Think of the ball as delicate." Joe slid Stan's forefinger down the side of the ball a little. "There you go. Just walk around town like that, cradling it like those eggs and you'll be fine. Then let it rip."

Stan stood, remembering Lefty Grove and his egg throwing. He couldn't believe it. He and Joe'd thrown together a million times. Taught once as a youngster, he could do this without thinking, his body somehow always knowing the exact right way to throw, to hit, to do anything related to sports.

Joe hopped up and backed away with his glove, gesturing for Stan to pitch. They threw fifty-one pitches, and Joe waved Stan to come closer.

"Way better there. Wild pitching will only go so far."

"Now. Hitting." Joe plugged his glove against his hip. "What in the blessed hell was that you were doing today? I felt like I was watching Monocle circa 1932."

Stan smiled and looked down. Joe was teasing, but still, Stan wasn't accustomed to not building on what Joe already saw as talent.

"Listen, I could tell you what went wrong. But I want you to tell *me* what went wrong."

"Well, first hit, I was…" Stan couldn't even find the words. He shrugged. He never had to figure out what had gone wrong on the baseball field. He had no idea how to capture what he'd done in words.

Joe squeezed his shoulder to steady him. "Close your eyes. Replay it."

Stan exhaled, recalling everything from the first at bat. "I dunno. I got into my stance and swung like always."

Stan opened his eyes, and Joe shook his head.

"No. Not like always. You got into a stance all right, but it wasn't yours. What the hell was that? You looked like a starched shirt on a hanger."

Stan rubbed his temples.

"Show me. Batter's box is there. Walk up, replay it."

Stan did.

"Freeze," Joe said. Stan followed his order. Joe latched his hands around Stan's. "Feel that. Game's over, and just the memory has you strangling like you're catching up a chicken by the neck for dinner."

Stan grimaced.

"Loosen up. Why'd you start doing this? Standing straight, your feet far apart, up on the plate. What the hell is that?"

"Heard Rowswell saying Suhr's stooped over and read an article in *Baseball News* and—"

Joe shook his head and cut Stan off. "Cut that shit out. Feel that? Your grip? Never saw you hold a bat like that before. Golden boy Benjamin got in your head that bad?"

Stan slouched. "He did."

Joe gripped both of Stan's shoulders. "You're not perfect, but what you do naturally, it works. But…" He shook Stan. "There. Tight as braided wire. That's what I've never seen you do before."

"What?"

Joe adjusted his baseball cap. He paced. "First it was whatever little tune-up you did on your mechanics, but it was more than that. Watching you play, I couldn't figure it out. You've been tumbling around with the Falcons and playing basketball forever. You're smooth and easy in every movement. For the love of Moses, you can hit bottle caps with a broomstick into tire holes a hundred feet away."

Stan nodded. That was certainly true until today.

"Your whole life you've managed to concentrate and relax all at the same time. Today? You were agitated on the mound, at the plate. Hell, I think I saw you checking out the girls coming across the railroad tracks halfway through the seventh inning."

Stan chuckled. "They were cute."

"See? You were."

Stan waved Joe off. "What if I can't fix it now that I've messed around with everything?"

"There's nothing to fix, Stan. You just need to let your body settle into its relaxed stance. Like stretched out coiled wire. Just let it spring back to where it easily goes. Notice when you feel like you're getting behind or upset. This, everything baseball, is your gift. Don't ever forget it, and you can do anything."

Joe had Stan take some swings. Stan took deep breaths and let his body settle into its normal movements.

"That's it." Joe punched the inside of his glove. "That's the strange-ass, peek-around-the-corner stance of yours. Don't ever let anyone mess with it. Long as you live."

Stan smiled.

Joe put his arm around Stan. "Now come up to the house for some dinner. Shot six rabbits this morning up on the ridge near the cemetery. Kate's got the meat marinating, potatoes roasting, orange cake with vanilla frosting. And little Joe wants to throw with you."

Stan's eyes widened. Joe's energy could not be contained by anything, it seemed. "And tell me you'll be my batboy this year."

Stan thought for a moment, all that he had to do—all that Honey and the girls did to add money to the coffers. Honey had already gotten a job delivering groceries. The girls cleaned offices or homes. Batboy would take up any time Stan might have for paying work. Pop would kill him. Pop didn't love Joe the way Stan, Honey, and Mom did. For some reason, he seemed to overlook that Joe didn't just play and coach baseball, that he also worked the hottest shifts in town at the zinc mill. Stan had to be careful how much he mentioned Joe, how much Pop was aware of the time the two spent together. This—what he had with Joe—his father could have shared in it. But he didn't want to.

"Might even be able to sneak you into some games a few innings this summer."

How could he decline the chance? Stan's eyes went wide.

Joe tossed the ball into the air, catching it while walking backward uphill. "Yeah. You're that good, Stanley Musial. You could easily play with men on my team twice your age. And you know that. I've told you that before. You understand that, right?"

Stan nodded.

"Don't let me see you forget it ever again."

Chapter 30

Stan

"Stormy evening, Stan." Honey caught Stan coming into the boot-room at dinnertime.

Stan set his glove behind the winter coats. Guilt at having enjoyed a meal at the Barbaos' engulphed him. He'd been careful not to eat too much of Kate's baked rabbit. Mom had made bread that day, and he wanted room for it—ten loaves, and it wouldn't stay around long. He had to leave enough hunger to get the cabbage stew down, too.

"Thunderstorm?" Stan said.

"Quiet cyclone." Honey shrugged.

"We don't get cyclones. Andrew said—"

"Yet here we are with a cyclone."

Stan inventoried his chores—he'd dug the coal that morning, taken the laundry baskets to the cellar. He eyed the stove. The beans and stew were cooking, but he had missed being the one getting them going. Mom might be mad about that, not Pop.

Mom turned from the stove, cradling her serving spoon over an open palm. "Really? Doesn't feel like storms."

Stan glanced at his feet, searching for a way to conceal a topic that would upset Mom. "Well. Maybe. Can I take something to the table for you?"

"Bread," Mom said, finishing at the stove.

Stan cut two loaves and added the slices into the basket.

"Find work yet?" Helen asked, pulling utensils from the drawer. "Heard Mitchel's Hardware's got openings."

Stan unfurled a napkin and laid it over the bread the way Mom liked it.

Pop stepped into the kitchen, one hand on the doorjamb as he rubbed the hollow between his shoulder and chest with the butt of his palm. "Saw Stashu heading into Barbao's. Maybe he doesn't need a job."

Honey's head snapped toward Stan.

Mom handed Stan a bowl of soup. "For Pop," she said.

Stan's hands quivered, hot liquid sloshing over his thumb.

"Don't waste food, Stashu," Pop said. "Maybe you don't care. You feast already? Cabbage no good for you?"

Stan looked down and shook his head. "No. Starving."

He edged past Pop.

"*Obrzydliwy* cabbage," Pop snarled as Stan entered the dining room, stuck again with the last open seat, right next to his father.

Rose put stew at Stan's seat while he retrieved the bread and placed it in the middle. Everyone seated, Mom said grace. Stan crossed himself and opened his eyes. Pop was frowning at him. Stan forced a smile and turned to his soup.

"You look for job?"

Stan's throat closed. He didn't want to lie, but he didn't want to serve as the weather front colliding with Pop's quiet cyclone. Though his father had been hired back on at the wireworks, he continued to harden. Instead of flexible resilience, like the wire he bundled, he was growing brittle, like pig iron before it was transformed to steel.

Stan had no idea if Honey or the girls had seen him with Joe, sitting on the hillside shooting the shit after the game. Caught in a lie after being seen entering the Barbao home would bring more trouble. Not what he wanted. Why did Pop have to be so angry all the time? Why couldn't he be like Joe?

"What'd you say?"

Stan's breath froze in his chest. Had he spoken aloud? He shook his head, his stomach filling with acid.

"You play games like ten-year-old. You're fifteen. If one hundred percent production was open, I'd make you work there now. Like your mother did. You know that, Stan? Your sisters work and…"

Pop's tirade went on, his half-English, half-Polish words belting the room, constricting Stan's lungs with an invisible clasp. Ida had left first chance she got. The others would leave soon, too.

Everyone except Mom.

Stan raised his eyes to see her watching Pop. Brow furrowed and eyes turned down, she looked like a different person, pleading silently with Pop to stop, sad like she was mourning a death somehow. Soon her jaw clenched, her fist clamped around her spoon, and Stan thought she looked like she might beat her husband with it. He hated that Pop made Mom look like that. She worked three jobs to his one and sometimes his none, blaming his hand and lungs and stomach.

Pop latched his giant claw around Stan's arm and shook him. "Answer me."

"I went a-a-after the game." Stan stopped wanting to smooth his words before speaking them.

"He tried the gas station, Pop," Honey broke into the conversation.

"Gas station?" Pop glanced at Honey, then stared back at Stan. "That true?"

Stan prayed the lie would be hidden away, unexamined. He nodded. Pop released him.

Honey clinked his spoon against the side of his bowl. "Mr. Dehaven said Uncle Frank spoke to him and Stan could work in between games."

Mom relaxed, sighing with her whole body. "Ida's husband? Because of the car connection?"

"Yeah. His car lot and…" Stan said, not knowing the exact connection that carried a job with it. He pulled a piece of bread to bits before eating it. He eyed Honey and gave him a little smile.

"I'm sure old Mr. DeHaven'll love to have you manning the pump when you can."

Stan was confused.

Honey shook his head. "What? You don't know that you're a draw of sorts around here. That's funny, Stan. Funny. Pretending you don't know all eyes are on you."

Stan didn't quite know what to make of Honey's tone.

Pop shoved more bread into his mouth, tension released in his neck, and it felt as though a pressure valve had been turned. Relief. Stan breathed full and deep, but the anger at his father remained. Why did Pop make them feel that way? What had they done to make him so hard?

Mom passed the soup tureen to Honey. "Keep some for Matka. Her belly's acting up, and I'm going to take hers upstairs when we're done."

Conversation began to flow. When the girls reported on the day's work and the gossip around town, Honey leaned into Stan.

"Give me center stage in your prayers tonight. I earned it."

Stan pushed his bread toward his brother. He'd earned that, too.

"It was rabbit tonight. You wouldn't have liked it anyhow," Stan said.

Honey just grinned and shook his head. Stan's brother didn't stammer. Honey didn't worry. Honey didn't feel a bit of the pressure that Stan did at school or when Pop was around, or any other adult. The only thing that seemed to upset Honey was Stan. Yet he'd saved him that night. And Stan was grateful. So later, he stitched Honey's name into his prayers extra tight, same as he sewed a worn baseball shut. But he left Pop's name out. Just that one time. Another act of rebellion. One—his admiration for Joe. Two—secret meals at friends' houses. Three—he'd been asked to be the Zincs' batboy, and he would have very little time to work. The only one no one would ever find out about was omitting Pop from his prayers. No one except God. And for that he'd beg forgiveness in confession, then fill the air to the rafters with Hail Marys and Our Fathers as penance.

Chapter 31

Stan

Stan and the team had splintered in a dozen directions when the skies split open. Almost home, Stan heard his name being called from farther up Marelda. Andrew. Stan jogged toward him as a sliver of sunshine slipped through the clouds and smoke, falling over his friend. When Stan reached him, they squinted into the shoot of light.

"That's weird." Andrew dug into his backpack.

Stan shielded his eyes, scanning the sky for signs of sunshine in other parts. "How was the dentist?"

Andrew spread his lips to show his gleaming teeth. "All's well and ready for practice later."

Stan pulled his glove out from under his T-shirt. The half that had been against his belly was dry.

"Buckets of rain," Andrew said, looking at the glove as Stan turned it back and forth. "Vats."

"Dumped a ton, then stopped. But by then we'd all scattered. Guess we'll practice at the top lot later."

Andrew's mother stuck her head out the door. "Lunch, Andrew. Oh, Stanley. Come on in. I've set some sandwiches up on the observation deck. Have you seen it? Andrew and his father have done a fine job finishing it."

Stan slowly shook his head. That must have been the project Andrew mentioned earlier that month. "Observation deck?"

Andrew slung his bag over his shoulder and waved Stan along to follow. "It's more of a perch. *Observation deck* makes it sound a lot more grand than it is."

Stan followed Andrew up three floors to their attic. They made their way toward the daylight on the back side. The large space was lined with neat trunks and boxes, a clear aisle leading toward a door cut into what Stan assumed was originally a window.

When Andrew flung the door open, Stan stepped through, feeling like he was entering another world, one drawn into a storybook. He gasped. The view, though muddled by swirling smoke and heavy clouds, was, in its own gritty way, spectacular. The sun-shoot that had fallen over Andrew outside, on the other side of the house, was nowhere to be seen over the river, but the sheer spaciousness of having a deck overlooking McKean and Meldon Avenues, the zinc works, and the Monongahela *felt* extravagant. Across the river in Webster the white zinc smoke was draped like cotton batting strewn over a tabletop.

Stan removed his hat. "Wow."

Andrew pulled a black-handled case out of the attic, flipped open several latches, and pointed. "Telescope."

Stan's eyes went wide. "The good one?" Andrew had had other telescopes over the years.

"Yep. Can you believe it? Dad got it on loan from Carnegie Tech."

"Well, set it up," Stan said.

"This one has to be put inside every night." Andrew wiped a finger along the railing that enclosed the deck. "The old man and I finished this banister two days ago. Look." He held his finger up—thick yellow soot. "Can't risk that on the lens or dials. Not a good one like this. Hopefully I'll have one like it to take to college. I'm saving."

Stan eyed the food Mrs. Morrison had set up. Shuffling in the attic drew their attention. She appeared with a pitcher of lemonade and another tray. Andrew and Stan relieved her of her load and she laid striped cloth napkins on the small table. "Eat, eat."

"Thank you, Mrs. Morrison. I shouldn't."

"Of course you should. Sit, enjoy this beautiful view."

"Thank you so much," Stan said. His mouth watered at the array of sandwiches. Her roast beef was Stan's favorite, left over, even cold with cheddar cheese. He made himself eat the ham first, savoring each bite while Andrew gobbled his up.

"College," Stan said. "Three years away. Bet they'd make you line boss in two days if you hired into the wire mill. Half the managers learned on the job, not in college. The engineers, too."

Andrew chuckled and stuffed the last of a ham sandwich into his mouth. "You know me better than that, Stan. And it's possible I could go early if I score well enough on exams."

Stan nodded. "Head's in the clouds, going to MIT or Harvard for engineering or biology or weather—is there weather studies at MIT? Anywhere? Do folks really study that? No matter what you do, you'll take it with a helping of the stars and moons, I know."

"You could go to college, Stan."

Stan let the meaty juices and his saliva combine in his mouth before swallowing his bite. Andrew was always generous with his compliments even for the things that Stan wasn't yet good at. "I'm lucky Pop's letting me finish high school. And woodshop's my thing. You know that. I don't even have the right classes—"

"That *is* a great bat you made at the end of the year. And those balusters you carved for Mr. Humphries's house… so intricate."

Stan nodded. He was proud of the woodwork for his teacher's renovated staircase. But he was most pleased thinking he'd found just the right circumference on the baseball bat he'd made. Stan looked at his hands. "Pop was really good with his hands before he got injured in the mill. Now his fingers hurt to do small things. Still works in shipping at the wireworks, but Mom said he used to make her presents. An angel. Some rings. Can't quite imagine it."

"Love'll do that," Andrew said.

"Suppose I have yet to see."

"Mr. Duda said you could play basketball at Pitt. I could name six schools you could go to for basketball or—"

"Baseball, Andrew." His voice was tight, irritated that Andrew would attempt to steer Stan from his true love.

"I know. You have stars in your eyes, too. Baseballs launching into outer space."

Stan sipped lemonade, feeling an odd discomfort in his belly. "You don't think I can play pro ball."

Andrew popped a potato chip into his mouth. "Oh, I *know* you can. But then what? Can't play forever. No one plays forever. Five years, maybe. Lefty Grove's an exception. Babe Ruth, all of those fellas raking it in, are exceptions, not the rule."

Stan was unsettled by Andrew's thinking. "I don't need what's after that. I just need the chance. *I'm* one of the guys who'll play forever. I know that deep inside. Just like you and your weather observations. Just like you know what's coming based on what's come before. My God, you said you wanted to someday go to the moon. As if that's possible. Yet you think someday people will be bouncing around on the moon. No one thinks it's important or possible, but you do."

Andrew pointed a carrot stick at Stan. "True."

"And I know, God, I know, Pop's reminded me a million times how much time I waste on a game, but it's the only thing I can imagine doing. And as much as you give me credit for having a bigger brain than I do, and I'm forever grateful that you think that, I know what I'm good at. And though I've been in a slump the last two games, I am a baseball player, like Lefty Grove and— "

"I know, like Pie Traynor, too."

"If I don't play baseball, I don't know how I'll live."

Andrew sat back in his chair, fingers woven behind his head. "So we'll both leave Donora."

Stan felt the unstated words. The fear that once people left they lost touch with their home, with their friends. "I'll play for the Pirates. That's just up the road."

Andrew shrugged. "Gotta go with the team that takes you. Even if it means going all the way to Boston or St. Louis."

Stan knew that. But he was confident if the Pirates had a look at him, that would be his home.

Andrew shifted in his seat and pulled out his notebook. "I've been thinking."

"Always," Stan said.

Andrew paged through his book and stopped. "We could go to Mars and still not really leave Donora behind."

Stan ate a potato chip, unsure what Andrew meant.

"See that." He pointed at the townscape he'd drawn. The horseshoe-shaped Monongahela River squeezing the land nearly to an island, the mills drawn in, McKean, Meldon, and Marelda, where the two sat on the observation deck. "See the red dust I drew on these houses in south Donora by the blast furnaces, and the black in the middle of town, and yellowish white over here by the zinc mill?"

"Live it every day."

"Well, I figure all this metallic dust'll mark us for life. We inhale it, it lands on our skin and everything we own, and no matter how we scrub at it and try to keep it off, it comes back. It's part of us. You know our skin is the largest organ on our bodies. It absorbs everything. So I figure if the two of us go our separate ways, we'll still be connected. I'll be sitting in some fresh classroom, professor filling a blackboard with formulas and impossible things, windows open, cool fall gusts rustling through Massachusetts oak trees, peeling away their colored leaves, and someone'll walk by me and take a swipe at dirt on my arm, and it'll be this grime, probably the yellow zinc debris that seeps out of my skin and just won't wipe off. And they'll be confused as to what it is and why I'll probably stare at it and let it sit there, marking me. And I won't care because I don't want to leave completely. I'm actually glad I won't be able to leave the place behind fully. And you won't be able to either."

Stan thought about what his friend was saying. His eyes burned. He could blame the gathering tears on the sulfurous yellow dust if he wanted to. He couldn't quite imagine being so far from home that people might not recognize different types of mill dirt.

"Heck, if a surgeon sliced us open, they'd find rings of smoke in three colors, with more of each color depending on which mill we lived closer to."

"Like rings inside a tree," Stan said.

"Just like that."

Stan finished his sandwich and wiped his hands together to remove crumbs. He was comforted by Andrew's thoughts, as though him speaking them had revealed Stan's own thoughts and feelings for him. That someone like Andrew would hold Donora and Stan close for the rest of his life, made him know he'd do the same.

"This deck is amazing, Andrew." And he scanned the space again, the scrap wood and mismatched shingles, yet it felt like a palace. "I can't even imagine what your observation deck will look like when you're all grown up."

"Well, I gotta wipe it down before we go to practice," Andrew said.

"I'll help."

And so they took the rags sitting inside the doorway and wiped the banisters and tables down, not put off by the idea it would have to be done again the next day. It was just the way it was. It was just who they were—a couple of fellas from Donora.

Chapter 32

Stan

Stan and his band of Heslep All-Stars gathered at the *rovinatý pozemok,* or flat land, to attempt to practice. This space up on the old Heslep mine property was where they went when they didn't have access to a "real" field. Since the mothers of Donora forbade younger kids from playing up there on account of little Mac Maroz disappearing into a coal-barren sinkhole, it was mostly older kids from the north end of Donora who hung out there. With an eight-team league made of neighborhoods in Donora taking turns with the other fields, Stan and his friends were going to have to make use of the space they hadn't frequented until then.

Sitting high on the hills, the surface was raggedy, like a kid growing his first beard, sprigs of growth springing up every few inches or so, leaving lots of stony bare space. Aside from its mostly flat surface, there was a sloping left field, which made it difficult for the best fielder to properly work that area. This space commandeered by the kids was so unappealing to whoever owned it that it remained a field they played every sport on, including tennis. This flat land was where Stan worked to perfect hitting to left field as a left-hander.

Stan got into his stance, alternating between a broomstick and a piece of pipe, swinging as Buddy Griffey tossed bottle caps and Smokestack tossed pebbles for Stan to hit toward left and center fields. Cheeks, Skunk, and Moonshine stood in the field five feet apart, closer and farther from home plate so Stan could practice his touch. Soon Honey arrived with Stan's handmade bat after using it in a game he played with some younger kids that morning.

"Too light, too long," Honey said, handing it over. "Handle's too thin. And just put some of Hazel Youngblood's pine tar on it rather than mess with making grooves. Some deeper than others and—"

"Perfect for me."

"'Course. You made it. The magic bat."

It did feel like an extension of Stan's body. Feeling good, Stan took swings, snapping his wrists, stretching them, strengthening them. Finally he exhaled and wiggled his bottom, relaxing into his trusty, spiraled stance, the repeated clinking and pinging contact making music to his ears. He started humming Benny Goodman's "Goody Goody" and the rest of the gang came in humming too, breaking into dance.

Clap, clap, clap.

Stan turned. Benjamin and his merry gang of Cement City Cardinals mocked the Heslep All-Stars from the path that led to the hidden field.

A wave of self-consciousness worked through Stan, remnants of their practice game remaining. Stan ran Joe's encouragement, Andrew's too, through his mind. Whatever had gone wrong at that first game, he wouldn't allow it to happen again. Unlike when faced with teachers or math problems or handwriting drills, instead of Stan becoming more shaken, he felt something in his core solidify. Almost like God himself settled his nerves, he remembered who he was and his purpose in life. He would erase that game from his mind.

"Must be lost," Stan said. "You fellas all the way up here on this scruffy field. Cement City closed for repairs or something?"

The rest of the All-Stars slid closer to Stan, the Cardinals inching forward, too.

Benjamin smirked and crossed his arms.

"Benji here hit all our balls into the river," Hound said.

Stan smiled. "Did ya now? Isn't that somethin'."

Schmitty rolled his shoulders back. "Now we're in the same shape as you fellas hittin' peas off our mamas' broomsticks."

"And there's the matter of uniforms," Benjamin said.

Stan glanced over his shoulder at his teammates. Their uniforms would again consist of T-shirts and denim that matched as well as possible. Canvas shoes would have to do. Maybe they could match up the pattern of holes to better present as a team for their games.

Stan's awkwardness sprang to the surface again. Lack of money and its obvious markers on his life always did. It didn't matter that most of Donora was in the exact same straits as the Musial family. He felt the lack deeply.

Only Mom knew and understood that. It was something they could never discuss in front of Pop, the sense of people looking at Stan's pants rising to flood-dodging heights. The way Mom searched tirelessly for denim scrap that matched his worn trousers in color, stitching extra length on the bottoms or waist if she could. Honey had shorter legs, so his pants never seemed to need this exact surgical sewing maneuver. But Stan saw how Andrew's family lived. Melonhead's, too. And he knew he would never let himself live poor once he was old enough to make money. He'd make sure of it, and he'd make sure Mom had what she needed. All of them, even Pop.

Benjamin, in his practice baseball pants and leather baseball shoes, scanned the Heslep All-Stars, then lowered his hands, assuming a nearly vulnerable posture, his face soft, no smirk, shoulders slumped, mirroring Stan's insides near perfect. This threw Stan off. He shifted his feet.

Hands. Benjamin's were dusty, but under his nails was clean. Stan remembered how Andrew had described the Hicks' home. Stan eyeballed the All-Stars's blackened fingers.

Benjamin tossed a stone into the air, bounced it off his elbow, and caught it. "Been thinking how we might be able to make this league a real thing."

"Thinkin', huh," Smokestack said.

"Even got a line on getting our results into the paper. Few articles, maybe."

"Do you now?" Moonshine said.

"Got a plan."

"Out with it, then," Honey said, shouldering forward.

Stan was perfectly comfortable with his teammates doing the talking. It lessened the chance he might stumble over his words. Stan braced himself for some sort of attack on the financial situations of most of the All-Stars, how none of them could rustle up balls for games or baseball shoes and pants.

"Four things," Benjamin said. "Raffle, uniforms, balls, box scores after every game. Hoping to play ball at Harvard, and some legitimate press would help me out."

"And it'll git me a date." Hound licked his lips.

Matthew Jones got into his batting stance and took practice swings with an invisible bat. "Nothin' on this planet's gonna get you a date, Hound."

Everyone laughed, and the tension broke. Hound rolled his eyes.

Benjamin brushed dust from his pants. "My father got eight stores in town to agree to sponsor a team. They'll donate shirts with the names we picked on the back."

"And the balls you mentioned?" Andrew said, biting on the end of his pencil.

Benjamin widened his stance and rubbed his hands together. "Balls are a different matter. The boys and I went to every other team, and we all agreed if we work together, we can rustle up enough cash for balls. Maybe a drawing."

Cheeks pushed through the All-Stars and stood beside Stan, hands plugging hips. He nodded. "Little raffle, aye?"

Benjamin smiled.

"No," Cheeks said. He drew his hands over his head as though opening a banner. "Sweepstakes. A raffle."

Both teams nodded, smiling.

"My uncle ran one for the church last summer. Learned enough from him to make this work."

"So you're sure we can make enough money? We only got a week and—"

"Easy as pie," Cheeks said.

Stan couldn't imagine that they'd succeed at this. Asking for money? When most had none? He could feel his words inflating in his throat already. He imagined his father hearing about such a plan. The explosion that would follow.

Cheeks grabbed a stick and squatted, signaling them to pay attention, to step back so he could use the dirt as his paper.

He dragged the stick, making a square and tapping it. "That's our policy bank. Me."

"You?" Matthew Jones scowled.

"Yinz want this to run like cool crick water or not?"

Both teams agreed to that, convincing Benjamin that Cheeks was the man for the job, having been raised at the knee of Donora's best-known bookie.

"Simple and clean is how we'll structure this venture," Cheeks said.

Everyone nodded.

"If I were lookin' to make a livin' outta this, I'd use the middle three digits of stocks traded each day, or we'd generate some excitement by making a policy wheel to spin."

"Those sound like great ideas. Everyone will know we're on the up and up."

Cheeks drew three lines in the dirt and pointed to each line. "Shirts, balls, newspaper."

"Yeah, we established that."

"Well, two of those things are secured out of kindness and more likely favors owed to Benjamin's old man."

Benjamin shrugged and nodded.

"If we want real, new balls to start the season we need to be assured we make the money fast. People can't just hand over cash for our games. Not when half the town still gets steelman's steak on credit at Labash's."

Agreement all around.

"What are we talking here?" Stan asked. "Playground balls? Wilsons? Single-seamed?"

Benjamin pulled two pamphlets out of his back pocket. He handed one to Stan. Wilson brand, nine balls depicted—five baseballs and four playground balls. Stan rubbed his chin, looking the choices over. The fellas gathered closer. "Eight and a half per dozen for the amateur league…"

"Look at the Babe Ruth at the bottom." Smokestack pointed. "That's his signature on that. I've heard about those balls."

Stan's eyes went back to the amateur league ball. "Wrapped in good quality yarn. Standard size and weight. Costs a load. Dozen per carton." His mouth went dry. He'd much prefer scrounging up old balls or looking the other way if Moonshine swiped one foul from down the road into the Monongahela when he was watching a game while visiting his pap.

"Or does it mean each ball comes in a carton?" Stan asked. This was crazy.

"Why would a ball come in its own carton?" Tank asked.

Benjamin thrust the second catalog into the middle of the group. "Boys, boys. You're aiming too low. Take a gander at these Spaldings. Cream of the crop." He pointed. "Official National League ball with a patented cork center."

"What's patented?" Skunk asked.

"No idea," Smokestack said.

"Means only Spalding can use whatever cork and method they employ to put it inside that ball," Andrew said.

"Means we want these balls," Benjamin said.

Stan read aloud. "Only ball used in championship games since 1878." He knew that in the back of his mind. Spaldings were big-league balls. To buy some seemed impossible.

Stan kept reading, his eyes growing wide.

"What?" Monocle asked.

"Each ball is wrapped in tinfoil, *gold* tinfoil, packed in its own box, and sealed with some special formula for sealing things according to the baseball gods."

"Whoa," they all muttered at the same time, drawing back. Stan imagined peeling the wrapping, each ball its own special gem.

"Like those little chocolate Easter eggs we get."

Stan broke away from his imaginings and looked back at the price. "A buck twenty-five! Each!"

"Oh, that hurts." Smokestack gripped his head, rubbing his hat up and down.

Cheeks pushed in to see better. "Fifteen smacks a dozen."

"That's more than my pop makes in two weeks," Stan said. His face heated as he realized he'd said it aloud. Honey nudged him.

"More than a month for my dad," Smokestack said, giving Stan a wink.

Stan appreciated Smokestack jumping in with a lie. He didn't even know his pop. Everyone acted as though it was normal to have no money. And in some ways it was. But if a fella drank half his pay or got it lifted out of his pockets at the Bucket of Blood, it was different. It wasn't just the depression lightening his billfold. It was the man himself. It was why Stan's mom had three jobs instead of none, like Mrs. Morrison.

Stan wished he could separate how he felt about the family situation from how he felt about Pop, from how it made him feel about himself.

"Listen." Benjamin pointed to the balls. "Let's buy four of these beauties for the championship game. The rest, we'll get those Wilsons with the rubber center. They're still double-seamed and half the cost, better than anything we're gonna sew up ourselves, from the looks of things now. We can only hit so many bottle caps and scrap iron and still call it a real game."

Hound blew out a load of air and pulled the ad close. "Can we do it? Any way you slice the jumbo bologna, it's a *ton* of money."

Cheeks raised a hand. "Fellas. Please. Yinz're insulting me. Like yinz don't even know me."

Stan smiled.

"I'll work up the tickets. Definitely a raffle. Not a drawing. Drawings are free. We're looking for profit. Yinz just put on your best salesmen routines every day. Let people know the more they buy, the bigger the pot, the more money they win."

"But isn't that the game that got shut down when Mr. Peters rigged the whole thing?"

"Let me handle that. But if I catch any of you slackasses not sellin', you're gonna have to hit off a ten-year-old mushball with the guts squirting out of half-sewn seams."

Cheeks scanned the group. Stan wasn't comfortable asking for money. Pop had instilled a sense of distress in the act of asking for or accepting charity, as though somehow not asking or accepting would make their money problems go away. Stan couldn't imagine getting the words out of his mouth to ask someone for money when no one had enough.

Andrew held up his pencil. "Letters. Merchants love letters. We'll go to those sponsoring our shirts to get their friends to donate. We just need to write the correct letter."

Mumbling filled the air.

"*I'll* write the letters. Relax, fellas," Andrew said.

Stan smiled at Andrew. It would be his biggest contribution to the game he'd made since he warned them to cut out of practice before the tornado skirted Donora the year before. "If anyone can write a sales letter, it's Andrew."

"Well, that's settled, then," Benjamin said. "We'll head back to Cement City, stopping to tell each of the other six teams what's required."

Cheeks backed away with most of the Cardinals. "I'll work up the tickets. This is gonna be good."

Benjamin stuck his hand out to Stan. "Good luck this season."

Stan took his hand. "You, too."

The Cardinals started back toward the path, Benjamin tossing his new glove into the air and catching it. He made a football move, reminding Stan that he'd heard Benjamin was also being recruited to play football at several colleges. That kid had everything, and Stan wanted the same things. He wanted the easy confidence Benjamin displayed in every area of life. Stan felt deeply confident about baseball, but that was about it. The way Benjamin just stuck his hand out to say good luck, there was something utterly likeable about the kid even as Stan had disliked him just moments before.

"So, Weatherman. You'll be our man to submit the scores to the paper. Right?" Moonshine asked.

"Right," Andrew said, smiling ear to ear.

"And predict the weather. As usual," Stan said.

"Always," Andrew said, slinging his arm around Stan's shoulder. "This is your summer, Stan. I can feel it like I feel a high-pressure front undulating in, hidden behind the smoke."

Stan scratched his cheek. "Funny word. Undulating. But you're right, Weatherman. I can feel it, too." But he also felt worry kink in his belly. He would never get the words out to ask for money at any of the businesses in Donora. And he didn't quite know how he could manage not to fail his friends.

Chapter 33

Stan

Cheeks called a meeting with representatives from each team. Everyone needed to sell.

Honey ran his hand through his hair. Smokestack let out a whistle.

"We could go to five movies for the price of one of those balls."

Tank rubbed his belly. "Fifteen gallons of milk."

"But the foil," Benjamin said, digging his thumbnail into the yawning seam of the ball in his hand. "Can't rely on these castoffs for the entire season. Not if we want to look like actual teams in the box scores."

"It is a lot."

Cheeks shouldered in, cigarette dangling from his mouth. "Give it a couple of days of raffles to see what we come out with. But each of yinz guys is gonna have to sell. Your teammates. All of us. If no one buys tickets, there'll be no moolah, and all this mooning and dreaming over balls wrapped in foil will be as distant as the sun."

Everyone looked at him.

"Wow. That was eloquent, Cheeks. Didn't know you had it in you." Benjamin put his palm out.

Cheeks rolled his eyes then slapped some tickets into Benjamin's hand.

As Cheeks passed out sets of tickets, Benjamin and Stan gave the orders to make as many balls as they could for practice. "My mom's got a ball pattern cut from orange slices. We can use that."

"My grandaddy's got a pair of rubber overshoes he said we could use for the centers."

"Great, great."

"Mrs. Kraft donated stockings she's tired of darning." Howard Hempfield, from one of the middle Donora teams, handed them over to Stan.

"Great," Stan said. "Anyone comes across anything else, just bring 'em to Cheeks's house. Later tonight we're gonna make some balls there while he counts our proceeds from the first day's raffle."

Stan had been worried about asking people for money, barely slept at the thought of it, but now he was emboldened. If they were all going to do it, he could.

Andrew pulled a stack of papers out of his satchel. "Twenty letters to get us started."

"Whoa," Stan said. "Did you sleep at all?"

Andrew shrugged. "Fair weather at home last night. Whole family helped. Even my sisters."

Stan nodded. This made him think of his home the night before. It had been a tornado of activity and tension. A broken bowl meant each Musial poured some of their soup into Matka's and Rose and Helen shared. Stan knew his family needed a new bowl, yet he was going to go around asking for money for balls. His father's voice rattled inside Stan's head as though Pop had run radio speakers into it. Between Stan's lack of contribution of money—working at the gas station just here and there—and Pop edging dangerously close to the kind of mood that sometimes got him in trouble at the wireworks, Stan started to second-guess this plan all over again.

Mom had asked Stan to meet Pop at the gate after his shift, to make sure he got home without stopping off at the Bucket of Blood or the Falcons. And he'd promised he would, just like Moonshine did. Just like half the town did. Stan's belly ached, and he thought perhaps he was taking after his father where his stomach was concerned. Mom had been taking Pop soup for lunch every blessed day just to make sure he didn't miss a shift because of it. Or worse, leave to get a sandwich at the tavern.

Weatherman went on to explain that when they stopped at select merchants, they should explain why the teams were selling the tickets and also leave the personalized letter for each. Then he'd be writing more so each team could have one with them in case a random citizen wanted to see it.

"Oughta be able to unload the whole lot of tickets come payday. Just stand outside the Bucket of Blood," Nicky Christmas said.

The thought of running into Pop outside of the Bucket of Blood sent Stan's heart falling to his feet.

Cheeks put his hand against Nicky's chest. "Gotta watch our step. Uncle Marty's lookin' the other way on our little game here, but we can't go and undercut his whole payday business."

"Yeah, yeah," they said. "No Bucket of Blood."

"And," Cheeks said. "Buddy, Nicky, Tank, team up with Stan, Andrew, or Honey if you aren't sure a business is friendly to folks with darker skin."

"I can't solicit at Murphy's. Let's just say we have a discrepancy regarding elderberry bushes and property lines between my family and theirs," Moonshine said.

"And I can't go to Mr. Pavlesic's," Smokestack said. "Claims Auntie Hazel's hair tonic fried the last of his off," Smokestack said.

"He used to have hair?" they all sounded off.

"Got it," Nicky said, eyeing Tank and Buddy. "We'll stay away from Winter's and Plum's. Everyone else should be good."

"Are we gonna make any money at all on this?" Benjamin asked. "Why so many people to avoid?"

"One reason or another," Moonshine said. "But when times are bad, we stick together. We do."

"Trust me," Cheeks said. "Raffle will be held on the daily at 4:00 P.M. at Americo Field before whichever of us teams are attempting to have a practice game. That oughta draw a crowd and let them see us smacking river rocks off of broomsticks and pipes. And hopefully they'll buy more chances the next day."

Skunk took his stack of tickets. "And if any of you hooligans wins the pot, turn it back in. Same goes for family."

Stan adjusted his hat and eyed Honey. They shared a smile. Pop wouldn't buy a ticket, and if Mom did and won, she'd be the first to return the money, even if the Musials could use every dime of winnings. She knew what baseball meant to her boys. *"It's the most American thing they can do, Lukasz,"* she must have said a thousand times each summer.

They divided up the letters for the merchants among the teams, and Stan, being the most likeable and best player on the team, was charged with asking Mr. Rosenberg to buy a block of raffle tickets to get things going.

Honey took two letters and dashed off with Smokestack, headed to Mulvaney's Restaurant and Perkins' Smoke and Guns.

Stan nearly choked at the thought of approaching someone like Mr. Rosenberg—owner of the most exclusive clothing shop in town. He'd known they'd all have to ask people to buy tickets, but he hadn't been expecting to have to make one of the formal pitches with the letter. Stan looked at the paper again, the words dissolving in front of his eyes, his heart racing and feeling like he'd been asked to give a recitation on what he'd read on world history the night before. When he looked up, all the boys were gone.

Except for Andrew. "Want me to go with you?"

Stan nearly hugged him. "Would you? You talk like... It'll go so much better if you go and..."

Andrew slung his satchel over his shoulder. "Sure. But you don't need me, Stan."

Stan stayed put. "You know I can't..." His words were already getting caught in his throat.

Andrew jerked his head and started walking. Stan followed behind.

"You got lead in your shoes today?" Andrew said over his shoulder. "Trying to level the playing field for me, what with my slow, clumsy feet?"

Andrew chattered about the strange temperature inversion, he called it, that seemed to have settled over the town two nights before. Stan hadn't noticed it any smokier or darker or colder than usual. But Andrew sure made a stink about it all—asthma and oxygen depletion and mill waste. On and on about the weight of air, of all things, and the steep valley walls. Though he didn't follow the monologue completely, Stan appreciated not having to say a peep, Andrew's droning a comfort of sorts.

When they reached Rosenberg's Clothiers, they entered, the door setting a bell to ringing. Mr. Rosenberg put down his scissors and glided from behind the oak counter that spanned across the back of the shop.

Andrew sauntered up to Mr. Rosenberg. The two shook hands, and the man reached out for Stan. He took his hand, but yanked it away as fast as he could, noticing that the man wiped his palm on his pants once they were finished. Stan spent most of those first moments staring at Mr. Rosenberg's shoes that reflected the light from above like sparklers, and that's how he noticed him wiping his palm. Stan's thoughts raced. He wiped his own palms against his pants—his trousers doctored with scrap denim. His clothes never felt worse for wear than right then in the middle of a store that specialized in fine wool trousers, coats, and hats.

Andrew nudged Stan's side with his elbow. He looked up, shocked that Mr. Rosenberg was looking at him expectant, eyebrows up.

"Your average so far, .400, right?" Andrew asked, straining to get Stan to answer this question that had clearly been directed at him.

Stan's tongue felt thick as nerves kicked in. "For practice games."

Mr. Rosenberg cocked his head as though Stan were a puzzle to solve. He took Stan by the elbow. He'd been so nervous he hadn't even heard what Andrew said. Had he asked him to contribute to the cause? To buy tickets? Was Stan supposed to ask?

"Come see this, boys," Mr. Rosenberg said. "My biggest prize in life." He looked over one shoulder, then the other. "Don't tell Mrs. Rosenberg that, of course. I tell her our daughters are my biggest prizes. Which of course they are. But you boys'll understand once you see this."

He pulled out a drawer in the back room and set it on a worktable that was draped in fabric with chalk markings outlining the wool into sections.

"Andrew here tells me he has dreams of landing in the stars quite literally. And you have dreams of stardom, too?"

Stan nodded.

"Well, some of us are ordinary men with boring, unshiny lives, hopefully quiet ones, but this… this is the closest I'll ever get to the stars, real or figuratively."

Stan and Andrew leaned in as Mr. Rosenberg opened the box. He slid a work lamp closer, illuminating the velvet lining and the baseball nestled inside it.

He took it out and turned it. "Babe Ruth's signature and…" He spun the ball slowly, moving it closer to Stan. "A little bird told me you love Lefty Grove and Pye Trainor." All three signatures were etched in between rough, dirty spots. Stan couldn't breathe, and this time he couldn't speak because of the awe that had swept over him.

Andrew grabbed his hat and put it against his chest. "Wow," he said.

Mr. Rosenberg let the boys cradle the ball, study it, explaining that he and his son had spent an entire baseball season following the Phillies, Pirates, and Yankees. "Saw the Bambino hit his 714th home run at Forbes Field."

"Whoa." Chills ran over Stan's arms as he recalled listening to that game on the radio with Andrew and Joe Barbao. Stan pointed at the ball, his finger shaking. "That's not *the* ball is it?"

Mr. Rosenberg chuckled. "Oh no, boys. I wish, but no. This will have to be enough, won't it? Can you imagine the greatness scrawled right there into the leather, three sets of magic hands touching it? I just…" His eyes started to glisten like the reflection off his shoes.

Stan let out a big sigh. "You don't have to tell me." He leaned in and ran his finger over Lefty's autograph, wanting the great man's skill to somehow seep into his fingertip. Just a little would be enough.

Mr. Rosenberg slipped a pen out of his pocket. "Here. You sign."

Stan drew back, hands up.

Mr. Rosenberg pushed the pen closer. "Don't be shy."

Stan shook his head, staring at the ball. "It'll ruin it."

Mr. Rosenberg shrugged and held it further into the light. "Your signature will make it the most sought-after ball in history someday."

Stan's palms began to sweat again. Was this man kidding?

Mr. Rosenberg shifted his weight, studying Stan again. "You're superstitious, aren't you?"

Stan wiped his nose. "Yes. I…"

"You'll come back and sign it for me when the time is right?"

Stan nodded, face flaming. A stew of self-confidence, self-consciousness, and pride bubbled inside him.

"That's really neat," Andrew said. "He'll be back to sign that before you know it. He's gonna be Donora's biggest name."

"Well, he's got a gift. That much I know."

Mr. Rosenberg settled the ball back into the box as though it were priceless crystal. "My son went off to the army this January. Our tour of baseball stadiums and search for those signatures was the most precious thing I've ever done in my life."

Stan and Andrew nodded. Stan's eyes welled. He was too easy to cry, as his father always reminded him. He wished he could control it better.

"So you." Mr. Rosenberg gestured at Andrew. "You're the engineer and team manager and weather prognosticator, and this one here's a magician with his hitting. You're a smoking pitcher, too. But I've seen you hit like… Well, since you're superstitious, I won't say it for the chance of saddling you with a cloak of bad luck right over your shoulders like a fine topcoat. Except it wouldn't be fine at all. It would be terrible. So I'll zip my lips. But I do know talent when I see it. I will say that."

Stan couldn't stop smiling. "Thank you."

Mr. Rosenberg nodded, hands on his hips. "Now. About that contribution for the team and the tickets."

Stan couldn't breathe when he left the store; the feeling of satisfaction and strength was like when he hit the grand slam to win the Championship game the year before. But this time all it took was someone talking about his talent. Just kind words and the invitation to sign a ball with the greatest baseball players on earth was all it took.

A hand on Stan's shoulder stopped him from walking. He turned. "Mom."

"You were in there?" she asked.

"Just collecting for the balls. I told you."

She squinted at him and then took her gaze down to his hemmed pants and back up. She held her purse tight against her belly. "Don't forget to meet Pop. Just walk him up the hill, and I'll be home by then."

**

Stan met Pop at the Sixth Street gate after work, and the two walked home, nearly like pals, discussing mill politics and how things were changing, how striking might be an option if the burgess didn't stop blocking William Feeny from holding his organizing meetings.

Pop ticked off a list of conditions they were fighting for. "Eight-hour shifts. Vacation. Sick days. Decent pay. Safety equipment. Help when a fella's injured or killed or… It's what I always imagined for me, for you." He tossed Stan an apple he'd had left over from lunch, and Stan gobbled it down, agreeing with every word Pop said about worker's rights and safer mills.

"Those men, the bigshots, even tried to influence my vote once," Lukasz said. "Can you imagine?"

Stan shook his head. He couldn't fathom anyone trying to change Pop's mind about anything, even an employer. They must have underestimated his stubborn strength. Stan did remember conversation about it, Matka's grumbling, Mom's worries, Pop's anger as he stalked around the house, barking at everyone.

But this time, just talking with Pop alone, walking up that hill, it felt like when Stan was with Joe or how he saw Andrew with his old man. By the time they reached home, Mom was ready with a big bowl of cabbage stew.

But Stan declined. "Working later, lots to do before—have to make balls and… I'll see you later tonight."

And he was out of the house before too many questions were asked. He wasn't going to miss dinner at Cheeks's. Especially since Honey would be there, too—this time Stan wouldn't be lying to him.

Heslep All-Stars spent the evening on Cheeks's porch being served Italian sausage sandwiches by Mrs. Carvelli and sneaking beers from their cellar. Smokestack rolled cigarettes and as many boys as could help, sewed balls.

Stan's job was to gently dismantle all the wool stockings they'd collected. Buddy Griffey cut discarded rubber overshoes into pieces and formed them into balls. Next down the line, Melonhead wound the newly unraveled yarn around the rubber ball, eyeballing it for the right size. From the collection of mismatched, discarded boots, Monocle cut using the pattern they'd made from the orange and then sewed halfway up the pieces. Then Honey slipped the yarn-covered ball with the half-sewn boot leather inside, and Skunk and Nicky finished the sewing job.

And so for the balance of that week, they and the other teams practiced with weather-beaten balls, handmade, misshapen mushballs, and anything they could find, making their case for needing the raffle funds, making people want to buy a chance at winning money and helping these boys buy decent equipment. And somehow four out of eight raffle winners were associated with a player on one of the eight teams. Even the Donora *Herald-American* reported on the boys' efforts, taking every chance they could to draw the citizens' attention from the dire straits of their lives.

When the week of raffles had passed, they gathered for a final night of ball making.

Monocle spoke around the needle in his mouth. "Don't you think Mr. Hill's gonna be bent out of shape that all those tickets he bought, the shirts he sponsored didn't win him a thing, not once?"

Cheeks shook his head and lit a cigarette for him and Smokestack. "Mr. Hill's just fine with the arrangement."

"Arrangement?" Honey said.

Cheeks rolled his eyes and surveyed the fellas. He shook his head. "We got the money; we ordered the balls. Case closed, fellas. My uncle was a great help. He got his cut. That's all yinz need to know."

**

At the end of the next week, the balls arrived. All eight teams gathered at the field to unbox them. It was like Christmas morning, and every single present was what they'd asked for—and brand new. The Wilsons came by the case, the leather scent filling the air as they poked their noses into the case. They opened the individual carton lid of one of the foil-wrapped Spaldings, passing it around to see. "Don't unwrap it, not even a little," Benjamin said. "We'll save that for the championship game."

Any of the Wilson balls was better than the ones they made themselves, and they were proud for getting the funds together to make it happen. They kept the Spaldings under lock and key at Mr. Rosenberg's store, the vision of them coming out at the end of the season enough to inspire the best play of their lives.

The first few weeks of the season brought the Cement City Cardinals win after win.

Stan hit like a big-league batting champion and struck out large swaths of players every time he pitched. Yet the Heslep All-Stars couldn't beat the Cardinals for anything. The All-Stars were growing touchy. One by one, they started to question whether they'd be one of the teams to play with the foil-wrapped balls.

Chapter 34

Stan

The summer league baseball games went on, several a week. During week four, the Cement City Cardinals were on top, Heslep second. On most of the days Stan pitched, Heslep would win, but when it came to playing the Cards, even Stan couldn't quite bring the All-Stars together for the win. The last game Heslep had nearly beaten the Cardinals, but close wasn't enough. After the game, everyone scattered, irritated with the way each other played, pointing fingers. Honey took off with Smokestack and Cheeks to sneak beers at his uncle's house. Andrew's family stuffed him into their car and drove to their grandpa's farm for a few days, where they would stargaze by night and crick-walk by day.

Though the team was peeved with one another, Stan seethed. The rest of the team forgot losses immediately, on the hunt for the next fun thing to do. But Stan hated losing, and though he was playing beautifully himself, the team not being able to beat the Cardinals was really getting to him. His pitches were solid, but if he was honest, if he was pitching as well as he wanted to, he would be throwing no-hitters. So after that game, he didn't accept invitations to join others to sit out on porches. With no Zincs game to be batboy for, he stuffed his hands in his pockets and walked the town, clearing his head until his shift pumping gas at the station would begin. He passed Weston's Drugstore and heard his name being called.

Mr. Weston, the owner of the store, stuck his head out and waved Stan inside. He appeared friendly, but his son played on the Thompson Tigers, and Stan knew from seeing this man that he did not take kindly to his son's team losing or his son playing badly. In fact, this father was one who made Stan grateful Pop didn't attend his games. Because if he did, he might behave just like this guy.

"How about a nice milkshake? Rootbeer float? Pop?"

Stan looked behind him, then pointed to himself. The radio on the counter was playing Ray Noble's "Got You Under my Skin," giving the place an air of lightness and fun.

"Yes, you." Mr. Weston fussed with the radio channel, clearing up the static.

Stan didn't have any spare change after he'd donated his extra to the raffle ticket fund for balls. Plenty of people didn't have extra money to spend. Most of what he earned working at the gas station went to Mom for expenses.

"It's on the house, buddy. Come on. You'll be doing me a favor sitting here, chewing the fat."

Stan wrinkled his nose. Was Mr. Weston serious? A milkshake on the house? Why?

A harmonica on display near the soda counter caught Stan's eye. He stopped and ran his finger over the box. "Kid like you should have a harmonica," Mr. Weston said.

Stan nodded. He did love music and dancing.

"It's yours."

Stan backed away.

Mr. Weston took it from the display and slapped it on the counter. "Have a seat, Stan. I've been thinking about our Pittsburgh Pirates this summer. What'd you make of Vaughn?"

"Mighty good."

"Smokin' 'em, isn't he?"

"Sure is."

They talked for an hour, Stan forgetting how this man treated his son at games, talking as though he did it for a living. Jerry McMullen made the milkshake and cleaned the area behind the counter, quiet even though he was talkative at school normally. It confused Stan, the attention, the gifts of food and harmonica from Mr. Weston. Stan wiped his hands on a napkin. "Thank you for the milkshake, Mr. Weston. But I can't accept this harmonica."

The man drew back. "Sure you can."

"But why?"

Jerry eyed Stan as he cleaned up.

"Because you're a great ballplayer, and I enjoy every hit you crank out of the park and every pitch you hurl." He slid another napkin toward Stan. "People like people like you. It's simple."

Stan still wasn't sure what to say or think. He felt horrible for the man's son but was grateful the kid was nowhere in sight. And Stan was saddened that Pop didn't feel this way about him. His own father never saw what others did.

Mr. Weston set the harmonica on Stan's napkin. "It's yours. Helps calm the nerves. You'll see."

Stan shrugged and put it in his pocket. "Thank you." He eyed Jerry, wishing he had something to tip him with. Stan's palms began to sweat. He was nervous when he had nothing and unsettled when others gave him things. The only place he felt comfortable was at the ball field—on the mound and in the batter's box.

Mr. Weston waved at a customer coming in the door and followed her back to the pharmacy window.

Stan headed toward the gas station, putting the harmonica to his lips. He would bring Jerry a tip after he worked at the station. The harmonica, the metal sections, slid easily back and forth as he experimented with notes, attempting to play tunes he knew from the big-band sounds at dances and popular songs from the radio. The evening passed quickly, Stan shooting the breeze with everyone who pulled in for gas or to have their tires filled with air.

In between customers, he played the harmonica, doing his best to find a recognizable tune.

As his shift ended, he was surprised. He realized all the worry and darkness he'd been feeling when he approached the drugstore, the unease he'd felt at being gifted the harmonica, was gone. With a couple pennies in hand, he jogged back to the drugstore to tip Jerry and tell Mr. Weston he'd been right: Stan's mood had lifted to the moon with just a few notes, bad notes, not even the right notes, but that the harmonica was wonderful.

As he approached the store, he heard the sound of glass breaking. Stan rushed in to see what was the matter. Mr. Weston was leaning over Jerry, screaming as the boy cowered, eyes wide with a rag in his hand. Mr. Weston threw the spoon across the room and broke a second glass into the sink. "We don't serve Negroes. And we surely don't give money to them comin' in here to support their team. I have a son on a different team, you know. Cost of those glasses is comin' out of your pay."

Jerry's face went white as a vanilla milkshake. "But he's on Stan's team, and you talked with him for an hour. I figured you— "

Stan surveyed the space. No one else was there. The radio played "Good Night Irene" just soft enough that although Stan didn't want to believe what he was seeing and hearing, he couldn't deny it. The music wasn't that loud. *This* was the version of Mr. Weston who came to games to scream at his son.

Jerry started to respond, but Mr. Weston's glare stopped him. "I don't care if he does dress like a dandy and hit the ball like the dickens. I don't care if he ends up on full scholly at Notre Dame. He'll ruin my business, so…"

It took a second for Stan to realize they were talking about Nicky Christmas. Stan looked around again. Was Nicky there? There were certain places that only allowed whites in Donora, but the kids in town went to school together, lived side by side, played sports together, had kids of every nationality to their homes. Stan's stomach churned. Even knowing Mr. Weston wasn't a kind man to his son, Stan hadn't known that Mr. Weston was one of the fellas who wouldn't serve Nicky.

He started to back away, hoping they wouldn't notice him when Nicky sauntered out of the bathroom. Mr. Weston's face went beet red as he watched Nicky cover every inch of space from the back toward where Stan was waiting. Nicky's face was tight, and Stan knew—he'd heard what Mr. Weston said. Stan wanted to slam that harmonica into Mr. Weston's face.

Nicky finally noticed Stan, his face lighting up at the sight of him before he glanced around the rest of the store. Stan smiled noticing Mr. Weston glowering. Stan started to feel sick. He should speak up, tell Mr. Weston that if he wouldn't serve Nicky, then he shouldn't serve Stan. Perhaps it would have more impact if Stan had actually bought the milkshake he'd enjoyed earlier.

Nicky drew closer to where Stan stood, Nicky's gaze flicked back just long enough for Stan to fully absorb the hurt he'd felt, the pain behind his eyes. Stan threw a glance at Mr. Weston, then back at Nicky.

"Hey, Nicky." Stan grabbed his arm.

Nicky stopped, the inside wound visible through his eyes. How could this have happened right there in Donora to a guy like Nicky?

Nicky lifted his chin.

"You up for a card game?" Stan shouted the question, making sure there was no stammer to interfere with his words. "My house?"

Nicky lifted the brim of his hat. "Sure, Stushy. Sure."

Stan put his arm around Nicky, and the two walked out the door.

Outside, up the sidewalk a little ways, Nicky stopped and bent over, hands on knees. He brushed the front of his slacks, breathing deep. "Boy, was I glad to see your mug in there."

Stan shook his head. "I'm so sorry that happened. I… You just took the paper, the letter in there and he treated you like that, like…"

"Bought their most expensive malt and… yep. That's what came of it."

Nicky exhaled then suddenly looked at ease again and if you didn't look for what was hidden inside his smooth sauntering style, you wouldn't know he was just treated like a… Stan wasn't even sure what to call it. Inhuman?

Nicky had obviously gone home to clean up before approaching Weston's. Stan didn't even own nice slacks or a jacket like Nicky's, let alone the… what did they call his sharp, shiny brown and white shoes? Spectators. Nicky was the one Mr. Weston was worried about eating at his soda counter? Good God, Stan's wardrobe consisted of moth-eaten sweaters, cotton shirts, and denim sewn onto denim. Yet all it took was two boys with different shades of skin to allow for fawning conversation, a free milkshake and harmonica for one and a humiliating ruckus for the other. Mr. Weston's words turned Stan's stomach like Matka rung out a rag. He forced himself to calm down.

"Texas hold 'em?" Stan said.

Nicky pointed at Stan and winked. "Nah. Got a date," he said and sauntered away, whistling, his posture hiding the sadness Stan had seen in his eyes. "Thank you, Stushy Musial. You're a good soul, top to bottom," Nicky said over his shoulder.

"So are you!" Stan felt the weightlessness of such a response. So are you? It sounded ridiculous out loud. But what could Stan say to erase what just happened from Nicky's mind? How could anything Stan might say lift that ugliness out from under Nicky's skin? A kid who didn't deserve any of it?

Nicky raised his hand, not looking back, disappearing into the hazy summer night.

Stan's hands quaked. He returned to the pharmacy, Mr. Weston standing in the window, jaw clenched. Jerry, behind him, saw Stan and gave him a nod. The tip. Stan stomped past Mr. Weston, digging the money from his pocket and handing it over to Jerry. "Thank you for the milkshake, Jerry."

Jerry forced a smile and Stan figured Mr. Weston would probably take the money to help pay for the broken glasses. He wanted to say something to Mr. Weston, at least question what he'd done, but no words came. Stan shook his head, disgusted, then jogged home, not realizing he'd gripped the harmonica so tight that the outline of the squares had embedded in his palm. The unfairness turned his stomach.

He grabbed his belly and wondered how many people he came across each day felt like Mr. Weston. Was it something that happened when a person became an adult, that suddenly they smashed valuable milkshake glasses just because someone with dark skin drank out of it? He shook his head and breathed into the harmonica, then pulled it away, staring at it, thinking he should return it.

If Mr. Weston wasn't going to treat Nicky right, Stan shouldn't accept a gift from him. Stan started back toward town, toward Weston's. He stopped. No. No. The harmonica would be a reminder for Stan every time he played it. A reminder that the world may be one way, but Stan didn't have to be that way, too. A reminder to never enter that store again.

**

The Heslep All-Stars had a day off from games, and Stan's shift at the gas station was later that evening. Though he was missing the chance to watch the game between the third and sixth place teams in the junior city league, Stan didn't let it bother him too much. During that time, he was serving as Joe Barbao's batboy when the Donora Zincs played Monessen, always a close game.

Stan was quick to retrieve bats, balls, to get a drink for a player—anything the men needed. Andrik Dulka was the Zincs' backup pitcher, going into the game after Joe was struggling. But when Dulka started to fade with several innings still to go, Joe paced, teeth clamped over a cigar, mumbling to himself. Their third pitcher had gotten too close to a zinc retort and burned his hand. He was out for at least a week.

"Dammit," Joe said. He removed and replaced his hat a dozen times before taking Stan by the back of the collar. "My arm's hangin' from the game yesterday. Dulka's ace has apparently unionized and got two weeks' vacation. His changeup's got typhoid. You're goin' in."

In? Joe couldn't possibly mean *in*—in the game? Stan stared at Joe for a moment. His mentor dug something out of his pocket and slammed it into Stan's palm. "I know you like your gum."

Stan looked at the Dubble Bubble in his palm.

Joe took off his shoes. "Put those on. Too small for your big boats, but you can't go out there in canvas. They'll think you're a kid."

Stan was speechless. He moved quickly, exchanging shoes. An order like this from a teacher to do something big would have left him stammering for days. This time there were no words at all.

Joe took off his jersey and handed that over to Stan as well. The thick wool in summer heat itched his neck and arms as he slipped it on and fastened the buttons. Still it was a uniform, its heaviness adding to his nerves. Joe stomped over to Monessen's bench pointing back at Stan. Americo Park went silent in Stan's ears. His focus on what was next took precedence over everything. His heart beat heavier, but it didn't race. It didn't make his breath shallow or uneven.

He pressed his chest, waiting for panic to hit. He nearly asked Joe if he was sure, that there was no way he, a fifteen-year-old, ought to be playing against grizzled old mill men. What was he thinking? But when Joe looked back at Stan, his worried brow softened and he just nodded, chomping on that cigar. And Stan knew. There was no way Joe would ask Stan to play if he didn't think he could. Baseball meant too much to Joe. And he wouldn't insult the game by putting in a hack.

Next thing he knew, Stan was on the mound with a nearly new pile of balls at his feet. He threw some warm-up pitches. Joe sent signs to the catcher, Lenny Abrams, who conveyed what he wanted to Stan. Unlike playing on the junior league team, Stan didn't dream of throwing something different than what was signaled in. With Joe at the helm, Stan had no need to second-guess. They knew each other too well.

Where sometimes his pitches were particularly wild and even dangerous, utterly unhittable for some of the high school batters, he felt his body stretch out on the mound, as he knew each of these players could level one back at his head with the greatest of ease. That day his wildness worked for him. The opposing players hadn't really registered who Stan was or what he could throw, so any of the pitches that were hard and inside or too high just set them more on edge.

Not even a few bad pitches could remove the smile from his face. Six innings that day, the day that changed everything about how Stan understood what he was capable of. Six innings: thirteen batters went down whiffing. The team surrounded Stan with the usual backslapping and pats on the head. And then, with Stan still in the field, with the dust settling, he looked into the stands. Honey jumping up and down, hands in the air. Nicky Christmas and Cheeks were there, too. Stan could not have imagined feeling higher, utterly drunk on what he still couldn't quite fathom. His teammates being there to witness it all made it that much sweeter.

Stan was changing his shoes when bickering drew his attention. He took the leathers to Joe, who kicked out of Stan's canvas shoes. Marshall, the center fielder, poked Joe in the shoulder. "I pay two bits to the union. My brother does, too. And he don't get to play. Some kid does? No way, you. We took a vote, Joe. You're out."

Stan's mouth dropped open. He quickly slid his shoes on, wanting to hit the road.

Marshall grabbed Joe's arm. "You can play. But no more managing."

Stan's heart sank mortified that Joe lost his managing duties because of him.

"All right, fine," Joe said. He looked at Stan. "I like playing better anyhow."

Was Marshall about to can Stan? He looked away, waiting for the hammer to drop.

But Marshall took Stan by the shoulder, squeezing. "This kid can stay though. We all agreed to that."

Joe winked at Stan and he was high once again.

**

Stan's results were noted in the paper and the reporter wrote, "Fifteen-year-old boy playing against men… 5'4" and 140-pounder made pitching debut against Monessen… [Stan's] got a world of stuff and a brainy head, [but] he is too small for steady playing now…" While it thrilled Stan to be mentioned in an article about a semi-pro game, the mention about his height and weight unsettled him. Brainy? He did study baseball like Andrew did the wonders of the world.

In addition, a new man, Steven Koskoski, was made manager when the players ousted Joe. And though Koskoski saw Stan's talent, he was gruff and impatient, and his manner brought Stan's nerves to the surface. Still allowed to play with the Zincs, Joe focused on his pitching, the zinc shakes from hot hours in the mill causing his hands to sometimes disobey his mind's orders.

Despite all of that, Stan found solace at Americo Field. Most of his responsibilities remained the same—keeping track of all the equipment, player preferences, chasing down balls, and all the mundane things that shouldn't have seemed wonderful but were to Stan. He had the chance to watch Joe play and get into the game sometimes himself. The players might have ousted Joe as manager, but they wanted Stan at the ready if they needed him.

Joe's brusqueness with teammates, his habit of getting tossed from a few games a season, showed Stan one way of coaching. He was a little gentler when it came to Stan, but Stan did every single thing just the way Joe wanted. And the reward came when Stan was permitted to hit batting practice a little bit before each game. Like pitching, batting practice had come to feel like he was stretching out to where he belonged, like his body was unfurling, fitting into its proper space.

The field, laid out just outside the zinc mill, was hemmed in by a short left field, cut off by trolley tracks. First base line was crowded with train tracks. This was the second field that Stan played on that gave him the chance to work on hitting to the left, something most left-handers never learned to do well.

With his harmonica his trusty companion, always in his pocket, he found that he played it or simply hummed anytime nerves threatened to take hold. Always finding his stance the same exact way, he practiced the art of minute adjustments once a ball was pitched. He knew what was coming once the ball was halfway to the plate, and when he moved out of his crouch, he would tweak his foot placement to hit the ball in the direction he wanted it to go. The swing, level and even, every single time, when he just fell into the groove of the game, natural as his breath.

He found he needed even more practice now that he was hitting against men. But it wasn't as though he felt a deficit that he needed to address, it was that he was thrilled at the chance for fine-tuning, the way every pitch thrown gave his eye a chance to better see what was coming. Being a pitcher himself, he picked up on the slight twist of the wrist as it released a curve instead of a fastball.

One particular game, Koskoski was unusually bristly. Chomping on his gum, Stan watched as the Zincs' lead dwindled down to nothing. In the sixth inning, the pitcher having worn his elbow thin and the batters needing to catch up with several runs, Koskoski told Stan to pinch hit. The order from the new manager hit him like a fever, sending a mix of chills and heat through him, right down to his fingertips.

Joe came closer. "What? Waiting for a set of trumpeters to herald your approach?" Joe let a smile snake through his grimace. "Don't let Koskoski rattle you."

Stan shook his head and eyed the stands. Must have been a thousand people there. Stan reminded himself that he'd just lit up the field during batting practice. He rolled his shoulders, took the bat he liked, and headed to the plate.

There was something about the light that day, the shine it put on him, and he felt the weight of all eyes like he hadn't the first time he'd played for the Zincs. He was accustomed to fans in his junior league games. But thousands of people didn't show up to watch the Heslep All-Stars play the Cardinals.

"Stan!" He turned. There, squished in the middle of the fans, were Honey and Nicky Christmas.

And Pop.

Stan could not remember the last time his father had attended a game. He shook his head, trying to dislodge the nerves. If his father saw how good Stan was, he couldn't help but be proud of him.

"Musial. Today? I got a shift after the game," Koskoski said.

Stan stepped into the batter's box, taking his place far back from the plate.

The first pitch came in. He didn't even see it.

"Strike." The umpire punched his fist.

"Come on, Stushy." Joe smacked his hands together.

Stan stepped out of the box and spun his wrists in a circle to loosen up. *Concentrate.* His eyes went to the stands. Honey and Cheeks sat forward on their seats.

Pop was gone.

Stan scanned the fans for Pop. And Stan found him. Already leaving the park, the back of his head, broad shoulders, the way he carried himself bigger than his 5'5" size, all recognizable. He wasn't even staying for Stan to finish his at bat.

"Get in the game, kid, it's a good one," a spectator yelled.

"No batter, no batter, no batter," the entire Charleroi bench chanted. Their fans roared, voices blurring into a pulsing wave of sound.

Stan shook his head and rolled his shoulders trying to loosen the tension grip. He chomped on his gum and stepped back into position.

Concentrate and relax.

The pitcher wound up, and Stan blew out his air. He watched every motion the pitcher made, trying to discern the pitch that was coming based on his movements. *Zing.* Right by Stan's nose.

He stumbled back, swallowing his gum. His nose was actually hot from the ball whipping by so close.

The crowd roared.

Stan beat his chest, trying to move the gum into his belly. What was happening? It was like none of his body parts were attached, least of all his eyes and hands.

"Strike," the ump called. Half the spectators disagreed with that. Stan's nose did as well. He stepped back in the batter's box, determined. He gripped his bat, repeated his mantra to concentrate and relax, and held the bat even tighter.

The Charleroi bench started to chant, "Struuuuuuuugggling." Their fans picked up the verse, and the rhythm of it fell over Stan, making him lose track of the ball as it bulleted toward him. He wasn't going down standing there looking at the ball, so he took a giant swing.

And that was that. Stan's up with the Zincs when they needed his bat the most ended in blast-furnace orange flames. He dropped his head and backed away from the plate, wanting to hide.

"Whooo," the pitcher said. "Thanks for the fan, kid."

Stan stalked back to the bench, face blazing. He tossed the bat aside, the sound of wood hitting wood as it smacked against the others lined up against the fence reminded him that it was he who'd put them in order of the next hitter.

He kept his eyes on the ground.

Pop. Had he seen Stan strike out? Had he turned back to watch before leaving? Could he hear the announcer declare Stan Musial had struck out? Batboy might be the furthest he went in baseball if that at bat was any indication. He was mortified. He bent down to organize the bats he'd just knocked over and saw Joe's feet standing there, clearly waiting for Stan to notice.

He stood. "I'm sorry, Joe. I just…"

"Here." He held out two pieces of gum. He was chuckling. Stan waited for his tongue lashing.

"So?" Joe said as Stan unwrapped one piece.

"Well. I wasn't expecting to go up, and my head was fizzing like seltzer." He almost said he'd seen his father there and that only added to his nervousness, but he kept that to himself. "And I tried to relax and concentrate and obviously... I didn't."

"Obviously," Joe said.

Stan's breathing started to iron out just talking to Joe.

"But... looking back. I know what it was." It shouldn't matter who was in the stands. The realization came. "My breathing. I held my breath. And that wrecked my calmness and my concentration—"

"And you swallowed a wad of gum."

Had it been that noticeable? Stan put a fist against his breastbone. "Stuck right here." He laughed, Joe's observations never feeling like accusations, allowing Stan to see the humor in them.

"You chew a lot of gum." Joe started to walk away.

"Joe?" Stan waited for more advice.

Joe turned, his arms open wide. "Nothing else I can say, kid. You know what you did wrong. You know what to do to fix it. My work is done." Joe turned back and dragged Andrik by the collar, scolding him for chatting with a girl over the fence.

Stan reorganized the bats. Joe's kindness and coaching deepened Stan's sadness that Pop might've left the game early, that he didn't care. But complicating that was the idea that Pop might have stayed and witnessed Stan's failure. He put his mind back on Joe, their relationship. And he looked back into the crowd, some still heckling him. Beforehand, he couldn't have imagined the embarrassment at striking out that way, in front of all those people. His initial worry that he'd let Joe down, the humiliation, the fear that it was all over for him in Joe's eyes, had been displaced by the way Joe had responded to Stan's strikeout. Joe believed in him, and Stan was convinced that was worth more than anything he could have assigned a value.

When the game ended, Honey, Nicky, Andrew, and Smokestack stayed behind. Despite his poor performance, they jumped on his back, rubbing his hat all over his head, teasing him for his memorable whiffing.

"First-class strikeout," Nicky said.

"Only the best from me," Stan said. The boys helped Stan load the Zincs' equipment into the storage shed, sorting out a few balls Stan brought from home along with his bat. They locked the shed just as the sun was setting.

Andrew pointed across the river. The unusually clear night mixing with lighter than usual mill spew created bands and splotches of spectacular blues, pinks, and oranges, making the naked hills of Webster burst to life.

Honey turned and pointed in the opposite direction. "Wait, the sun sets back there."

Andrew nodded. He traced his finger along the horizon over the river. "That blue curving color is the earth's shadow. Above it, the pinky purple is the Belt of Venus."

"The earth has a shadow we can see?" Honey scratched his chin. "Oh man. Earth's almost as big as Stan here, I suppose."

Stan squinted at him. "What's that mean?"

"Earth's so big we can sit in its shadow. Your shadow falls over me all the time," Honey said.

"Earth's shadow is night," Andrew said.

"Oh, so half the time I have to sit in Stan's shadow."

"Same for all of us, Honey," Andrew said.

"What's wrong now?" Stan squinted at his brother.

"Nothin'."

"What? What'd I do now? I just embarrassed the shit out of myself in front of the whole town. That's not enough for ya?"

Honey shrugged.

Stan wasn't in the mood for this and started to walk away.

Honey grabbed his arm. "It's that Mr. Rosenberg dropped off a box of clothes."

Stan's eyes went wide. "Well, that's really nice. We could use something new, right?"

"For you. *For you.* Made it clear it wasn't for Pop or me or—"

"When?"

"Just before this game. I was just getting home from work and—"

"You can wear my… whatever it is. Pop can, too. I'm sure it wasn't just for me," Stan said.

Honey shrugged. "It's not the point. Everyone knows you, and no one—"

Stan turned fully to face Honey. "Quit moaning. You know you're as good as I am. I'm playing in the big leagues someday. You can, too, Honey. You just have to set your mind to it."

Honey shrugged. "Set my mind to becoming the earth when I'm just a guy standing on it, hidden in its shadow? Right."

"You just get all negative. Too often. There's barely any difference between us."

"Barely is big. And Pop said—"

"Why would you listen to anything Pop says about baseball? You know he doesn't want either one of us to play ball. Hell, he'd make me go to work in the mill right now if he could."

"Let's just hit some balls," Honey said.

"In the dark?" Stan asked.

"Yeah, we talked about this earlier when you were already at the game. I got the old man's car," Andrew said. "You said you needed some extra hitting the other day, so I asked my dad and he said sure. I got some of our bats and balls, you have your bat, Stan, I piled in some beers, and get this—the old man built a radio and attached it to the inside of the car door. We can even listen to tunes while we hit." Andrew left to get the car.

"Night ball," Nicky said. "Imagine that."

"Apparently we don't have to imagine, Nicky," Stan said.

"Well. I gotta get rollin'."

"Date?" Stan asked.

"Gotta find people in need of my services. You know, running errands and such. Got a cash situation that needs resolved."

"At night?"

"You'd be surprised how many folks are in need of twilight deliveries. Beer to Mr. Mizgorsky from Mr. Hawkins, knitting needles to Mrs. Jones from Mrs. Hasselton. My ma had trouble getting flour at the Red Cross. Ran out just as she got there. So… work is calling. Ma's accustomed to being the one who shares, not the one who takes and…"

Stan knew the impact that could have, how that made parents feel. "Take this." Stan reached in his pocket and pulled out earnings from the gas station.

Nicky stared at Stan's open palm, the money in it. "I can't."

Stan shrugged. "Pay me back when you can."

"No. You said you were saving up to take the inter-urban to a Pirates game."

Stan opened his arms. "Pirates will wait for me. Just not meant for me to get down there yet. I was to go to Babe Ruth's last game. Missed that one. After that, what's it matter how long it takes me to get there?"

"Oh, Stan." Nicky looked at his feet.

Stan handed Nicky a ball. "This flour situation bringing stormy weather your way?"

Nicky met his gaze. "Blizzard, tornado, monsoon. All at once."

"Monsoon in Donora? Can't have that." Stan took the ball back and shoved the cash into Nicky's hand.

"I'll get it back to you."

The lights from Andrew driving the car onto the field, angling the headlights so they hit the mound and home plate from the side, interrupted. "Let's just play, Nicky. Let's have some fun."

They set up as best they could. The sound of the ball cracking off the bat, the mills serenading, the music on the radio, all made for the perfect night.

"You know President Roosevelt switched on the lights that lit the Cincinnati Reds' stadium, and they played night games against every team in the league," Stan said.

"Minor league teams have been using lights in certain towns for years," Andrew said as he fiddled with the radio dial.

"Must be spectacular," Honey said, picking up a few balls.

The boys agreed, but Stan didn't think he could have a better night than right then. That night, with their makeshift night-lights, as they drank and smoked and hit, music playing, Nicky and Honey taking turns pitching to Stan while Andrew and Smokestack chased balls, the boys wouldn't have chosen another place to be in the world.

"Turn that up," Smokestack said as the song "Summertime," by Billie Holiday came on the radio.

Stan sang along. "And the livin' is easy…"

Crack, crack, crack. No bad vibrations, no *thunks* in the lot of Stan's hits that night. The bat, in Stan's hands, felt like he'd been born with that exact pine seeded in his bones, grown right out of his palms and shaped just for him.

They sang to every song that came on, the mills spewing and grinding into the night faded into the background, somehow it all collected to feel like silence, and a calm filled Stan. An hour of him hitting passed in a blink, and he realized he needed to give Honey and Nicky a chance too.

One more. He held one finger up to Honey.

Stan told himself he'd never choke on his gum again.

The next hit sailed until they couldn't see it. Andrew turned, gaze following the ball, removing his hat. They walked toward each other, switching up.

"There's a moon shot," Andrew said handing Stan a beer.

"Sent that one to the stars." Stan sipped the beer. "Just laid it up there for you to find when you start school out where there's clear skies and quiet nights and the best telescope in the world."

"I'm quite sure I'll see your hits landing all over the universe, Stan Musial. Don't doubt it a bit."

Honey spun around in an exaggerated way and spiraled to the ground. "That was so beautiful. That sound!"

"Makes me want to go to church and praise our beautiful God with you Musials come Sunday. How'd you do that?" Smokestack said, coming across the field.

Stan shook his head. He understood their reaction. That one had felt different, looked different as it rose up and out over the river, lost in the smoky night. He almost heard it land on the hillside of Webster. "That beaut doesn't mean a thing if it's not recorded on a scoreboard or box score in the paper."

"It won't be the last one you hit like that."

Stan knew that was true. "Your turn, Honey."

And Honey staggered into Smokestack, laughing about something Stan couldn't hear. "You serve 'em up for me, brother. I'm gonna send mine into the black spaces between those stars where no one, not even Andrew'll find 'em."

All of Honey's discontent seemed to dissolve as he laughed and enjoyed the practice, the beer, the smokes. "Sweet Home Chicago" came on and the moody tune slowed their rhythm.

"Someone oughta write about Sweet Home Donora," Honey said. "Maybe that's what I'll do." And though Stan knew he wasn't going to go writing and performing music, Stan assumed Honey had passed through his dark valley, that in the same way Stan came to realize every time he played that baseball was what he was meant to do, that Honey felt the very same thing. That he'd figure just how to mesh hard work with his desired lifestyle.

Stan swigged, finished his beer, and wiped his brow with his forearm. He spun the ball hidden in his glove, his fingers finding the horseshoe curve. He stopped and drew the ball out, studying it. He held it up. "Hey. Just realized the shape of the laces follows the path of the Mon river around Donora."

Honey took a few practice swings. "Just serve 'em up, Stushy. I've got lots of catching up to you to do."

Stan jammed the ball back in his hand, choking it for his curveball.

"Give me the hot stuff, Stushy," Honey said. "Right down the middle."

Stan paused and readjusted his grip for a fastball. What his brother needed was practice with every other pitch, not the heater. Stan ran his fingers around the laces and settled them in for a curveball again.

The smile on Honey's face made Stan stop. His brother waiting in his stance, the tip of his bat circling just a bit, Nicky with catcher's mitt poised, music playing, metal dust glimmering in the glow of the headlights, the blast of furnace fire marking their play, Smokestack lighting his cigarettes, Andrew adjusting the radio, and chasing down balls. This moment would stay with Stan, this place, his hometown scooped out of the flats, built into hills, and hugged by a fat river. He might one day leave Donora, but Stan knew it would never leave him.

Chapter 35

Mary

Endings or beginnings. Mary rarely had the time to consider the concept. But she felt as though she had been forced to do so a lot recently. Earlier, Lukasz had declared he'd heard Stan sometimes played with the men on the Zincs team, so he was going to attend the game. He was long overdue back home. She assumed the boys must be roaming town with friends. The girls were at a dance at the Slovak Home, and Mary had just tucked Matka into bed after a long day of pain in her abdomen and chest. She had shortness of breath that reminded Mary of Papa's lung problems.

"See, Mary. I do have a heart." Matka pressed her chest. "Hurts like hell, and the pain here is just… I swear I could draw the exact placement of my heart without even seeing inside."

Not even Mary's cabbage or fresh chicken soup eased the discomfort. Dr. Lindsay had stopped by and suggested that sips of whiskey as needed would help Matka sleep. He wasn't sure why her breathing had gotten so bad, but he suspected she might be facing a cancer of some type. "If the pain doesn't ease, I'll take a better look in the office."

Mary's eyes watered at the thought of Matka being so ill, of suffering, sounding like every inhalation and exhalation required her actually thinking about it to make it happen. Matka had accepted rounds of whiskey and finally started to slip into sleep.

"I'll fold laundry tomorrow. I'm no freeloader." She reached for Mary. She couldn't remember a time Matka reached out in need.

Mary kissed her hand. "You've worked harder than anyone I know. Time for you to rest." And by the time Mary had finished that sentence, the whiskey had done its work and her mother had fallen asleep.

Faced with Matka's weakening, Mary was forced to page through her catalog of heartbreak. When Papa had stopped talking to her, when her sister Rose died of the flu in 1924 at the age of sixteen, when Papa died in 1928, when Ida's baby died at birth in 1934. It was absurd to wish there were no endings in life, the agony that came with them always fresh, even if sometimes familiar. And so Mary, like many women her age who were tasked with holding family memories, got good at parceling off the aching that came with them.

She gathered laundry for washing, saving the boys' room for last. She pulled the covers off the bed and got on her knees to search for several of Honey's socks that hadn't made it into the hamper. She located them under the bed and could see piles of newspapers and baseball books on the floor on Stan's side. Mary set her clothes basket aside and got on her knees. She pulled everything out to organize. Notebooks were filled with drawings of pitch grips and statistics and questions he had about the game. Baseball books and a slew of newspapers flayed open to pages with box scores and articles about pro teams and players. He'd circled the Pirates' scores as well as Lefty Grove's wins and losses with notes beside them. The thought that someday young boys would be circling Stan's or Honey's names in the paper shot to mind. She drew a deep breath. She crossed herself and said a prayer. They wanted that more than anything.

As always, prayers buoyed her, like being at church did, too. In prayer and at church, she found herself less bothered with family, thanking God for the opportunities coming their way. Stan never missed church. Honey was a different story. As she squared off Stan's collection of papers and notebooks, she considered Honey. In some ways, she fussed less about him. He said he had the same dreams as Stan. But he wasn't as sensitive or driven. In that quiet moment, she admitted the differences between her sons. Stan was better at baseball in a way that most wouldn't notice if they hadn't seen Honey right up against Stan. Honey didn't fret, like Stan did, not about anything. He didn't feel their lack as though they were the only family in town struggling to make ends meet.

If they never made it to the pros, Stan might not be able to live happily. But Honey? Whatever it was that worried him, he didn't seem to let it shape his behavior. He did what he wanted, shorter-sighted than his brother. Perhaps it was a matter of their age difference.

No. She sat on the bed. It was just who each was. She sighed. Honey hadn't checked out library books, borrowed them from Andrew Morrison, spent hours poring over newspapers. It wasn't Honey who left the house with a ball and glove every single time. It wasn't him whose head was filled every second with nothing but the baseball life.

Mary pulled the laundry basket onto her lap. She loved her boys dearly, equally, if not the same. But she wasn't always sure what to pray for. She knew when it came to Lukasz, Matka, and the girls—for God to soothe Lukasz's soul, keep his job, lighten his load, for God to save Matka from a long, excruciating illness, for the girls to find fine, hardworking men to marry—but the boys? There were times she worried that her prayers, if answered, would be all wrong for what they needed in order to be happy, healthy men.

Chapter 36

Stan

Andrew dropped Stan and Honey off at their home after a night of playing "under the lights."

"I feel like a rich man," Honey said, leaning over the front seat, patting the leather.

"I might like having a car, I have to admit," Stan said.

"Someday we'll all have cars," Andrew said.

"I think you're right," Stan said.

Honey and Stan got out.

"Well," Honey said, "if I don't have my own, I'm borrowing from you two."

"Anytime," Andrew said.

Stan and Honey entered the house, and immediately Stan's good mood soured. The air was still, heavy, scented with whiskey and fresh-lit cigarettes. If there had been a way to get up to their bedroom without having to pass the kitchen from where they'd entered the house, Stan would have taken it.

"We could go back out, put a ladder up to the window," Stan said. "I broke the trellis last time."

"We should invest in a ladder as soon as possible."

"Psst." Honey gestured at the bench near the door. He picked up a box and turned the lid so Stan could see. Gold lettering spelled out Rosenberg's. The clothes Honey had mentioned at the field. Empty. Gold tissue paper was strewn on the bench, scattered over the shoes lined up in front of it. Stan picked up a card. *Can't wait to see you around town in this, Stan. We finally got something in the store as sharp as you! Keep up your hitting. You make baseball worth watching.*

Honey inched toward the kitchen then turned back mouthing the word "Matka." With a sigh of relief Stan followed. Slow, bluesy musical strains of a brass band at the winding-down end of a set came through the radio. Maybe the neighborhood ladies were visiting to drink and smoke, even though due to her high blood pressure Matka wasn't supposed to do either. Maybe the ladies had hung up the clothes that Mr. Rosenberg brought by. "Matka, you're not supposed to—" Stan ventured completely into the kitchen, wanting to stop her from smoking. The sight of Lukasz sitting opposite Matka, wearing what Stan assumed was "the suit," made Stan stop short. Honey was at the sink chugging a glass of water.

"Nice fit. Expensive." Lukasz brushed the collar.

Stan didn't know what to say. In another home, these same words might just be harmless. But in Stan's home, the words came with anger stitched around them like baseball laces.

Lukasz held his arms out. "I've been needing something new. Something to show off the important man I am. Head of the household."

Stan felt the familiar closing of his throat. "Looks nice."

"You're a boy. And the best clothes man in town drops off a suit with your name on it. A boy. You asked him for a suit? That's what you've learned? To beg?"

Stan shook his head. "'Course not. I didn't—"

"I saw you play today. I saw. You're not good enough for a suit like this. Strike out. Yet here it is." Lukasz lifted the whiskey bottle and slammed it against his lips.

Of all the games for Pop to see. "Off. I was off my game tonight. But if you would have seen—"

"Where's your pay from the gas station?"

Stan reached in his pocket, remembering he'd given it to Nicky. "Someone needed—"

"Someone?" Lukasz rose out of his seat, swaying. He latched on to the edge of the table. "You're the someone who needs the money. Your family needs that money."

Matka sipped her coffee. "Always bring the money to the family."

Fear gripped Stan. Even with his father being sodden with whiskey, his presence felt enormous.

Mom came up from the cellar, untying her apron. She quickly scanned the room. "Lukasz? When'd you come home? Matka, you're up. Boys? When did you all—"

Lukasz pulled at the lapels of the suit. "Home long enough to put on my new suit. And your son gave away pay to a friend. After getting free gifts. I suppose he ought to try living on Modisette Avenue. What's next, Stashu? A free home? For a boy. A little boy. And his little games. And I…" Lukasz held up his hands.

"Lukasz, please," Mary said. "It's a nice thing that Mr. Rosenberg… You should be proud of your son. You should—"

"I am the man of the house, Mary. You can't tell me I *should* anything."

Mom gestured to Honey, who stood in the doorway, shrinking away. "Take Matka upstairs. She doesn't need the stress."

Honey did as he was told, and Stan stepped toward Mom and Pop. "I'll return it. I didn't ask for anything, I swear."

Pop glared, his eyes unfocused yet piercing, a night's worth of whiskey reddening and watering them. For a moment, Lukasz looked small, hard-shelled like a walnut, but tiny, like Stan could put him in his palm and close his fingers around him.

Pop pointed at Stan, looming enormous again, the way he always had. "No baseball until chores and work are done. I despise that Rosenberg and his free clothes. An insult to think I can't buy my family clothes." He continued to rant, his voice spreading, suffocating as he jerked from English to Polish and back again.

Stan held his breath, anger and fear swirling inside him. He hadn't done anything wrong. His father should be proud of him.

"Please, Lukasz, calm down," Mom said, inching toward him. "Your son is—"

"Rosenberg drops off gifts like we are *poor*. For a boy who strikes out, who—"

"We *are* poor!" Stan screamed, shocking himself, his voice booming like a man, not a boy. His vision went blurry. Long-rusted words flew out of him, shelling like fireworks. "I'm good enough to play on a men's team, and Mr. Rosenberg did something nice because he believes in me. Joe Barbao believes in me. The *whole town* believes in me. Everyone but—"

Mary put her hand on Stan's arm. "No." Her eyes went wide, pleading, with the slightest shake of the head.

Stan refocused on Pop. He tried to bite back the words, but they were out, making Pop's glare pin him harder. "Everyone but *you*. I'm your son, but they treat me better. Why? Why is that?" Loose words were a first for Stan, and when he'd spent them all, he stood frozen, bracing for what might come next.

But instead of attacking, Pop stumbled back, palm on the wall, steadying himself. With a deep breath, he lurched forward, swiping a newspaper from the table. He shook it at Stan, then held it up and drew a line with this finger across a column as though physically trying to tie his vision to the paper. He glowered, the hardness in his face breaking Stan's heart. Why couldn't he be proud of him?

"My son. You think you are big. But did you see this?" He stumbled. Mom caught him under the arm and he shook her off, pulling himself up, reading from the paper. *"Only 5'4". Too small to play every day."* He lifted his gaze to Stan, lips drawing in a tight smirk.

Stan couldn't breathe. Was Pop finished? Stan wanted to flee but couldn't make his feet move.

Pop shook the page. "The *whole town* believes in you? The whole town knows you are little and—"

With Pop's mocking, the words wormed deep inside Stan, making his body turn rigid and wobbly at the same time. His hands shook. He balled them, trying to keep his emotion stuffed inside. He'd been taught to respect his parents, to understand his role as a child in their household. He'd wanted his father to be proud of him. He'd spent his life tightrope-walking the valley between twin walls—dodging Pop's gaze and hoping he noticed his prowess.

What father treated his son's success as though it were a crime? He bit his tongue, wanting his stutter to save him. But it was too late. He was beginning to see the gap between father and son as giving the space to be truthful. If Pop was going to say what he believed about Stan, he would return the favor.

Mom tugged at Pop, trying to get him to sit. She shushed at him, wanting to calm him. He resisted like granite slabs easily weathering rain.

Stan laid thoughts to what he'd seen his whole life. Mom soothing Pop. Succeeding, but only until the next time he was angry or sad or lost. Like sparks that formed then flew, the words shaped inside Stan, rising up from his feet. He leaned forward, letting them out with a blast-furnace roar. "I'm little because of you! You're the shortest man in Donora."

Mom's jaw dropped. Pop flinched, but his expression remained hard as ever, boring into Stan. But when Pop widened his feet, hands fidgeting, Stan knew his words had landed.

Fear crashed through Stan, the release of long-held feelings jolting him. He stepped toward his parents. "Whatever you don't like about me is because of you! You never like when I'm good. From the time I let you win at the Falcons when I was eight years old. Eight. Even then I *let* you win."

Mom leapt between her son and husband, one palm on each chest. "Please stop. Don't do this." *Please*, she mouthed at Stan. He hated to see Mom bridging husband and son, as she'd done Stan's entire life. His insides collapsed in on themselves, sickening him. He tingled from his scalp to his fingertips. He latched his gaze on Pop. "I'm never talking to you again!" He jabbed his finger. "I hate you, and I will never live in a house like this. Not ever. I hate that getting something nice is bad. I hate—"

A squeaky sound made Stan notice Mom. Tears welled in her eyes. Stan hadn't meant to do this to her, to hurt her, to sound like Pop, ungrateful. He hadn't meant to let any of what he said into the world.

"I'm sorry, Mom. I didn't—"

Lukasz lurched toward Stan again, but Mom's hand kept him back. "A *game*," he said. "You never *let* me win. Never. And now you play a game and pretend it's big shit. Those people just use you for—"

And that last bit was all Stan could take. He ran from the kitchen, unable to constrain what might come out of his mouth next, worried he might punch his father to shut him up. He didn't want to make things harder for Mom or make things so he couldn't reverse them later.

For the first time in his life, Stan saw his stammering as sometimes saving him from what he shouldn't say. This time it hadn't. He ran down the hill, stalking around town, trying to release every bad thought that fluttered in his mind and tangled around his heart. He hated what he saw in Pop's eyes and couldn't believe a father would dislike his son's achievements, dislike his son so much that he could want to keep a person slight and insignificant. How could Pop feel this way? Stan was strong, like Pop. Why wasn't that good? Stan felt as though he lived with a creature he didn't understand, couldn't talk to, couldn't love like a person should. And that dug a hole out of his heart that he wasn't sure could ever be filled.

**

The sun was rising when Stan had burned off the tirade, when he'd finally tucked his rancid words back inside. Knowing Pop would be dead asleep or gone looking for work, he approached the house, familiar voices lifting over the morning quiet.

Honey and Andrew. They must have been up all night, too.

"I smell what you're cookin', Andrew. But can't deny. He's left me behind."

Stan stopped and watched them from behind the tree near the porch. The two sat on the top step of the stairs, Honey tapping a broom handle between his feet, then tossing a stone and swatting it across the street in perfect rhythm. "Officially right there, that Zincs game, the newspaper articles. He's no longer one of us," Honey said.

Stan dug his fingertips into the crevices cutting between raised bark sections of the oak tree.

Andrew shook his head. "No. No. You're seeing it all wrong. Stan Musial left the rest of us behind the day he was born. You're not the only one. He's special in a way that no one else is. See how people gather around him, want to be near him. And he just smiles and answers their questions and makes everyone feel welcome. You *shouldn't* feel so—well, it's the same for everyone. Believe me."

"But I'm the only one who has to live with him. I'm the one with the same last name."

The thought that Stan should correct Honey, that he should give him a pep talk about his own talent came to mind, but he was too tired to stoke the conversation. Not after what happened with Pop. He backed up to keep out of their sight, then faked a cough to let them know someone was coming. He didn't like that whatever it was he was good at made Honey jealous, that it created this anger in their father. But baseball was what Stan had to hold on to. And the more people gave him things or disliked him for it, or the better he got playing in a league for grown men, the more sure he was that his life would include baseball.

"Hey, guys," he said, coming up the stairs, sitting just below them, leaning against the banister slats. "Long night? You didn't have to—"

Andrew put his hand up. "Honey and I did some moon gazing and… well, we just wanted to be sure you were all right."

For all the emptiness Stan had felt walking the streets all night, being with his brother and his best friend right then, in that slim sliver of early morning light, he felt the empty spot inside him fill a little. He trusted them; he knew they loved him, even if he'd "left them behind."

He tossed a stone for Honey to hit. And then another. "Ever notice how it smells up here? Walkin' the town, the night to myself, I realized not every neighborhood in Donora carries a slight scent of sewage."

Andrew tossed a stone to Honey. *Whack*, it flew into the street sign with a metal ping.

"Nice one," Stan said.

"Must be our house that smells like that," Andrew said. "Dad's got some guys working on the toilet."

Stan looked at his friend. Andrew was always quick with some way to dispel discomfort. Always making other fellas not feel bad about something, as though the homes that still had outhouses or had shoddy indoor plumbing might not be the sources of the odor.

Stan smiled. Andrew's very existence was instructive. A kid with so much, always willing to sacrifice—his body in baseball, his pride in all other matters. "You're wild, Weatherman. Wildly humble."

Andrew pulled something out of his pocket. "Oh hey. Here." He tossed sticks of Dubble Bubble at Honey and Stan.

"You had that all night, did ya?" Honey said.

And Stan hoped he'd be just like Andrew when they grew up. Like the sun and moon and stars, these incredible, wondrous bodies shone down on all of them, sharing their greatness, simply obligingly doing what they did, Andrew was just like that. When a person was truly big, when he had enough, when he understood how impressive he was, he could share all of that with others. Andrew, young as Stan, taught him over and over there was always enough in the world, somewhere there was, and when a person got his hands on it, he ought to share.

Chapter 37

Mary

The night Stan let all his thoughts out, all over Lukasz, Mary barely slept. Not because Stan was out alone, roaming. She was quite sure he was safe, and he clearly needed to expel the rest of the pent-up anger he'd been stowing inside. But the argument had laid bare the feelings she'd hoped somehow Stan might escape having. Same as she'd wished for all her children. His reference to the handstand contest at the Falcons, so long ago but still clear in his mind, confirmed, like Ida's experiences had, that although Mary had done her best to protect her children from a particular view of their father, they had their own eyes, minds, experiences.

They could see plainly what was in front of them. She knew that would happen, how could it not? But she had hoped to shield them from the pain it could cause. Her deepest sadness came in recognizing Lukasz's failure to entertain the relationships he desperately wanted, that human beings needed, but instead he continuously strained, almost as if he were compelled to repel and harm. She felt the heavy responsibility of being the person he needed the most, loved the most, wanted the most. And though her own disappointment grew each year, she couldn't deny loving him still, loving him so much she still believed he could soften and let his own children's affection inside him someday, let his out.

Lukasz had been sleeping hard for about five hours when a knock at the back door drew Mary from bed. Albert MacKenzie removed his hat, saying that they needed some extra fellas for a shift at the wireworks. Mary wasn't sure Lukasz was in the shape to take it on, but he was out of bed and headed to the mill before she could even determine if he remembered what had happened the night before.

Matka shuffled into the kitchen, face ashen. Mary rushed to her. "You all right?"

She nodded but pressed her chest.

"I'll get the doctor."

"No. I don't want that man poking round. I'm fine. Just need coffee. Coffee soup with the thick bread. Lots of sugar. Headache's all it is."

"But you're grabbing your chest."

"Doc said high pressure'll do that. Told you that."

Mary settled Matka at the table then put the water on for coffee. "How 'bout eggs, then, or toast?" Seeing Matka in pain or discomfort, with shortness of breath and her reduced ability to walk caused Mary to feel her own age. There was only so much she could push Matka to do.

"Eggs'll be fine. Along with my soup."

Mary nodded, saddened.

"Stashu and Lukasz—they all right?"

Mary moaned, but waved the question off. Like she ignored the feelings that came with Matka's declining health, she did the same with her son and husband. She'd learned that lesson from Matka well. Just keep going. Things were easier that way. And after she'd let the sorrow drape her the night before, even through the early morning, she was ready to face the day.

She went toward the front of the house to retrieve the eggs Mrs. Morrison said she'd drop on the porch. As she approached, she heard voices and realized Honey must have been out all night as well as Stan. She pulled the curtain on the front window aside, peeking at Andrew, Honey, and Stan sitting on the stairs, smacking stones across the street with her broom, their voices soft, tired. All three were good kids. Two of them would lead lives far different from most in Donora. Honey could do that, too, if he just believed in what was possible and then worked for it.

Mary opened the door and picked up the egg basket. "Come in for breakfast, boys. Pop's at work. Matka's up, and the jumbo's lookin' good. I'll fry it up with eggs." They hopped to their feet. Stan finally met her gaze and gave her a smile. She roped her arm around his shoulder and kissed his cheek. He squeezed her around the waist as they entered the house. Inside, she turned. "You, too, Andrew. Your mom brought me these beautiful pink and beige eggs from your grandpa's farm. I won't take no from you."

Mary sent them to wash up. And with morning's arrival, she allowed herself to embrace the goodness in her life, grateful her boys had friends like Andrew. It gave them a view into a world that showed possibility, not prescription. It was like when she worked at the Dunns' as a girl, all that they'd given her to see the world's expanse past what her upbringing had allowed. And she'd taken most of it. But she'd left the biggest offer behind and had chosen a life with Lukasz instead of moving with the Dunns, giving baby Ida up for adoption in another city. Things could be different for her sons and she was sure it would be.

Stan and Honey kissed Matka on the cheek, and Andrew shook her hand.

"Well, always a gentleman you are," Matka said. She narrowed her gaze on him. "Don't trust men with *too many* good manners."

Stan burst out laughing. "You can trust this fella, Gram. He's a good one."

And as the girls wakened, their voices mixing with the boys' while Mary cooked, she was struck with satisfaction, breathing room. Matka seemed to feel good enough to eat, and she had a glint in her eye as the kids' conversations swirled around her, interrupting them to scold one of their bad ideas now and again.

And Mary marveled at how she'd circled around in her relationship with Matka.

At one time, Mary's mother could not give her anything she needed. And now Mary was caring for her, seeing her fragility, remembering her strength, and far enough from any of their disagreements for them to hurt anymore. All that was left was the love that had been there all along. She felt as though she was reaching back for Matka and forward for her children, healing what had been wrong in her own life through accepting things as they were, not as she had wanted them to be. Her siblings had long since left their home, even Donora. Looking at Matka, Mary realized her fortune to be the one to meet their mother all over again, to know her differently.

The power of contentment felt better than any soaring great news Mary could imagine. Despite Lukasz's limitations, her dreams that dissolved, she'd been a good wife. She never stomped on his opinions; she endlessly made amends on his behalf and buffered everyone who came into contact with him. These weren't facts she could submerge into often, but in keeping their family together, it gave her the chance to be the mother she'd always wanted to be. So she would try again to soothe Lukasz, to invite him to see the world and his children the way they actually were.

She pulled her stock pot onto the stove, sliding it behind the frying pan. He would need some soup for his belly. Maybe pierogi. She would take it down to him at lunch and then she would set things right again. She crossed herself. "Please make Lukasz change. Please, God, somehow." And for the first time her prayers for life with Lukasz pleaded for something else. She no longer just wanted to buffer him, to try to love him into improving. She wanted him to just turn into the person he'd promised her he'd be.

Chapter 38

Stan

Stan avoided Pop best he could, doing his eggshell walk when both were home, but he played as much ball and worked as often as possible. And when weather patterns on the home front grew hot and threatening, Andrew was always there with an invitation for Stan to join him on his perch. Out there, on sweltering summer nights, the two talked the night away. It was perfect, even when it was too smoky and cloudy to see a speck of starlight.

The Heslep All-Stars played well enough to make it to the championship game, facing off against the Cardinals. Benjamin Hicks was his normal arrogant self at the game, but when the boys gathered to unwrap those special gold-wrapped balls before the championship game, the whole lot of them were giddy like little kids, like brothers with Christmas presents delivered right from Santa's hands.

The bleachers were stuffed with fans of all ages as the raffle and sponsorships had made citizens even more interested than they might have normally been in junior league baseball.

The Cardinals and their fans were mouthier than usual, agitating sleepy Heslep fielders. One inning turned into three, rattling Stan so much his pitching went wild, knocking two kids in the back and sending balls over Tank's head twice. The saving grace was that Stan's feral throwing kept batters unsettled, whiffing as often as they hit.

In the fourth inning, Stan, though hitting well, began to feel that familiar tightening in his throat, the kind he experienced in school when cornered by a teacher who wanted a particular answer at a very exact time.

Stan tried to take deep breaths and concentrate on every element of his pitching, so focused that he nearly didn't respond to the rising amount of bickering between his teammates. Honey was especially impatient with what he saw as atrocious play by Monocle and Smokestack.

As Honey lambasted Monocle yet again, Stan stepped off the mound. He thought of the earth's shadow they'd talked about when they practiced with the car lights. Maybe others felt the same vastness, small because of it. Andrew shouted for everyone to get in the game and reminded Stan of how the Weatherman always lifted others, so confident in his bigness that he could share it. That was it. Everyone told Stan how great he was, wanted to help him, and it made him work harder, made him want to please those people. That was it. It was worth a shot anyway. Stan jogged toward Monocle, waving him in. "You're fine, Monocle. Just do what you've been doing all season." Stan put his glove on his shoulder but stared at Honey as he talked. "Monocle's gonna have a red-letter day."

Honey blew a bubble in reply, clearly irritated that this conversation was as much for him as for Monocle.

As they headed back to their positions, the fans took the opportunity to dig in. "Okay, Schmitty, send a pea to right. Kid's got a rusty glove, and they know it."

Stan made eye contact with Melonhead at first base. Carson, the baserunner, had been taking a good lead. When he saw Stan glance his way, he inched back to the bag.

Not close enough, Stan thought. Carson had a habit of stealing bases, and with Heslep being off their game, Stan was sure the guy would take his chances.

Schmitty sauntered to the batter's box, chomping on tobacco, grinning with black seed between his teeth. "Hey, Pitch. Rough one today."

Stan clenched his jaw, circled the mound, noting that Carson had slipped a couple steps farther toward second base. Stan rolled his shoulders. *Relax.* He exhaled, started his motion, then fired the ball to first base, Melonhead catching it with his fast hands and the runner off base for an out.

"That's it, Stan. That's what we want to see," someone shouted from the stands.

This relaxed Stan and the team further.

"I'm feeling like a home run today," Schmitty said just before spitting.

Stan let the words wash past him like smoke over the river. He flowed through his motion, the release perfect, allowing his slow ball to wiggle toward the batter before sinking just as it crossed the plate. Schmitty got a piece of it, the ball taking a hard but odd arc that caused Monocle to flinch and rotate his glove.

And in one of those baseball miracles, the result was the ball landing in the glove with a *thunk*, shocking him as much as anyone watching. Monocle's wide eyes as he stared at the ball in his glove made Stan laugh—belly laugh. "Oh, there's some hands," Stan shouted. "Nice one." And from that point on, Heslep played loose and better than they ever had. Their team's tension had broken, and the momentum shift was clear to both teams. Even Honey softened up.

When the All-Stars batted next, Moonshine was picking at Nicky's stance, which he'd already changed up for each of his first three at bats. Stan called Nicky out of the box and leaned close to his ear. "What the hell're you doing?"

"Finding my swing."

Stan had heard this kind of thing plenty of times. Loads of times the batter actually needed to find a swing. He thought of what Joe had told him and thought the same would apply to Nicky. "Well, stop it. You know exactly where your swing is. Same swing as all season." He wasn't one to normally give unwanted advice. But this time he felt it was important. Walking back to the bench, he scanned his teammates' faces. "Don't mess with Nicky's stance—leave him be."

And so Nicky reverted to his typical, easy stance, the one that almost looked like he just accidentally found himself in the middle of a baseball game, and he hit like always. They all hit like Nicky the rest of the day.

As Heslep started to come together, finding their bats, coming up with every bad bounce for outs, the Cardinals unraveled. Heslep beat their nemesis, the Cement City Cardinals, 22–4. The Cardinals were so put off for having lost that they stormed the All-Stars with raised fists. They'd never lost in front of a big crowd before, and it stung like mud-wasps.

Stan and Andrew kept their team back. Nothing Cheeks liked more than a rumble, but even he was too happy with the win to throw punches. The game was written up in the paper, and Stan couldn't have been happier that his team had gotten press coverage, that they'd won it all together.

**

That night, the league sponsors threw a dance at Palmer Park to celebrate all the teams, complete with live music and refreshments. Stan wore the jacket from Mr. Rosenberg, and Honey borrowed one from Andrew. The feeling of having beaten the Cardinals stayed with Stan and the team throughout the night. Stan was grateful that although he'd never taken fancy dance classes, over the years Mom had taught them fiery polkas, the choppy Charleston, old-fashioned waltzes, the Lindy Hop, and even taught them the silly Grizzly Bear that made her belly laugh, as though it put her back in time recalling things she wasn't sharing with her kids. Stan's parents danced around the house many times, times when Pop found a smile and sometimes even a laugh.

Just before leaving for the dance, Mom reminded Stan, Honey, and Andrew of how to ask a girl to dance. "Always a gentleman. That's most important when it comes to dancing and courting. Ask everyone, even the shy girls, even the…" Her voice caught. "The tall girls who look bored in the corner. Ask them all."

Stan saw a glimmer of a girl behind his forty-year-old mother's eyes, the mention of height clearly being something that must have bothered her at one time, though he couldn't imagine it. She ran their home, and if you subtracted the concessions she made to account for Pop's moods, she was the rule-maker who made sure everything worked. She donated time and anything she could to those who needed it; she was vocal about American ways and values and politics and what that meant for their family. She played catch with her boys, loved baseball, and her laugh—it was as big as she was tall, the contagious kind that made everyone around her double over, too. She was the family's sun—always reliably there, even if hidden behind thick clouds. So while he knew girls were sometimes left to the corners and edges of the dance pavilion, he was sure that had never happened to his mom. It was simply her reminding him to be nice as she would have been any chance she had.

The boys trooped off to the park, and when they arrived, they and the rest of the Heslep All-Stars were met with congratulations from dancegoers, even from the Cardinals. The sting of their loss had worn down. There were still rough edges between the two teams, but they were full of cheer for the dance. With pats on backs all around, Stan didn't notice the energy shifting until Andrew elbowed him.

Above the throng, he saw Benjamin's head moving toward them. Closer, the sea of kids parted to make way for the suave, sauntering Benjamin. With his fine linen jacket, boater hat, and white shoes that glistened under the lantern light, he embodied the sense of a movie actor. He grinned at Stan, putting his hand out. "Great season, buddy."

That meant a lot coming from Stan's greatest competition.

"I'd give ten years' allowance for a touch of that magic you have in spades."

Stan was startled. He felt his tongue thicken, worried for a moment that he'd lose his words. But he told himself there was no need for that. This was an equal, not an adult, not a teacher. "You're right there with me every game."

Benjamin shrugged. "That's the thing about you, Stanley Musial. You make everyone feel like your friend. So I have a hard time taking you to task. I can't deny what I don't have compared to you."

Stan's gaze lit over Benjamin, the fella with everything. "Now come on. Surely you're getting calls from Yale by now. You beat me up plenty. Still got the wounds to prove it." Stan pressed his chest. Benjamin had humbled him plenty.

Benjamin shook his head and backed away. "There you go again. I'm trying not to like you, and you just won't permit it."

Stan's cheeks warmed. "Now get yourself a dance partner, friend."

"I'm trying to get on several dance cards before you do."

And a girl in a pink dress that lifted like flower petals in the wind when she spun was batting her eyes at Benjamin, distracting him completely from any thought of Stan.

Stan let the first dance go by before fully recognizing he had to ask the girls to dance—they weren't going to ask him. Spinning and turning the night away, laughing, filled with popular tunes and old standards, Stan took each song with someone different. Except, he saved the sixth and the twelfth dance for the girl huddled by the drinks, the one who made him wonder how it was possible his mother might ever have felt shy, had ever stood alone waiting for someone to notice her.

It capped a wonderful day, the attention from the girls nearly as intoxicating as the win that day. And he went to sleep, his prayers mostly full of thanks for what a great day it had been.

Chapter 39

Stan

Fall 1936

School started in early September. Stan took mostly non-academic, commercial courses, woodshop and electrical shop being his favorites. When in English and History, he'd sneak *Baseball Magazine* behind his textbook, lost in the world he most wanted to be a part of. And when he could, he'd steal away spending time in the library, where Miss Helen Klotz always had new sports books to recommend.

One morning he was called to the office.

"Stanley Musial." Mrs. Hampshire waved Stan to her reception counter. "My grandson is your biggest fan. Saw every game you played. Pack of his friends, traipsing after you big boys like you were laying a gold-dust trail at your heels."

Stan smiled. "That's nice. Thank you."

"But you were his favorite. *Stan struck out grown men, Stan launched two out...* all summer long. Stan, Stan, Stan. And," she leaned in, "he reported you helped him with his grip on the bat and his swing. Oh my, I haven't heard such swooning since my niece married the oil baron out Texas way."

"Thank you." Stan grew hot, as he always did when attention was turned on him, even though grateful to hear it.

She gestured toward the chairs along the wall. "Sit and wait there for your teachers."

Stan could hear his shop teacher, Mr. Reese, guidance counselor, Mr. Duda, Coach Russell, and English teacher Mr. Clark talking in the counselor's office.

"He's a gifted carpenter," Mr. Reese said. "Could be a master in no time."

Stan couldn't see them, but he knew their voices like his own.

"The kid oughta go to college. Doc Carlson at Pitt says he'll take a look at him for basketball," Coach Russell said. Stan straightened. Coach Russell had been central to getting plenty of fellas connected with great colleges.

One of them sighed.

"Let the kid be," Mr. Clark said.

"College, yes," Mr. Duda said. "Baseball. Maybe both sports. I see that."

"Gotta shine up the transcript though," Coach Russell said. "Commercial course load won't cut it at any college."

"College-prep math, maybe science will round him out nice," Mr. Duda said.

A strange sensation crept through Stan, hearing them discuss him like an inanimate object they were shaping into a sculpture of some sort as much as a teenage boy. The door slammed behind him, and Melissa Carney entered, her face red and blotchy. Mrs. Hampshire dashed around her desk to lead the girl into the nurse's office. The commotion made Mr. Clark notice Stan sitting and waiting.

Coach Russell came toward Stan, taking him by the shoulder. "Stanley. Come on in." Nested at the center of his mentors, Stan listened to each critique his strengths and weaknesses as they pertained to his future. College. The word ricocheted around his mind. Until then, Andrew had been the only person who'd ever mentioned it to Stan.

Mr. Duda knocked on the desk to get Stan's attention back toward him. "Mr. James at the junior high already said you can take algebra down there to make up for what you missed. Would be a little strange with the younger kids, but colleges won't take you without it."

Stan shifted, starting to feel hot and trapped. Algebra at the junior high?

"True," Mr. Clark said.

"Well, I think you oughta leave the kid be. He likes to work with his hands. He's a ballplayer after all," Mr. Reese said.

Stan's head swam. He couldn't imagine going to junior high for a math class, but he'd do it if it meant he could go to college. College? What was he thinking? That would take him eventually to baseball, but not straight there. What if he got injured and never had the chance to go pro? And then there was basketball. Did he even want to play it in college? He'd sure had a good time the prior season. The three men stared at him as though he could make this decision on the spot.

"Stan?" Coach Russell asked.

"What do you think?" Mr. Duda asked.

Stan thought of his parents. Mom knew his dream was to play baseball—she'd helped him build it. But he'd never seriously discussed any of these other choices with anyone. Pop wanted Stan in the mills, especially since they'd ramped up production to help supply other countries what they needed to face the threat of war. "I don't know. I'm just…"

Mr. Duda slumped back in the chair. "It's a lot. We're tossing all of it at you at once."

Stan nodded, relieved they didn't seem to expect a decision right then.

"But you'll need to do some things if you think college ball is in play at all. Just so you have choices. Nothing's written in stone."

Stan was stunned that although graduation was years away, post-graduation decisions needed to be made now.

"Talk to your parents," Coach Russell said. "And don't forget to ask if you can play football," he added.

Mr. Duda leaned forward on his desk. "Nothing like the college experience."

"Playing for Doc Carlson at Pitt?" Coach Russell said. "Getting an education? Well worth your while."

"Or he can build—things that last a lifetime," Mr. Reese said.

"He can take up carpentry anytime," Coach Russell said.

"Because it's not academic?" Mr. Reese rolled his eyes.

Mr. Duda shook his head. "You played like the dickens this summer for the Zincs. But playing ball in college, getting a degree, that gives you a full complement of life choices. And, well, we want to put a high school baseball team together here again for spring. Haven't had one since 1923."

"All right." Stan wiped his sweaty palms on his pants. "I'll think on it."

"You have so much greatness in you, and we don't want to see it go by the wayside," Coach Russell said.

"Thank you. A lot to think about." Stan couldn't find the right words to further express his thoughts.

Released from his conference, feeling like he'd just been fire-hosed, a clamp squeezed his throat. Choices. It was too much to consider. All he'd ever wanted was to play pro baseball—none of the rest of it. He passed Benjamin Hicks and several girls on their way to class.

"Hey, Musial," the boy said, one of the girls on one arm, her books in his other.

"Hi, Stanley," the girl said, looking as shy as Stan felt.

Confidence. Andrew and Benjamin had it in every aspect of life. Even with Andrew, who was a terrible athlete, his lack of success didn't bother him a bit, satisfied with having attempted to play at all. Their self-confidence filled them from the ground up, born inside them, bred in their households. Stan felt that, too, on the field. But maybe college was where he ought to go. Maybe it would give him what he lacked in areas beyond sports. Maybe Andrew was right. A person couldn't play ball forever. Maybe he should consider college, even if just to enjoy the possibility. Maybe that would change Pop's view of him if colleges wanted Stanley Musial to attend.

Heading for English class, Stan waved at Franny Litvak and Nancy Sobol. He tried to imagine them being yanked into the office for a fire-hosing of life options. Secretary or housewife? Nurse or teacher? He looked up to their librarian, Helen Klotz, more than he could say. Maybe she'd dreamed of being a doctor but teachers had steered her toward librarian. His sisters, like many kids, had quit school before graduating. Even Rose had chosen that year to leave and start working for a family needing full-time housekeeping.

Honey seemed on the edge of quitting every other day. Mom loved being a mother. Though she never said, Stan was confident that was what she'd dreamed of being. When she talked about falling in love with Pop, her eyes would shift up and she'd get a little smile, as though the clouds held her good memories for safekeeping. Life was simple when you knew what you wanted. It had been simple for Stan until he was suddenly given choices.

Matthew Zeman brushed past, apologizing as he dragged a wheeled crate overflowing with chemistry equipment. Had his teachers sat him down for a grilling between choices of scientist or mill foreman? Stan thought of Pop, the choice he'd made to come all the way to America knowing no one, with nothing but the strength that coursed through him. With his mother long dead, his father with a new family, with no jobs available, no path to remedy that, Pop had sailed toward freedom, huddled in a tiny cabin with nothing but a bag full of wire, the name of a sponsor in Donora, and the hope of living the American Dream. Pop provided only those facts. He never expressed how he felt about leaving, how it felt to not understand English, how it felt to never speak to his father again. Had it been hard to leave him? Pop had never said, never even expressed sadness about what he'd left behind. Perhaps that indicated a level of pain Stan couldn't imagine. The things causing the most pain were last to be discussed in the Musial home. If that held, then perhaps what Pop had left in Poland hurt so much that it worked like acid, liquifying the words to describe it.

Stan's parents loomed so large in his world he couldn't imagine not talking about them, not telling his children all about them someday. Pop left everything he knew to live the American Dream. If he could do that, Stan could make a decision. Having choices should make him excited, not unsettled. He simply needed to look at the array of options through different eyes.

Chapter 40

Mary

Suzanne Lancos's heart gave out just after midnight on September 30, 1936. Mary was by her side, holding her hand, reminding her about the forty years they'd shared as mother and daughter, retelling stories—the good ones—as Matka's eyes closed and shot open depending on which topic stimulated her.

"I'm so proud of ya, Mary. Yer papa was, too."

Matka pressed the final words out, then her labored breath overcame her ability to talk, catching then leaving her body for the last time. Mary's breath stopped, too, the finality shocking even though completely imminent. She laid her head on Matka's hushed chest, immediately wading into the emotional mix that came when a mother died and a daughter was present for it.

The next two days, Mary readied for Matka's funeral, fulfilling her request for one viewing just before the funeral mass and burial. It was quieter at the house, the boys moving lighter and softer, less demanding. Honey had even brought Mary coffee before she got out of bed those two days, surprising her further. Lukasz pulled day shifts and tiptoed around his wife in a way that told her he understood the loss.

Ida sent word that she and Frank would stay at the Donora Hotel but that they'd come to the house first. Helen, Vicki, and Rose took on all of Mary's jobs except the one at the big house on Thompson. Mary needed work in order to keep her emotions steady until everyone arrived.

And so the day before the funeral, morning broke with the kind of light that turned up gently, water-coloring over the deep night blue with shades of gray. No golden sunrise or dramatic weather, as though the universe wasn't aware that someone had died, someone who had often shaken the house rafters like a thunderstorm trapped inside. The first chilly fall morning light revealed fog in the hollow, strung tree bough to tree bough like wet cobwebs.

Waiting. Mary stood on the porch, surveying the cobbled-together home; like so many in Donora, it had been expanded as money came in or materials were found. It had been a good home overall, one that Matka and Papa had taken great pride in owning. The constant fight against soot and mill dust was difficult, but despite their limited resources, their home was warm and clean as possible.

The coal seam in the back fed them with fuel, the worn abode giving Mary her best and worst memories. With Matka's death, Mary felt shrunken—lighter, smaller, part of her life cut off, relief and grief intensified in equal parts.

She stared into the craggy valley beyond the hollow, grateful that Lukasz was getting regular shifts at the wireworks. An arm around her shoulder startled her. Stan. She waited for him to say something, but when he didn't, she slipped her arm around his waist, no words needed to understand this was his way of comforting her. A quiet presence to lean on.

She looked back at his profile. He'd grown a little bit, seemingly overnight. His face, more angular, having shed a bit of baby fat, exuded a kindness with every expression. His eyes filled and tears dropped. She looked away. "Thank you, Stashu."

He squeezed her tighter.

A car pulled in front of the house, jerking to a stop. All four doors flung open like bird wings setting to fly. Mary's brothers, John and George, and sisters, Ann and Victoria, tumbled out, arms open. Mary rushed to them, gathering them in, hugging them all at once. Tears and laughter spilled out, hugs and kisses were delivered with observations that everyone looked good; it felt like Mary was the one arriving home. Victoria fanned her face as tears continued to drop. Ann dragged a hanky out of her purse, dabbing at Victoria's cheeks.

"Come, come inside," Mary said.

They pulled casseroles, baked goods, and crates with whiskey bottles and beer out of the car then filed onto the porch. Stan greeted each aunt and uncle, all marveling at how grown he was, at what they'd heard about his summer baseball achievements. Stan's face reddened, and he had trouble making eye contact, but Mary knew he was pleased. She held the door open. Her siblings entered, suddenly hushed, wandering the space, drawn corner to corner, something important, but unseen compelling each in various directions.

Mary took their coats. "Looks the same?" The weight of her family's arrival was heavy. Memories of their childhood flooded through her as she observed her adult home as a child again.

Ann nodded. "So much so, but... not. Feels completely different. Just the feel." She looked toward the kitchen and followed Mary there.

"It's been so long," Victoria said. "I half expect Papa to come blustering in, bottle in hand, bitching about some new tax on some item he'd never even buy."

"And Matka, screaming about a mill boss or the burgess or some council member with the next bad idea," George said.

"Or some snooty mill foreman," John said.

"And our sister Rose," George said. His voice was thin, fragile.

"Oh, I miss her." Victoria hugged herself.

"Me, too." George unloaded an armful of whiskey bottles onto the table. He turned as Honey came in, then Helen, Vicki named for her Lancos aunt, and little Rose, also named for her aunt. He threw his arms open, hugging them all. "Holy mackerel, you've all turned into people! No more babies. I can't believe it's been this long."

This brought another torrent of tears at not getting together enough and laughter about things that had lost their sting and were now only seen as funny. Mary didn't spend her days missing her siblings, but with them there, she felt as though her world expanded back to where it ought to be all the time, wondering how she didn't ache for them on a daily basis.

Neighbors dropped off pierogi, kielbasa, haluski, donuts, ground coffee, and beer. The family ate, drank, and smoked, the kitchen taking on a blue haze as they shared a steady stream of memories that came from living toe to toe with eight Lancoses and countless boarders.

"The fireplace, that Christmas Eve," Ann said. She pointed her cigarette at Mary. "Still hide things there, Mary?" No. Now she hid secrets behind her heart walls and in the pockets of her mind. She shook her head and explained to the kids that she used to stow things in there to hopefully use as part of her engagement items.

"Engagement trousseau... Mom," Helen said, her eyes wide. "How wonderful."

Time had made the memory wonderful. Mary waited for someone to mention the boarder, his advances toward Mary and the sadness of that Christmas Eve, that it had caused the beginning of the rift between Mary and Papa that would last until he died. But her siblings let that bit sit quiet, unspoken.

"Oh man, Matka hit the roof when they discovered your hidden treasure."

"Yeah," Mary said. "But now I know. She did her best with what she had, where she came from."

"We all do that." George nodded. "The best we can."

"But boy, Matka could hit the roof like a rifle shot."

"The roof! Still leaking, falling in with hard rains?" Victoria asked.

Mary refreshed everyone's coffee and slumped into her seat. "Oh my. No. We haven't had a leak in… I can't even remember. Not even with this past March's flooding." She thought back to her sisters sleeping in the same bed, Ann's cold feet climbing up her legs, the ceiling that had collapsed right on the bed.

John dumped some whiskey into his coffee mug. He eyed Stan and Honey. "Wouldn't be a walk back in time if I didn't dirty my mitts in the old coal mine."

George lifted a finger in the air. "I brought a little somethin' to make things easier."

The boys and their uncles disappeared into the backyard with a box full of whatever it was George had brought.

Mary's sisters drank pots of coffee, getting reacquainted with their nieces, Ida coming in from Pittsburgh with her husband, Frank. They were elbow deep in coffee cake and Ida's painful stories of her difficulties having children when an enormous boom shook the house and rattled the windows.

They rushed into the backyard. Stan and Honey barreled out of the mine, their faces covered in coal dust. George and John came next, stumbling out, blackened from head to toe. George shook his hair, dust flying as he put on his typical crooked grin. "Worked! You'll have coal for years without stabbing at the seam."

Mary's mouth dropped open. She crossed herself when she realized they were all safe.

George yanked something out of his pocket. "Dynamite. Works every time."

"Oh my God," Mary said. "You did that on purpose?"

"'Course."

"Of course." Mary shook her brother by the shoulders.

And with the relief no one was injured, the chain of laughter began, one person's lighting the next, and Mary was suddenly crying through her laughing, overwhelmed by the death that had brought them together, the things that had sent them splintering—emotional dynamite blasted it all apart, easy to access for the first time. Woozy from pots of coffee, she put her hand on her forehead.

"You all right, Mom?" Stan rubbed her back. She choked on a sob and nodded, but she wasn't so sure.

The laughter swirled around her, half of them doubled over.

Mary's sisters dragged her back into the kitchen to ready the next round of food.

The three of them stood at the stove.

"I remember watching Matka stir the cabbage stew." Victoria took the spoon from Mary.

"Always cabbage," Ann said.

"And her hands. They looked so old to me," Victoria said.

"So red and raw and just… old, I know," Ann said.

Mary held up one hand. Her sisters did the same. "We have the exact same shaped hands as her. Every one of us."

"Mine are big though," Mary said. "Always hated that."

"Strong," Victoria said. "And when I think of Matka's hands now, I see them as useful, resilient. So much work and… Well, I see them differently now."

Mary nodded. "Time passing'll do that, I suppose."

"Ever wonder what our kids will remember 'bout us?" Ann asked.

"Baseball hands." Stan poked his head into his aunts' conversation. "Mom has baseball hands."

Mary turned her hand this way and that.

"So she does," Victoria said. "If she would've been a boy, she'd have been written up in the paper, too."

Stan smiled wide. "I believe it."

And in that moment another layer of emotion imprinted, this moment forever pressed into Mary. Like a fingerprint, it would remain forever.

Stan put his hand over Mary's like the players always did. Victoria followed suit, then Ann.

"Long as we have Matka's hands, we have her," Victoria said.

Stan winked at Mary, and she knew someday that would be what he'd remember about her, too. Baseball in the backyard, baseball hands.

**

Arriving at Matka's funeral mass at St. Dominic's on Thompson Avenue, Mary craned this way and that. No sign of Lukasz. Angry, but unwilling to let his absence take away from Matka's spiritual sendoff, she put her thoughts on Matka's soul and her ascension into heaven. Mary had always found much more comfort at mass than her mother, who had often experienced it as an obligation she didn't quite appreciate. With rosary in hand, Mary's fingers sliding over smooth stone beads, she looked down the pew at her siblings. She reached across her sisters and gave George a whap on the arm, like Matka would have to do multiple times a mass. George winked, then smiled. When the priest entered, John put his finger to his lips, mocking himself, a signal to his inability to stifle his chatter as a young boy for even a few moments.

Ann leaned across Victoria. "Where are all the swell fellas to ogle?"

"Matka's spirit must've blocked their entrance," Victoria said, making them giggle like teen girls.

The mention of Matka's spirit made Mary feel her closeness. Even though joking about her presence, Mary had a particular sense of saying a tangible goodbye.

The mass was long, the sanctuary packed with people who'd known Matka since Donora was practically born. Afterward, the luncheon at the house left Mary feeling warm and loved. Lukasz arrived with a pan of *galumpki* from his buddy Jimmy Wisnewski's wife. He greeted everyone with head nods and handshakes and set the pan on the counter. He took Mary's hand, whispering that he'd missed the mass due to the fella who'd promised to cover his shift not showing up till late. Mary cupped his cheek and thanked him, relieved he was home and sober.

With the kitchen, living room, and porch stuffed with mourners and family, Mary wasn't sure what to expect from Lukasz. She shuddered at the idea he might get lost in one of the bottles of whiskey people had brought. But he simply shoved his hands into his pockets and made his way around the house, thanking people for coming.

Father Dobowski gave Mary an eyelet tablecloth. "It was the one we used in the kitchen. No one did it up like her. She took such pride in it—even though it wasn't one of the fancy altar cloths."

"Thank you," Mary said, tearing up yet again. Everything Matka did, she always seemed to do with disgruntlement. But apparently that didn't carry outside the family. Peggy Picarro drew Mary aside as the crowd was thinning. "I wanted to tell you that your mother was one of the kindest people I've met in Donora."

Mary started to laugh but then realized Peggy was sincere.

Peggy leaned closer. "I got myself in a bad spot. Way back when…" She leaned closer still. "When I first knew a baby was coming, your mother found me at the church in tears. She helped get me settled at Mrs. Clancy's boarding home and gave me the quilt right off her bed so I would have something nice with me in that strange place. While I waited."

Mary grew confused.

"I only know that the quilt was right off her bed because your sister Rose, being a little girl still, just blurted it out." Peggy chuckled. "Your mother smacked her ass and shushed her good, but I was touched at a time when I needed someone to not think horrible things about me. She said she understood my predicament. And couldn't let a girl feel alone what with no husband or…"

Mary couldn't get her breath in or out.

Peggy shook her finger. "You'd just had Ida, I think… it was Ida, not your Vicki. Your mother told me about your baby, and I was so envious that you had this wonderful husband and family, that you weren't alone or scared. She said you were brave and bold. And that I should be, too. I never forgot that kindness."

"I never knew," Mary said, astonished to hear Matka said these things about her way back then. Peggy handed Mary a parcel and left with a sigh.

**

Hours later, drained in every way possible, Mary washed her face and hands, then sank onto the edge of the bed.

Lukasz handed her the package Peggy Picarro had brought. She untied the string and opened the paper. Matka's quilt, the well-used squares in shades of white, pink, and blue. Mary explained the story to Lukasz, memories ticking by, words quickly spent. Her shoulders shuddered, and she bowed her head.

Lukasz sat and took her hand, warming it in his. He slid closer, pulling her into him, her head on his shoulder. He kissed the top of her head. "My love, my Mary. I'm so sorry."

He got on his knees, undid the straps on her shoes and slipped her feet out of them, rubbing her ankles. He stood, pulling her to standing.

She exhaled. "I'm tired, Lukasz."

"I know." He unbuttoned her top, undressing her down to her slip, settling her onto the bed. He pulled the sheet up to her shoulders, then folded the quilt Peggy had brought and laid it across the foot of the bed, layering it over her feet. He opened the windows to get a cross breeze and knelt beside her. He smoothed her hair back and wiped her tears.

"You're a *good* daughter. And your mother treated me well. Sharp tongue like me, but she loved you, and that's why she questioned me. Until she saw. Then she knew I loved you."

"She came to our wedding. Hid near the confessional."

"And brought presents when your papa said no."

Lukasz kissed Mary's forehead then laid his palm against his chest. "It hurts deep inside. Like when my mother died. I hadn't felt this pain in... I didn't realize Matka had become mine... until now, I know."

"Oh, Lukasz." She shifted to her elbows, wanting to comfort him. But he pressed her back into the pillow, shushing her. "You sleep, my Mary. You rest your heart on mine."

She felt a rush of love inside her that felt new and old, completely unexpected.

He brushed her cheek with the back of his fingers. "You are so strong."

She closed her eyes.

"I wish I had half your strength." Lukasz kissed her, opening to page one of the storybook of his Mary mythology. "I said before, you stand like the valley walls. I don't do enough. You carry everything we need to live right inside you, like Donora earth that makes up the steel, the more heat and hot air, the better you are."

Mary opened her eyes and smiled before her eyelids drooped again. Comforted and loved, wrapped in his retelling of the story of her, in that moment Lukasz was the man she had married. But did he truly not know that sometimes she felt more like coal dust than valley wall?

Lukasz adjusted the covers. "You say sometimes you feel more like coal dust than valley wall. So I will protect you. You sleep and rest your heart on mine."

Mary sighed, losing track of anything other than the sense of falling into deep, needed slumber, finding respite for her heart, her soul, for everything.

Chapter 41

Stan

Grandma Lancos's death left the house emptier and softer. Even Pop seemed muted, more helpful to Mom, gentler with her in tone. Extra touches passed between Stan's parents, a gaze that lasted a little longer, something that told Stan that Mom had forgiven Pop for missing the funeral mass. They all missed Grandma Lancos, her rough ways well-intentioned, even when they felt mean. With her gone, they could laugh about the things that might have caused hurt feelings or a sore bottom in the years before.

Stan had spent a good deal of the fall of 1936 mulling over what path he should take after high school and how to talk to his parents about it. Mom knew his lifelong dream to play ball, and he was pretty sure if he decided to go to college, she would see the value in that. But Pop. For him, so far the only answer seemed to be for Stan to go into the mills, to begin to earn money and contribute to the family. "Unions are coming. Then you make more money than we can imagine. You work five days. Eight hours. It is why I came here."

Mr. Duda, Coach Russell, Mr. Clark, Mr. Reese, and Joe Barbao were always there to listen and advise. Coach Russell even approached Pop once, trying to open up a discussion about Stan's future, but Pop apparently grumbled about Stan finding a place in the mill, and that was that for the conversation.

Mr. Duda kept encouraging Stan to have a talk with his parents, to at least let them know that he was considering college seriously, that there would be scholarships. Donora had a strong history of putting their high school athletes into colleges, and from there those men went on to prosperous lives, gentler lives than those provided by the mill. This impressed Stan and made him feel good that they had included him in the idea of being one of those college scholarship men. But he hadn't yet changed his schedule to include algebra or other prerequisites for college, and although he was Mrs. Quinn's favorite English student, he did the bare minimum. And she let him, always noting that he was an A+ fella if not an A+ scholar.

Still, he needed to talk to at least his mother and knew she would be home early on this Tuesday afternoon. She would know how to best approach Pop, especially after the argument the two had had that summer. Stan and he had barely spoken since. Every moment of that situation stayed with Stan, but Lukasz had been too drunk to keep memories of it straight. Mom had told Stan that the mood of what happened was clear to Lukasz, aware that the fight had widened the divide between the two. That he felt bad about it.

Stan had assured Mom he didn't need to discuss it other than to apologize to her for making her sad, for his part in making things hard for her. He liked the way his family let tension pass, delegating painful experiences to the backs of minds so people could move on with life.

Stan entered the house after school, hearing the kettle whistle in the kitchen. This was his chance to talk to Mom. He drew a deep breath and headed that way.

"Your Mr. Rosenberg dropped off a parcel."

Pop.

Stan stopped short.

Pop slid the kettle off the heat and turned, crossing his arms.

Stan eyed the table, the tissue-wrapped bundle.

"Open. See what we got."

Open it yourself. Take it. Stan didn't want it. But he did as he was told, feeling Pop's heavy gaze on him. Stan's very existence seemed to bother his father, stabbing at him. The tissue paper crinkled as he lifted up a crisp white shirt and a blue sweater like Benjamin and Andrew wore to school daily.

Lukasz scoffed but didn't yell. Instead, he silently turned back to the stove, pouring the hot water into a mug, pulling his dark shroud over him as he left. Stan stared at the clothes, wanting them so much, but not wanting the trouble they brought. His parents' bedroom door slammed.

From a distance, yelling came. Stan couldn't hear Pop clearly or Mom's responses, but the rising voices, clashing, filling the house made him want to throw up. He ran his hand over the blue wool sweater, the knitted yarns warm, and the handsome shirt. The yelling grew louder then softer, but the tension came like heat waving off a hot summer street. Stan could return the clothes to Mr. Rosenberg. He could thank him heartily and tell him one day he'd come back and buy one in every color.

Stan didn't realize he was holding his breath until a crash from upstairs shook the kitchen windows.

Mom.

He sprinted to the bedroom and burst in, ready to leap in between the two as she had done for him that summer.

But when he burst through the door, a massive mound in the middle of the room made him hurdle it, his parents catching him, keeping him from going headfirst into the dresser on the other side of the pile.

Breathing heavy, he turned. What in the hell? Daylight shot through the roof, illuminating the mound, the window was sagging out of its frame, too.

They stood gaping as Honey, Helen, Rose, and Vicki joined them.

Mom covered her mouth, and her shoulders started shaking. Stan patted her back. "Don't cry."

"She's laughing, Stan," Helen said.

"It's not funny, Mary," Pop said.

She shook her head. "This happened before. When I was a kid and… Remember the story we told you kids before the funeral?" She couldn't stop her brash laugh from rolling out. And the kids couldn't stop either.

Lukasz finally cracked a small smile just before heading for the shed to retrieve a shovel to remove the debris. *"O mój boże, dach,"* he said.

"The roof, yes. Oh my," Mary said. "I suppose it's time for a patch job, isn't it? New windows."

"I'm glad Grandma Lancos isn't here to see that," Honey said.

And they imitated all the ways she would have screamed about it.

"Maybe it *was* her. Wants us to think about her," Helen said, taking a bucket from Mom.

"Impossible to forget someone like her," Stan said as he started to toss some of the plaster into the bucket.

And while it was a relief that the crash wasn't the result of Lukasz's temper, Pops being so angry about everything, even good things, was infuriating. His father was the most miserable person Stan'd ever known. And like the ceiling pile in the middle of the room, Pop was an obstacle to be leapt over or shoveled away. Stan wasn't sure he'd ever see humor in his father the way Mom and her sisters and brothers now saw humor in their parents. Some things couldn't be softened no matter how much time passed.

**

Basketball season would be starting soon, so Stan worked as many shifts at the gas station as he could. After pulling a double one Saturday, finishing after dark, he headed for a milkshake, threading his way down McKean Avenue. Stan ran his recent conversation with Mr. Duda and Coach Russell through his mind. They'd cornered Stan at the end of the school day Friday, telling him it was time to speak to his parents about life after high school. Walking down the sidewalk, a few folks headed toward movie theaters and restaurants and ethnic halls, but it was late enough that most were already tucked into the place they were going. Stan jammed his hands in his pockets and went over how he would phrase what he needed to say.

Just as he got to rehearsing how he would ask his father to please support him, Pop's distinct roaring filled his ears. Stan snapped out of his ruminations, heart racing. Disoriented, he put his back against the wall between Turner's Hat Shop and Antonio's Shoes and surveyed the nighttime crowd for the source of the voice.

Across the street, Pop stood with two men. The streetlights were too weak to completely fight through the smoky fog. Stan slid further down and ducked under Turner's storefront awning, confident his father hadn't seen him. The men were dressed in fashionable overcoats and fresh hats with black silk ribbons that looked liquid when the dim streetlight caught them just right.

"No! Wrong," Pop said. The bellow washed over Stan as he watched. He began to sweat. Who on earth was his father bullying?

A third man stepped out of the tavern, towering over Pop. He bounced his fat black leather briefcase. "Enough of this," he said, his deep voice carrying across the street, but he wasn't yelling as Pop was. Stan tried to make sense of it.

The man with the briefcase gestured, and the other two stalked away. The remaining man leaned in to Pop and talked at a volume Stan couldn't hear. Pop's face creased, his shoulders slumped.

"Let the runty Pollock go. Can't reason with a moron," one of the men yelled from down the street.

Pop's shoulders folded in, appearing so small that Stan nearly ran across the street to interfere, but he couldn't move. It didn't make sense. His father was hard and big and stood up to powerful men who tried to tell him who to vote for. Yet… Here was Pop looking tiny, boyish. No. Fragile. The man Stan was watching right then didn't resemble the force of nature who lived at home one bit.

Stan strained to hear what was being said.

The man turned, his voice angled so that it carried. "You're just a little man with a little job in a mill, barely keeping that job. A cog in the machinery. That's all you are." He shoved Lukasz who stumbled back a couple steps.

Stan couldn't breathe, feeling like he was watching a movie instead of something in real life.

Pop actually cowered, slumping against the tavern wall. Stan, still frozen in place tried to shout for the men to stop. Nothing came out. The man lorded over Pop in a way that seemed impossible. Finally, he turned and jogged across the street toward Stan, passing right by Turner's, so close Stan could smell a mix of spicy pipe smoke and whiskey. Another man appeared and shook the first fella's hand. "Everything all right?"

"Damn Pollock mill-hunky." The briefcase man shook his head and straightened his coat. "Not worth a thing past the hands at the ends of their arms."

Stan had heard people called Pollocks hunkies plenty of times, but not like this, not in a way that was pointed at his father with such superiority. The Musials didn't socialize with people who didn't just stop over for a beer on the porch or coffee in the kitchen. And like the day Mr. Weston had broken that soda glass after Nicky drank from it, Stan felt his world shift. He didn't recognize any of the three men who'd berated Pop, but obviously they worked at the wireworks.

He peeked back out. Pop, still against the tavern, was breathing heavily, his hat pulled down over his eyes. The three men were just a block away, relaxed, seeming to have already forgotten the incident that had completely diminished Pop right in front of Stan's eyes.

Stan's stomach filled with acid, nauseating him. He ducked back into the shadow. All his life he had wanted Pop to seem smaller, to *be* smaller, weaker, harmless. But he'd never imagined that the world didn't see him as Stan did, that the world wasn't afraid of him. Humiliated, threatened, completely without power—Stan couldn't have fathomed it. His heart pulsed, pushing blood right into that hole that the summer argument with Pop had caused. It filled with sympathy for his pop. No wonder he returned from work the way he did. Maybe he faced this kind of thing daily.

He shouldn't let his father weather this alone. The first kernel of sadness, deep despair for Pop, formed inside. Understanding had been born. Stan drew a deep breath and stepped out from under the awning, into the streetlight, readying to jog across McKean to aid Pop. But as he crossed the street, looking back and forth, it was clear. Pop was gone. Stan went a block in one direction then the other. He even poked his head in the tavern, the thick scent of hops hitting him. No sign of Pop.

And Stan knew he'd missed his chance to help. He kicked down the street, stomach growling for that milkshake, undone by what he'd witnessed. With the moment over, he'd never mention what he'd seen. He felt the shame like it was his own. Partly because he was Pop's son, he was a Pollock, too. But the bigger share of shame went to his own behavior, for how he'd never known his father was made so small by those outside the home, that he might feel it in some way every day of his life. The change in how Stan saw his father came like a thunderclap, jarring then reverberating in his chest like a Fourth of July parade full of drums and tubas thumping by.

He searched for the men. He would tell them what Pop had been through, how he bravely came to Donora alone, with nothing, how he made beautiful Christmas angels, and dreamed of a house he'd build and believed all men were equal. Stan stalked up and down the block on both sides. There were other finely dressed men, but none were any of the three that Stan had watched turn his father from a hulking giant to a helpless soul with the ease that the open hearth turned cold iron red hot and liquid, as though the men had been designed to do just that.

Chapter 42

Patryk

Fatigue clouded over Patryk, and he closed the book. He looked up to see that not only were Owen and Dr. Lewis there, hanging on every story, but the room had filled. Lucy had arrived, and two nurses crowded in along with the head of maintenance, an orderly, and the CEO of Blue Horizon.

"That's it?" Nurse Perkins threw her arms open.

Patryk couldn't believe what he was seeing. "No, that's not all."

"Read some more!"

"I will… maybe. But I want out of this prison first. You can all come up to the house to hear more."

Everyone looked at one another. Lucy pushed to the front of the group, pouring water into a cup for Patryk. "He just means he misses home. He doesn't really think this is a prison."

"Adjusting can be difficult." Dr. Lewis crossed one ankle up on his knee. "And I have to say thank you. This has been amazing. Hearing my grandfather's name like that, to think someone knows his story. It really just took me back to his stories, to him." His beeper went off, making him check his phone. "Oh boy. Gotta go. But I'll dig through some boxes at home. I think—"

A loudspeaker crackled with a voice calling Dr. Lewis's name. He punched something more into his phone as he backed out of the room, everyone separating to let him pass.

Just before he left, he stuck his head back in. "I remember hearing all about Mr. Duda and Coach Russell. They kept watch out for all the players in Donora. But Stan was a special deal for them. They *adored* him. They definitely wanted him to go to college."

"But Mr. Duda supported him playing baseball?"

"Dr. Lewis," the voice called over the intercom again.

"Same with Miss Klotz," Patryk said.

"Who's Miss Klotz?" one nurse's aide said.

Patryk set his cup down. "The librarian. Remember? She gave Stan the library books and told him to follow his heart. Am I getting ahead of myself?" He looked back at his book. "In spring 1937, Stan and his basketball team for Coach Russell were section champs. Musial, Norton, and Ercius were named to the conference all-star team. They were legendary."

"So Coach Russell was still pushing college, and basketball?"

Patryk shifted in his seat. "Wanted him to come back for the high school 1938 season mostly, but yes. He wanted the kid at Pitt."

Patryk pointed to some wording then started back into his tale. "As big as 1936 had been for Stan, 1937 was huge. Ida's husband, Frank, set up the arrangement at the gas station again. But this time Stan would make twenty-five dollars a week instead of what he'd made the summer before! He gave fifteen of it to his mom and kept ten. Honey got disgruntled from time to time because Stan would make him take his shift when he had a Zincs game. Played like a firecracker for the Zincs, for American Legion, trying out for pro teams in Monessen. Even broke Joe Barbao's ankle with a shot down first base line. Joe finished the game but the kid dumped him right on his backside. That summer the Cardinals took a look at him and these two fellas—Ollie Vanek and…" Patryk snapped his fingers, "something French. Frenchie, I think. They were hot on Stan's trail to sign with the Cardinals that summer."

Owen dropped his head. "A dream come true."

"Not so fast. Even for someone gifted like Stan, someone with magic in his fingertips, he didn't get everything he wanted all at once."

Owen gestured to the closed book. "Want me to read some?"

Patryk eyed everyone in the group. A second orderly wheeled a patient into the room. Her fine white hair was gathered into a bun, bright blue eyes sparkling.

Patryk cocked his head. He'd seen this woman before. At bingo the other day? Dinner? He shook his head, scrolling through time.

"Hello, Patryk."

He drew back and narrowed his gaze on her, his memory spooling back, back, back. Finally an image came clear. A dazzling redhead with these same eyes. "Maria?"

She pushed out of the chair and walked slowly toward him, everyone in the room keeping watch as she drew closer.

"My blue-eyed Italian princess."

"It is." She grinned.

Patryk swung his legs over the edge of the bed, making everyone gasp. Everyone but Maria, who was shuffling toward him, reaching out. And as their hands met, everything else in the room faded away.

Chapter 43

Stan

Fall 1937

Stan had started his junior year of high school still pulled in several directions, unable to decide what he wanted for the rest of his life. Over the years, the protective netting that Joe Barbao, Mr. Duda, and Coach Russell created grew stronger, but more expectations were placed on him. Though his summer success reinforced his original dream and he kept veering toward the idea of signing on with a pro baseball team, he did agree to take the required algebra course in case he decided on playing basketball and baseball in college.

Mr. Duda made arrangements for Stan to begin his course at the junior high, walking down to First Street School at the end of the day. The first day Stan felt as shy as when he'd actually been in junior high, waiting for heat to rise up the back of his neck, bringing a sense of doom or shame as he sat in a room with kids three and four years younger than him. But like Andrew sat comfortably with his lack of athletic prowess, Stan found himself confident in having made the choice to at least set himself up for college. Mom was supportive of it, but Pop had brushed the idea off, mumbling about every moment Stan didn't go into the mill was a dollar lost. It wasn't a discussion—just a declaration that he expected Stan to eventually live up to, adhering to the Musials' way of easing past trouble rather than turning it over, examining it, discussing it on and on.

Stan did fine in algebra, wondering what he'd been so afraid of, waiting for his stammer to intrude, but it never did, even when asked questions. It seemed, in addition to what he'd learned from Andrew, Stan figured the confidence he was gaining in baseball was carrying over to his academic coursework, even if his practice habits didn't.

Like young versions of the Andrew Stan recalled in junior high, the younger students eyed him oddly at first, but several boys were happy to talk baseball and give Stan math pointers when needed. And he returned their pointers with his own when they brought balls and asked how to throw various pitches.

Even with Stan's genuine attempt to make sure he earned the necessary prerequisites for college, his mind consistently reeled back to pro baseball. No matter which choice he made, neither was what Pop wanted for him. Coach Russell had asked him to try out for football that year. His parents forbid him to play—Mom because she didn't want him hurt for baseball or otherwise, and Pop? Who really knew? And though Stan really wanted to give football a try, he knew he had bigger arguments ahead, so instead of his tongue getting tied and starting to sweat when Pop began to pace and grumble, Stan studied him. After seeing him humiliated, seeing Pop's limitations in a way he never had before, he understood him differently, with kindness, no longer butting up against his hardness, no longer seeing himself as causing it. Stan finally grasped Pop's anger often had nothing to do with him. And though he knew his father would never be what Stan wanted him to be, other men in his life were, and this also lessened his anger toward Pop.

Depending on Joe for summer and pro baseball advice, on Mr. Duda and Mr. Clark for high school and college baseball, and

Coach Russell for basketball, Stan was given more than he could have expected from even one of them. Yet wanting to please each meant his decision would disappoint at least two of them. Though he loved Mr. Reese and his classes, Stan knew his path wouldn't go the way of woodworking.

He trusted each, but as Mr. Duda and Coach Russell were pushing him toward college, Joe saw his baseball giftedness and saw no point in wasting a bit of it on school. That could wait. Over the summer, Joe even made sure that Stan tried out for Ollie Vanek and Andrew French several times. The men were part of the Monessen ball club of the Class D—Penn State League—part of Branch Rickey's St. Louis Cardinals system. Mr. French had been eager to talk to Stan's parents about signing him, but Stan hadn't invited him to do so yet.

Over the winter of 1937, Stan had grown a lot, was flexible and strong, and had a great slider with this slow, mesmerizing spin that started just before dropping over the plate. Nice curveball, decent fastball, and Stan could hit.

So when the end of September rolled around, Vanek was pushing again for the Musials to invite Andrew French to their home to sign Stan at the age of sixteen. Several unsuccessful attempts to sign Stan earlier that summer, as he was torn between what to do, left Andrew French at the end of his patience.

Stan had become a master of avoiding conflict, ridding his life of it like a housewife scrubbed soot from walls. He'd learned to enjoy modest things—baseball and the hope of a steak dinner even while Donora was just staggering back to financial health. And now not only was conflict around him and tangled inside him, it was solely because of him. He understood why college could be important. He wanted to please his high school coaches and give the winter and spring 1938 teams a chance of winning championships. But Ollie Vanek dropped Stan off after his last workout telling him he would stop by with Mr. French on September 29th. And that could be his last chance to sign.

Just a few days before that appointment, Stan worked up the courage to tell his parents what he wanted. Honey was working that day at Mercer's Grocery. Pop and the girls were still at their jobs as well. It was time.

Mom was in the kitchen at the stove, where she seemed to be more than anywhere in their house. He drew a deep breath. His mentors flashed through his mind—the disappointment for Mr. Duda and Coach Russell. The thought choked Stan, yet when he separated himself from everyone else's ideas, he knew what he had to do.

He approached Mom. Her initial reaction was the biggest smile and hoot he'd ever heard. She dropped the spoon into the pot, her laugh spiraled around the kitchen as she cupped his cheeks, kissing him on the forehead, then she knocked his breath out with bear hugs. This was what he'd hoped for. But when she stopped hugging and pulled away, her brow furrowed, serious and steady, like when she discussed the electric bill or siding on the house that needed to be repaired. She paced the kitchen, mumbling.

Stan grabbed her hand. "Pop?"

She nodded.

He couldn't let her take the heat for his dream. "I'll talk to him," Stan said. "If I'm going to sign up for the beginning of my adult life, I should be man enough to approach Pop."

"I agree." She crossed her arms and leaned against the countertop behind her. "A calm approach from you will surely…" She shook her head. "Let me think about just who should talk to him. But timing. You said these fellas are coming with a contract on Wednesday? Oh, that makes sense."

"What?"

"Did Duda talk to Pop about this?"

Stan flinched, thinking. "Mr. Duda wants me to go to college. I haven't told him or Coach about Wednesday yet."

Mary sighed and fixed her bun. "Maybe Joe told him? He's close with Ollie Vanek, right? Maybe he told him about it."

Stan nodded.

"I think Duda may've changed his mind and had a little talk with your father, telling him to let you sign with a pro team. Pop said something to me about the Cardinals coming to call on the twenty-ninth. I just waved him off, thinking he misunderstood. Told him to let it go."

"What'd Pop say to Mr. Duda?"

"Said you're lucky to still be in high school, that he wanted to march your ass down to the wireworks, where you could make money with your hands and forget about all of these games before all the good jobs disappeared."

That sounded like Pop. Stan couldn't believe Mr. Duda tried to talk to him, that he'd done that for Stan, even though he wanted him to go to college. "You and I've talked about this since we first threw catch in the back."

She nodded. "We have. Since you crushed me in the belly with that first real baseball."

Stan covered his eyes. "Oh man, I felt so bad."

"No matter. I knew then what was coming."

"And you like me playing baseball, right? You believe in me? Still?"

"Oh yes." She bit her thumbnail.

The sense of his dream being tangible, coming true, expanded through him, thrilling him. "I can't believe it."

She took his shoulders, with him now taller than her after he'd worried he might never surpass Pop, he looked down on her. He grasped her wrists.

"You're not there yet. Your father's quite the hurdle."

"He can't say no. He just can't."

She pulled him into a hug and patted his back. "Are you sure it's what you want? This fight with Pop? Because he has to sign since you're only sixteen."

"I know. Yes," Stan said.

"So few make it in baseball. So very few."

They stared at each other. Was she going to discourage him? "We need Pop's signature for sure. I'll sign. And you. You should sign, too." A smile slipped across her face, the kind that a person got when they didn't really want it but couldn't keep it away. And he knew she was on his side. She couldn't help it.

Moving forward with pro baseball—anything that wasn't going into the mills for a job—could cause Pop to explode. If they pushed him into signing, the ramifications could linger. He thought of the men in the street humiliating Pop. That wasn't what Stan wanted. But he knew his mother could finesse this, could get Pop to see Stan's way.

He had to say yes. Stan surveyed their home. Though it held happy memories, laughter, it told the stories of storms as well. A home passed down, with furnishings nearly forty years old worn from scrubbing soot and smoke away as much as from wear, the scent of cabbage overpowering Mom's attempt to freshen the air. Would Pop overpower them too?

He thought of Andrew's house, their library room, the steaks, Honey and his dreams of baseball and post-game, well-done T-bones. Stan had been proud to give Mom fifteen of his twenty-five dollars a week. The pay was the result of Uncle Frank convincing the gas station owner he'd make the money back just having Stan there to draw car owners in. With baseball, Stan could earn so much more. He could give his parents everything. Yes. This was what he wanted. Mr. Duda and Coach Russell flashed to mind.

Stan adjusted his baseball cap. "We just have to be sure the Cardinals don't file the paperwork until next year. No money's exchanged, and then I can play high school baseball and basketball."

Mom pulled back with a sigh. "Your pop can say no, Stan. But I'll do my best to get a yes."

"If anyone can coax a yes, it's you."

She chuckled and fished her soup spoon out of the stew, stirring the cabbage, lifting it, the green shreds falling apart into threads. "I'm afraid this is more of an axe-and-crowbar operation. I just don't know…"

"He'll see. After Mr. French and Vanek talk to him. He'll have to see it our way."

"Say your rosary, then, Stashu. We're gonna need all the novenas we can get."

Chapter 44

Mary

September 29th arrived much faster than Mary had anticipated. She and Stan decided that she'd be the one to tell Pop and to tell him on the very day that the Cardinals were coming. That way Lukasz wouldn't have the chance to badger Stan, or seethe and argue with Mary for very long. Stan would come home early from school. Honey would still be there and the girls still at work. Stan would greet the Cardinals reps but then wait in the kitchen to allow her and Lukasz to talk without him being there. Not because Stan was too immature to contribute to the conversation, but because the entire thing was more about Lukasz than Stan. And knowing how competitive he was with his son, Mary thought it would be smoother without Stan sitting there, watching his father have to change his mind—something Lukasz might see as losing.

Midday, she was on the porch sweeping away as much soot as possible, as much of her worry as she could, too.

"Mary."

She looked up.

Joe Barbao.

She leaned on the banister, wanting to invite him to the signing but knowing it was out of the question.

"Big day," he said.

She nodded.

"Well…" He started to walk away, well, a slight limp reminded Mary of Stan breaking Joe's ankle earlier that year.

She dashed down the stairs and pulled his arm. "You're still limping. Not better?"

"Oh, Kate puts some stinky rub on it every night." He lifted his foot and circled it. "Nearly good as new."

She shook her head.

"A little parting gift from the greatest ballplayer in Donora."

Mary chuckled, grateful for this man's presence in Stan's life. "Thank you. You know. For everything."

Joe adjusted his hat, looking surprised. "He did it all, Mary. I don't have to tell you."

She nodded. "He works hard."

"Endurance of a plow horse but light and scrappy and… he's been brushed with the gifts of the baseball gods' gold dust laid right down in his bones. It's quite a combination."

Mary thought of Mrs. Mazur and how she'd said Stan was born under a lucky star. "We both know having unnoticed talent doesn't get a kid to the pros. You made sure he got seen as much as you helped him get good."

"He's got luck in spades, doesn't he?" Joe grinned and kept on down the street, shoving his fist into the air. "Onward."

"Onward indeed."

**

Ollie Vanek and Andrew French arrived at 1137 Marelda Avenue with Mary's stomach alive with nerves—excitement for Stan and worry that Lukasz would choose this time to exert the only power he might have over Stan's life. She'd made cinnamon rolls and prepared pierogis and a plate of cold cuts.

Mr. French came into the house, leaving Vanek in the car. He removed his hat and shook Mary's and Lukasz's hands and declined anything to drink or eat. This made Mary acutely aware of the worn chairs and threadbare carpets. She reminded herself none of that mattered. Her son had the kind of talent that was born of something bigger than the house he was raised in. Lukasz clenched that square jaw, jutting it out like she'd seen him do so many times, unimpressed with Mr. French, the man who could give Stan the life he'd wanted since he learned a guy could make a living playing ball. And as his first act of impeding the negotiations, Lukasz refused to speak English. This left Mary to translate.

Mr. French went on and on about Stan's naturalness as a ballplayer. He highlighted Stan's power and flexibility and athleticism, the way his lean body hid its fine, steely fibers. Not an imposing young man, but stealthy, fast, surprising in so many ways, at every appearance on the field.

These words took Mary's breath away, confirming what she'd seen in Stan nearly his whole life. She glanced at Lukasz, whose mouth had dropped a little, as though he was hearing these things, realizing these things for the first time. He started to talk, but his voice cracked. He cleared his throat. *"Odziedziczył to wszystko po mnie."* He leaned forward, fists on his thighs.

Mary nodded and patted her husband's hand. "He did get every bit of that from you." It was true. Stan's genes and his experience at the Falcons enhanced his abilities. "Lukasz had Stan train at the Falcons Nest 427 when he was young."

Mr. French raised his eyebrows and grinned. "That certainly explains his agility and strength, so much."

And Mary thought of all the men she'd heard talk in the homes she cleaned, when she worked in the wireworks, and around town. Mr. French understood the value of flattery when making a sale.

This made Lukasz smile, and Mary's heart quickened. She squeezed his hand. "What are the contract's terms?"

Mr. French dug into his briefcase. "We file it in the spring. No money is given until after school ends. No bonus of any sort. Stan can play high school sports this entire year. He'll be assigned to a team sometime in spring. He'll be the property of Branch Rickey and the Cardinals system."

Mary straightened. It felt strange to hear her son described as being owned. She didn't want to ask the next question but had to. "His salary?"

"Sixty-five dollars a month, ma'am." Mr. French smiled, shuffling some papers.

Not enough. Lukasz had said he wouldn't accept less than eighty. But it was just an excuse. She eyed her husband.

He shook his head.

Mr. French slid to the edge of his seat, holding up one page. "It's the going rate."

Mary was panicking inside. Lukasz had to see she was on his side with this. "He's worth more than that. His potential. He's pure raw talent. You see it yourself."

Mr. French leaned forward. "Do you know how many—he's not even *seventeen years old*, ma'am."

"But he's *good.*"

Mr. French looked at Lukasz, then Mary again. "He is. But the salary's fixed."

Lukasz got up and stalked away.

"This is an offer, not a negotiation," French said.

Lukasz froze halfway up the stairs.

Mary willed him to come back down, to have common sense.

But he kept going up. The bedroom door slammed upstairs. Mary's hands shook.

Stan poked his head in from the kitchen, his smile snapping away when he saw Mary's face. This made her leap to her feet. Mr. French was reaching for the doorknob.

"Please," Mary said. "Stay. Give me a few minutes. Please."

The gentleman sat back down, drumming his fingers on his knee.

Mary pulled Stan back into the kitchen. He'd already burst into tears. She gave him a hanky. "This won't be your last chance. I promise. When you turn eighteen, you can sign without his signature. Mine doesn't count. They're not willing to pay enough. You don't want to play for a team who doesn't pay you enough. More money would've helped sway your pop."

"Sixty-five a month isn't enough? Pop earns twenty-two when he's lucky. You can't be serious."

The pain on Stan's face sank into Mary, his eyes pleading. He was a sensitive person who cried easily, but these were different tears.

"It's not my decision," Mary said, understanding her role in the family more deeply than ever.

Stan turned away, grasping the countertop, sobbing, trying to keep his crying quiet. She held him and patted his back.

"What do you mean it's not your decision? You've decided everything my whole life. You're the only one who *can* make decisions."

She'd done such a good job of working around Lukasz that her children didn't even see her true position as wife. Mary's anger swelled at herself. She shouldn't have allowed this to happen, to set them up to think she could control the outcome of something so important, something Lukasz didn't support. Stan was right. No matter what the Cardinals wanted to pay, her son had the right to prove he deserved more by competing.

"You know Branch Rickey actually hides kids away until their eighteenth birthdays so other teams can't sign them. Would Pop like that better? I could go hide in some cornfield farmhouse until November 20, 1938, and then he'll have nothing to say about it because I'll be eighteen."

"Oh, Stan." Mary's breath caught. "Please. Let's think this through."

The kitchen door opened and Honey waltzed in, smiling, Ollie Vanek in tow. He shook Mary's hand and reintroduced himself to her. But when he focused on Stan and Mary and saw Stan's tears the smile snapped away.

Above them Lukasz stomped down the hallway, then down the stairs. Had he changed his mind? She had to make this work. She'd been a good wife to him. It was time for him to be a good husband. In the way she needed it.

Mary motioned for Honey and Stan to stay put and for Ollie Vanek to join Mr. French. She jogged back into the front room.

She caught Lukasz as he was leaving. She slipped between him and the door and pressed it closed with her back. Mr. French had turned in the chair, staring at the two of them, irritated, questioning. Vanek sat on the couch.

Lukasz's jaw clenched. He sliced his hand through the air. "No college, no baseball. The mill. The union will—*I came here for that.*"

He came here for *that*. The words sparked a slew of stewed memories, but suddenly what she needed to say was clear. She pressed Lukasz's chest, keeping him from reaching for the doorknob. "Wait."

Honey and Stan peeked from the kitchen. Mr. Vanek's eyes were wide as he slid to the edge of the couch.

"Why did you really come to this country, Lukasz?"

He pursed his lips. "Mills."

She patted his chest and nodded. "But *really* why? What you've always told me for as long as I've known you."

He glanced at Mr. French and Mr. Vanek and pulled himself up straighter. "Freedom. I leave a land of kings and barons and I came for a life I could make and choose."

Mary patted him again. "Freedom. You came all alone, leaving everything behind, so you could have a son who's free to choose baseball. You came here for this." She jerked her head toward Mr. French and Mr. Vanek.

Lukasz glanced at the Cardinals representatives. Mr. Vanek slid a pen out of his breast pocket and held it up. Mary grabbed it. Lukasz looked at his feet. He reached for the doorknob.

No.

Her mind flew. She wanted him to remember the choices they'd made as a young couple—using freedom to choose each other when her father didn't want that match, when Papa wanted someone else for her. She laid her hand on his shoulder, like she did when they danced. She leaned in to whisper. "We chose each other even when others said no. You have to remember that. The shed, the… *everything*."

Lukasz's shoulders relaxed. He leaned into her and murmured, "Choices."

"Please," she said. Her heartbeat pounded in her head.

Finally he pulled away, hand to his temple.

Mary glanced over his shoulder. Stan and Honey were inching further into the room. Mr. French stared, face red. Mary held her breath. She felt as though everyone was. *Please. Hail Mary, full of grace…*

Lukasz exhaled and finally fixed his gaze on Mary. She held the pen to him. "Please."

With a little nod, he reached for the pen. "Fine. *Podpiszę.*"

Honey scooped Stan up and spun him. "Yeah, you're going to the pros, Stan! You did it!"

Stan held his brother and finally turned, fresh tears staining his cheeks. Mary raced to him for her own hug, the surge of joy like nothing she'd ever felt. Lukasz, bent over the table, signed the paper, then plodded past Vanek and his outstretched hand, ignoring Mr. French as well. No congratulations to his firstborn son, the one he desired so much he hired a midwife with a track-record in encouraging just the right gender baby to appear. The son Mary thought would help change everything. And he had, but not for Lukasz, not the way they'd all wanted. Mary's heart swelled and broke at the same time watching the door shut.

Ollie Vanek's attempt to shake Lukasz's hand had been rebuked, but he shook Stan's and Mary's. Her heart beat so fast she could barely breathe. Mr. French gave them the papers to sign. Mr. Vanek forked pierogi into his mouth, watching, smiling. Mr. French organized his paperwork and discussed what would happen in the spring.

And with that, the representatives from the St. Louis Cardinals went on their way. Mary pulled both boys into her, kissing their cheeks, feeling a high, optimism like she couldn't have imagined when the three of them first dreamed this dream, throwing catch barehanded in the backyard. They finally separated and the boys rushed out the door to hunt down Joe Barbao with the news.

The silence of the empty house hit Mary like a train, not even a moaning barge or whining train reached her ears. Alone. She gathered the snacks she'd prepared, still disbelieving that it all happened. Stan got the chance he needed. It was simply wonderful. He was set to be everything great a person could be. But in winning that, Mary feared he'd lost his father, and she might have lost her husband, too.

She exhaled and filled the sink with sudsy water. No one would ever know what it took for her to do what she did that day. To push Lukasz, to subvert his demands, to make him do it in front of others, to shove her way to the top of the family order. It had to be done. And even if she lost her husband in the process, her son had gained everything. Nearly everything. And what more in the world was a mother to do than give her sons what they needed to make their dreams come true?

Chapter 45

Stan

Even keeping his signing with the Cardinals relatively quiet, knowing it was done changed something in Stan. He felt connected to his future as strongly as he was to his past and was comforted that he could still decide to play college ball as long as he didn't accept money for anything. Joe and all the men who'd invested time and energy in Stanley Musial drowned him in congratulations, expanding his confidence further.

And for the first time Stan was struck by something as baffling as a pitch that curved and sank as it crossed the plate. Love.

"It settles in when a person least expects it, threading through every aspect of life, sitting in the heart, expanding into the bloodstream, infusing every second of life with wonder and *wonderfulness*. Oh, it's just the best thing that a person can feel. Even dirty soot looks exactly right landing on every surface that's still when a fella's heart is filled with love. Everything's new and bright," Dick Ercius said in between sips of his chocolate malt.

Stan cocked his head and squinted. That certainly didn't resemble anything he'd witnessed about love before.

"Don't mock me, Stushy. You'll see."

Stan couldn't imagine it. Well, no. When he thought of the Morrisons he could, but like so much about them, that sort of love seemed unrealistic for the rest of the world.

"Come on," Dick said. "Ann's sister's better lookin' than she is. Funny as hell, too. Shrimp, they call her. You know her, right? Tiny thing? Heck, if I hadn't fallen for her sister, I'd have my eye on Lillian Labash."

Stan thought about it for a moment. He'd seen her breezing through the school halls with her pack of girlfriends, her at the center as they laughed and talked. She *was* pretty. Very. And he'd put away a few dollars from working all summer. He could afford a date. Still she hadn't paid him any special attention. Would she even want to go with him?

"She knows who you are. Her dad's been following your baseball life for ages."

Stan drew back, surprised. "Sure. I'll go."

"Good. So you'll meet her at Herk's at four. Ask her then. For Saturday. Double date."

"All right, all right. I got it. I know who you mean. Her pop owns the grocery near the edge of town."

"That's him." Dick stole Stan's hat and tousled his hair. "I owe you." He tossed the hat back.

Stan clutched it to his chest. Lillian Labash. Big, bright, brown eyes, huge smile. Stan thought perhaps it was he who'd owe Dick in the end.

**

Stan walked into Herk's, greeting everyone—customers and employees—as he scanned for Lillian. A hand waving at the end of the row of booths caught his attention.

He neared and saw her. Chin on her fist, her face lit up like the sun, looking so happy that he thought maybe she'd been expecting someone else. Someone she'd already dated.

Still moving toward her, he looked over his shoulder, struck with self-consciousness. No one was behind him. He hadn't thought this through. Other than Blue Louise who talked baseball as much as him, and a few girls in classes, he'd never really sorted through potential dates or dating in general.

He slid into the booth across from her, struck with fear, worried he'd stammer. Sodas. He didn't carry cash around—some coins here or there. It hadn't occurred to him that meeting at Herk's to plan the date might be a date in itself.

"I just ran into Dick," he said, "and haven't been home since school, so…" His mind quickly calculated ways to fix this dilemma. Dave McElhinney was behind the counter. Stan could ask him to spot him some money if needed, run home, and be back in a flash. The newspapers didn't call him "The Donora Greyhound" for nothing.

"Stan?"

He met Lillian's gaze. Her full attention knocked his breath away.

Movie starlet good looks, a sly smile crossed her mouth, the kind that came to him when he found just the right pitch delivery to make an infallible hitter swing like a toddler. He obviously wasn't the first fella she'd struck dumb with her mere presence. He forced an exhale.

Stan's gaze followed Lillian's dainty fingers as she unclasped and clasped her barrette, then smoothed the flip at the bottom of her hair.

"Would you like something to drink?" he asked.

She shook her head. "I'm sorry. I told Dave behind the counter we wouldn't be ordering. My mom has dinner waiting." She pulled one sleeve of her sweater down over her dainty wrist. "But how rude of me. You might be starving."

His breathing evened out, relieved. "No. I'm fine," he said even as his stomach growled. "Dick thought we could double with him and your sister this weekend. Saturday."

She tilted her head.

"That all right?"

She lit a teasing smile. "Where we going?"

Stan's eyes went wide. "Oh gee. You know…" He shook his head. "Turns out I forgot to ask."

"Well then, I'm not sure I want to go."

Stan's breath left him again. How could he have forgotten to ask where they were going?

She squeezed his hand, then released it, sending electrical shocks through him.

"I'm kidding. 'Course I'd love to go with you."

He forced a swallow down, his cheeks going hot.

"Who wouldn't want to go somewhere, anywhere with Stan Musial?"

He studied her. Was she irritated or flirting?

She winked.

Teasing. That's what it was. Her boldness took his breath away again. He pressed his chest and reached for the glass of water to his right. The ice jiggled as he sucked half of it back. The coldness gave him a brain freeze. He squeezed his eyes shut and rubbed his head.

"Brain freeze?"

He nodded, shaking it off as it receded. "That was…" He was embarrassed.

She smiled, her gaze hard, delving, fascinating. "So Saturday. Okay."

He felt like a little boy compared to her, her ease and poise. Brain freeze? Really. "Six P.M. I think that's right." Was it possible for him to have less information? At least she lived with Ann and could easily ask her for details.

"Well, okay." Her curls flounced as she talked. "I'll see you then. With bells on." She slid out of the booth and ambled away. "If bells are appropriate for where we're going, that is."

Ouch. He turned to see her sauntering along, waving to friends. And just before pushing out the door, she flashed a parting grin over her shoulder, leaving Stan utterly breathless yet again, tingling from his head to his toes, as though a high fast pitch had just whizzed past his ear—exhilarated, stunned, ready for the next pitch.

Chapter 46

Mary

Mary's daughters had been dating for years by the time Stan came home to say he was going on a double date with Dicky Ercius and two Labash girls. She was accustomed to the hubbub that Helen created with each new love, convinced of marriage with a fella just before dumping him, her eye drawn by an ever more handsome, smart, or funny young man. Vicki and Rose had never been as interested in finding a husband as Ida and Helen were. All three single daughters worked in homes or as secretaries but were content to stay at home with Mary, Lukasz, and the boys. So it shocked Mary when Stan came with his news, asking if he ought to buy flowers, what he should wear, whether there were things he should know before going on this first date.

Mary helped him clean up, adding enough grease to his hair to tame his waves but not slick it back. She did up his nice suit and shirt from Mr. Rosenberg and sent him out the door with a very tiny bouquet of witch hazel from the back hill and pansies from the hollow across the street. She'd cut the stems short and wrapped them with brown ribbon that had once held letters together in a drawer in the kitchen.

Part of her was so happy for Stan. Not only were the Labashes good-looking and personable, they were generous. She didn't want Stan to know the Labashes had once extended credit when things were really bad and the only work Lukasz found he lost or quit almost right away. She reminded herself that everyone had been living on grocery credit at that time. And Mary had given away to people in need far more than they ever took. Still, it unsettled her that Stan's date might not understand just how hard things had been for them to reach the point they accepted credit or stood in soup lines.

When Stan left, Helen put her arm around her mother. "Those flowers—the witch hazel's a shrub, flowering beautifully or not. They were sort of…"

"Wild?"

"Weird. You think she'll appreciate them?"

"If she can't, she's not the girl for Stan."

Helen moved toward the kitchen, pulling Mary. "He'll probably be the next of us to marry. After me. Soon your nest'll be empty."

Mary leaned into her daughter. "He's sixteen, Helen. But you. You've found a man you actually like for marriage?"

"Might have. Think so. Name's Clyde. Sweet dimple in his chin." She pressed hers. "Sort of off center, the dimple. Yeah. I think I like this one."

Mary squeezed Helen around the waist. "You love doing this to me, don't you?"

"I do." And she pranced away, the ruffles around the hem of her skirt rippling as she ambled out of sight.

Chapter 47

Stan

Dinner went well with Dicky and the Labash sisters. Stan barely had to say a word as the girls and Dicky flitted from one topic to the next with the greatest of ease, their conversation bits strung like the Christmas lights they would hang on McKean in a few weeks. Stan enjoyed every moment.

After they finished, they headed out to walk to the theater. Dicky and Ann held hands and walked ahead at a brisk pace. Stan, unsure what to do with his hands, jammed them into his pants pockets. Autumn leaves, nearly all crisp brown by then, skittered along the sidewalk. Some still flashed red and yellow bellies as wind opened and closed them like butterfly wings.

Lillian pulled her coat collar up. He reached for her, to shield her against the wind, but then stopped himself, not wanting to be too forward. "Not too cold for you?"

She shook her head and held her hat down. "You know, Stanley Musial, I wasn't so sure this date was actually happening."

He drew back, her candidness surprising him. "Wasn't sure? What? Why?"

"All week, didn't hear word one after we met in Herk's. No phone call. No bump into you in the hallway. No pebbles tossed at my window. This sort of neglect was nearly inexcusable."

Stan couldn't stop smiling, her tone playful. He didn't know what would come out of her mouth next.

She shrugged. "I thought to myself, *Okay, I'll put up my hair and pink my cheeks and press and puff my sleeves just right, but if he doesn't show up, I'm going to his house to take him to the movies myself.*"

Stan stopped, bemused. Every second was an assault on his senses. From her outspokenness, her beauty, her openness, to the details of what she said. "I was supposed to call you?"

She finally stopped and turned back.

She strutted toward him, eyes wide. "How's a girl supposed to know a boy is serious about a date if he doesn't call to confirm by Wednesday?"

Stan didn't know what to say, and he couldn't stop his goofy smile. He re-buttoned his coat and pressed his chest, trying to ease the sensation he felt there. It was the same as when Tank took batting practice and launched one right into Stan's breastbone. But this time the hit was good as much as it was bad. He threw open his arms. "I'll call next time."

She took a step closer. The wind dug under her hat, peeling hair from underneath. She pushed the lock back under the brim of her bowler, the front edge covering her eyes when she didn't look up at just the right angle. He could only see her cheek and perfect, bow lips, causing his stomach to flutter. When peeked from under her hat, meeting his gaze, the energy between them nearly knocked him over. Right in the chest again, that feeling, like a whole world had exploded inside him.

"There's a next time?" she asked.

"You want a next time?" Stan asked.

"Definitely." She paused. He didn't know what to fill the space with.

"You're adorable," she said.

After a lifetime of his tongue-tying, he'd never found it as knotted as it was at that moment. He wanted to tell her she was beautiful. He wanted to shout that he'd never met a girl like her, even though they shared the same school halls, that he'd never paid her much attention. But instead he said, "I don't have a phone."

"Hmm." She shrugged. "Slip me a note in the hall, then."

He nodded.

"Hey, you two!" Dicky yelled from ahead. "We're gonna be late."

Stan and Lillian rushed ahead, but then she stopped, making him do the same. She looked up at him and pulled the bouquet from her purse. "You didn't call me, but you brought me the most..." She stuck her nose in the blooms. "The most wonderfully peculiar flowers I've ever seen."

When she pulled them away from her face, they'd left yellow pollen on the tip of her nose.

Stan gestured toward his nose. "Pollen."

She batted at her nose with her delicate, gloved hand, then started after her sister again. And somehow, without even trying, his hand found hers, and they bounded together toward the theater.

She looked up at him again as they did. "You'll have a phone in every room someday. I can just see it."

"Who needs a phone in every room?"

"Sounds good to me."

"Well, I can't even imagine it."

"I'll imagine for you, then."

And with every nerve tingling the rest of the evening, Stan walked Lillian home as slowly as he could without coming to a complete stop. At her front door, they said goodbye, and without thinking it through, he kissed Lillian Labash's cheek, the scent of pears and the feel of velvet skin staying with him, running through his mind a million times before he saw her again in school on Monday morning.

Chapter 48

Stan

Winter of 1938 was different than past years for Stan. He kept on with the academic courses required if he chose to go to college instead of acting on the pro contract he'd signed with the Cardinals. Though his mentors and close friends knew he'd signed it, most people weren't privy to that information. His college prep courses demanded more time than his former commercial coursework had, but he still wasn't what he would consider a scholar. Certainly not like Andrew. But there were times they met in the library and he helped with Stan's algebra, and it gave him a quiet time to complete work quickly and then head back to the gym for extra basketball practice.

"Hey." Andrew snapped open the school paper, the *Varsity Dragon*, when he'd finished his physics homework.

Stan looked up from his notebook.

"I might graduate early," Andrew said.

He'd talked about that before, but Stan never really expected it. He put his pencil down.

"If I stay for senior year, I can easily double major in physics and chemistry when I do go off to college."

"Easily." Stan scoffed. "Ha."

"Easy as it is for you to find that sweet spot on a bat."

Stan nodded. "I hope you stay."

"Yeah."

"Wouldn't be the same. I just don't—" Stan started to imagine not stopping at Andrew's, finding him on his observation deck, gazing through heaven's window, attempting to draw back the thick Donora draperies that often blocked his view of moon and star. But if Stan started playing ball for the Cardinals in the spring, he would be the one who was leaving early. "You should do it. Even if you would be abandoning your best friend at a critical time in life. Senior year's no joke."

Andrew chuckled. "Sure. Sure. Let me just read this little section from our preeminent paper. It's 'reported' that Stan Musial and Lillian Labash have been keeping company after school."

Stan's face grew hot. "I spend more time with a basketball than Lillian."

Andrew turned the page. "Sure. Sure."

Stan yawned and closed up his books.

"You really like her."

Stan stood, not wanting Andrew to see the way he couldn't stop a clownish smile from covering his face.

"You're in love."

"No. No. But I do like her."

Andrew stood and poked at the newspaper. "Says there that you also keep time with Carol Hasselton."

Stan snatched the paper. "What? No way. No."

"Oh, Stanley Musial, is there anyone who doesn't want you?"

"You, too, Andrew. Please. Yale's calling."

Andrew put his pencils into a canvas pouch. "If I didn't know what a nice guy you were, I'd think you had to be an asshole solely based on the constant swooning with your name on people's lips. Girls, teachers, coaches, teammates."

"Oh man. Now we just have to live up to it all." Stan slapped Andrew's back, and they walked home, the grinding mills back at capacity—blast furnaces whooshing, men working for the most money they'd ever had, and things were looking good for the town to build back to where it had been before the depression took hold. "You afraid to leave Donora?" Stan asked as they reached Tenth Street.

Andrew was silent.

"Andrew?"

"No. I'll miss a lot. But—hey. Stan. I'm not leaving yet. I may not even go early."

"All right. We'll see."

And Stan checked himself for whether he was the one who was actually afraid to leave. He would have loved to play for the Pittsburgh Pirates, to be just an hour up the road. But really, there were away games, and a ballplayer's head was submerged in innings and hits and pitches, so what did it matter what towns his seasons cycled through?

**

A couple weeks into the season, Stan should have continued meeting Andrew to study, but he was unhappy with his basketball play. So, as he did for most of the month of January, he stayed after practice, the janitor leaving a row of lights on so he could perfect his jump shot, left-handed hook, and outside set shot. Exhausted and hungry, he finally left school, walking in the winter evening darkness. A tug on the arm as he moved along Helsep Aveune startled him.

"Lillian," he said. Her arms were full of grocery bags, light from the house above them illuminating just enough that he could still see the small freckle near one eye, the only mark anywhere on her perfect, creamy skin.

"What're you doing?"

"Delivering a few things for my dad. Mrs. Wislitsky up on Mulberry Way needed her teas. Mrs. Dougan's sick, too."

He took the bags from her. "I'll help." And so they dropped the food at Mrs. Dougan's on Eighth. They talked about who was dating who, what they might do on the weekend for a date, and how hard their English classes were that year. He walked her home, and she pulled his arm, stopping him a few storefronts before her father's.

He smiled and sighed, not wanting to end the walk but knowing both needed to get home.

"I love your smile," she said, making his stomach flip. "Sometimes I wish it was just for me."

"Who else would it be for?"

"Carol?"

He thought of what Andrew had read aloud from the paper. He looked away. "Nah."

She spun her wristwatch, brushing its face with her finger. She inhaled deeply before letting it out. "It *is* for me, isn't it?" She started backing away.

The clumsy grin that appeared when he thought of her, when someone mentioned her name, returned. How right she was.

"I know it is, Stan Musial. And mine's for you, too." And she disappeared into her family's store.

When Lillian was out of sight, he considered that her good cheer was for everyone. And that's what he loved about her. *Loved?* Starving, he picked up to a jog. And halfway home, he thought about what happened whenever Lillian was around. Every single time they were together, she knocked him out, reminding him again of being nailed in the chest with a baseball. Though more pleasant, the sensation of Lillian lasted for days, too, every breath, every toss and turn in bed, every movement seemed to begin and end in his chest and radiated throughout every inch of him.

Chapter 49

Patryk

Patryk's next few days were empty of Lucy, Owen, and the slew of Blue Horizon personnel who'd taken to his Donora stories. Lucy had gotten hired on as a temporary nurse at Monongahela Hospital and Owen had some travel games and extra workouts. But with their absence, his hours were filled with Maria. His blue-eyed Italian princess wheeled into his room each afternoon, and they talked about the old days in Donora before each had married someone else.

He shared the book with her and had to wrestle it out of her hands when she wanted to take it to her room after dinner one night. It wasn't just that he wanted the book at hand when Owen came back from his tournament, but he wanted to be sure Maria needed to return.

Finally given permission to move around whenever he wanted, he escorted Maria to her room for the night. Inside her room, he reached for her hands.

"Shouldn't we wait for James to help me?"

"No. Ya walked a little ways in my room. Why not now?"

"I just haven't been moving that way. Not regularly."

"No time like the present."

She latched on to his hands, sending little thrills up and down his spine. "Why're you doing this?"

"Because if the two of us are gonna shack up back at the house in Donora, yer gonna hafta be mobile."

"You always were a dreamer, Patryk."

"If one thing I realize lately, it's that dreams never die. Anything can happen. And you wheelin' into my room the other day is proof of that."

**

Patryk strolled back to his room, surprised to find Dr. Lewis there, sitting on the bed, paging through the Donora book.

He stuck his hand out to shake. "Patryk. Thought maybe you flew the coop again."

"Nah. Just visiting with a friend."

"Your Italian princess?"

"The very one."

Dr. Lewis's face drooped for a moment, but then he tapped a box he was holding. "I brought you some things."

"Nicky Christmas's stuff?"

"Yep."

"You know, he just clean disappeared out of my storybook, didn't he?"

"He did. I went back through my memories, some documents, and some boxes—"

"Dr. Lewis," Nurse Crispin said. "Mr. Rusek needs the information for tomorrow and—"

"Yes, yes, of course. We'll take a look at what's in the box after we chat."

Patryk's heart raced. This wasn't good.

"We've been drawing blood regularly for your blood pressure meds. But the checkup you had the other day was more extensive."

Patryk sank into the chair beside the bed. He felt like an actor in a play, these same words muttered a million times before the lead character was given his death notice.

"You've got cancer."

Patryk stared at Dr. Lewis.

"Prostate, maybe some metastasis."

"Cancer. Foul tip to the head, isn't that sure as shit just… Cancer. Next time how about you use a different script? Bring the news on the back of a circus elephant or something? Circus makes everything better, right? I feel like I'm in a circus."

Dr. Lewis gave a little smile then dug into detail and Patryk, not wanting to hear it, wanting to control where his thoughts went, started reciting what he could about Stan Musial in response.

"That 1938 season saw the Donora Dragons with the best basketball team of that generation. Section IV champs. Never done before Musial jumped in there. Almost beat Har-Brack in overtime at the Western Pennsylvania Championship game. Stan even got half-dead ill before a tournament. Coach Russell and his wife nursed him back to health due to Mary working so much that she couldn't do it all. They played the games at University of Pittsburgh. Went to a movie one afternoon before it started. Then to have dinner at the Schenley Hotel. Manager wouldn't let Tank in the door on account of him being black 'n that. Believe that shit?"

Dr. Lewis offered a concerned nod.

"You remember 'em days like that, Doc?"

"I know of them, that's for sure." He'd stopped trying to talk over Patryk.

"Stan was always aware of that—all the mistreatment of black fellas. He wasn't a big mouth, though. But he always included 'em."

Dr. Lewis nodded. "I know. My grandfather wrote that down about Stan. What happened in the pharmacy. You'll see it in the box I brought."

He'll see? Like he'd live long enough to look through the box? He swore he could detect the tumor growing as they talked. Up until a couple of months ago, Patryk hadn't cared about living. Now he didn't want to face dying.

"So what happened?" Dr. Lewis asked.

Patryk lifted his brows. The cancer news had disoriented him like the drugs they'd given him a couple of times.

"When the manager told the team that Tank couldn't eat there?"

"Coach Russell and the team said they'd leave if he wasn't allowed in."

Dr. Lewis nodded and rubbed his chin.

"Bastards made them eat behind a screen of some sort. Can ya imagine?"

"Seems impossible." Dr. Lewis rubbed his shoulder. "Yet not."

Patryk stared at the wall. "Very true. Very true."

Dr. Lewis put his hand on Patryk's, startling him. "You've got decisions to make. Treatment for someone your age can be… well…" And off he went with all his doctor talk, Patryk's ability to process it further dissolving.

"Mr. Rusek," Nurse Crispin said. "Should I call Lucy to help you decide on a course of treatment?"

He shook his head, desperate to live, but not sure which treatment would give him a life worth having. All he wanted was to be alone. "I'll decide tomorrow. I'll tell you then."

Chapter 50

Stan

When basketball season ended, Stan started right into high school baseball. But he and Lillian always found time to walk the town or have a milkshake at Herk's. It seemed as though each time he saw her, feelings deepened, and that baseball-shot-in-the-chest sensation stuck with him, thinking of her when he should have been falling asleep or hitting the books. One spring afternoon the two were walking into Palmer Park when Poppy Sukova and Susan Babov approached coming down the path.

"Lillian! Stan!" Poppy said. "We were just talking about the prom and graduation and... Well, Lillian, what *are* your plans again?" Though Lillian was just two months older than Stan, she was a grade ahead.

Lillian glanced at Stan. "Oh. Um, work at the store, of course. And Mother needs some help. Maybe some school. I'm just not quite sure."

Susan exhaled with her hand at her chest. "I know. Decisions. I'm trying to decide whether to study science at Pitt or just head off to Smith for a degree in literature."

"Oh," Lillian said. "Yes. Well you have a full year to decide."

Poppy fluffed her hair and adjusted her headband. "Well, we're off. See you lovebirds around town."

"Good luck with the baseball season, Stushy," Susan said. "Lots for you to decide as well, I hear."

Stan nodded.

"You're so talented," Poppy said.

Stan felt the familiar heat work up the back of his neck. "Thank you. You're talented, too. In science, I mean. Andrew told me."

Poppy batted her eyes. "Maybe we ought to double sometime." She looked at Susan and shifted so she boxed Lillian out of the conversation.

Stan nodded. "Sure."

The girls bounced away, their chatter rising up the hill, following Stan and Lillian as they ascended. They looped around the ball field, stopping at the tree that stood near the outfield fence. Lillian had been quiet. No—silent, the difference in the heaviness, the awkwardness of one but not the other. She'd never been silent ever since they began dating.

"What's wrong?" he asked.

"Nothing."

"Okay."

She glared at him.

"What?"

"What?" She leaned forward. "Are you kidding?"

He shook his head, confused. She stomped away, right back down the path toward town. He stopped her before she exited onto Meldon Avenue. "Please, Lillian, what's wrong?"

He pulled her hand, backing up the path. She wiggled out of his grip but followed him.

"You're awfully impressed with Susan and Poppy."

"I am."

"I knew it."

"Anyone who can do all those sciences and maths and… Like Andrew. I mean, I'm taking junior high math right now. Think about that. I'm seventeen years old in class with twelve- and thirteen-year-olds. Andrew lives and breathes all that stuff about the universe and stars and weather and physics… and it's impressive."

She snapped her fingers at him. "Stanley Musial. I'm talking about those two girls who just flirted right past me to you and how I'm graduating, and my plan no longer seems like a plan because…" She looked away. "You'll be with them a whole year more as they decide between silver and gold. And I'll just be…"

He'd never seen her appear vulnerable. He didn't know how to respond to it. He was used to her just telling him how things were. She was always assured, regal.

She drew a hanky from her pocket, dabbed at her eyes, and let out a forceful breath. "I want to be a mom. I want to have a beautiful home, not big, but nice and… I'm nothing like those two girls, so if that's what you are looking for, let's just put this…" She spread her arms. "Let's just slide *us* onto a stretcher and right into a hearse and send the whole thing up to Gilmore cemetery for burial."

Stan snickered.

"You think that's dumb."

"No chance."

"You're laughing."

"It's the way you said—never mind. I'm not laughing at the idea."

"I see you staring at Poppy in the hall, following her into English class."

"You said my eyes were always on Carol's sweater. Now I'm staring at the back of Poppy's head, diggin' in to see her beautiful brain?"

Lillian's eyes started to glisten in the sunshine. "Don't make fun," she said.

He shook his head. And that was when he felt it. The difference between the baseball shot in the chest and this, what Lillian did to him. She caused something to fill his blood, heat it to where he could feel it warm every bit of him, the sensation made permanently part of him.

He slipped one hand into the small of her back, pulling her against him, kissing her. She threaded her arms up around his neck, bringing him even closer, as she caressed where his hair met his collar. Her lips tickled his ear. "I love you, Stan."

He froze. He'd felt it for some time. Put words to it in his mind. But never said it aloud. He waited for his tongue to stop him from being able to get anything out. But then he realized that when he was with Lillian, he didn't feel any of that anxiety. "And I love you." She latched tighter to him, her head against his chest, and they held each other until voices coming their way made them break apart.

"Your stomach's growling."

He pressed it. "I'm starving."

"I'll make you something at the store."

And off they went, hand in hand, something alive and different in every step he took.

✳✳

At Labash's Grocery Store, Stan talked to Ann and sat at the counter while Lillian made him something to eat. When she turned with the finished sandwich, Stan nearly fell out of his seat.

"Holy cow, you used a whole cow for that one," Ann said with a wink at Stan.

"Pig and cow. He's a growing boy. Stomach growling so loud I could barely concentrate on our conversation."

Stan bent his head sideways and counted up the skyscraper layers. "Quadruple decker."

Lillian leaned in, drawing her finger upward. "Ham, rye, swiss, roast beef, rye, swiss, roast beef, tomato, swiss, and more ham and rye."

"Holy cow!" a man's voice boomed. Stan looked up to see Mr. Labash sauntering toward Lillian, apron draped across his middle. "A Dagwood! Someone must be very special to rate a Dagwood from Shrimp."

"Dad, please. Stan's special to everyone, you know that." She glanced at Stan.

Mr. Labash stuck his hand out. Stan wiped his on his pants and accepted the shake. "Good to see you again, Stan. Congratulations on the basketball season. Best team in a generation's what the papers said. You were quite the sensation. Doc Carlson at Pitt's had his eye on you since last year."

"Lillian's had her eye on Stan since last year, too, when she noticed his legs at a basketball game," Ann said.

Lillian threw a cloth at her sister, her face turning apple red, which made Stan's cheeks go hot as well.

"Great basketball season and now first baseball team in ages. I hear great things so far."

Ann grinned up at Mr. Labash. "Did Lillian tell you Dad used to play ball? Minor leagues."

"Oh yes. You must have been good," Stan said.

Mr. Labash leaned on the counter. "Not like you, Stan. Nothing like you."

Lillian folded linens as Stan and her father talked baseball teams and baseball life. "Whatever you decide between sports and college and all the rest…" Mr. Labash wiped the counter down with a bleach-dipped cloth. "You're gonna do great."

And Stan felt a swell of pride rise up.

Chapter 51

Stan

April 1938

Deep in the heart of the high school baseball season, the team was having a strong run. Stan was batting cleanup and alternating between pitching and playing outfield. Honey played first base. Their biggest team issue was keeping Tank healthy to catch Stan's pitching. No one else easily could. But Stan was juggling thoughts regarding his future even as he grew increasingly comfortable on the field, throwing out as many base stealers as striking out batters.

After being lost in the rhythm of each ball game, after the thrill of celebrating with teammates like Nush and Buddy, and the rest, anxiety quietly crept into his world at night. One source stemmed from the Cardinals having not yet contacted him with a minor league assignment. Another well of concern sprang from journalists branding Branch Rickey and the Cardinal organization as outlaws, breaking rules, like owning more than one team in the same league. Did he even want to play for them? Joe told him not to worry, that the assignment would come soon and he shouldn't worry about league politics.

Others were still urging him not to worry about pro assignments at all, to keep his amateur status. But after less-than-stellar grades for the year, except for the courses he put effort into—algebra and woodshop—he knew college wasn't what he wanted. Even if it brought him all the confidence he lacked in other areas of life. The baseball season—winning the section was exhilarating and only served to make him sure baseball was his path.

But not hearing from the Cardinals sowed some doubt in his mind. What if they'd forgotten him? Because he was no good? Because of how his dad hesitated to sign? What if… His mind churned endless scenarios, tossing and turning half the night. What if Pop was right that Stan should work in the zinc mill, play semi-pro, be a star in the valley, live a good life with health benefits, steady paycheck, paid vacation? Maybe Stan's dream had been foolish, and whatever was happening with the Cardinals was just God's way of telling him that. Pop still hadn't spoken to him and barely grunted at Mom since the day of the signing, seven months before, brushing past each other like they were ghosts. Though Stan weathered the shunning all right, guilt that he'd caused Mom to be marooned from Pop was ever present. Stan said plenty of rosaries that spring, but the momentary peace that came with them didn't last.

The Donora Dragons hit well enough to win the section, but their fielding ensured a tie for second in their league. Stan lost two high school games that season, with strong pitching but subpar fielding. There was only one game that Stan had truly played poorly. Against Charleroi, the errors were all his. The Dragons won 9-8, but Stan gave up five runs in just the last inning.

By then, the press was tracking his performance, reporting on everything baseball related. From there, the townspeople analyzed, guessed, and declared anything they wanted about him. His feeble pitching against Charleroi had grown men huddled in bars and ethnic clubs suggesting that Stan's arm wasn't good enough for the pros. They had chronicled his playing for the Zincs, musing that Stan had changed his mind about playing for the Cardinals, deciding that Stan was mollifying Pop. Or worse, they suggested Stan didn't think he was good enough either.

It was true; the sense of Pop's cold shoulder was as stark as his blow-your-hair-back rantings that had stopped since he was no longer speaking. Stan wanted his father's blessing. He wanted him to care about his baseball playing as much as fellas in every bar in town did. He wanted him to understand that he would succeed and that would make the men who'd called Pop a runt in the middle of town shut the hell up. But he couldn't say any of that to Pop. He couldn't say anything at all to him since the signing. And he did feel bruised from the way he'd played against Charleroi. But what surprised him wasn't that he'd had to push back on his own sudden doubts, but how quickly his biggest fans had decided his career might be over. Joe reassured him they were all nuts, including Stan, who was entitled to a bad game once in five years. He shouldn't be so hard on himself. Stan wasn't sure that was possible. Too much was depending on him.

**

At one point, Stan was invited by the sports editor for the *Donora Herald*, Johnny Bunardzya, to go see the Pirates play the Giants. His first Major League Baseball game ever. Even skipped school to do it. On the edge of his seat the whole game, awestruck that he'd finally made it to Forbes Field. Its iconic red-brick left-field wall, glimpses of Schenley Park beyond that. It was better than he'd imagined from listening to games. Mesmerized by every second of each inning, Stan began to analyze what he was seeing, matching pitches against his hitting and vice versa. "I could hit major-league pitching."

"You're a pitcher," Johnny said.

Stan nodded, squinting as he watched one of his idols, former Pirates third baseman, now manager, Pie Traynor, work his magic giving advice to Arky Vaughn. "Yeah. But I could hit. I know it."

Irv Weiss, a Donora businessman and Pirates booster, saw Stan and Johnny and introduced Stan to Pie Traynor afterward. Traynor was so moved by Irv's support that he humored him by asking Stan to throw some pitches to the guys still milling around the field. He held his own against Brubaker, Waner and others. Afterward, with Traynor impressed, Stan mentioned his relationship with the Cardinals as a means of adding another layer of proof he had big league potential. "But they forgot about me."

Traynor stepped back and looked at Stan top to bottom. "How old are you?"

"Seventeen."

Pie smiled, removed his hat, smoothed his hair back and replaced the hat. "Rickey usually smuggles kids like you into the forest until you turn eighteen so no one like me has a chance at you."

"My father signed."

Traynor leaned in with his hand out. "Oh, Stan. If those fellas who spent all summer lookin', if they stopped at your house, ate some snacks, and slipped a paper across your table for you to sign, if they got that far? They won't have forgotten you. Not for a second."

Stan struggled to maintain eye contact.

"But if the Cards do release you, come on back. But I'm quite sure they haven't forgotten you. Not a kid like you." And with that, Stan was left hoping that maybe the Cardinals had indeed forgotten him. That maybe he'd be able to someday play for the Pirates, just an hour from home.

**

The end of May arrived and with it came Stan's assignment with the Cardinals. He'd been told to go to training camp in Georgia on June 5th but had yet to tell anyone. After a dance, he walked Lillian home, and the two sat on her porch talking, sitting on the top stair. He finally got the words arranged and told her he'd be leaving.

"Hang on," Lillian said, hopping up and entering her house, surprising Stan. She returned out of breath and plopped down beside him, holding something in her lap. The light coming through the back door window only splashed through enough for him to see her eyes shining with tears. "Here." She pushed something toward him.

Envelopes.

"Addressed, stamped, and bundled with twine. Perfect for a baseball player's entrée into the world of pro ball."

He stared at her offering but didn't take it. He didn't spend much time considering not seeing Lillian for months. The light exploration of the idea stung, wringing his insides and so he was better off just not considering it at all.

"Prepared these a while back so when the time came, I'd be ready with encouragement and smiles."

He looked away.

"What?" she asked, pushing the envelopes into his belly.

He finally took them, fanning the edges. Twenty envelopes.

"I figured you'd be beat from so much ball, late games, bus travel and such…" She wiped at her cheek. "I don't expect that you'll write every day. But I wanted… I didn't want… Well, you see that they're addressed to me. And your mom. I put a couple in there for her."

Stan was touched by her thoughtfulness. She moved away from him slightly, looking off into the yard, her jaw clenched.

"You okay? All right with me going? I mean…"

"It's not for me to say."

"I'd like to know what you think." He gently pushed the envelopes back at her.

She untied the bundle and rearranged them before retying them, avoiding looking him in the eye. "Coach Russell's been asking me to talk you into reconsidering college and playing your high school baseball and basketball seasons."

"What'd you say?"

"Rah-rah, Donora Dragons." She shook her fist.

"That's what you said?" Stan chuckled.

"Who am I to say?" she shrugged. "*That's* what I said. I'm just a girl from Donora with a boyfriend barreling into the world toward fame and fortune."

"Lil. You know how much I—"

She swept her hand toward him. "I've plenty to do while you're gone, Stushy. Secretarial courses, maybe. The store. My family. My sewing. Then there's recreation, of course. You know I like ice-skating. Plenty of—"

He brushed her hair back and pulled her close, kissing her, wanting her to stop talking before she outlined the first ten names that would appear on her first dance card after he left.

Eventually Mrs. Labash flicked the boot-room light off and on.

"Time to go in." Normally Lil would turn this signal into a five-part affair of inching closer and closer to the door, with her mom eventually sending Ann down in her robe, demanding Lillian end their date. But this time Lillian went straight for the door.

She'd left the envelopes beside Stan. "Lil," he said as she opened the door.

She turned back but didn't release the knob.

"Don't tell anyone about June 5th. All right?"

Her brow furrowed.

"Lil, for the love of—I'm tired," Ann shouted again.

Lillian sighed, then turned her forefinger and thumb at her mouth. "Lips are sealed. Promise."

And Stan knew—one of the only things he knew for sure was that Lillian Labash would keep her word.

**

Edging closer to June 5th, Stan grew less sure of his plan to leave. His options coiled in his mind, each examination of them leading to less clarity. What he felt for Lillian was something he could only call love, but he tried to push that aside when thinking about baseball. Same as his feelings for Pop. If he put him first, giving up on pro ball to stay in Donora, it would satisfy Pop. He imagined work in the mill, hundred-pound bundles of wire to deal with, or work at the sweltering zinc retorts, with after-work boilermakers at Falcons Nest 247. He could have a good life. Satisfying? He didn't have to stop off for drinks after work. He was quite sure he'd be like Mr. Morrison more than Pop when the time came to start a family. Staying in Donora wouldn't be so bad. He'd never imagined it before, and visions of it felt as foreign as if he'd been shipped off to Poland to live in Pop's old village.

At one point, two considerations, Lillian and Pop, wrapped tight and paralyzed him. June 5th loomed, but Stan wasn't packing. Wasn't making rounds of goodbyes, was avoiding Joe Barbao, showing up to the field just in time for him to be distracted with another player's lazy fielding or weak hitting. He told everyone that he was waiting to hear the exact date to report—only Lillian knew the truth. A short conversation with Andrew brought college back to the forefront.

And then Stan did it. On the morning of June 5th, his eyes opened with the sun, staring at the ceiling in his bedroom. He held his breath. His lungs grew tight, and he was taken back in time when he used to do the same thing to get Grandma Lancos to not spank him, to numb away the pain if she had managed to get him in her claws. He just wanted everything to stop. And then it was too late. It was done. With a deep exhale, he rolled to his side, looking out the window he'd been looking out for seventeen years. He'd missed the trolley that would take him to the bus that would rumble him to training camp in Georgia. No last-minute, mad rush jamming clothing in a bag, no wild dash down the hill with glove and bat under his arm, hopping on the trolley as it picked up speed. He simply pretended nothing had changed, that his inaction wasn't the biggest gesture he could make in regard to his future baseball career. Why had he done this? He couldn't say even to himself. He simply couldn't move.

**

Two days later, Stan entered the kitchen for morning coffee. Pop looked up from the paper with his knife-sharp glare and smirk. Stan let it nick him, but not sink into his skin. Nothing could hurt him right then; he'd worn his nerves raw fretting for weeks. He poured coffee. Mom came in from the yard and kissed Stan on the cheek. He sipped his coffee, his back to Pop, hoping he'd slip out of the kitchen before Stan turned around. But instead Pop started reading from an article, parts in Polish, parts in English. Stan tuned him out, knowing his political tirades by heart.

"What did you just say?" Mom's voice came with a screech, jarring Stan.

He turned.

"Read that again." Mom flapped her hand at the paper.

"'Musial, ordered to a team in Georgia, failed to report.'"

Mom shook her head, her eyes wide. Finally both turned their attention to Stan. The fog that had been clouding his thinking for a month suddenly cleared. What had he done?

"Failed to report?" Mom kept repeating the words.

Pop scoffed.

"Stan?" Mom crossed the kitchen and took him by the wrist. "Is this true? What the hell did you do?"

"It's what he didn't do." Pop rose and left the room, grinning. "Welcome home, son."

Stan nearly threw up.

Mom paced then gripped his arm. "What the hell are you doing?"

He pulled away.

Tick, tick, tick, the clock sounded above his head.

"Nine months ago—the time it took to carry you in my belly, by the way—we forced your father to do something he didn't want to do. For you. For me. And you just *fail to report*?"

"I…" He shrugged.

"Those words are the last ones I'd ever expect to hear attached to you. You took a class with twelve-year-olds, for Christ's sake, just in case you chose college. You've had a glove and ball attached to your hand for as long as I can remember and now… Fail to report? You? I can't even believe it's possible."

She swiped the paper off the table, hands shaking as she searched for the proof.

Shame. It was predominant in Stan's well of confused emotions. His failure surprised him as much as her. He hadn't viewed his inaction that way. It was ridiculous. What had he expected? No one to ever know?

She tossed the paper into the air. "What's happening? You want college? Does Joe or Duda know? What are you planning to do?" She stared at Stan. "I'm sorry. I don't know what—" Her face hardened, looking at him in a way he'd never experienced before. Mom raised her finger. "Nine months we've all been ignored by your father. The tension and…"

Stan let her rail at him. He deserved it. "I'm sorry. I just couldn't…" He couldn't say he was afraid. The words, he realized, had never been said aloud. Afraid. He'd been petrified. And that stunned him.

"Oh." Mom covered her mouth. "Oh no. It's Lillian. You *haven't*… You're not just going into…"

She didn't have to say the last part. Going into the mills. Marrying Lillian? Mom looked horrified and sad.

What if he'd ruined his chances with the Cards? His mind began to clear, parting the mash of emotion that had numbed him out for days. What if his only choice at that point was the mills? "I'm sorry, Mom."

She glared from across the room, fists balled at her sides.

As long as he remained in this kitchen, he wouldn't be able to sort things out, the press of tension like he hadn't felt in the house in some time. But Mom had been feeling it. Stan had simply walked right past it, absorbed in his choices, not realizing what the September signing had meant for Mom. Cell walls—his were about to break wide open. Andrew. He'd gone to a science institute in Pittsburgh for the week so wasn't available. Stan needed a way to release the tension.

So he grabbed his bat and sprinted to the lot where he'd played since he was a boy. With a pile of stones, he tossed them up and launched each one a mile, arching toward the river. Every time he thought of failing to report, he choked. What was he doing? And how could he have no idea?

Chapter 52

Mary

The door slammed nearly off the hinges. Lukasz stalked back into the kitchen. Stan's exit had cut a line between Mary holding her tongue and not being able to do so anymore. She swung around to Lukasz, rage ripping through her. Instead of neatly siphoning it off and away from her as she normally did, she let it swamp them both. He poured some whiskey into his coffee. She considered storming out, expelling the anger somewhere else. Then she could retrench, returning home to make the household as calm and nice as she could. But this time—no. She'd let the anger spool out too far to retract.

She grabbed the newspaper from the table, rolling it up. Lukasz snatched a section away from her. She leaned over him. "This is all your fault." She'd never said those words to him before. "What are you doing? It's been *nine months* since Stan's signing. It's the one thing I haven't let you have your way on, Lukasz. *One. Blessed. Thing.* And it's for your son, for Christ's sake. All it took was five seconds of pen to paper, and you act like the Cardinals asked for your right arm. Your *son*. How on earth can you look at him, hear everything that's offered to him, hear all the magnificent things people say about him and…" She bit her tongue, breathing deep breaths, then just let it out. "Hate him for it? They love him. There's not one person who doesn't adore him. And you hate him?"

He stared at her.

"What is wrong with you?"

"He failed to report. Not me. I told you a game—"

"Because of you. He hadn't even told us when he was supposed to go. You did this. This is your fault. Those scouts scour every valley and nook in mountain walls and far-flung farmland, all over America looking for rookies. Your son was one of them. Now he's not. Now…" She shook her head.

He turned back to the torn newspaper page she'd left him with.

Her throat closed, disbelieving. "You don't care *at all*? You don't care he missed his chance? That's really how you feel?"

He stared at his scrap of paper.

"Answer me."

Lukasz dropped the paper, his hand trapping it on the tabletop. "I signed paper, as ordered, like a boy. He failed, my son, like a boy."

She smacked the table with the rolled-up paper a dozen times, then dropped it. "He's your son!"

Lukasz turned his gaze to her finally, his face blank. "I just said that." He went back to reading. Mary gasped and covered her mouth, backing away. She could strangle him, feel his skin under her fingers as she squeezed, scaring her to death. She stopped at the stove, its edges warming her backside. She gripped it to keep from swatting him.

She controlled her voice, reeling it back to talking volume. "Twenty-five years I've loved you and coddled you and done what you wanted, how you wanted, trying my best to show you how I see you. How the world would see you if you let them, see you as the man I chose because you understood me like no one else could. You saved me. Again and again. Until I had no choice but to love you, to see you as the man I should marry. Where's that gentleness? That hope you gave me? That love? Why'd you take it all away?"

Her muscles contracted in her neck, choking off the rest of her words. She put a hand to her throat. "Why do you want people to hate you?"

His hands shook, rustling the paper. "Why?" He lifted his gaze to her. "I feel most like me when I feel bad. And so then…"

Her chest ached, heart racing, prepared to come to a halt with the words her husband had spoken. Her anger whistled out of her like a balloon released air through a tiny pinprick.

"How do I stop being me?" He shrugged.

Mary couldn't remember the first time he looked directly at her and said something revealing, human.

"That's like asking why I don't peel back my skin and step out of it, pulling on Ken Morrison's or Joe Barbao's. It's impossible. It wouldn't fit."

Mary shook her head. She'd spent their marriage believing Lukasz's mythology that she was a strong mountain, believing that she had in fact stood up to the slow-moving, river-eroding forces of him, shaping his path as much as he carved away at her. She'd thought she'd been somehow showing him who he actually was inside. Now she saw—what he was in his own estimation was utterly different than who she thought he could be. So he was right. Looking at him with that ripped page, his inability to help himself, she understood. This she could not fix. As much as she wanted it to, American life simply did not fit.

Chapter 53

Stan

Stan followed his hitting in the lot with several more trips there that week. He hit so many stones out of their "field" that a farmer might be able to turn the soil for a crop. Exhausted, he collapsed and sipped from the dented canteen they used to use during practice. Doing his best to keep hidden from anyone who cared about baseball or Stan playing baseball, everyone except Joe. Stan even avoided Mom.

He was coming closer to making his decision, finding a way to open up conversation with the Cardinals organization again. Even smacking stones out of the lot felt better than anything else he'd done in ages.

Joe stayed steady with his advice. "I'll call Vanek and tell him you'll head to the next place they can put you, try to get him to convince Rickey to put you close to home."

Stan considered that, but the newspapers and everyone in town were relentless. Most meant well. They were excited that one of them had the potential to go where they could not. But oddly, he was quite sure that being further away might actually reduce some of his fear of the unknown.

During the time Stan waited for answers regarding his next options, the Yankees called, having seen him play the summer before. Stan declined their invitation, saying he'd signed with the Cardinals. But the phone call still got into the papers, convoluted, resulting in a crush of people asking how he could sign with the Yankees if he was signed with the Cardinals. People stopped his sisters, brother, and parents on the street just to say and ask the same things over and over. All of this helped blot out Lillian's gently placed questions, queries shrouded in things that she hoped were rhetorical. But being so overrun with press and concerns about whether he'd actually make it to a team that year, he barely registered what she was asking him.

The final uproar of the spring came when the press found out about Stan's trip to the Pirates game with Johnny and the workout with them that followed. People questioned whether Stan was serious about going to the minors at all. Plenty were thrilled with the notion of him staying behind to work in the mill and play for the Zincs, playing until the zinc-induced shakes or the baseball field broke him down for good.

Joe stopped Stan as he was heading to the lot to hit stones yet again. "You sure you don't want Vanek to try to get you set in Greensburg? We could all come, support you in person and—"

"No." Stan blurted it out. "If I fail, I don't want anyone who thinks I'm great watching. If I make it, friends can watch me all day long."

Joe squeezed his shoulder. "You are great."

Stan headed to the lot wondering when his sense of greatness and purpose would return.

**

Honey appeared at the lot just as Stan sat for a break, drinking his water. Honey picked up the bat. "Toss me some."

Stan unearthed stones and lobbed them toward his brother. "Heard your argument with Mom and Pop the other day."

"Hmm."

"Tried to sneak out the window, but it jammed."

"Trellis's broken anyhow," Stan said. "Remember?"

Honey nodded in between swings. "So I heard the blowup that followed after you left."

"Did they see you?"

Honey connected with one stone, hitting so hard they lost it in the smoky sky almost instantly. "Nooooo. I hid upstairs like a five-year-old. Huge tornado ripping through? No way am I stepping into it."

"I woulda hid, too. Remember when we would crouch under the table, balling up real small, Grandma and Pop swatting at us, ducking behind Ida's legs?"

Honey leaned on the bat. "You holding your breath."

Stan smiled. Honey got back into his stance. Stan tossed another few stones.

"You gotta leave, Stan."

"I dunno."

Honey glared at him. "I do know." He waved for more stones. "You're sooo good."

"You are, too. Just work harder." Stan and Honey said that last part simultaneously.

"Stop." Honey signaled for another toss. "You know you're different."

"We have the same parents, same everything."

"No lucky star though."

This stopped Stan mid-toss. "Oh man. That lucky star." He couldn't deny that caveat to their story. He completed the toss and kept it up one after another.

Honey paused and wiped his brow with his forearm then signaled for Stan to start tossing stones again. "I'm shittin' jealous of you." His breath sped up. "You and Andrew. Both brilliant. One with his mind and you with your body, the way you feel your way through the world. Just swat, crack, launch a pea right into that starlit universe far, far away, where Andrew's got his telescope aimed just waiting to see where you land all those hits."

Stan dug into the dirt to release more stones.

Honey held his hand up to keep Stan from tossing them. "You know all this." He leaned on his bat, leveling his gaze on Stan. "You don't have to pretend you don't. It's all right to be who you are. Like you said… remember that one time when you nailed me in the back for that automatic double and we were walking home and I was bitching and moaning and… well you said, baseball is who you are and you're never gonna be anything else. Something like that. You were correct back then. And if you ignore who you are now and don't go then you can't blame me. This time it's not my fault. Keep doing what you're doing."

Stan appreciated Honey that moment more than he ever had. "But that's just it. I haven't done anything. Signed some papers. Shit, *Pop* signed some papers. I haven't done anything except fail to report."

Honey shook his head. "Cut this crap out. Quit holding your breath like a four-year-old. You're going, and you're gonna like it. Donora's not big enough for both of us." He winked, making Stan smile as he tossed a hundred more stones and their conversation curved into easy talk about hitting streaks, losing streaks, beers after games and what they'd do when they played against each other in the World Series. And it was good; for the first time in a long while, it was good.

**

Later that week, Stan got home before anyone else, and so he took down the laundry for Mom, put baked beans on the stove, and stirred the simmering cabbage stew. With June edging toward July, Stan was still waiting for a formalized plan to be given to him. The Cards were irritated with his no-show, and the last he'd heard they were letting the beginning of the season settle before deciding where to send him. This hesitancy on their part left him washed in the now-familiar mix of confusion and relief that nothing was happening, that he was simply marinating in the same life he'd always lived.

A knock at the door came.

Lillian. She stopped his heart every time he saw her.

He invited her in. A basket slung over one arm, a pink-and-green scarf tying her hair back, the silk trailed over one shoulder. Her perfect, heart-shaped face and warm gaze made him pull her in for a hug. He was self-conscious for a moment—the weathered furniture and tiny rooms not as welcoming as hers, always giving him pause when she visited. The scent of beans and cabbage stew felt prominent in her presence. For dates, Stan always picked her up and walked her back home so she spent little time on Marelda. He told himself the Musial home didn't matter. More people in Donora lived like him than like the Labashes.

She held up the basket. "You've been busy deciding and thinking and changing your mind, back and forth. Spending every minute up on that lot smacking pebbles over the hillside, scaring the dickens out of Mrs. Walthrop when you pinged her house six times."

"Wait, how did you know that—"

"I'm not an ignoramus, Stan. I have ears. We sell the paper at the store. I can read as well as anyone."

"I didn't mean…" He should have kept her up to date, but after failing to report, he just couldn't keep explaining.

"I've brought you some things. Dad wanted you to have your favorite after your big win the other day with the Zincs. Fixings for a Dagwood. He likes to treat the local ballplayers once in a while." She patted the basket.

"Oh gee. That's really nice. Really." He guessed this meant the Labashes had decided Stan was going to stay in Donora. And maybe he should.

She shoved the basket toward him. He took it and headed toward the kitchen. The sound of Lillian clearing her throat made him turn back. "Are you inviting me in?"

"Yeah." He stirred the beans. "Wanna sit?"

She nodded but didn't sit. She opened her arms. "Are you going to fill me in on what you're doing? Or are you going to slip away to a team under the cover of a dark, smoky Donora night and I'll read it in the paper? Will you use those envelopes I gave you? Are we breaking up? Will you stay here and take the job in the zinc mill? I thought you cared about me. Or are we breaking up no matter what you do? Do I need to hang out in the Bucket of Blood to get these answers? Or do you still care about me?"

The thought of breaking up sent fear through him. He pulled the spoon from the beans and set it aside. "Lil. No."

She jerked back, arms crossed.

"I mean yes. I care. You know that. If anything, you know that."

"Then what? This is how it goes with you?"

"What? How what goes?"

"You, the way you pull me in and then cut me out and— what are you doing? How do you not know what you want to do after a lifetime of knowing? Suddenly you just let newspapers and men in bars tell tall tales about you? Shouldn't *I* at least know what's true? I'm assuming *you* know the truth."

His mouth went dry. Her direct questions were welcome yet frightening. "You'd be surprised about what I know or not about my very own life."

She sighed in an assertive way. "Just tell me the truth. Always. I can deal with anything else."

He leaned against the countertop, one foot over the other ankle. Five feet between them felt like miles considering how it usually was when they were in the same room or even walking down the street, their hands finding each other automatically. She looked like a queen standing there, her grace just… how could she even like him?

Her demand to know should have made him feel attacked, but it didn't. Her usual candor split open the shell that had encased everything he'd stuffed away—piles of thoughts and worries, years of dreams now loaded in like laundry, topped off by all these new choices he'd never expected to have. So many thoughts that he didn't know what to say first.

So he started with whatever was piled at the very top. She put him at ease like no other, she had threaded her way into his heart, her strength tangible. He knew he could trust her with the things he didn't even understand himself. "When I think of my baseball team, teams, from the time I was young… those fellas have been everything to me. When things are hard and…" He shook his head. What was he trying to say?

Lillian stood stock still except for digging her finger along one of the grooves in the pine table.

Stan relaxed when he realized her silence felt welcoming, not awkward. "When I play baseball, it's like a series of sensations, some sharp, like a heckle from some beefy man with a raspy voice that comes like a line drive. Or when the crowd roars long and loud, and it just hangs in the air like zinc coating, something that will stay with me forever. And when I bat and I'm looking at the pitcher and everything just fades away, all the voices, the fielders, my doubts, and I feel the pitcher's movement like it's mine, and in the back of my mind I register the grip and see the ball come off his fingertips—but that's not even what's important; it's what comes after all that stuff that I concentrate on, and before the ball gets halfway to the plate I know where it's gonna break or curve or drop, and I know whether to swing for short left field or smack one through the center right gap. And then I do. It's not like the kind of thinking in algebra or making sure I don't stammer or deciding to try college. It's like nothing else I've ever experienced. It's like magic. It's when I'm the most happy I could ever be." His eyes burned with the tears he too easily shed.

He could hear her breath quiver from five feet away. She shook her head, her eyes welling, too.

With the words out, his first full understanding of exactly what baseball meant to him, said to someone else, he expected Lillian to bolt. His praise of baseball made it clear that there wasn't much room for more. Yet. He pressed his chest, unable to ignore the truth about how he felt toward her.

He steeled himself against what she might ask. Would she tell him he could have all that stuff he just spewed out, right there in Donora, plus her, plus the chance to play until his body gave out? If he went to the pros and failed, he wasn't sure he'd ever pick up a bat again. It would make sense for him to just stay.

No.

With what he'd said sitting between them like smog strung between valley walls, his chest felt lighter. Better to be honest like Lillian had said. He closed his eyes. He'd never said such things aloud, about baseball, about anything. But now he knew. There really wasn't a choice to make at all.

"I have to go."

She smoothed her skirt and cleared her throat. "Oh, Stan."

He wiped his wet cheeks with the heels of his palms.

"You can't possibly stay."

Was she angry?

She pressed her hands against her belly. "A fella can't feel that way about something and turn away from it, that very thing that makes him happiest in the whole world."

She understood. He covered the space between them in two strides and scooped her up, holding her tighter than he'd ever held anything. "Thank you, thank you for understanding."

She sobbed into him.

"I love you, Lil," he said.

"And I love you."

Her tears, wet against his neck, her now muffled sobs against his skin, made him vow to hold her heart close forever, as close as it was right then.

**

Stan rushed to Joe Barbao's home, panicked for the first time that he had truly missed his chance with the Cardinals.

Joe waved him into the house. "What's the matter?"

"I figured it out, and I need your help." Stan removed his hat and brushed sweat from his brow.

"All right, calm down, calm down," Joe said, waving him into the kitchen. "What's the matter?"

"Can I use your phone?"

"Sure. What's wrong?"

"I need to check in with the Cardinals and get my assignment. I need to make sure they know I'm in. I just need to— "

Joe pulled a spiral notebook from a drawer. "Got the number here." He picked up the phone and waited for the operator to ask where to direct the call.

Stan paced while Joe paged though the notebook. He'd been so good to Stan over the years. The father of his baseball life and so much more. And here Joe was doing just what Stan could always depend on—laying another bit of foundation for him to stand on.

"Wait." Stan took the phone and hung it up.

Joe shook his head. He actually appeared frightened. "Look, Stan, you can't just go back and forth again. It's time to—"

"I know."

"What, then?"

"It should be me. I should call. I should tell them—no, *show* them I'm ready. I'm not a little kid and…" He exhaled deeply. "You've done everything for me. Everything. And now I should take care of the rest."

Joe lifted his hands in surrender. He smiled and backed away, leaning against the counter, smiling, watching Stan finally grab hold of his future.

**

It was done. This time Stan was going. They'd first slotted him into a team not far from Donora in Greensburg. But he reminded them of his request to go farther away for rookie ball, and so he was set to move to Williamson, West Virginia—just far enough to fail or succeed on his own. On a hazy, humid July day, Stan said goodbye.

He brought his bags downstairs, then stole away to Andrew's, climbing into the attic and out onto the observation deck. Andrew sat on the wicker settee, surrounded by books and notebooks, pencils strewn over the space, the only evidence Andrew was ever scattered.

"Need someone to run your latest 'Theory of the hidden parts of the miraculous universe' by?"

"You're always the first one I call." Andrew shoveled his books aside and stood, hands shoved in his pockets. "So it's you leaving me."

"I have to be first, you know."

Andrew shrugged. "Donora Greyhound strikes again."

"All right, okay, Wild Weatherman of Donora."

"The world awaits the Magician, the—"

Stan shoved Andrew's shoulder. "Just Stan. That'll do."

Andrew rubbed his shoulder. "I'll miss you."

Stan looked at his feet. The image of the two of them in Miss McKechnie's class, Andrew tossing him the hanky, shot to mind. He lifted his gaze. "Thank you."

"For what?"

Stan shoved the words out, but not nearly enough of them to express what he wanted to say. "For everything."

"Someday I'll say I knew you when," Andrew said.

"And…" Stan tried to wrangle out a witty response. Tears stung the back of his eyes, and he was about to bawl.

Andrew pulled Stan into a bear hug, slapping his back a couple dozen times before pushing him away. He folded a piece of paper and handed it to Stan. "For the ride."

Stan put it in his pocket.

"Go on. Can't miss another wagon train, or you'll never get out. And then…"

And so Stan entered the attic doorway, a glance over his shoulder at Andrew among all the things he loved so much. The ache it brought to think of parting was too great to stay a second longer.

✳✳

Back in his kitchen, Stan found Mom fussing with a grocery sack, folding the top over. Lillian! She leapt up from a seat at the table and scrambled to Stan. They held each other tight, laughing, Stan's tears finally dropping. He and Lillian released each other, glancing at Mom who smiled, but looked as though her mind was somewhere else. He and Lillian had said goodbye the night before, but he was so happy she'd showed up that morning.

"I got some time off from the store," she said.

Mom held up a sack. "Brought sandwich fixin's. Said it's all your favorites from her pop's store."

"No milk." Lillian wrung her hands. "Wouldn't hold on the hot train and all."

"Thank you." He took her hand, wishing he could smuggle her down to Williamson.

Mom dried an apple she'd washed and started on the next as Honey came flying in from the front room. He grinned and threw his hands in the air. "This is it." He tossed something at Stan, who dropped Lillian's hand to catch it, rosary beads trailing through his fingers.

"Take mine, too. You've been burnin' yours up, and I figure you'll need another soon."

Stan glanced at Lillian. She backed away, hand over her mouth like she was holding back the emotion he felt at the gesture. He looked at his feet.

"So I'll see you in a few months. Two. Right?" Honey said.

Stan met his gaze. "Play hard this summer. You know you're just as good. No daydreaming in center field."

Honey nodded. "Retire that pick-off move. No balks in the big leagues."

Stan furrowed his brow. "No way. That's my pride and joy."

"And you're ours," Honey said, head down. He raised his eyes then scrambled out of Stan's grip as he tried to hug him. Stan caught Honey just as he was crossing the threshold to the front room and squeezed him tight.

Honey banged on Stan's back. "That's enough. You hugged me last night. That'll do. I can't start blubbering again."

"I was the one blubbering," Stan said.

"Well, I can't afford to catch the habit from you."

Stan stepped away leaving Honey to exhale and steady himself, gripping the doorjamb.

Lillian dug a pristine white hanky from her purse and handed it to Honey who was still trying to keep from crying.

"Well." Mom pulled the sack from the table. "I guess—" but instead of Stan taking it from her, he pulled her into a hug. She stiffened for a heartbeat's time and then squeezed him right back, rubbing circles into his back as she had a million times over the years.

"Thank you for this," Stan said. "For everything. All these years."

Her embrace rolled his memory back in time to all the ways she'd held him close and up throughout his life. He wasn't sure he could actually leave. "Everything, Mom. Everything." This time he wanted to leave, but it burned and ached all at once. Even the thought of saying goodbye to Pop made him weak.

The back door opened. There he was. "Pop," Stan said.

Lillian stood. "Hello, Mr. Musial."

"Hey Pop," Honey said. "Wow."

Stan knew Honey was as surprised as he that Pop had shown up for this moment of seeing Stan out of the Musial family nest.

Pop nodded at each and removed his hat.

Stan released Mom and took a stutter step toward his father, then backed up, dropping his arms, afraid to hug his father after a lifetime of not expressing affection that way, after barely a word between them for nearly a year.

His father froze, then met Stan's gaze. "Good luck."

He didn't look angry or hard, his face soft like that time Stan had watched him sleep under the tree out back. He thought of those brutish men on McKean calling him a runty moron. And without considering it more, Stan rushed to Pop and wrapped him up in his arms, lifting him off the ground. He set him down almost instantly, patting his back, then backing away. "I'll make you proud." He vowed to give Pop something to make men like those on McKean shut the hell up. It would be Pop's success as much as Stan's even if Pop didn't yet realize it. The man deserved something that others would admire about him. If Stan fulfilled that, it would be worth it all.

The sudden quiet made Stan look up at the kitchen clock.

Mary snatched the sack lunch from the table, strangling it. "Time."

"But Rose and Helen and…"

"Your sisters were supposed to come say goodbye. Ida and Frank said they'd pick Helen and Rose up from work, and get Vicki but…" She lifted his duffel strap over his shoulder. Lillian handed Stan his suitcase. Mom stifled a sob, the tension so great Stan needed to get out before he exploded or imploded or just melted right there.

Out on the front porch Stan exhaled thinking he could let his nerves settle now that the difficult goodbyes were finished and he was relieved they'd all agreed to let him walk to the trolley alone. "Nice smoggy day to send me off. Silvery sun and all."

"Donora sunshine," Lillian said.

He winked at her.

The sound of familiar cackling filled his ears and Stan looked up the street. Ida. She'd parked her car and leapt out with her husband Frank. Helen, Rose, and Vicki spilled out as well. They rushed to the house, taking the porch stairs a few at a time.

Hands.

Stan dropped his luggage and lunch sack and the sisters grabbed him up, holding him, pinching his cheeks, memories and stories tumbling from their lips told in shorthand that only family members who'd been present for the original happening could understand.

"Oh, when you were born," Ida said, adjusting Stan's baseball cap. "What a… well, it was…I'll never forget that."

The pain on Ida's face was clear to Stan knowing that she'd not been able to have a healthy baby yet.

Honey blew his nose, a loud honk breaking the sad note of loss making everyone buckle in absurd laughter.

Ida started to dig into her purse and Lillian swept over handing Ida yet another hanky, the crisp whiteness practically glowing against the hazy fog. "I came prepared," Lillian shrugged.

"Greetings, Musial family." A voice rang out from the sidewalk.

Andrew.

"You're gonna miss your wagon train."

Stan turned. It wasn't just Andrew. Tank, Smokestack, Moonshine, Monocle, and Melonhead stood with him.

The Musials whooped at the sight of Stan's gang, the celebratory feel like booze filling the bloodstream, the moments before it turns things bad.

"Trying to get left behind all over again?" Smokestack asked, the red glow of his cigarette bouncing as he spoke.

"Then what?" Tank shrugged. "Hit some more stones off fence pickets up on the flat lot for the rest of your life? Plow it for corn or something?"

"Can't grow anything but stone up there," Monocle said. "And I'm pretty sure Stan harvested every available scrap for hitting in the past couple weeks."

"No, sir. Time to go," Stan said, picking up his luggage yet again.

His family's laughter and excitement died away and Stan finally descended the porch stairs. Each friend took a piece of luggage for the walk down the hill.

"We'll send him off good," Monocle said, patting Stan's shoulder. "Kid like this needs to fly like those balls he smacks over the river."

Stan couldn't breathe. He turned back for a final look at the house on Marelda, the family home.

Mom stood at the center, top of the stairs, her daughters scattered around her. Lillian leaned against one porch column, smiling through tears, wiggling her fingers in a small wave goodbye. Pop sat on a stair, below Lillian, beside Honey, lighting a cigarette, expression unreadable.

Stan paused, branding the sight into his mind. The picture of Donora and all it was. Right there. They were great and small, loud, bold, so strong even when sometimes broken, and sometimes they were even utterly silent. They were the reason Stan was who he came to be. And as the smog hung in ribbons of every shade of gray, partially obscuring Vicki's arm, and Rose's leg, Mom's cheeks reflecting light off tear-stained skin, Stan wondered what parts of them would be the same when he returned. If he could have painted a canvas of them just like that he would have.

A flash of movement drew Stan's attention. Honey. He patted Pop's leg then leapt down the stairs. "Think I'm staying at the house to drown in all the stories of Stan Musial, wonderful, handsome, star-bright, dancing fiend? I don't think so. Self-preservation as a life goal is underrated." He grabbed Stan's wrist and yanked him, moving him toward his future, the boys who'd meant so much over the years escorting him into the rest of his life.

Chapter 54

Mary

The night Stan left, his absence hit Mary like a bullet, leaving a hole that peeled back her flesh smidge by smidge all day, different than what she'd felt when her Ida or Helen had married off.

Lukasz had talked even less since their recent argument over Stan so she continued her habit of talking at him. It had been a long ten months. "Lillian Labash dropped off fixin's for Dagwood sandwiches. Stan's favorite. She thought you and I might like them, too."

"Good sandwich," Lukasz said.

Mary startled, turning to him, mouth dropped open. It was the first pleasant, offhanded comment he'd made since last September. She turned back to the meat and cheese and tomato and lettuce, piling it high.

"I think Lillian's in love with Stan."

"Hmm," Lukasz said, opening the paper. "Looks that way."

"Said rooms light up when he walks in. That smile. His shyness, the way he doesn't know his worth. It's endearing, she said when she helped me with the dishes after lunch." Mary lidded the sandwich stack with a slice of rye and set the plate in front of

Lukasz, sitting beside him. She covered his hand with hers. "Like you, Lukasz. She sees Stan a lot like I saw you."

A smile tugged at his mouth, but he wouldn't let it out.

Mary leaned into him and touched where the smile was threatening. "He's great, and you're part of him." She cupped his cheek, then pulled back, satisfied that hardness between them had begun to soften.

"The hankies," Lukasz said.

Mary narrowed her gaze on him. "Lillian certainly came prepared. I gave him five fresh ones and with the dozen Lillian stuffed into his bag, he can start a huckster wagon on the side if he's short on money."

Lukasz slid his hand behind Mary's neck, into her hair where he caressed her skin with light swirls. "No. I meant the hankies I brought from home—"

Mary leaned into his hand, and latched on to his wrist, edging closer to him, relaxing into his touch. She hadn't thought of those hankies in years. Lukasz had brought a pair of embroidered hankies from Poland, one for him and one to give his true love. When he'd arrived in Donora, a Polish immigrant had been his arranged fiancée… "Aneta," she said.

"Descended from kings," Lukasz said.

"Your betrothed."

He shook his head and pulled two handkerchiefs from his pocket. "Found them the other day in an old toolbox, on top of a bundle of wire. Just sitting there."

It had been arranged for him and Aneta to marry, but the hanky he'd given to her found its way to Mary. And so did Lukasz.

"I'd forgotten about that…" She smiled. "That part of us."

"I never forget." He leaned in and kissed her slow and soft like he used to way back when.

"You surprise me all over again, Lukasz."

"And I fall in love all over again," he said taking her hand. "Thirty-sixth time."

"Thirty-six?"

"There were others since we last mentioned it." They kissed again then pressed their foreheads together, Mary feeling the earth between them soften even more, making her feel like she was falling, just for a second. The sense of falling in love, being in love, wanting nothing more than love itself washed through her. "Eat," she said, pushing the plate toward him.

He nodded. "Two months. He'll be back."

"Season's over in two months. Yes, he'll be back."

"Hmph."

She thought again of Stan leaving, of the way he looked back at the family waving goodbye. Her insides jellied. This season would be short and no one knew what to expect. She almost started to explain to Lukasz that Stan wouldn't be Babe Ruth the second he hit the field, that this one piece of Stan's career wouldn't see him catapulted into the World Series, but that that wouldn't mean failure. But she stopped herself. Sitting with him, peaceful, loving, she held her words on the matter of Stan's future success. Instead she focused on the idea that the short time away was simply the beginning of the end.

"Well." Mary took a bite of the sandwich. She swallowed and sipped her lemonade. "He's never coming *back*, back, Lukasz. Not really. He's been set to go since he arrived under that lucky star and that pink moon."

"Hmph." Lukasz took another bite.

And so that was what she told herself to be a comfort. Stan had never been theirs to keep, just to hold until the rest of the world got a look at him.

Chapter 55

Stan

The rumbling and bouncing of the bus that took Stan on the last leg of the day-long trip to Williamson gave him plenty of opportunity to feel the shock of disappearing from the life he'd lived for nearly eighteen years. He played his harmonica softly, letting the notes soothe and numb before sleeping most of the trip. When he woke he remembered Andrew's note not far from his destination.

You might feel unmoored having left Donora.

Stan chuckled at seeing the unfamiliar word, *unmoored*. It was only unfamiliar in print, because Andrew used it extensively over the years in conversation. Its usage like having Andrew right there.

But don't fret about that. Your mom's your sun—always present even when covered in black, smoggy fog draped over cumulus clouds. Joe's your moon, everything you're shooting for. And your pop's gravity itself. And that's not a bad thing. It grounds you, it records where you've been so you can appreciate where you are. All these things go with you everywhere and so, well, maybe I've got all those people attached to all the wrong celestial bodies and physics principles, but I'm no Henry David Thoreau so… anyway. See you soon.

Andrew
WWoD

And with that, Stan burst into tears, ducking into his seat to hide away from fellow passengers, debating whether to stowaway on the bus for an immediate return trip to Donora.

**

Lefty Hamilton, the general manager of the Williamson Colts, met the bus and introduced Stan to the tiny town of Williamson. This man and his wife made Stan feel at home, and soon Stan's name was on the lips of every fan in the rugged mining town as one of the most likable players on the team. Stan's truncated season was successful, but not glamourous or glorious.

Over his two months away, Stan wrote letters to Lillian, but not nearly the number he should have. He wrote regularly to Joe. And he even sent a note to Honey, putting it inside a letter to Mom. He had to admit Honey's prediction had been correct. The first time Stan pulled down the brim of his hat, hiding his eyes, and started his motion to pitch before throwing to first to pick off a baserunner, he was called for a balk. And again and again. "You were right! My slick pickoff is dead and buried. Finally got it through my thick skull. My pride and joy six feet under, buried with sadness and resentment. But I suppose I'm better for it."

Deemed the friendliest player that year, the fans loving him, as he was never too rushed to talk or sign a program for some kid who liked the way he pitched, Stan found that grown-man baseball gossip in Williamson didn't bother him like it had in Donora. Nights full of beer and pool and the occasional movie with a gang of players and town girls led to days of ball. And though Stan still missed home, he'd adjusted to the baseball life fine.

He went 6-6 pitching and batted .258. But he'd made the leap and left Donora. One reporter from Donora came a few times, hovering, watching and letting his town know that Stan was making his way even if not lighting the league afire.

His final organization assessment for the 1938 season read, "Arm good. Good fastball, good curve. Poise. Good hitter. A real prospect." These weren't headline words, but they added to Stan's confidence. He had something to build on, reinforcing the idea that he would work his way into the major leagues, even if most of the fellas he played with in Williamson would not.

Chapter 56

Stan

Stan returned to Donora on September 8, 1938. Mrs. Roberts granted Mom a long lunch break so she could meet him at the trolley. They trundled up the hill, Mom crushing him with bear hugs that continued at intervals as they dragged his luggage, each unspooling the news of their summer months. It felt good but turned upside down to return. Nothing had changed in town, but everything felt different. With distance from the place that shaped him, he returned with new edges and curves laid into his skin, his mind finally having cleared from all that had plagued him leading up to his departure. Pop was working a shift, Honey had taken over Stan's job at the gas station and was there, and Rose was still at the house where she cleaned.

"Thank you for sending some of your salary back," Mom said.

Stan's chest puffed out. "You're welcome. I loved doing it."

After sandwiches and cabbage stew, Mom took Stan's face in her hands, kissed his forehead, then bear-hugged him all over again. "You are home, and I might never let you go again."

"You have me until spring, that much is for sure. I'll finish school."

"First Musial to do so," Mom said.

"I've been asked to play for a semi-pro basketball team. I'll train and work in between."

"And Lillian?"

Stan sighed. He couldn't wait to see her. "Yes. I sort of thought she'd be there with you to meet me."

Mom cocked her head. "Well, she's just letting you sink back into home. She's thoughtful that way."

"She is thoughtful." But Stan wasn't so sure of her motivation behind not showing up.

"And then you'll be off again."

"Yeah."

"Well," she said, "I'll take these couple months with you." And she kissed him and left to finish her day at Mrs. Roberts's home.

The silence that emerged when Mom left was probably the most unfamiliar thing he'd felt that day. He roamed the kitchen, noting everything. Mom's notepad with grocery list was where it always was. Coffee mugs rinsed and drying in the strainer, the same chips along the lip of Pop's mug, a clean tea towel folded in three parts near the stovetop. He sat at the kitchen table. He drew his fingers over the scarred wood, his forefinger dipping into the one rut he'd watched Lillian's finger trace the day he knew it was time to leave.

He needed to see her, but something held him back.

He unpacked his bags, remembering the day he'd left. As the bus had rumbled nearer Williamson, a surge of terror had come with each pitted, dirt-road hole the wheels hit. At that time he hadn't been able to get the image out of his head of Pop and the three men who'd been so rude to him, treating him like a child or a moron more than a man just like them. It was that scenario that had haunted him at first as he was introduced around the team of fellow professionals.

He wouldn't fit, he wasn't as good, he was just a guy from a small town where most people never left once arriving. Though nothing compared to Pop's journey from Poland, Stan worried he'd set himself up for a similar fate—to never belong anywhere else. But that worry had left quickly as he fell into the rhythms of the games, sleep, pool, movies. His sense of feeling at home came when they played their first night game under lights that lit the field about as much as the headlights on Andrew's car that one summer night.

He'd exhaled into his pitching that night, realizing Andrew had been right. Though far from home, home traveled with him. The good parts.

He opened his duffel and pulled everything out, seven envelopes still addressed to Lil, stamped, but empty, now loose in the twine she'd tied them in. He put the letters he'd received from Joe and Lil and Mom and Andrew into his drawer, under his shirts.

He sat on his bed and lifted the last letter Lillian had sent to his nose. Lilac. A new perfume? Perfume from another letter that had traveled with it? That last letter had been short. No love words or statements of yearning and good wishes for the end of the season.

She'd simply reported on the number of counter guests they had at the store the day she'd written it, grocery store stats, like baseball box scores and scouting reports. Upon first reading, this had made him smile, her sense of humor always succeeded in doing that. But as the bus had drawn closer to Donora, he'd reread the letter. Rereading had made him smile again but then delivered a stab to his heart as well.

This reading had his eyes drifting repeatedly back to a name. Donny Harshman, one of the counter-sitters, apparently bought three and a half sandwiches, preferring his meats spread among short stacks rather than the Dagwood that Stan had called an architectural wonder one time when Lil had stacked it five high. "Major league staying power—three-hour sit. Strengths—shooting the gas. Weakness—doesn't realize when to stop with the gas. All-star tipper."

At the time the letter was delivered, Stan had been focused on the last stretch of the season and a mess of going away. Post-game pool marathons prevented him from replying right away and before he knew it, he was stuffed in a hot bus headed back home.

Old Donny. Fine fellow, but one who'd asked Lil out any chance he got. Something Stan had never worried about before. But now home, in the silence, the late afternoon light revealing every blemish in the Musial home, the blemishes on his writing record the past eight weeks wasn't holding up to scrutiny. And he was struck with uncertainty, a question boiling to the surface. Had he been traded?

**

Six-day losing streak. Twelve at-bats. Zero hits. Not even ugly foul-tips. Lillian Labash was giving Stan the brush-off. At first he played along, understanding that he needed to work a little to remind her he'd returned. He dropped off a bundle of flowers picked from the back hill. Mrs. Labash thanked him on behalf of Lillian, but he still hadn't heard from her directly. His more veteran teammates in Williamson had warned him of the pitfalls associated with "re-entry into your hometown" following a season. He hadn't expected this little bit of baseball life advice to hold when it came to Lillian.

Still in high school, Stan had to work his attempts to see Lillian around those hours. Now that his pro status had wiped out him playing ball for the high school or college, he was back to taking an easier complement of courses that even included shorthand. Turns out that a guy still had to do his shorthand homework if he wanted passing grades.

He did what he needed to get by. To keep his mind off Lillian, he made a list of places to apply for off-season jobs, started workouts at the Falcons, and confirmed that he would play semi-pro basketball for the Garagemen.

But unlike his slender letter-writing offerings while away, Stan'd been stellar at showing up in the places he expected Lillian to be. The Donora Women's Club sewing bee, leaving church, but he missed her every time. He'd stopped by the store, but she was never available. Andrew let him use their phone to call her. "Scraping out the oven, Stan," Ann had said.

"Well, could you—"

"She wants her envelopes back," Ann said. She chuckled then lowered her voice. "I know it's silly. But if you have any interest in Lil at all, you better get your fastball-hitting rear end over here soon."

Stan didn't know what to say and Ann hung up before he figured it out.

On and on, the excuses for her unavailability came and with them a deepening sense of loss for Stan. In school, his mind slid to Lillian, making each class creep by like a day. Over dinner his mind would go to imagining her with Carnegie Tech student Donny Harshman, riding in his slick car, dancing the night away. Donny's future in vinyl and nylon reminded Stan of his choice to avoid college.

It pulled his life into sharp focus. Stan's sweat-soaked summer in Williamson, thick dirt stuck to his skin, under his nails, Saturday nights spent playing pool with a dozen of his favorite teammates and a hundred off-duty miners, meant he and sharp-dressed Donny Harshman were living in completely different worlds. Donny's stable path meant money—no, shiny, modern *luxury*. Stan's path offered uncertainty and... well, infield dirt. He'd realized his error in not paying enough attention to Lillian, even if from afar. He'd been busy, yes, but he could have written more, even short letters would have been better.

The thirteenth time Stan approached Labash's Grocery store, he spied Donny at the counter. Lillian leaned on it, watching Donny enjoy a good sandwich. Stan's insides rumbled with hunger of every sort. Was that Donny's first stack or third? Was he on his first hour sitting there or fourth?

A towering load of schoolbooks sitting beside Donny's plate signaled commitment to being there for the duration. Stan wasn't looking for a confrontation. If Lillian didn't want him anymore, then perhaps that was for the best. It wasn't as though he couldn't have gone on dates in Williamson.

Had he not been so wrapped up in baseball and those pool tournaments, the comradery of it all, he could have worked a dinner or two with a nice girl into his lineup with one of them who hung around with the crew. If Lillian didn't want him, then... He let those words sit with him, wanting to see how it felt to separate from her mentally. Like slag poured off steel, perhaps it was simply the way things went. He'd left Donora, and maybe that meant he'd left her, too.

But as he backed away and started toward home, the sense of Lil gripped tighter. He didn't want to leave her. He wanted her in his life. Ignoring the homework he had, missing dinner, he circled town, taking twenty minutes to loop to his house and another twenty looping back to Lil's. Seeing Donny at the grocery left him with that same crush of worry and confusion that had shadowed him when deciding to leave. But with his third loop around town, darkness settled over his path back toward the south end, back toward Labash's. Nausea swept through him. He realized he wasn't confused. He'd never been confused when it came to Lillian. He had just been asleep.

**

A quick glance through Labash's storefront window revealed an empty counter. And Lillian behind it. She wiped down the spot where Donny had been sitting for, what? A decade probably. Stan pushed through the door, the bells alerting Lillian. Her head snapped toward him. She stopped mid-swipe of the cloth and stared as he approached.

"Stan."

His body came alive, aware of breath, heartbeat, his words catching in his throat.

"That seat open?"

She glanced toward the back. Was Donny still there? She sighed. "'Course."

He slid onto it, stomach growling. This made her giggle.

"Your stomach gives your intentions away every time."

He nodded, expecting her to ask if he wanted his usual. But when she didn't, when she just looked at him as though they'd just met, he said, "Can I have a sandwich? Please."

"Sure." She started wiping at the counter again. "Menu?"

Menu? She knew his order. "Lil, what—"

Laughter startled Stan. He turned, legs dangling from the counter stool. Mr. Labash and Donny sashayed toward them, cutting a path down the aisle that displayed canned vegetables on one side and laundry soap on the other, looking like lifelong friends.

"Stanley!" Mr. Labash's face lit up.

Donny pushed his chin out. "How nice. A celebrity."

Stan stood, wanting to ignore Donny, but deciding not to. He said hello, looking at his feet as often as he looked the two men in the eye.

Mr. Labash held his hands up. "A solid first season in Williamson. Reports from the field indicate they're changing their name to the Redbirds for next season."

Stan nodded. "They are." He'd only seen one reporter from Donora a couple of times in Williamson. That seemed like a strange detail to report with so few articles written.

"So, six and six?" Donny said. "Hmm. That's something."

Stan finally held the guy's gaze. Stan may not have been headed for business glory, but he certainly understood his baseball world better than this guy. If Lillian was choosing Donny, Stan wasn't going to be belittled.

"Yeah. Learned a lot. Solid work."

"The Donora Greyhound, the player with magic hands and bewitched bat, *still* had stuff to learn? Can't imagine it," Mr. Labash said. "That's wonderful."

Stan straightened. "Sure. Lots to learn about signs, reading them, stealing them, backing up bases, relay throws, and cutoffs. You know. Local ball got me started, but this was different. It was…"

Donny crossed his arms, scowling.

Mr. Labash grinned and pushed his fist into the air. "A success, far as I can see. And small as Williamson is, seems like there was plenty for a fella to do. Movie house, tavern, poolhall."

Stan nodded, feeling like there was much more behind Mr. Labash's words.

"Fishing. We did some fishing, too."

"Hmm," Donny said. "Sounds about right."

"It was great, Donny. Everything as it should've been."

"That right?"

Donny studied Stan, reading him for what? His continued interest in Lillian? His chances with her? "Sure."

Donny shuffled his feet, looking awkward for a split second before rolling his shoulders back. "Gotta go. Big talk at Carnegie Tech on fluoropolymers and future applications in home products. You wouldn't believe the stuff on the horizon in home goods." With that sentence, he'd recovered his poise and stuck his hand out to Mr. Labash to shake, his other hand on the man's shoulder. "See you around, Sam. Golf, next Sunday. Ten sharp."

Stan rolled his eyes. *Sam*? He glanced at Lillian's hand. Had he overlooked an engagement ring or something? The jingling bells on the door marked Donny's exit.

Mr. Labash rubbed his palms together. "I've got some cartons to unpack, so I'll leave you to talk. But, Stan, if you're looking for work in between basketball and school, I always have something."

Out of the corner of his eye, Stan saw Lillian digging at the same spot in the counter that she'd been working on when he arrived. "Thank you," he said, unsure about the idea. He slid back onto the stool. It was time to work this part of his life out, too.

Lillian slid the menu to Stan.

"Forgot my order already?" He wanted to see her smile.

She tossed the rag into the sink and dried her hands. "Nope. But things have changed so…"

Stan raised his eyebrows.

She tapped the menu.

"Same order." He slid it back. "Nothing's changed."

She set it aside. "Hmm."

"You look real nice," he said.

"Thank you."

"And you're doing well. Obviously."

"Hmm."

"Lillian."

She gathered meats and cheeses from the deli case, dealing them out like cards on a plate in front of Stan. She pulled bread and condiments toward her, her hands flying, setting everything up.

When she finished, she pushed the plate toward him. "Four stories. Five was a little too high to manage last time if you recall."

Stomach growling, hours since eating, he still couldn't take a bite. He stood and went around the counter to where it was open. He wanted to hold her. He needed that more than food.

She shut the refrigerator and turned. "Eat up."

He looked away then back. "Can we talk? Before eating, I mean."

She looked at her watch. "How about while eating?"

"Got a date?"

"What if I do?"

"Well. I'd like to know about it, then."

"Really?"

He nodded.

"That's all you have? Questions about what I'm doing? You could ask anyone in town and get those reports. Just like I take my news of Stan Musial right from the locals' mouths. And newsmen? Well they seem to know it all."

He deserved that. "I'm sorry, Lillian. I should have written more."

"Hmm."

"You're sore, and I understand that."

"You do? Hmm."

"Stop that."

She stared at him.

"I mean, talk to me."

"Do you plan to return the favor?"

He raised his shoulders and dropped them. "Yeah. I mean, that's what I just—"

"You didn't send many letters back, so…"

"We were on the road, and you said you knew I might not write all the time."

She scoffed and shook her head, grabbing the rag. She scrubbed at the counter again, that same spot. "That's not the thing, that's not…"

"Then what? Tell me. Talk to me."

She whizzed the rag from across the room into the sink.

"Nice arm," he said.

She crossed hers.

Sense of humor completely gone.

"Lillian, please. Talk to me."

"You sure that's what you want? Because I've done a lot of thinking and digging around my heart and searching my soul, and I've got an awful lot to say, Stanley Musial."

He flinched. She was madder than he could imagine. But yes. He wanted to talk, to tell her how he felt, that he loved her every bit as much as baseball. Didn't he? It sounded stupid to think in those terms. "Let me say something first."

She swept her hand aside, giving him permission.

"I'm sorry."

Silence.

"I am."

"For what?"

"For not writing. For… I guess I haven't said what you wanted. And I'm sorry."

"Okay."

Silence. The sound of footsteps overhead made the two look up. "Mom's heels. She and Dad are going out."

Other than the first time he'd sat with Lil at Herk's, he'd never felt uncomfortable with her. And he never realized that she must have done most of the talking when they were alone, that she'd shepherded them through conversations, allowing him to always have his bearings. He'd been comfortable with her. And now… this.

"If that's it, then, I guess it's my turn to talk," she said.

"Yes."

"Before you left, we said we loved each other. Said it many times."

"And we did. We do. Don't we?" Stan asked.

"I don't think you realize what I—"

"It's not like I didn't write to you, Lillian. I know I'm not a wordsmith like…" Stan pointed to the chair Donny had been sitting at all day.

Her lips went thin and tight. "It's not the letters. I know you were doing the very thing that you love dearly. I never expected you not to be with your friends or sit in the room writing to me after every game. But it was brought to my attention that you were keeping company with some gals there in Williamson, a whole movie-going gang of gals and guys and I just want to have clarity on the matter."

Stan's eyes went wide. "I caught a movie with some fellas and some girls came along. How did you know that?"

"Reporters, Stan, they pick up every crumb you leave behind to report and surmise and discuss from one end of town to the other."

"There's not another woman in the world who could possibly… I certainly never—I love you. You see that, right?" He wanted to hold her but could tell that was not welcome at the moment.

"I see you better now than before. That's for sure."

"Then you should know I love you."

She cocked her head, examining him as though she could suck the truth right out through his skin.

"You know that, right?"

She sighed and leaned against the counter.

"You know?"

She looked up at him.

"I won't do it again," he said. "Not even with a whole gang if it worries you. I won't make you feel like that, hurt you again."

He half expected her to rush into his arms. Pop had never said so much to apologize to Mom before she quickly started to smooth things between them, to soften his sharp edges. But Lillian straightened, a few feet away, calm, measured, beautiful, but absolutely unmoved.

"I know you won't do it again, Stan."

He moved to hold her. She planted her palm against his chest, pushing him back.

"I won't be waiting for you if you do."

Her graceful delivery of this sentiment sent fear though him. He believed her. "I don't want to lose you. I just got caught up in all of… everything."

"I know. I think about that day in your kitchen all the time when you finally decided to leave, when you realized you had to. The way you described what you feel when you play baseball. It touched me deep inside. I understood what it all meant to you more than ever before. And I was happy for you. That you finally were lining up your dream with reality and… I never in a million years would have asked you to stay back."

"I know you understood, and that's partly why I love you so much." He grasped her arms. She stiffened but didn't wiggle away.

"You are great, Stan. You are so good at being that. You make everyone feel like there's no one else on earth when you talk to them. It's like you bring the very oxygen they need to breathe."

"I'm shy and strange. I'm completely inarticulate, Lil. Except with you or when talking baseball. But I'm not great. None of that stuff."

"You sign autographs when other players are gone. You actually discuss your baseball release when someone stops on the street with suggestions, even if he knows less than me about some damn curveball grip. You make others feel good. You just do it, and that's aside from your actual baseball talent, which makes everyone feel like there's magic in the world. You are great whether you admit it or not. That's what people love about you."

"But I love you," he said. "It's you I feel comfortable with."

She moved back and waved a hand through the air. "Love comes and goes. I'm telling you this because I need you to understand me."

"I think I do."

"No, you don't."

"Tell me, then."

"What you said about baseball, your love for it, getting lost in it, I understand, and I know that will be… everything to you in some ways. Whatever team you're on works as your family to some degree. And I don't think you shouldn't go to movies with a gang of people."

He couldn't breathe. He felt as though she were winding up to dump him.

"But I won't stand there watching and cheering you if you don't feel that same love for me as you do for—fielding questions about who you might have an interest in besides me."

"I do—"

"I'm not done yet."

He nodded, their gazes latched.

"You have to figure out how to be ordinary, too. Because the ordinary stuff is what really matters. The rest—all that cheering for you—is actually for them. What you said about focus and your breath while pitching and hitting, how the world fades away, all that natural ability, the wonder of it when you play. It's all for other people, something you're giving away. Because if you think all that praise for your baseball greatness is something they're giving to you, it'll never, ever be enough. And then nothing else in your life will be enough either. And I can tell you for sure, Stan Musial, I am ordinary. I love ordinary. I want that with you. And I am fine with standing in the footlights of all your charmed baseball talents, but I will *not* be waiting if you think for one second I'll look away while you choose others over me after the fuss of the game ends. If you look at me like I'm not good enough for you…"

"No. Stop it. You're spectacular. I would never call you ordinary. You're not."

"But I'm not a ball player."

"I don't think I'm permitted to date ballplayers."

Finally a smile.

"Stop. Don't make me laugh when I'm mad as a hornet."

He nodded.

"What I'm asking is if you think you're good enough for me. Because I know I'm good enough for you."

Now he was confused. "I don't understand what you're saying."

"This town is half full of men boo-hooing that their wife wanted more in life than they can give and so they go and dilly-dally around town and blame it on the woman. Whole town ends up chatting about who's at fault for specific actions and turns out it's that one doesn't feel good enough for the other so… he treats his wife like…"

"Wife?"

She nodded.

"You're leaping ahead."

"Same principle for girlfriend."

"But no one would talk about us, you that way. They—"

"Yes, Stan, they will and did. All summer. And I won't be pitied behind my back. I need to know where I stand and make my choice. If there's anyone else for you, tell me, but I won't be made a fool of for being with you."

Her words sank into his skin one by one, hitting every target she aimed for.

"I swear," he held up his hand. "I got overwhelmed and didn't do right by writing letters but I didn't so much as hold another girl's hand."

She blew out her air, but didn't look particularly relieved or convinced.

He didn't want to be someone she used to love, or used to know. This was not a woman who would simply, silently, sink back into their relationship without him making clear what he felt.

This was not his mother and he never wanted to be his father. So this was it. This was his chance to set things completely different. She went back at the stain that wasn't on the counter, her hair bouncing with every scrub. His emotions swirled, making him feel like he might cry. He tried to hold it all back.

He cleared his throat, steadying his voice. "You probably think I don't love you as much as baseball."

She froze then straightened, meeting his gaze again. "Well."

He thought of all the hours since he'd been home, all his thinking that led to this moment. But really it was what he felt about her. He gasped. His eyes stung. "I do."

"Don't lie."

"I'm not."

"To me or yourself."

He shook his head.

"At least shed a tear."

The ones welling dropped down.

"Now you're being dramatic," she said, tears streaming down her face, too.

"Oh my God, Lil. Please give me a break." He couldn't wait another moment. He grabbed her up. The fresh smell of her hair, her body warm as her heart pounded against his chest, lit his body on fire. He realized she hadn't said she still loved him.

"Do *you* love me?"

"Yes, yes, yes."

He exhaled and set her down, wanting to see her when she said it.

She took his hands and squeezed them. A serious look spread over her face.

"What?" She's promised to Donny?

She wiped her eyes with dainty flicks of painted fingers and tossed Stan a towel. She fanned her face. "Okay. I won't have this conversation again. I won't be the girl fretting till the point of explosion, and we argue and tread this terrain over and over, breaking up, getting together again, all of that. No. I will love you

fiercely. I'll take a backseat to baseball, but I won't worry that
there's anything else happening."

"I won't do that to you. Not ever. And if you say you're
choosing Donny over me, I think my heart will stop beating the
minute your words leave your mouth. You really like him?"

"I do," she said.

"I see. He's got that car and all that vinyl and nylon and golf
with your pop… and smooth as silk… Lil. He's nothing like me."

"Nothing at all."

"So we have to share you until you decide?"

She dropped her head back then threw her arms in the air.
"I don't want Donny, Stanley. Can't you see that?"

"You're sure?"

She sighed, dropping her arms. "Completely."

He thought with all this up and down his heart might give
out right there. "Well okay. I think it's all clear now." He stepped
toward her. This time she didn't back away.

"We understand each other." She stepped closer.

"Better than anyone." He reached for her, pushing his hand
into her hair, the nape of her neck, warm against his palm.

She pressed into him, wrapping him tight, and he realized for
the first time what it meant to love. Just like Dicky had promised
he would nearly a year before. When everything had been moving
parts flying past his head a million miles a minute. Now, the parts
were placed, locked into position where he could tend to them
just as each bit deserved.

He buried his face in her neck, never wanting to let her go.

The sound of her parents coming down from upstairs made
her wiggle away. She shooed him around the counter to his stool.
"Now eat that sandwich before it tumbles over."

And that's what he did. She pulled a step ladder up to the
counter across from him and sat on it, the two of them falling into
his stories and hers, the two months apart now woven back into
each other's lives.

Chapter 57

Owen

Owen arrived at Blue Horizon with news for Gramps. He'd been permanently—at least as far as the rest of summer was permanent—shifted to center field and was instructed to focus on hitting, that he could leave the grind of pitching behind him. He hadn't even realized that something like that could be a relief, that after ten years of being picked to pitch, even a starting pitcher in high school, that he'd been ignoring the fact that his skillset was slipping. The rotations per second had slipped from 2200 to 1800 and sometimes not even that. His speed had started fluctuating between 84 and 92 miles an hour.

"But you've got speed, and man you can hit so we'll slide you over for now and see what happens."

Owen had nodded, not sure what it all meant at first.

"You're going back to Michigan at the end of the summer, right?"

Owen hadn't thought about leaving. It was just the beginning of August. The question struck him as so shocking that it took him back to when his mum had forced him to go to Donora at the beginning of that summer. Sprang it on him, hitting him like a pitch in the back. Yet, now… he couldn't imagine heading home to Grosse Point. Not even to patch things up with his girlfriend and play ball with his old buddies. "I don't know what my mum's planning yet. I guess we're going back."

"Well, let's focus on the next four weeks. I want to get a better feel for your hitting and fielding now that we've taken pitching out completely." He patted Owen on the back. "You've got something, kid. Just need to sort it all out."

And with that Owen was released from practice, his ride dropping him off. When he knocked at Gramps's door, the room was empty. Though there were no alarms or the telltale way Blue Horizon marked each room's indicator with information regarding where the resident was. It said Gramps should be in his room, yet he wasn't. He collapsed into Gramps's chair and pulled the big book onto his lap, careful to dust off his pants before setting the book there. He opened to where it was marked, checking to see if Gramps had moved ahead without him. Owen had been told Harrison and his family might be heading back through town after vacation and so maybe they'd taken the book over again. But no. It was marked where he'd left off. He dropped the bookmark and picked it up. A bunch of numbers were scribbled on it, looking like medical information. Owen set it aside and started reading the page aloud.

It was an outline glued onto a couple of pages, a piece that described some of what Stan experienced after that first season in Williamson. It was typewritten in a straightforward way, missing a lot of the detail that the author of most of the book included that drew the reader into the story with scenes that leapt off the page. But it was telling with some of the phrasing.

> Musial and anyone asked declared Stan's 1938 summer in Williamson a success. In Fall 1938 through Spring of 1939 Musial busied himself with school, semi-pro basketball, club teams at school for tennis and ping-pong, and of course Lillian Labash. The two spent many evenings double dating with their 'old' teacher Ki Duda and his wife, Verne.

Basketball team: Garagemen—owned by Monongahela Auto dealer Frank Pizzica. Stan was youngest player by years, but Frank and his wife, Molly, were very close friends of Stan's for the rest of his life. Though the games brought little money for the players, they enjoyed Molly's Italian cooking on a regular basis."

Owen turned the book to get a better look at handwritten prose on the next page: "I met Stanley when he wasn't even twenty years old. Just a couple months on the road at Williamson, he was still green in many ways. Not physically. He was ferocious on the court, never letting anyone best him if he could. That beautiful left-handed hook. And I guess that's what it was about him. So much talent and ferocity, yet graceful as hell and kind as shit. Whipsmart, too. Even if not bookwise.

But… Kid had the grace of God's breath inside him, but had a lot to learn about social graces. There he was naïve and clumsy as my ninety-year-old grandma driving to the basket. But thing about Stanley was that he absorbed every bit of advice me or those other great men in his life had offered. Can't say how many meals Molly and I served him with the purpose of not only feeding the kid with the bottomless pit for a belly, but to teach him business manners. Down to how to dress and for the love of Pete, taught the kid to look another man in the eye, offer his hand, and to firm up that dead fish handshake of his. I mean I'd say to Molly, Hey Mol, ease up on the Miss Manners routine or he'll stop coming around. I need him for the next game.

But I think Stan was relieved to learn all this stuff. All the stuff that helped him later, the stuff that a kid in a mill-town might not need to know. He was a good soul in every single way a person could be. And even though his girl was a stunner and they were too young, he was practically a family man. Even back then. Helluva kid. Helluva man.

It was signed—F. Pizzica for the purposes of Musial archives and interviews.

The next page went back to the outline, sketching out his next baseball and life developments.

Reported to Williamson again—$75/month gap in playing time due to shoulder tenderness. Report to St. Louis home office indicated Musial's pitching was wild and not dependable, though at times was electric. "I'm led to believe his wildness is his effectiveness."

Owen gasped and reread that line. The report referenced in the outline wasn't attributed to someone specific, but it sounded like Stan Musial was not having the kind of second year a fella would want.

The notes added that Stan had exceptional practice habits and was a fine person.

Owen blew out his air, reminding himself he knew the ending of Stan's story, he didn't have to be nervous. Yet, he'd never heard any of this before, all that wasn't perfect about Stanley Musial. Owen sank further into the chair, oddly comforted to know Stan's path to greatness wasn't perfectly straight. In the end, Stan finished the season 9-2, but his ERA was sky high. Too many walks.

Batting average .352. Owen let out a whistle. "Well there you are, Stan the Man," Owen said aloud. "I knew you were in here somewhere."

He scanned down the page for more.

1939 Personal Life—Graduation from high school—left for spring ball. Lillian walked in Stan's place to get his diploma.

Marriage—November 21, 1939—Secret wedding.

Official wedding date filed in Florida—May 25, 1940.

Dickie born—August 1940

Owen stared at the book again, turning the pages back and forth. The outline mapping all the stats someone could ever want to know about Stan, but it was the story behind his stats that Owen had fallen in love with. "This can't be it," Owen said, flipping forward. "They can't have left out Stan and Lil's secret wedding."

"You read ahead, did ya?"

Owen's head snapped up. Mum and Gramps stood there, arms crossed, scowling.

"I uh... I just opened it and... well... this outline in here and this writing isn't Gram's and... well, all of this." Owen pointed at the page.

He got up to make room for Gramps to sit. Mum helped him over and wiped up the table, picking up the paper Gramps had been using as a bookmark.

"Gramps?" she held up the document. "What happened... you weren't going to tell us?"

Gramps sighed into his chair and rubbed his temples. "Can't I read the rest of this section with the kid here? Then we discuss all that."

"What?" Owen asked.

Patryk retied the string on his sweatpants. "Cancer. Just some damn cancer. It's nothing."

Owen felt like he'd been smacked in the head with a line drive. "What?"

"Nothing. It's nothing. I haven't decided a thing. Let's just get back to the story."

"Gramps," Lucy said. "Please—"

He slid the book onto his lap. "No. You please. Let me read this with the kid and then I'll tell you everything."

Owen wanted to hear about the cancer. But he followed Gramps's lead. He'd rather save it for later and fall back into the pages of this great, mysterious fairytale, the place where none of them who read it had to wrestle with their own problems. At least for the time being.

Chapter 58

Stan

Stan returned home from his second stint in Williamson, West Virginia, standing on solid soil built on confidence and accomplishment, but the assuredness was cloaked in a bit of instability. His 9-2 record wasn't terrible, the last three wins helped significantly. But his shoulder had bothered him half the season, making his pitching less predictable than it had been in ages. This is what led to the shrouding of full self-confidence in his pitching. Over the course of the summer, he'd counteracted this by constantly asking for coaching feedback, practicing before and after games, and playing out of his mind every chance he got. *His hitting.* Now that felt right. Easy, natural, like it had since the first time he swung something at a ball heading his direction. But he'd been signed to pitch.

Stan and Lillian had grown closer despite the distance that summer. He wrote more letters and with every day that put him nearer to going home after the season, daylight grew shorter but his days felt longer and he thought more than ever about holding her again, wanting her close by even during the season. This time when he returned to Donora, Lillian met him at the trolley. He leapt off as it rolled into the station, lifting her, spinning her so long that he nearly missed getting his bags off before it pulled away again.

The lovebirds traipsed up the hill to Marelda and blasted into the house, smothering Mom and then Rose in hugs as well. Pop was at work, Honey and Vicki, too, and so the four enjoyed the usual Musial meal of cabbage stew, pierogi, bread, and *placek*—an Easter sweet bread Mary made especially for Stan's return. She asked a million questions about every pitch, his shoulder, next year's prospects. And hitting.

"That was always when I saw you smile most, Stan. Have they seen you hit yet?"

"'Course, Mom. I do it all. It's just they signed me as a pitcher."

Mary nodded as Lillian and Rose fell into conversation more interesting to them—the upcoming holiday season's fashions. When Honey rolled into the kitchen the conversation turned back again to all things baseball. Finally, with nightfall tight around them, Stan started to walk Lillian out the door to take her home. Pop was coming up the steps when they left the house.

The two eldest Musial males greeted each other. Stan felt like they were strangers again, the time between leaving and returning, causing their lifetime of unease to reveal itself. Stan awkwardly stepped around him, Lillian following.

"I brought you some sandwich meat, Mr. Musial," she said, her voice light and airy.

"Thank you," he said, punctuated by the door shutting.

Free from any family, Stan and Lillian grasped hands and started down the hill. She squeezed his hand. "It'll be all right. He'll warm up."

Stan nodded. He didn't need to hide things from Lillian. "Heard Pop told Mr. Labinsky who told Tina McCandless who told her mother who mentioned it to the reporter who came to interview me in Williamson that Pop wasn't surprised to hear I'm not setting the world on fire. This wasn't my best showing."

Lillian stopped and pulled Stan into her, forcing him to bend down to where her lips brushed his ear. "Put anything those reporters say or ask right out of your head. I told you. That's the most important thing for you if you're going to do this. Be *this*. A ball player. Don't read what they print, and put any stupid questions they ask away with the dirty laundry. Tell them you and your pop have the deepest understanding of one another's intentions and that's that."

She pulled away and brushed his shoulder like she was dusting him for lint. Her self-assuredness stunned him like always. He couldn't imagine living without her.

"I will. I'll remember."

And so they started up walking toward Labash Grocery store on McKean, stretching out the walk like kids pulled their bubble gum, looping it around fingers and then chewing it all over again.

Chapter 59

Mary

Mary dropped the second of two laundry baskets near the clothesline then dug into her apron pocket. With three clothespins in her mouth and three in her hand, she started her rhythmic movements of plucking a shirt from the basket, plunking the pins at each shoulder, sliding the basket down and doing it with the next piece. She'd turned the radio up loud enough to hear it through the kitchen window and so was startled when Stan tapped her on the shoulder.

She clasped her chest. "You scared me."

He smiled and dug into her pocket for a share of clothespins. He moved the basket between them and moved along with her, silent at first. He'd obviously been doing his own laundry in Williamson and she smiled at the fact he employed the exact same method as she. "Should I stitch you up a wash apron for next season?"

He chuckled.

"Thought the woman you rented from did laundry, too."

He sighed and dug into her pocket for pins again. "Saving money."

"You're doing fine."

"I'd like to send you more."

"Pop's working and I have…"

"Sixteen jobs, I know. Ran into Mrs. March on my way back from the Labashes. Said she's got you down to wallpaper her entire home before Christmas."

Mary paused, not quite sure what meaning was buried inside Stan's words about the facts of her worklife. "We're good, Stan."

"Someday I'm going to give you a brand-new home with only good memories and…"

"Stashu," she took his hand, his big brown eyes luring her back in time to when he was a little boy, to when he needed her. "What's going on?"

"I don't know. I mean…"

"Did you hear something from the club?"

"No. That's all fine. Good."

"And Pizzica? You're playing for him?"

"I am."

"Then?"

"I want to marry Lillian." He stared at Mary.

She plunged back into the basket for something to hang. She pulled a pillowcase out and shook it before plugging the pins over its edges.

"You like her, right? I can see it."

"She is very nice… but she reminds me of…" Lukasz's former fiancée, Aneta, flashed to Mary's mind.

"Then it's our ages? She just turned nineteen. I turn in six weeks or so."

"It's so much more than that."

"We love each other, Mom. I mean you can't worry that we'll be like you and Pop. That I'll be like Pop."

His mention of her marriage shook her. "Oh, Stan. There's so much you don't know or understand about your father, about us."

"I heard Matka say you secretly got married."

Mary stopped mid-hang and studied Stan. His words felt sharp, but his expression conveyed his usual kind self. "Oh, Stashu. There's so much more to that than you know."

"I'm sure. But just because you and Pop don't love each other—not like Lillian and I—"

She reached into the basket but kept her gaze on Stan. "What makes you think we don't feel the same?"

"Because I've seen how he's treated you for… my entire life."

That stung at Mary's core. She straightened pulling the wet garment against her belly, the wetness soaking through her dress, chilling her skin. "I understand what you saw and that it makes you think we don't love each other as well as we could. And you're not totally wrong. But you never know what's happening inside a marriage that isn't yours."

"But he doesn't treat you right."

"Certainly not always. Certainly not. But you have the whole world in your grasp. And Lillian has… so much, too. Just wait until you're on solid ground with your contracts and—"

"But I love her in a way that I don't think I can survive if— "

"She's a loyal girl. She won't—"

"I know. It's not that. It's that I need her. I want her to be my wife, to call her when a game goes bad, to have her with me when possible."

Mary clutched the laundry tighter against her. "Once Lillian brought us some soap and lunchmeat and she said she was interested in converting to Roman Catholic from Byzantine Catholic. She'd been so full of questions and well I assumed she was hinting that she wanted to marry you, but it takes a while to convert. You can't say hey I want to be Roman Catholic, wave a wand and it's done."

Stan raised his eyebrows as though he was surprised to hear that Mary knew of Lillian's plan.

"And you're so young."

"Older than you were."

She nodded. "Things were different back then."

"So you say." His jaw was tight.

Apprehension curled around Mary. She didn't want to argue. Not with Stan. She stepped away from him and flicked the pillowcase into the air, shaking it out, sending something flying out from inside it. Two things.

Stan snatched the clumps with one hand before they hit the ground, leaning forward and spinning around like he was making a run-saving catch in the outfield. "Hankies." He said shaking them out. "Good God, what happened to this one? Mop up a crime scene with it?"

He held both up. Mary felt her eyes widen. One was stained. The sight of dark rounded splotches catapulted her back to the day Aneta, Lukasz's betrothed, had elbowed Mary in the nose when they were trying to win a contest that would determine who would find their true love. St. Andrew's Day eve—the night that Czech girls, Poles, Hungarians—they would gather with church women to play games, cook, eat, and hopefully find out who their husband would be.

One of the traditions called for sleeping with a man's clothing to ensure he'd be one lucky girl's future husband. So silly, even back then it was. But with Mary's nose gushing, Aneta had stuffed her hanky into Mary's face and she walked home with it, still bleeding. That night, not knowing that it was Lukasz's hanky, Mary slept with it. It took another couple years for her to discover there were matching embroidered handkerchiefs and that she had one of them. They'd been given to Lukasz when he was leaving Poland—one hanky for him, one for his beloved.

Close to when Mary accepted Lukasz's proposal, she was still unsure of him as a husband. Then when the second hanky in the pair made its way to Mary and she realized she'd slept with the first on St. Andrew's Day eve years before, she knew he was intended to be hers. The two hankies had found their way to her and Lukasz had found his way to her, over and over, saving her repeatedly. Suddenly it was all clear and well, the secret wedding, the baby conceived before it, all of it made sense in her heart even if not in her mind.

"Andrzejki," she said.

"And what?" Stan said.

"St. Andrew's eve. I never mentioned it to you?"

Stan shook his head.

She chuckled. "It's really silly thinking back." Standing in the yard with half the clothing hung and flapping around them in the fall breeze, she told Stan the story of the handkerchiefs. And then as they started to hang the rest of it, he told Mary about the night he saw the men berating Lukasz on McKean, about how seeing that changed what he understood about his father.

It was getting dark when they realized they'd stopped hanging the clothes halfway through Stan's story. They laughed and finally finished, quietly, moving along the line, both lost in thought.

She wanted Stan to wait to marry Lillian until he had a solid contract in place, one that would ensure he could take care of a wife and children that would surely follow quickly. But she recognized that when it came to the emotions held deep in a person's heart, outsiders were kept away.

She grasped that she was now fully an outsider in her son's inner life. Though not yet nineteen years old, he was grown, he was in love, and she couldn't force him to make one choice or the other on the subject of Lillian Labash. She knew that in her bones. How could she not?

Stan nested one laundry basket inside the other and carried them under one arm and slung his other around Mary. She studied his profile as they headed up the stairs to the back porch. He was just as sweet and kind as he'd always been.

She wasn't sure Stan fully absorbed the essence of his parents' marriage, didn't quite buy the story of a gentle, chivalrous, Lukasz Musial, but he had learned that no one was just one way or just one thing. And for the second time in her life, she clearly saw Stan as standing apart from their family, needing a specific type of fatherly approval less and less in order to be whole. He was making his way in the world and their conversation had answered her own worried questions without her even asking them.

She could let go because Stan was already gone.

Chapter 60

Stan

The 1939 offseason was easier than the 1938 one because Stan was a high school graduate. He worked for Lillian's father, took a couple safe shifts at the zinc works and spent time with Lillian whenever he could. The two of them delivered store goods, laughing all the way, getting to see inside nearly every home in Donora, and from that the two of them plotted and planned out the type of homes each would like someday.

They walked along, each with a box under one arm, hands clasped between them. "I'd love a big kitchen where we can stuff a dozen people around the table," Lillian said.

"Like your house?"

"Like yours, too."

He squeezed her hand.

"And two phones."

"I thought you wanted one in every room."

"Two will do. Along with some nice dinnerware. A nice, soft shade of fresh cream."

"I just want a big bed. A new mattress I don't have to share," Stan said. "And steak for dinner. Once a week. I told you about that."

"You and Honey and the steak, yes. I know. But Stan." She set her parcel down and put her hands on her hips. Stan set his box down.

"No sharing, huh?" she asked.

In the soft moonglow and streetlights fighting through November fog, Lillian had never looked more beautiful. He kissed her and eventually she wiggled away.

"We can't just stand here kissing all night on the street." She whispered the word *kissing,* making him laugh.

He stuffed his hands in his pockets. "You're right about that."

"Yeah." She picked up one box.

He shoved his hands in his pockets, looking to moor himself. "So marry me."

She flinched and shifted the box.

He took it from her, set it down again, and then knelt in front of her, taking one hand. "Marry me." He kissed her fingers.

She let out a little laugh and looked away before she finally got that he was serious. "Oh, Stan. I just started my Catechism. I haven't even told my parents I'm leaving our church. And my dad won't just let me get married. I just turned nineteen. Mum wants a big wedding for me, I'm sure, and you'll be gone to spring training. A full season this time… and you have responsibilities to your family. Your mom will kill you. Kill both of us. And you'll be gone again…"

Her voice trailed off. The sidewalk gravel dug into his knee. "Sounds like you've been thinking about… Donny Harshman?"

This made her throw back her head in laughter. "You're never going to let me forget that little detour I took, are you?"

He stood, still holding her hand. "Just want you to examine your options properly."

"That's absurd."

"Please. Then marry me. Now. Next week." Stan snapped his fingers. "My birthday. Thanksgiving's right after it and Andrew will be home and you can have Ann stand up for you if you want or…"

"Stan. My parents won't say yes until you make enough money. It's important to my father."

Stan grimaced, confused at the idea Sam Labash might not want Stan to marry his daughter. "But he believes in me more than anyone. He's always encouraging me and…"

"He adores you, yes he does. But I can't disappoint him by doing this all out of order."

Stan paced, heading up Heslep a ways before crossing back to Lillian. "Mom and Pop got married without telling anyone. They snuck away and even lied about Mom's age. We don't have to lie, but we can get married privately and then when I come back next fall we can do a fancy wedding."

"Stan, it's still a lie."

He shrugged. "You're already lying about the Catechism."

She looked away.

"This way, it's a secret for us. I'll ask your father for permission to have a wedding next fall. And then all next season, even if we're not together, we'll be joined together like… you know, no man can tear asunder."

"Or woman," she smiled up at him.

Stan thought she was coming around. "Why not? Unless you're holding out for nylon and vinyl man to sweep back in with a giant diamond ring."

"Stan, please."

He drew a deep breath. "I'm not making light of it, what it means to have all the stuff that a guy like Donny could give you. But I promise, I'll make enough to provide for you. And every time I walk in our front door I'll have a smile for you, for our kids for our life."

She rubbed one temple with her pretty fingers.

"And I can give you my whole heart, forever. I already have in fact. I've never stopped thinking about you when I was away, even if letters weren't sent or I played pool too late with my buddies or I was down in the dumps and couldn't get my words out onto paper. I love you more than anyone has ever loved a person before. And like I know I will make it to the majors and win a World Series and… well, I know that I love you more than anyone else has loved a person in all of history."

She opened her mouth then closed it.

"Don't you want to wait for all that hoopla? Do it right, once?"

He pressed his chest. "I have all the hoopla right inside me that I could need to last a lifetime."

She put her hand over his. "It seems crazy." She stepped closer to him. "But yet not."

He got back on one knee. "I'm asking you to step under my lucky star, to hold my hand for the rest of our lives, to laugh with me and pick out household items like creamy dishes and a huge mattress…"

"Very important," she grinned.

"And come to the ballpark and… let me take care of you the way that's good and honorable and loving… and… Lil, for the love of God, I've never said this many words in a row to anyone so please stop me while I'm—"

She pulled him to standing and flung her arms around his neck. "Yes, yes, yes," she said. "I'll marry you. Let's get married."

And so they did.

Chapter 61

Stan

Stan and Lil lived the months between November and when he left for his first full spring training, three miles apart, dating, but officially single according to paperwork that was procured, never signed or filed. They were according to the world, unmarried. But because they'd vowed they would take no other and love each other until death in a ceremony by a real priest, they continually stole away under the veil of their secret marriage, loving each other the way newlyweds did, being as careful as they could not to bring a baby into the world before they had officially, publicly been married. But two nineteen-year-olds, secretly married in Fayette County by a newly initiated priest who'd been visiting his mother for Thanksgiving, in a ceremony witnessed by Andrew Morrison and Abagail Hastings, were finding it difficult to follow their own rules for "being careful."

Lillian was well into Catechism classes to convert to Roman Catholicism when Stan left for the Daytona Beach, Class D Florida State League. His pay had grown to $100/month and he still sent a portion to his mom. He was careful to save every bit he could so when he asked Lillian's father for permission to marry, his future father-in-law would see Stan as being a solid man with the means to support his daughter.

But. As life often did, the best intentions were laid to waste when least expected. And in March, Lil phoned Stan with news. She was pregnant and she'd told her father everything after she'd passed out in front of him. "Spilled the whole thing, secret wedding and all."

Stan listened, hearing the fear in her voice. "Well then. I'll send money for you to come down and… Let me talk to your father. Please." His voice quaked.

"Yes." Mr. Labash's deep and clipped words in the background made him queasy.

Stan said a silent prayer that his words would come out fresh and clean this one time, when he needed to redeem himself in front of the man whose blessing was most important in the world to Lillian. "Sir. Your daughter married me and I love her deeply. She wanted to do everything right and I talked her into eloping and we thought perhaps we could manage for it to be our secret, taking it to the grave—"

"She loves you, Stan. She has since… Well, who even knows."

Stan exhaled. "Thank you for saying that. I'll wire money and—"

"No," Mr. Labash said.

Stan's breath knocked away. No?

"I want to pay to send her down. I love my daughter more than life, which is something you're soon to find out. What that feels like to have a child, a part of you who's outside of you and now you have to care for him or her and things can get hard in marriage but you have to hold it dear, the whole thing, your wife, your children, your family. Children change everything. But in all good ways."

Stan choked back a sob.

"And though you still need a formal, official wedding, you can do that in Florida. I won't stand in your way anymore, even if I didn't know I was in the way."

Stan's eyes welled, astonished by Mr. Labash's understanding. "I love her like nothing else."

Silence.

"More than anything, more than… not one thing more. She is everything I can ever imagine in a wife and I know I'm the luckiest man to live having found her and gotten her to agree to marrying me."

"Well," Mr. Labash's voice cracked. "With that lucky star of yours and all… Of course you found my daughter. I'm glad you see her that way. I always thought you did even if you were shy about it."

With shaking hands and jellied insides, Stan phoned his Mom.

"Trying out the new phone?" she answered cheerfully and Stan could imagine her smile on the other end.

"Sounds perfect," Stan said.

Silence.

"Something's wrong," Mom said. "I can feel it sure as I'm holding this brand-new phone to my ear."

Stan cleared his throat.

"She's pregnant," Mary guessed.

"We're married. And having a baby."

"You… you're married? But I saw her the other day at Crawley's, trying on Easter gloves and I gave her a basket of my painted eggs for her family and… oh dear God… I'm so confused." Stan could hear Mom pull a chair out and sigh as she sat. "Stanley, what on earth made you… when? She's turning Catholic? Oh my God. Her parents?"

"She's converting. And her parents just found out, too."

"And a baby. You said baby."

"I did."

He could hear Mom weeping. "Mom, please. Remember when you told me about you and Pop and how you just knew and…"

She cried harder.

"Mom, please."

"Oh, Stan. You are going to be the best father."

"I hope," he said, relief sweeping over him. "I'll try my hardest. I will work so hard at it."

And that was that. Lillian arrived in Florida.

The next months and years flew by. Their baby boy, a little butterball, Dickie was born in August 1940. He was named for the coach, Dick Kerr, in Daytona whose wife and he took Stan and Lillian in when the baby was about to arrive so the Musials could save money and have what they needed to care for a newborn. The Kerrs bought them baby things and got them started, picking up where Lillian's parents left off.

And with Dickie, this beautiful addition to Stan and Lillian's life, Stan was met with his first real bad luck. Chasing down a ball, he tripped and landed on his shoulder, taking his arm out of the business of pitching.

This development petrified him. But in taking this unlucky, painful tumble through his baseball life, losing his big-league arm, standing at the edge of being let go from the professional baseball world completely, someone finally noticed. Someone remembered to look at his batting stats and someone else recalled Stanley Musial, waltzing up to bat, coming into the park swinging for the fences and landing half his hits over them. The injury peeled back the real talent he'd had since he was small, the skill that he should have been plucked out of Donora for in the first place, his hitting. Starting the 1941 season, he was assigned to Hollywood, Florida, for spring training. There, sports editor Barnard Kahn wrote: "Musial runs like silk hose, throws like a bullet and hits like, well, like hell."

Still, the managers fumbled Stan, juggling him from one team to another still using him to pitch. From Hollywood to Albany, and Columbus, Ohio, to Columbus, Georgia—the lowest rung of professional baseball—Stan stayed positive, working as hard as he could, taking every opportunity given.

But with no one quite sure what to do with him, an old acquaintance stepped out of the shadows into the bright Columbus, Georgia sun. Stan put his hand out like Frank Pizzica had taught him and shook hard, keeping eye contact steady. "Mr. Vanek. It's been a while. Stan Musial. From Donora."

The older man squinted. "Oh, yeah… Musial. Your father's the one who—"

"That was him. Yes."

"And the pierogis."

"Mom makes the best."

"She's a tough nut, ain't she?" Ollie Vanek finally smiled.

"She is."

"Well… what can I do for you? You all set with a team, I imagine. Kid like you. What? Twenty now."

Stan nodded. Vanek was heading up a team in Springfield, Missouri. Stan moved toward the bats lined up along a fence. He felt the weight of this one and then that and then signaled Vanek to follow him to the batting box. "I get some batting practice in before I have to throw it. Shoulder's been—"

Vanek shook his finger. "That's right. I know. Bum arm, dead…"

Stan nodded, taking the first pitch thrown. He launched it over the fence. Again and again.

Vanek let out a whistle and adjusted his hat. "But your bat's alive and well, now isn't it, son? Craziest stance… oh yeah, now it's all coming back."

And as Stan explained his journey from the time of signing until that 1941 season of… "I'm sort of…" his mind searched for the word. Andrew's voice lit inside him. "Unmoored."

Vanek scratched his nose. "What you feel about Missouri?"

Stan dropped his bat and stepped out of the batter's box.

"Field can carry a stench from the sewage works from time to time."

Stan's heartbeat sped up. "I'd say I'm plenty accustomed to industrial stench."

Vanek crossed his arms looking at Stan up and down. "I was thinking the same thing."

Stan grinned and leaned on the bat.

"But not taking you to pitch. That's over."

"That's great, that's…"

"Lots to learn in outfield…"

"I'll be your best student ever."

Vanek waved him along. "Well, let's get this done then. Let's get that bat you swing like a baseball God unwrapped and out into daylight, why don't we?"

And so Stan bolted home, spinning Lillian around the kitchen, and into his arms, tighter than he'd ever held her. "Someone recognized me today, Lil. And we are on our way."

That night felt like Christmas as they packed and made plans and let everyone in Donora know they were moving on and leaving pitching behind. Ollie Vanek claimed Stan for the second time that day. And he phoned that night to check in.

"I couldn't believe it, Stan," Ollie said. "Sitting in that organizational meeting, manager after manager passed on you."

Stan gasped.

"Now don't take this bad. Because you have something pure and wonderful and… that goddamn stance."

"I can change it."

"Don't touch a damn thing with that hitting of yours. I'll send you back down if you do."

Stan laughed, gesturing for Lillian to lean into the phone receiver and listen.

"Hid the biggest grin of my life," Vanek said, "until I was sure all those fools were out of sight and the ink was dry on you coming with me."

So Vanek snatched Stan right out from under all those other higher up managers who hadn't known what they were looking at. Vanek took Stan with him and released him into the outfield wilds of Springfield's White City Park.

And then he handed him a bat.

Chapter 62

Stan

The Musials set up house near White City Park in Springfield. Stan made fast friends with Blix Donnelly and Fats Dantonio. Lillian, Hilda Dantonio and other wives created a community to fill the gaps when their husbands had gone to play. Stan worked extra hours with Vanek, honing his outfield skills, catching up to all he hadn't learned when he'd been busy trying to make it as a pitcher for three years.

It didn't take long for Branch Rickey to attend one of the games in Springfield. Stan was struck with a case of the nerves. His hitting hadn't been as consistent as he'd wanted it to be, but he felt good. With Rickey in the stands for the game against St. Joseph of Missouri, Stan settled his mind by revisiting everything he and Joe had talked about over the years. Deep breaths, relax and concentrate. Simple.

That night's game, while warming up, Stan remembered playing "under the headlights" of Andrew's car. That night in Springfield, the feel of hitting with Honey and his friends, the ease, it all rushed back. This was Stan's game and now that he'd found his position, he was surer than ever he had the tools to compete at the level he wanted to.

So, with a triple, a homer, and a single, scoring all the runs that Springfield made that game, right in front of the grizzled, seen-it-all-before general manager, Branch Rickey, Stan's confidence grew.

**

Batting daily gave Stan the chance to further shape and perfect the minute, blink of an eye adjustments needed to keep pitchers from getting comfortable when he was up to bat. Lillian, with nine-month-old Dickie, kept busy with each other and their friends in between games. Lillian did her best to wedge Dickie's naps into slots outside of gametime so she could attend as many games as possible. Stan loved to glance into the stands and see her constant smile even when a play went bad, Dickie in her lap, gently bouncing him, holding his plump hand to wave at Stan, watching as he carved his place in that baseball world.

At the game against Topeka, Stan further found his path. He hit a home run and circling the bases, smiling like a kid, glanced into the stands, unable to see Lillian in her usual spot. Dickie had been recovering from whooping cough, but the doctors said he was clear to go out and about.

No matter, he'd just hit Lillian and Dickie another one. And so he did. And then another. With three home runs his teammates and Vanek chased him down to cheer and celebrate.

As the team headed into the clubhouse, Vanek squeezed Stan's shoulder. "Goodbye, Stan."

"Yeah, nice day off coming for us," Stan said.

Vanek started to say something else when the groundskeeper called him back onto the field with a question. Stan showered up fast as he could and dashed into the parking lot to find Lillian.

He couldn't stop grinning as he wove through a small crowd in the parking lot, signing programs that were shoved in front of his face. It didn't take too long to finish those off and finally catch up to his wife.

She burst into tears just as he reached out to hug her. Panic swept through him as he realized she'd been missing from the stands several times he looked. "What, Lil? What's the matter?"

He patted Dickie's back. He was fast asleep on Lillian's shoulder, perfectly fine. She didn't respond.

"What's wrong? What's wrong?" He pulled her close.

"Oh, Stan I missed your—"

"I know, I saw you weren't in your seat. But the other two…"

She choked on her tears, but had already started to sputter out a laugh. "Oh, Stan I missed them all."

"All *three*, Lil? I hit three, you know!" It didn't seem possible.

She nodded. "You know Dickie's feeling better but some of the cough is lingering and I was occupying him with sips of water bottles and… well, a little too much water. And I had to take him out to change him."

"Three times?"

She nodded. "All three times you hit a home run."

"Oh, my God, Lil." Stan held her cheeks, her beautiful brown eyes glistening with tears and sunrays and he'd never felt more in love. He pulled her in for a kiss. "I love you so much. Oh, Lil."

They left the ballpark that day, laughing that the Musial family must have seemed a little odd if anyone had been paying attention. With Lillian's sobbing and Stan's infectious grin, they must have looked as crazy as the day had felt.

**

On Stan's day off, he and Blix and Fats went for a little fishing trip. Catching close to nothing, they were irritated when a voice, calling their names, came from around the bend in the White River.

"What in the hell?" Fats said.

A man emerged from a thicket.

"That's…" Blix said. "No. Why would he?"

"That *is* him." Fats elbowed Stan. "Looky there."

Stan looked up. It was one of the reporters who'd been hanging around the parking lot after games.

"All the way out here?" Blix said.

"What, he wants my recipe for fish bait?" Blix asked.

The man lifted his hand. "Stan!"

Stan pointed to himself.

"You're the only Stan out here," Blix said.

"Yep, it's me," Stan said, narrowing his eyes on the man who lumbered toward them, huffing and puffing.

"Well, time for you to go."

"Lil? She all right?"

The reporter leaned forward, grasping his knees. "Nope. Rochester. You're heading out today."

Stan shook his head. "But that's—"

"Yes, it is." The reporter straightened. "Just one hair's width from the major leagues."

Stan's mouth dropped open. His friends whooped and cheered.

Fats smacked Stan between the shoulder blades. "Well, go on. Don't blame us if you miss the train."

Stan nodded and set down his rod. "But, Vanek and… you guys…"

Blix shrugged. "Time for goodbyes later. For now, just go. We'll get Lillian all set… the wives'll all be bawling but, well. Personally, I'm glad to see you go. All your dark moods and negative thinking. Get out of here."

Stan laughed.

Fats turned and coughed, sounding an awful lot like the whooping cough Dickie was still recovering from.

"You don't have to hide your tears, Fats," Stan said, his voice cracking. "I cry all the time."

Fats's shoulders shook.

"Jeeze, Fats. You're really crying?" Blix asked.

Fats turned, hacking away. "I'm seriously coughing. I think your kid infected me, Musial."

Stan shook his head. "Something to remember us by," he said and finally turned and left.

He felt as though he floated the entire way back to the apartment, barely conscious of what he packed or what he even said to Lillian as he left with just one suitcase. He pulled her into his arms, holding tight, afraid to let her go.

She finally pushed him away. "Go. We're fine. Dickie's getting better and we'll meet you in Rochester just as soon as he shakes this cough."

Stan left and once he was settled on the train he realized what Vanek had really meant to say when he told him goodbye the day before. Three home runs in one game would mean the two would say goodbye for good.

Chapter 63

Stan

Stan arrived in Rochester and immediately hopped into their lineup. They were in fourth place and pushing for a playoff spot. For the second time Branch Rickey had come to watch a game Stan played in. And again, he put on a show—four hits. Success.

The next games brought plenty of opportunity for Stan to show off his continually growing skill. The games also brought the surprising chance to dust off trick plays that took Stan's mind right back to the fields of Donora when his athletic gifts were enough to make any crazy attempt at his pick-off move work or his plowing past third to score when others would have just stopped, a success. Here he was, playing baseball for his job, being asked to fake a bunt. And not just once but twice in the same game to help pull off an improbable win. He couldn't have imagined that the serious upper levels of pro-baseball could be so much fun. Stan finished up the run for the playoffs with hit after hit, making him even look at his bat a little longer from time to time and wonder if it had somehow been bewitched like others suggested over the years.

With Rochester playing Newark in the playoffs, Lillian went home to Donora to wait to see what happened. They lasted five games with Stan hitting well, but Newark had more overall power and experience. So with the season ended, the deflation that came with losing, Stan hopped the night coach back to Pittsburgh where Lillian and her sister picked him up and drove him back to Donora. They made it home in time for church, for a good Dagwood sandwich, and a much-needed nap on the Labash family couch. Then he'd go see Mom and the rest of his family who were just about as excited as him with his meteoric rise to almost the major leagues in just one season. Pop would have to be proud of that.

**

The feel of someone shaking Stan drew him from a deep sleep. He opened his eyes to see the flowery couch that reminded him of where he was—Lillian's childhood home.

She shook a piece of paper at him. Were they late on a bill or… his mind was too cottony to even guess what problem they were about to tackle.

"A wire came." Her breath was short, but controlled, her eyes wide.

"Wire?"

"They want you in St. Louis."

Stan rubbed his eyes. While it was good news, great news, unbelievable news—next season wouldn't be starting until spring. Surely…

"Now," Lilian said.

His mind was still with Rochester whose season just ended. There was no more ball to play in the Cardinal leagues. None except…

"Right now."

"No way."

"Yes."

"The major leagues."

"The one and only."

Stan was finally awake enough to register the chaos happening around him. Lillian's mother and sisters had already unloaded his suitcase, were washing and drying his clothes and getting him ready for the sendoff, for the big goodbye the one that kids dream about when they hit stones off of broomsticks into fat, black rivers that hug miles of mill-property.

And so with the faint fragrance of Lillian's perfume lingering on his collar, he left again.

Chapter 64

Stan

September 17, 1941

Stan entered the clubhouse at Sportsman Park, a big-league house, just for those who were deemed good enough, who'd come across enough luck to make hard work matter. Stan was greeted by the two most important men in the Cardinal's operation: Manager, Billy Southworth and equipment manager, Butch Yatkeman. Still in awe that there was a man assigned to set Stan up with gear and a locker, he wasn't bothered a bit by the hole in the wall area that the team had designated for rookies to change and prepare for games.

Though there were some grumblers in that tiny, hot room for the lowest men on the roster, Stan could not have been happier. Perhaps the others hadn't felt the thrill of rising from Class D all the way to the major leagues in just one season, before turning twenty-one years old. Perhaps it was just that much that turned potential disgruntlement to electrifying thrill for Stan. Every single day.

With the number six on his back and the team having lost bundles of players to injury, Billy Southworth told Stan with his high energy, deep voice that he'd be playing right away.

Right away. The words were jarring. Stan was tossed back to when Joe put him, the teen batboy, into the first game he played for the Zincs. He reminded himself that just the act of Joe doing so had reassured Stan that he belonged. This was no different. Billy Southworth wouldn't put Stan in if he wasn't ready. Breathe, concentrate, relax.

They played a double-header that day. His first up came with a knuckleball that he'd never seen or thrown. It shimmied and wiggled and caused Stan to swing with an odd cadence and he popped up to thirdbase.

The second time he saw this pitch, the next at bat, Stan hit a line drive that smacked off the outfield wall giving him time to double and drive in two runs. There it was. There was the batter he'd become, the one he'd felt like he'd been since he was a little boy. First big league hit, Christmas in September. Another hit that day and he was two for four. It couldn't have gone better. The Cardinals won and the team was coming together despite the rookies called up to fill in for seasoned big leaguers. And they found themselves in the running for the playoffs just a little behind Brooklyn.

**

Nine more games in what felt like an entire season even though Stan'd barely unpacked. But every moment he had to pause, he looked around and remembered where he was, and he burst out laughing, disbelieving how far he'd come since spring 1941. The only thing that could have made it better was if Lillian, Dickie and the rest of their family could have been in St. Louis to watch.

Next up, a doubleheader against the Chicago Cubs. Stan played left field in the first game and was quickly beginning to feel at home far from the pitcher's mound. His performance was solid in the field and he doubled at bat then singled, stole second, then doubled again. His fourth at bat, with the score tied at 5-5, he singled then moved on to second while the batter was thrown out.

He watched the Cub's manager, Jimmy Wilson, growing more irritated by the minute along with his team. Wilson ordered his pitcher to walk Frank Crespi. With Stan still on second, Coaker Triplett took a massive swing but only nipped the ball enough for it to worm along the field about fifteen feet toward third base. Stan took off for third, the catcher made the play, getting the ball to first base just a little too late and Triplett was called safe.

First basemen Babe Dahlgren began the business of screaming at the umpire, arguing his case for Triplett being out. The Cub's catcher stood there following along with the argument like a housewife listening in on neighborhood gossip.

This gave Stan just enough time to process what he was seeing and without slowing a bit at thirdbase, he poured it on, heading for home. By the time the catcher got into place Stan was sliding across the plate, scoring the winning run.

The rush of teammates to congratulate, pounding on him, lifting him up, smacking his back left Stan laughing harder, feeling better than he ever had in his life. In that one play he'd been pulled into the gang, like when Andrew had finally become one of the North Donora team, really part of them.

The second game of the doubleheader the Cardinals won again and Stan put on a fielding show complete with Falcons Nest 247 approved double somersaulting and diving catches. Two more hits and Stan couldn't have written a more perfect major league baseball day in his childhood notebook if he'd tried. And the Cubs' manager agreed, stomping around, hitting his hat off his leg screaming that, "No one can be that good."

And yet Stan was.

**

As the season was coming to a close, still with the chance for the Cardinals to win the pennant, they took a little trip to

Pittsburgh to play the Pirates. Stan could not have grasped beforehand what it would feel like to walk into Forbes Field, home of his childhood team, an hour from Donora, the stands packed with half the Monongahela valley, there to see the Pirates, but also one of their very own sons who'd made it big.

They played a doubleheader and St. Louis lost the first one in a shutout, with Stan shut out from hits as well. But then game two came along and Stan found his magic bat once again. Three hits and one of them a home run, smacked right into the hands of Donora high school football player, and friend of Stan Musial, Steve Posey.

After the game Steve traded Stan the home run ball for a new one causing him to find a sense of joy that only came when one magnificent day was piled on another, when a dream was coming true repeatedly, like someone had sprinkled Stan and everything around him in magic fairy dust. With long hugs for Lillian, Mom, his sisters and the Labashes, a hush was settling over Forbes Field as the stands emptied.

Pop stood at the fringes of their group, quiet as usual. Stan went to him. "This way," he said guiding him toward the clubhouse. The lockerroom was nearly vacant and Stan took his father inside and introduced him to Billy Southworth and Butch Yatkeman.

Pop was his usual economical self when it came to spending words, but he was polite… no, he was thrilled even if quietly so. The wonder in Pop's eyes made Stan sure that his father had finally grasped his potential, that it was already being realized. Just three short years after Stan played hooky to attend his first Pirates baseball game. He'd been a confused, hopeful high school student. And now… Pop grinned and nodded along as Southworth and Yatkeman treated him like he'd descended from kings. Pop didn't say that's how he felt, but Stan could see it. He knew what it looked like when a person felt important, was treated as he deserved, because Stan had felt it too.

When the men were busy talking, Stan turned and wiped a tear before anyone saw. That he'd done this for Pop, made all the success matter even more.

**

The Cardinals had one last game against the Pirates and if they won, they'd move along in the post-season. This time an even bigger Donora gang showed at the game because the school district had given the kids the day off and Stan guessed that half the businesses closed just to come see him play. A respectable outing for Stan, he earned two hits, but St. Louis, and with the loss went the pennant and the chance to play more. With the last out in the final inning, the awesome strength and hope that the Cardinals had been living and breathing since Stan and the other rookies showed up, was sucked away like air from a tire.

Stan felt the sting of the season's abrupt ending deep in his bones. But he also took stock in where he'd started that season— Class D. He was disappointed their journey was over, but not frustrated with what had transpired overall. He was the first Donoran since 1908 to make it to the major leagues. And in his first twelve games at that level he earned twenty hits and batted .426. Just replaying those words in his head sent shivers through him.

He was on his way.

Chapter 65

Mary

Mary shut the scrapbook she'd been keeping for Stan. Actually, it was the second one. Her friends were keeping their own, too, in case Mary was to miss something. They also added articles and stories written about Stan as well as all the happenings in Donora, Pennsylvania. Mary's was stuffed full of anything that she found in the paper or letters people sent. She sighed, and ran her palm over the cover.

"You ready?" Lukasz said setting down his suitcase.

Mary nodded.

"You're sad. Like we've been invited to a funeral."

Mary chuckled. "Not at all. Just thinking about how much has changed since... Honey's working with the Civilian Corps, the girls are, well, you know..."

He took her hand. "We're going to miss the train."

Mary was pleased that Lukasz was excited to go. They shut off all the lights in the house and left. They were on their way.

They held hands heading down the street to the train station, watching where they stepped in the dark.

Suddenly the reality of what was happening hit Mary. She halted, making Lukasz jolt to a stop.

"What is it?"

A wave of excitement spilled through her. She started hyperventilating. "Oh my God." She gripped Lukasz's arm to steady herself.

"Your stomach?"

Mary shook her head. "Fine. It's just… I just realized… The World Series. I can't… even though I knew he was so talented and Mrs. Mazur said he was special and… all those years in the yard and playing with broomsticks and soft balls sewn up by hand and…"

"Now we go to Yankee Stadium. We see our son in the sunlight, like I imagined it would be when I dreamed of coming to America."

Mary drew back, shocked at Lukasz's words. Not that he felt that way, but that he'd said it all aloud.

He pulled her hand again. "So we go."

She took a step. "We go. Yes, yes. Let's go."

They arrived in New York, whisked off by a driver, dropped at a hotel, and then escorted everywhere they needed to be. Stan met them with hugs and big smiles and though the Cardinals had lost game one in St. Louis, Stan couldn't have appeared more relaxed.

When he wasn't playing or practicing, he took Lukasz around the stadium, Mary following at least as far as the locker room. Before those doors closed she saw Stan gently guiding his father around, introducing him to everyone they saw, strangers fawning over her husband and she nearly burst into tears, tears she'd held back for decades. She watched Lukasz scan the room, turning slowly until Mary caught a glimpse of the awe on his face, the smile, the appreciation he finally felt for all his son had dreamed and accomplished.

And so the Cardinals won the series and Stan was handed a check for $6,192.50. A fortune. The amount boggled Mary's mind. *"When baseball pays the bills, let me know."* Lukasz's words from years past knocked around her head. She marveled at how a man who left his home country with nothing and no one else could have been so cynical about the possibilities for their son. It never quite matched up for her, but then, it didn't need to. He was complicated. Life was too. But it was good. It was as it was supposed to be.

Chapter 66

Stan

With Lillian having gone to Donora when the Cardinals went to New York, Stan took the train back there instead of heading to St. Louis with his teammates aboard a fully outfitted, party car. The conflict he'd felt in deciding to return home alone caused him to burst into tears right in front of his World Series winning teammates. Their grizzled, rough ways would mean teasing when spring training commenced, but Stan had become one of them. They claimed him along with all of St. Louis.

Coming into Donora late at night, not letting anyone except family know he'd decided to skip the train to St. Louis, Stan was stunned to walk right into Andrew. "Oh, man. Andrew. What are you doing here?"

"Oh, you know. Just home for the old man's birthday and to celebrate a fella winning the World Series. Twenty-one years old and a World Series Championship."

Stan's body was electrified at hearing those words said aloud. He threw his arm around Andrew. "Well, I heard from someone at Pitt who knows someone who knows someone at Harvard that you got a study published in some big shit thing that I can't even name."

"Oh, Stan. Can you believe it?"

"I can."

"Yeah, you knew it all along."

Stan sniffed and dried his cheeks. They stared at one another. "I'm sure you know this," Stan said, "but seeing as we haven't talked in a while… I actually met the real, the original Wild Horse of the Osage."

Andrew adjusted his glasses. "Pepper Martin, sure. He's a player-manager in the Cardinal organization or something now, right? I took note of him being a former Cardinal the minute you slid onto their roster."

"Well, when I met him, and you better know I told him that the actual, original Wild Weatherman of Donora is my best friend."

Andrew laughed. "I sure as shit hope you did."

"I did. I did."

"What'd he say?"

"He just looked at me like I was… I dunno, some kid from a place he'd never heard of, rambling about another wild man he'd never met."

"Hmm." Andrew straightened, looking offended. "Maybe we'll just have to meet."

Stan chuckled. "Shoulda seen his face when I started to tell him about the weather and moon and stars and using words like unmoored and juxtaposition."

"Oh man. I thought you were sleeping all that time I was chattering away."

Stan paused. "Heard every word, my friend. Every one. But now I'm in a bind because he immediately thought I was smart and started asking me all these damn questions about constellations and… I just started throwing out words I heard you say before and… shit." Stan ran his hand through his hair. "I reeled all that brainy talk right back into my mouth, threw out a couple of stammered words and all was back to normal."

Andrew shook his head. "Oh Stan. You are smart."

"I'm no mental heavyweight."

"You're a lot moreso than you think."

Stan shrugged, words lost.

Andrew shifted his weight. "The World Series!"

"I know. I still can't believe it."

"What'd it feel like to walk onto that field for that game with those guys and…"

Stan looked skyward and closed his eyes, letting the sensations come crashing back. "Wow. I can't even say what the first half of that first game was like because I went numb and was joyful but…"

He paused, unsure of what he wanted to say.

"What?"

"*Magic.* You know. I hate to say that because all my life people have been saying that kind of stuff and I felt it and believed it, but not like now… not like this out of this world, crazy sense of amazement that this is my life. That I can play this game and be this… good." He was embarrassed to say that aloud. "Like it'll all dissolve or maybe never even happened."

"You are that good."

"It's a miracle. The game, the fact I'm playing at that level after nearly getting buried in the lowest ranks, that Vanek was there just at the right time, that he remembered and then actually watched. Lillian, a family." He sighed, reminding himself he didn't have to hide anything from Andrew. He rubbed his forehead. "A damn fairy tale. I hope it never—"

Andrew grabbed Stan's shoulder and squeezed tight. "Don't."

"Don't what?"

"Say what you were going to say."

Stan wasn't sure.

"Stop questioning and just go with it. Because it's all yours and it is great. Just appreciate it the way you apprciate every blessed thing that comes your way."

Stan thought back to all the years he'd been friends with Andrew, how this was just one more case of him showing Stan who he was and what he deserved.

"Thank you," Stan said.

"You can repay me with World Series tickets next year."

Stan was about to humbly say this might have been his only chance at that, but stopped. "You got it."

"Musial!" A voice came from down McKean as Stan and Andrew were crossing over it.

Stan looked this way and that, but then realized it wasn't Stan the person was yelling for.

"Pop," Stan said as he and Andrew stopped to watch.

"Well, would you look at that?" Andrew said.

Stan's mouth dropped open. It took a few seconds before it was clear. But it was. There was Lukasz Musial strolling down McKean, tossing a baseball into the air and catching it, then tossing it to… someone. A friend? Stan couldn't know at that moment.

He sighed and patted Andrew's back. "How about that? Lukasz Musial tossing a baseball around."

"How about it."

"Everything really has changed now, hasn't it?"

Andrew jerked his head in the direction of Labash's Grocery. "All good, though, Stanley F. Musial. It's all good when you waltz into town."

Suddenly Stan was desperate to see Lillian. "Let's go. Lillian will have fixin's for a Dagwood in the fridge. And I can't wait to hold her tight."

"Well, let's go."

And they did.

Chapter 67

Patryk

Owen and Lucy rushed into Patryk's room to find him struggling with the zipper on his duffel bag.

"Gramps." Lucy hugged him. Owen hugged him, too. "What's going on? Is it true? Are you all right?"

"Should you be up like this? Sit, sit," Owen said.

"What are you, my mother, two mothers?" He swatted them both away.

They backed off.

He pounded the bag. "Sorry. I just… I'm a little testy this morning, and yinz're all over me and…"

He could see both were worried. Lucy's eyes were filling with tears. He pressed his throat where his air had gotten caught.

"Now don't you do that, Lucy." He looked at Owen. "And don't you worry a second neither. I've never felt better. Never."

"So you're going to do the treatment?"

He drew a deep breath. "Still got that crack steel-man insurance package. So hell yeah, I'm doing it."

Owen and Lucy grabbed each other's hands. "I'm so happy, Gramps," Lucy said.

"We'll get you up and running for the last series of my season," Owen said.

Patryk sat. "I'd like that, Owen. I intend to be there. This is a blip—nothin' more."

"I'm so glad," Lucy said.

"Yinz changed everything for me. I was ready to die when you two arrived, dragging me out of my attic like I was the interloper. And now look at me."

Maria wheeled into the room.

"I've got to get this lady up and around so we can live at the house. So much life to live. And…"

He flipped his fingers toward the box Dr. Lewis had brought. "Take a look at what's in there. The doc dug the stuff out of his attic."

"Nicky Christmas's grandson?"

"The very one. Dr. Lewis can't wait to read more of the book and… I told him yinz could take a gander while I'm… gone… but I expect to go over it fresh when I'm back."

"We'll keep it safe, Gramps," Owen said. "Promise."

And with surgery and radiation looming, Patryk took Maria's hand and watched his family open the weathered box as though it were holding millions in cash and prizes.

"Oh my God, is this really it?"

Patryk nodded. "An IOU written to Stan Musial for the two dollars Nicky'd borrowed and never repaid."

"But here it is attached to the note," Owen said.

"Dr. Lewis said his grandfather fell on hard times after leaving Donora—the kind that put him in and out of a bottle. When his grandfather was finally out of it for good, he'd forgotten, the note buried in the box and just… who knows. Dr. Lewis doesn't know exactly what happened. Maybe just like so many people who lived back then, they just lost touch. Nothing special, just the natural way of things, I suppose."

"Oh wow," Owen said. "That's really something."

"One more thing in there."

Owen reached in. A smile inched across his face as he registered what he was looking at. "No way. No way…"

Patryk leaned in, his forefinger quaking as he pointed. "There. Stan's name. Spin that, there—Melonhead." Owen turned it a little farther. "Honey." He gasped. "Monocle. Oh my goodness."

The red stitches on the ball that had once been wrapped in gold paper, a precious jewel to a bunch of boys who practiced with broomsticks and balls sewn with shoe leather over wine cork, stockings, and string, were splayed open, evidence of being a well-loved part of a boy's life.

And as Patryk watched Owen mesmerized by the ball that wouldn't mean much to most, unless they knew the story behind it all, he was ready to fight that cancer. He envisioned it in his body, and he focused on the tumor shrinking, dissolving right out of him.

Maria squeezed his hand, and he thought for the first time in ages that he loved his life, that life was everything it should be.

Acknowledgments

The Magician is a work of fiction inspired by baseball Hall of Famer Stan Musial's childhood years in Donora, Pennsylvania. Like all the novels in the Donora Story Collection, the town of Donora acts as a character itself, shaping everything else in the book. Musial's autobiography, numerous biographies, articles, presentations, videos, and interviews with historians provided facts that acted as anchors and jumping off points for fictional scenes. In all the years of researching, reading, and listening, I didn't come across one item that painted Stan Musial as anything other than exceptionally talented and hardworking yet somehow able to convey the heart-warming ordinariness of a person who understood he lived an extraordinary life. Stan Musial was a kind person from the day he was born. And lucky. Apparently he was lucky as can be.

Next up in the Donora Series—*The Circus Dancer*.

Thank you to Mark Pawelec and Donora Historical Society. Your generosity in providing a historian's point of view and feedback related to Donora, the way the community functioned, and the ways the mills shaped everything is priceless. Any fictional depictions or errors related to historical fact are mine. Thanks especially for the note that my fictional Mr. Kaminski is similar to Mark's grandfather, Frank Musial. Frank Musial, a decorated Polish Falcons Nest 247 athlete and coach, wasn't related to Stan Musial's family, but would have known them well. Frank Musial's dedication to helping countless young Donorans learn to be good, strong people inside and out, supported them as they grew into solid American citizens. Thanks for resources and information related to the men and women who mentored Stan Musial over time, helping him develop into the athlete and person he became.

To historian and teacher Brian Charlton and the Donora Historical Society. Thank you again and again for the information presented and shared over the years about Donora (Cement City) and Stan Musial's life. Your historian/caretaker role, being the holder and disseminator of important details and atmospheric/contextual elements, have allowed me to make *The Magician* fuller in every way. Any errors or fictional representations of people, places, things, and events are mine.

Ted Musial, born and raised in Donora, but not related to Stan Musial's family, provided many wonderful details related to working in the mills and life in Donora. Thank you so very much for the long, colorful conversation. Ted's family members were (and some like Mark Pawelec still are) active, invested members of the Donora community and the Polish Falcons Nest 247. Your memories are alive and well in my books!

A million thank yous must go to the gifted author, Christina Fisanick, Ph.D., Associate Professor of English at California University of Pennsylvania. Your writing is inspirational and gorgeous. Your work in teaching students the value of learning history, theirs and other people's, illustrating how to contextualize it and share it in meaningful ways helps ensure the American way of life is safe going forward. They are so lucky to have you! I am so lucky to share in all you do.

Many thanks to David Lonich, retired California University of Pennsylvania professor and Donora historian. Your novels are fantastic representations of the storyteller you are in person. Thank you for always sharing and encouraging.

No book is created or released in a vacuum. Thank you to Demi Stevens, Jenny Quinlan, Barbara DeSantis, Julie Burns, Marlene Roberts, my mom, BooksForward, Michele Harden, Donna Hanlon, Lisa McShea, Alex House Writers, and readers who ask for more and share their thoughts with others. Readers who love the stories, Donora, and all its people, make telling the tales worth it. I hope you love this one.

Other Books by Kathleen Shoop

Historical Fiction

The Donora Story Collection:
After the Fog—Book One
The Strongman and the Mermaid—Book Two
The Magician—Book Three

The Letter Series:
The Last Letter—Book One
The Road Home—Book Two
The Kitchen Mistress—Book Three
The Thief's Heart—Book Four
The River Jewel—A prequel

Romance

Endless Love Series:
Home Again—Book One
Return to Love—Book Two
Tending Her Heart—Book Three

Women's Fiction:

Love and Other Subjects

Bridal Shop Series:
Puff of Silk—Book One

Holiday
The Christmas Coat
The Tin Whistle

Made in United States
Troutdale, OR
09/07/2024

22654611R00309